ALAN

BY

E. F. BENSON

British Library Cataloguing-in-Publication Data
A catalogue record for this book is available from the
British Library

E. F. BENSON

Edward Frederic Benson was born at Wellington College (where his father was headmaster) in Berkshire, England in 1867. He was educated at Marlborough College, where he proved himself as an excellent athlete, representing England at figure skating, and published his first novel, *Dodo* (1893), when he was 26. The novel was quite popular, and Benson eventually expanded it into a trilogy (*Dodo the Second*, in 1914, and *Dodo Wonders*, in 1921). Nowadays, Benson is principally known for his 'Mapp and Lucia' series about Emmeline "Lucia" Lucas and Elizabeth Mapp. The series consists of six novels and two short stories, and remains popular to this day, being serialized for Radio 4 as recently as 2008. Benson was also a respected writer of ghost stories – indeed, H. P. Lovecraft spoke very highly of him, especially his story 'The Man Who Went Too Far'. Benson died of throat cancer in 1940, aged 72.

BOOK I

ALAN

BOOK I

CHAPTER I

THOUGH half April had already spent itself, there was as yet no remission from the northerly winds, which since the beginning of the month had raged with peltings of cold rain, stiffening on their stems the unwary buds which warm March weather had fostered, and to-day, as Agnes Graham and her husband set out for his afternoon walk, these blasts had relaxed none of their Arctic rigours. But when Alan was at work on a book, this daily walk was of cosmic regularity, and only an unprecedented down-pour, something as exceptional as an eclipse, caused it to be abandoned. Otherwise, within a couple of minutes on one side or the other of three o'clock, he and Agnes left his house in Goring Square on their way to Hyde Park. One weekly exception there was with regard to their destination, for once a week he had tea at the Athenæum Club. But even then they left the house together at the same hour.

As concerning the Park, there were two walks of different lengths but largely on common ground. If the weather was pleasant they crossed the lower end of the Serpentine, proceeded along the north bank to the top of the long water in Kensington Gardens, and so, making the complete circuit, left the Park again by the footpath adjoining the Knightsbridge barracks. On inclement afternoons they walked along the south bank of the Serpentine as far as the bridge across it, and then retraced their

outward journey. If there was any doubt as to
whether the major or the minor of these expedi-
tions was to be undertaken, that point was settled
when they arrived at the Serpentine. Agnes always
brought with her a small paper-bag containing
broken bits of bread and biscuit from the luncheon
table, with which she fed the ducks and the gulls. By
the time that these fragments were dispensed, Alan
would have made up his mind. The longer walk was
in fine weather the normal walk : it was only in very
chilly or in very warm weather that reflection was
necessary.

"I think, dear, we will confine ourselves to our
shorter walk," he would say on such occasions.
"Our shorter walk will, I think, sufficiently freshen
us up."

To-day, so Agnes imagined, there would be no
question of the longer walk, for not throughout the
winter, when the shorter walk was the commonest,
had there been an icier afternoon. The wind squealed
shrilly round corners, laden sometimes with smarting
particles of dust from the road, sometimes with a few
bullet-like drops of rain or little pellets of frozen sleet.
She had even been prepared for Alan to cancel the
walk altogether, or postpone it in the hope of the wind
abating later in the afternoon. Thinking that in any
case the shorter walk would be the limit of their
activity she had arranged to go to see her mother at
four. Mrs. Mowbray had been confined to the house
for three days with a cold which she interpreted into
influenza, and her voice in the telephone, alluding to
neglect, had been hoarse if not querulous. . . .
After the shorter walk Agnes would have time, therefore, to spend an hour with her, before returning to
give her husband his tea and record the dictation of
his book for another couple of hours.

They made their way along the Brompton Road,

leaning against the wind. They were both of them tall, she noticeably so, and he clearly taller than he looked. His spare frailness, with his bent shoulders and his grey hair which he wore rather long, already turning quite white above his ears gave him an aspect of being older than the fifty-five years which were really his. His face, ascetic and distinguished, had curiously contradictory features. The eyes, dark brown and set markedly wide apart below fine black eyebrows, were of extreme softness and observant brightness, but about his mouth there was an egoistic hardness and toughness : it was set in the uncompromising lines and stiff corners of the habitual spokesman of settled convictions. He walked with short low-lifted steps, which made Agnes's longer and looser gait seem like the strolling of an adult beside a trotting child, and gave her a competent protective presence. Fully as tall as he, she strayed along beside him, and the wind which drove the blood from Alan's face only flushed hers a vivid and rosy resistance to its chilliness. She was twenty years his junior, and whereas he looked more than his age, some serenity and smoothness of ripening girlhood, uninvited and unconscious, sparkled in her easy vigour.

Here then, at the corner of the Serpentine they paused, and Agnes distributed her broken largesse. Some pieces she tossed in the air for the benefit of the chiding gulls which swooped to catch them before they reached the water : if they were too late the mallards and tufted ducks bobbing up and down in the windy ripples rushed to receive them. Alan, huddled in his coat, stood behind her sheltered a little from the wind and observant of the wheeling birds.

" There's a bold fellow," he said, pointing to one of the gulls. " I think he would almost take a piece from your hand, dear, if you kept very still. Hold a piece up : try him with it. Ah, he doesn't quite dare! But what mastery of these blasts! See how he takes advantage of the wind, does he not, like a child's kite that soars the higher the more violently it blows. What beautiful poisings! I must visualize, I must remember that."

"Nice wild things," said Agnes, thinking for the moment, more of her gulls than of him. "Just going where they choose——"

"Ah, the opposite of that struck me. Such tame things, surely. There! Is that all your bounty? Is your little bag quite empty? Let us go on, then. Really I was almost a coward, and nearly proposed that we should give up our walk. But now I find this wind merely invigorating. Let us take our longer walk."

Agnes recollected her engagement.

"My dear, I'm afraid I can't," she said. "I promised mother to look in about four. I never dreamed that you would take your longer walk on such a day. But I'll come with you as far as I can."

His mouth compressed itself while his eye remained softly observant.

"But surely you will have time," he said. "We shall be back again in an hour. If you are a little late for your mother, does it matter? It is a very dismal business walking alone."

Agnes hesitated. She knew that Mrs. Mowbray's eyes would be undeviatingly fixed on the clock from four onwards. On the other hand Alan disliked walking alone.

"I don't like keeping mother waiting," she said. "And she's had several days in the house."

A certain congealment, familiar to her, came over Alan.

"Ah! You must settle it for yourself, dear," he said. "I do not wish to influence your decision in any way. Of course I shall not go our longer walk alone."

Agnes wished he had not said ' Of course.' It implied that she ought to have known that. He was influencing her decision. She looked at her watch. " Come along then," she said. " I shan't be so very late. Why, what a long time it is since we went round by the north side. It will be cheering to see it again. And as for my lateness, dear, I shall lay the whole blame on you ! "

His mouth relaxed and unfroze. There was no tough ice about it at all since Agnes was coming the longer walk.

These walks, longer or shorter, were never very conversational. The object of them was to provide the relaxation of air and exercise for Alan, but his mind was usually busy brooding over the work which he would resume again after tea. Agnes's companionship, however, conduced to that : he could not meditate peacefully and prosperously on these walks unless she was with him. When a book was still in the stage of being planned and plotted, he would give her a sort of partnership in his designs, finding that to talk of them clarified them to his own mind, but when, as now, he had got to the actual business of dictation, her presence was to him much like the ivory paper-knife which he stroked and handled as he walked up and down his room with a glance every now and then at the notes which bestrewed the table where she wrote. Dozens of little slips were spread out there too, each inscribed in his minute delicate handwriting with some polished gem of a sentence embodying a casual impression of some sort. To-day, for instance, he would certainly have ready by the time his walk was over some phrase about kites and wheeling gulls which, sooner or later, would make a metaphor, or be inlaid into some fine piece of descriptive writing. He was always gathering these, and when in his dictation, he came to some appropriate niche, his marvellous memory would tell him that he had, ready to take its place, just the phrase he needed. This method, therefore, was by no means a wilful or haphazard patchwork; he but quarried in his mine of just observations so simply and flawlessly expressed, and put the limpid little stone into its appropriate setting.

Agnes, having made her choice that, at the cost of her mother's waiting, Alan was not to be curtailed of his longer walk, made no attempt to hurry him on. There was no use in giving him what he wanted and withholding graciousness from the gift, and, in consequence, when they had got back home, she was already half-an-hour behind her proposed schedule.

"You're not so very late, dear," said he. "And I have enjoyed my walk, Agnes. It has briskened me up wonderfully: this morning I felt very lazy-brained."

"That's good news," said she.

"And you'll be back for tea," he asked, "so that we can get to work again by half-past five?"

She took a handful of daffodils from a vase that stood on the hall table and shook the wetness from their stalks.

"Yes, dear," said she, "but if I am a little late begin tea without me. I shall be ready for work by the time you are."

"You are taking those daffodils with you?" he asked. "Beautiful things: what purity of outline, what Hellenic design! I always think of daffodils as Attic flowers. The table looks bare without them, dear."

This time she was firm.

"Mother will like them," she said. "I'll get some more to-morrow."

Mrs. Mowbray lived just opposite the Grahams on the east side of the square and Agnes hurried across with her flowers. Though she had warned Alan that he was to be made scapegoat for her unpunctuality, she had no notion of putting her threat into execution.

"I'm late, darling," she said, kissing her mother, "but I've only just got in. Look, I've brought you some flowers. They make a sort of sunshine, on this grey day."

Mrs. Mowbray made no spoken reproaches, but she glanced at the clock on the chimney-piece, putting on her spectacles to do so. Then, without any comment, she took them off again : they had done their work.

"Thank you for the flowers, Agnes," she said. "Pretty."

Agnes had observed (as she was expected to observe) that glance at the clock. It was rather uphill work sometimes . . .

"And how goes it, mother?" she asked.

"I have not very much to boast of. Thank you."

"Well, I really think you're better off indoors to-day than out. An awful squealing north-east wind. I hate a cold wind. It gives me elephant's eyes; little, red, wicked eyes."

Mrs. Mowbray decided not to know what Agnes meant.

"I beg your pardon, dear," she said. "Elephant's eyes? What are they?"

"Oh, you know what I mean. Elephants have little, red, wicked eyes, and so have I when I've been out in this sort of wind. But surely we must get some proper spring soon."

Mrs. Mowbray seemed to have no observations to offer with regard to spring or indeed anything else, and in silence took up her needlework. This assumption of needlework had always a paralysing effect on Agnes : it was a storm-cone, indicative of an approaching severity of weather, for usually she only worked at it when alone. But Agnes had come with the object of giving her mother distraction and entertainment, and she talked on.

" Alan is very much pleased with his new book," she said. " It is getting on famously. Another three weeks, he thinks, will see the first draft finished. After that he will be very busy revising his earlier novels for the collected edition. He loves the idea of the collected edition, for it looks as if his earlier books, some of which are out of print, are wanted again. But the revision will be a tremendous business. I doubt if we shall get away for his holiday before the end of August. He will not tackle the second draft of his new book till the autumn."

When Mrs. Mowbray was in the mood symbolized by embroidery she could find some depressing inference to draw from the most cheerful conversation. In the strange ways of the human heart she liked then to hurt the people who cared for her. You could not hurt a stranger, for indifference is never wounded : affection alone is vulnerable. She had the feeling also that Agnes was sorry for her and was trying to divert her mind from her afflictions, and that was a great liberty to take. . . . She could hurt Agnes most through Alan. Her small white face seemed to draw itself in towards her mouth.

" I have often wanted to speak to you about Alan," she said. " As you know, I don't see him much, for, so rightly, he prefers to spend his time over his writing than waste it over me. I quite understand that : I quite realize how right he is. I liked Alan's earlier work, in fact I was one of the first to appreciate it, as you know very well. But what a sad falling off in these last years ! What is the matter with him ? Is he happy ? "

Agnes had an unlimited tenderness for people who were being disagreeable on purpose : she looked on them as children. Like children who yell and scream and hit, they were probably uncomfortable, and that made them fractious. Certainly her mother felt uncomfortable after her bad cold : besides she herself had been late for her appointment, and Mrs. Mowbray hated unpunctuality. But what secret discomfort her remark gave Agnes, she could not know, for Agnes, so far from admitting certain qualms, certain misgivings of her own about Alan's work to anyone else, was still trying not to admit them to herself.

" Yes, dear, I think Alan's very happy," she said. " And as regards his work there's no one so critical of it as he is himself."

" The critical faculty may suffer the same degeneration as the creative," said Mrs. Mowbray with a sigh. (That was rather neat.)

Agnes would not allow the surface of her radiant placidity to be disturbed. Her mother had been mewed up in the house for several days : no wonder she took a gloomy view of whatever topic.

" Oh, I don't notice anything of the kind in Alan," she said. " He's almost too critical of himself. There was a chapter the other day which he had just finished after a fortnight's hard work, and at the end when I read it to him he would have none of it. ' It's slack stuff,' he said. ' Tear it up, and we'll begin it over again.' And away it went into the waste-paper basket."

Mrs. Mowbray took a dozen fierce silent stitches. Her needle made movements as of a wasp's sting, stabbing the fabric.

" And you won't get your holiday till the end of August, I think you said," she observed. " I am sorry for that."

" Oh, August in London is not so bad," said Agnes.

" I didn't mean that. I was thinking, no doubt very selfishly, of myself. I shall be getting back here at the beginning of September, just when you go away. Alan, of course, knew that as usual I should spend August in the Isle of Wight. Unfortunate, to say the least of it, that he should have fixed——"

Agnes could not quite let that pass. There are, limits to what even a child should say.

"Oh, mother, you really speak as if Alan had planned his holiday to begin just when yours was ending," Agnes said. "Alan didn't think anything at all about it."

"I shall hope, then, to see you in October," said Mrs. Mowbray.

Agnes laughed; that, after all, was the best thing to do, for Mrs. Mowbray was positively parodying herself this afternoon.

"But it's only April yet, dear," she said. "There's a lot of trouble to get through first. And you really mustn't be so vexed with us all. You've had a horrid cold, and that always makes the world seem hollow. Now what shall we do? Would you like me to read to you? Or shall we talk? And what a lovely cap you've got on. You look like a Rembrandt lady. I shall wear caps the moment my hair begins to grow grey."

"I'm not happy about Alan," said Mrs. Mowbray ruthlessly. "I often think about him, though he's sadly changed, Agnes. I wonder you don't notice it. Of course the change strikes you less, seeing him as you do every day and all day."

Agnes's face darkened into trouble and emerged again. It was being rather hard work to-day, but she proposed to stick to it. . . .

"I really don't think that much which concerns Alan escapes me," she said. "If there are two people in the world on whom I keep my eye, they are you and he. And you look fifty times better than you did yesterday. You're looking really quite yourself again. See if Dora doesn't agree with me."

Mrs. Mowbray held up her hand with the stinging needle poised.

"April the twenty-third!" she said. "I last saw Dora precisely two months ago. February the twenty-third was the exact day and then only for a minute. Two months, calendar not lunar, are a long time in which not to see one of your only two children."

There was nothing better to be done than to look on the bright side of Dora. Perseveringly Agnes looked at it.

"But Dora's been abroad," she said. "She got back only a couple of days ago. I haven't seen her yet. One doesn't see Dora for several days after she has had a journey. Journeys disarrange Dora terribly. I had a line from her in Paris, where she was spending a week on her way back from the Riviera. I wonder how much she owes her dress-maker there at this moment."

"You always take a hard view of your sister," said Mrs. Mowbray with a disconcerting change of attitude. "Poor Dora!"

"But, darling, what do you mean?" asked Agnes. "Dora's inimitable. I love Dora. I shall also be wildly jealous of her when I see her new Paris gowns. Oh me, oh me! How I adore nice clothes! But what's the good of them to me when they're wasted on Alan? He has no appreciation of them, bless him. He doesn't know sackcloth from satin, and as for cut—if I appeared in an ulster for dinner with some bird's-eggs in my hair he wouldn't notice. He hates going out, as you know: just now and then on Sunday nights when he's not working, he'll let me accept something. In fact we're dining out next Sunday with Mrs. Probyn, who has been very persevering. Going out distracts him: he thinks he does not work so well next day. And when he's having a holiday he likes to go away to some perfectly empty place where he can really rest.''

There was quite a variety of topics here on which censure and gloom could be hung. Mrs. Mowbray chose the topic of Alan, for artistic draping.

''I hope you may never feel that you've behaved unwisely about him,'' she said, ''in letting him sink into a hermit's life. To my mind that accounts for the falling off in his work, which I notice so terribly, though I am sure I hope that nobody else does. A fading of all vitality, of all distinction. . . .''

Agnes came out of this enlivening interview with a leaden heart. Certainly not even she, so habitually dissatisfied with her tale of service for Alan, could accuse herself of selfishness with regard to her mother's latest indictment, for often she pined with the poignancy of hunger or thirst for a larger human intercourse. But now she wondered if she had been wise. Would she have done better for Alan if she had insisted all these years on a less sequestered existence? Yet how could she have set up her judgment in defiance of his? The thing was not thinkable : the conditions that he felt he needed for his work were dictated by him, and by her rigidly obeyed. She must not disquiet herself over that, and yet how could she help wondering. . . .

There was some cause for perturbation. Her mother, it seemed, had noticed a loss of vitality in his work, and there she put finger on to a sore, a tender place. How often had Agnes asked herself whether that was true, and shrunk from facing the answer ! That question had long hovered over her ; like some fluffy seed it had hung in the air. Now her mother's words had caused it to settle, implanting itself in her mind, the soil of which was fruitful with tenderness and affection, and when it had sprouted a little, she would have to scrutinize it. Till then, it would be better, as far as possible, to avert her attention from it, letting the subconscious processes of her mind effect the ripening of it. It was no good to watch the growth of a thought : you had to look away from it, so she reasoned, and after giving it time to mature, regard it again. That process was a familiar one; often she saw it at work in Alan. He would take little seedlings of thought, and plant them in his mind, that aloof and candid mind, which nourished by processes unknown the growth which burst into exquisite flowerings. But, so her mother's question prompted her to ask, were these flowers of his growing scentless and devitalized, mere artificial wreaths of bloom which drew no nourishment from the kindly earth? Some faint tremor as of the solid structure of her path rocking and stirring, conveyed itself to her.

She steadied herself against it as she crossed the windy square. She had no time for such idle phantasms of the imagination. It was a sufficient task, and one that filled the day to co-operate with her husband when he needed her manual aid, to be always ready at his elbow with her companionship on which his comfort so much relied, and to be acute with criticism when he, more rarely, desired it. To do that she had to give a constant and vivid attention to his work, so that the finer shadows and lights of his design should not escape her. And then, when he could spare her, there was always her mother on the other side of the square, not so much (to look at it quite frankly) appreciating the pleasure of her presence, as taking note of the hours of her absence. . . . At that a thought totally unbidden popped with ripeness in Agnes's mind, even as gorse-pods pop on a sunny day on the hillside, and scatter their seeds. It was wonderful, in fact, how two people could use the entire time and energies of a third, and

yet leave her with the sense that she might be doing
so much more for them. Just now that seemed de-
pressingly true : she ought to have been at home before this, giving Alan his tea, and yet she had the
sense of neglecting her mother. Mrs. Mowbray had
alluded, just before Agnes left, to the solitary evening which lay in front of her, indicating, without
possibility of mistake that it was her daughter's duty
to make it less desolate. But in that case what would
happen to Alan and the hour of work which followed
dinner, prolonged sometimes till the parlour-maid
brought in the tray of lemonade and Marie biscuits?
'Oh, where shall wisdom be found?' thought she,
half amused at her own despondency, as a gust of
sleety wind blew her from the threshold on the turn
of the latch-key into the house. But the question remained unanswered,—or perhaps the answer consisted in hurrying upstairs, already late, and keeping
Alan waiting no longer. Agnes's mind was more at
home in directing her actions than in considering
problems in the abstract, and whatever general solution wisdom might inspire, it certainly inspired the
particular one of being in her place at the writing-
table, ready for his dictation, as soon as possible.

He looked up as she entered, and his relief at her
advent was clearly predominant.

"Here you are at last, my dear," he said. "I
began to be afraid that something unforeseen had
delayed you seriously. Have you had tea with your
mother? No? Then I insist on your having it now.
There is plenty of time : it still wants nearly ten
minutes to half-past five, and we seldom begin before
that. There is no hurry at all, though as soon as
you are ready, quite ready—and how was your
mother? Yes, you are looking at the water which I
so awkwardly spilt as I was filling up the teapot for
you. I deserve to be scolded. But I was very much

absorbed in the slips I was putting out. I did not
see that the teapot lid was shut. I scalded myself a
little. Nothing to matter : a drop or two only."
His enquiry about her mother had been quite dis-
missed from his mind in the greater news about the
awkward accident with the lid of the teapot.

" Oh, what clumsy folk men are," she said. " All
over the tea-cloth, Alan ! But you are forgiven : I
should have been here, and then it would not have
happened. Now I'll take my cup over to the table,
as you have everything ready, and drink it as I write."

He raised himself rather stiffly from his low chair,
and took up the big ivory paper-knife which he
always handled as he strolled about the room dictating to her. This was a highly-prized object, for it
had belonged to Flaubert. The tradition was that
the master had been wont to handle it in his frenzied
pursuits of the ' mot propre,' and Alan found some
suggestion of inspirational wizardry in using it
in the same way.

" Well, dear, if you're quite sure you'll be comfortable like that, let us begin," he said. " As I was
waiting for you, I arranged all the notes and slips
that I shall require. But wait a minute. Perhaps
you will want another cup of tea after our long walk
to-day. I should dislike feeling that you wanted
that, and were unwilling to interrupt me. I know
how unselfish you are. You would sooner sit still,
wanting more refreshment, than risk throwing me
out of gear by getting up. So take five minutes more,
dear. We shall still get our clear two hours before
dressing time. As a matter of fact—oh, I'm a selfish
old fellow, I'm afraid—there is just one more thought
I should like to scribble down before we begin. So
drink your tea at leisure, and don't think you're de-
laying me."

Agnes did not want more refreshment than she had

provided herself with, but she must appreciate his consideration for her.

"I am thirsty after our windy walk," she said. "Just one cup more."

The five minutes of indulgence had not spent itself before he was on his feet again with Flaubert's paper-knife in his hand. She moved to her seat at the writing-table.

"Shall I read you the last paragraph?" she asked, opening the dictation-book in front of her. "You stopped with an unfinished sentence."

"Yes, read," he said.

He picked up the last few words of the unfinished sentence and repeated them over to himself once or twice below his breath. Then he spoke aloud.

"The very fact of these complications," he said. "Yes, dear—write, please— 'The very fact of these complications, comma, the difficulties which faced his decision seemed to give him new stability. He no longer wavered and floated, comma, he had something definite to attach himself to, semi-colon, the very difficulties became his anchor, full stop.' No: erase 'became his anchor.' The very difficulties" . . .

He walked to and fro, stroking the paper-knife, then peered among the slips which covered the writing-table and pounced on one.

"Aha, I have it," he said. "Go back to 'He no longer wavered and floated,' and erase all that comes after. Then go on. 'He no longer wavered and floated, semi-colon, the very opposition which his mind encountered served to keep it steady in the air, full stop. Like a bird with pinions spread to the wind, comma, like a child's kite that uses the force of the breeze for its soaring.'" . . . . He crumpled up the slip from which he had just read, and threw it into the waste-paper basket. It had fulfilled its destiny.

"That is exactly what I want," he said. "How

quickly our observation by the Serpentine this afternoon has proved valuable! Read, please, once more
from the beginning of the paragraph, and then I
fancy we shall sail along."

But this optimism was not justified; inspiration was
not flowing freely with him this afternoon. He dictated a sentence, had it read aloud and then erased.
He fumbled for a word he wanted, impatiently fingering Flaubert's paper-knife, and had to leave a blank
till it visited him : he searched in vain for a slip on his
table which he was sure contained a phrase which
aptly expressed his thought.

Finally, after three-quarters of an hour of alternate
dictation and erasure, he told Agnes to cross out the
two paragraphs which were the meagre output of this
session.

" We must be ruthless, dear," he said, including
her, as he always did in his work. " We must not
let anything stand that does not pass our censorship.
If once we begin to let slack sentences, sentences not
clear-cut and crystal slip into our work, we shall go
all to bits. Let us treat ourselves to five minutes relaxation, and then tackle our problem again. A
cigarette, perhaps, a few whiffs at a cigarette would
clear these clouds. Odd, isn't it, that we can never
tell what is going on in the machinery of our brains.
Sometimes, as for instance this afternoon, I thought
our engine was ready to work, all bright and shining,
well-lubricated by our walk and with a full head of
steam rumbling in our boilers. But there's a bit of
grit, a speck of dust somewhere, which impedes it.
Five minutes pause, then. Perhaps you would play
me some little morsel of Bach or Mozart, dear, while
I relax, one of those delicate inevitable little melodies
that are such examples of simple perfect workmanship. Yes, that's nice. That's just what we need!
But softly, dear, quite softly, make a whisper of it."

The second attempt was more prosperous, and presently Agnes's pen was moving along without check. He always spoke very slowly when he was dictating, with frequent short pauses, and her hand easily kept pace with him. From long practice this writing had become a very mechanical affair to her : her hand as if by a distinct and local intelligence of its own took down the words without the conscious attention of her brain, which could follow its own line of independent thought unchecked.

How familiar were such hours as these! For fifteen years since, at the age of twenty, she married him, they had formed the main occupation of her days. Sometimes, as now, he would be dictating the first draft of a book, while he walked up and down with Flaubert's paper-knife in his hand; then, when that was finished, he would take her manuscript with little compliments on its exquisite neatness, and, sitting in his chair by the table, dictate it to her all over again with innumerable minute additions and omissions and alterations. Chapter by chapter, as finished, this was sent to the typist's, so that by the time they had arrived at the end of the second dictation, there was a pile of typewritten sheets ready for revision. Then it became her task to read aloud, fresh corrections were made by him, and finally there came the proofs from the printer's to be acutely scanned once more. With the electric light lit on dark winter mornings, and on long winter evenings, or with the room bright with the lingering sunlight of Spring and Summer, here she would be at her table, while the clock ticked out and recorded the flight of the hours, but gave no account of the innumerable days which had passed there.

Fantastically, as her hand followed his words with mechanical accuracy, she began picturing to herself the monstrous clock which would show that. Instead of sixty marks of minutes round the dial what multitude of days must be indicated there! Even if every minute's space stood for a week of these evenings of dictation, such a clock would only record the passage of a year; twice nearly would the pointer have to make this prodigious circuit before even one of the books which she inscribed and re-inscribed and then read to him and re-read, was ready for press. Opposite her now, as she sat here beside the green-shaded lamp, she could see, glimmering on the wall, the white vellum covers of the books for which she had been amanuensis. The first copy that came from the publisher's was always hers: it was specially bound for her and presented to her by Alan, with some graceful little legend on the fly-leaf, on the day of publication. He had given her also, as wedding present, a copy of all the books he had written before their marriage, and there in the dusk they all glimmered, a slowly lengthening line, which was the harvest of his laborious life. When many days were sped, the line would be an inch or so longer.

And in that glimmering white line, so now it struck her, was the harvest of her own life, as well as his. Fifteen, at any rate, of her own years were gathered and garnered there. But whereas he had imagined and wrought out those books, she had had little more hand in them (for all his asseveration of partnership) than the typist or the printer.

She became conscious that his voice was silent now : the cessation of it recalled her to her work, and she ran her eye over what she had written, in the unlikely case of his wanting to consult her about it. But presently he began dictating again, and the monotonous murmur served, as with her hand she automatically followed his words, to set free again the train of thought that flowed in her subconscious mind. . . .

She had at one time (she must not forget that) garnered rapture and revelation from these hours. That time was long past : now his dictation never ruffled her dead unemotional calm. But in the earlier years of her marriage these hours had been not less than sacramental to her : as if before an altar, she had witnessed the incarnation into words of those wondrous thoughts of his which in her girlhood had been her religion. Hers had been the ecstasy of being his evangelist, to whom he dictated his wisdom and his tenderness, which, when she had written and re-written and read (but not till then), would be given to the world. While the writing was in progress, she, so she used to hold her breath to think, was taking his thoughts down from his mouth and in her hand-writing alone did they exist. What pains she had taken with that, making it the thing of beauty which it was now, so that it might be less unworthy to record his utterance. Oh, wonderful, romantic hours, soft and fiery !

She strove in vain to recapture the smallest glimmer from that fire, the faintest glimpse of the blue hills where once she had wandered in caverns and bowers of enchantment. The memory of them remained, dried and pressed, without sap or fragrance. What had occasioned the change, what was the process of the disillusioning alchemy ? Had she altered, growing dull and stolid and unappreciative, or, far more disturbingly, was the change, as her mother had suggested, in him ? She would infinitely have preferred that it was she whose fire had faded : the other possibility she contemplated with blank dismay, unwilling to face it, but knowing that sometime she must look steadily at it. Supposing Alan, too, felt that his powers were fading ? What would there be left for him ?

She recalled herself to her work with a sense of coming back to it from a long way off. Her hand was poised motionless above the paper, and yet she had not been conscious that his voice had paused from its dictation. She heard him enunciate the end of a sentence, and realized that what he was saying bore no relation to the last words which she had recorded. Then he paused.

- " I am not so dissatisfied with that, dear," he said cheerfully. " Please read out all you have written since we took up our work again. A-ha! I thought we should progress well this evening."

It was with some dreadful misgiving that she had missed something, that her hand had ceased to act by its own intelligence, that she began. She came to the end of the unfinished sentence, which dangled in the air. The few words that came after made no sense.

" Yes," said he. " Go on, dear."

Utter dismay seized her.

" Oh, Alan, I've done something dreadful," she said. " I must have missed what you've been saying. That's all I have got down. Was there more?"

She heard some incredulous ejaculation come from him, as he moved to her side and looked over the page.

" But what have you been doing?" he asked in that shrill agitated voice which sounded like that of a frightened child. " For the last ten minutes you have taken down nothing. What has happened to you? Are you ill? Have you been asleep?"

" I don't know," she said. " I ceased to write ——"

" But without noticing it?" he cried. " It is incredible: I cannot grasp it yet. Was what I was saying so dull and uninteresting that you simply drowsed? I never ceased dictating for a moment. Ah, dear me, dear me! I am terribly upset. To

think that you should have failed me so utterly.
There was that difficult passage about Evan's return
which I have dreaded for days. I distrusted my own
ability about it, but this afternoon a wonderful clearness came to me : it flowed along without any effort
of mine. And that's all lost! What are we to do
now? I shall never be able to recapture it."

In and out of Agnes's mind there flashed the feeling "He's not thinking of me at all." But it was
instantly drowned in her own compunction. She laid
her hand on his.

"Alan, it was wretchedly, criminally stupid of
me," she said. "I am utterly sorry and remorseful.
You must forgive me. Such a thing has never happened before. It was an aberration, a madness!"

"Yes, yes," he said. "But how did it happen?
Was what I said so barren of interest to you that you
couldn't keep your mind on it at all? We have
often talked over that situation and its difficulties. I
am quite mystified : I am all at sea! Well, the thing
is done : it's no use crying over spilt milk. I must
keep my eye on you, I see, when we are at work together. It is a shock to me to find that when I am in
my happiest vein your attention can wander so much
that you sit there quite lost in your own thoughts.
But I make no reproaches, please understand that.
It is a misfortune which has happened to you and me.
Now let me pull myself together again, else I shall
never be able to recall what we have lost. Kindly
read over again all that you have got down."

Agnes heard that her voice was shaking. Bitterly
contrite as she was for her wanderings, she was also
profoundly hurt that he had no sense of sympathetic
compassion for her. Her penitence, her request for
forgiveness had gone unregarded : he could feel
nothing but the risk of losing the fruit of his inspiration. Never before had it been so plain to her how

his work was so paramount to him that everything else was without weight in the scales. But with an effort she controlled her voice; it would but upset him more if she allowed herself to be agitated too. She had to repair as far as possible the loss she had occasioned.

She read through again all that she had written up to this terrible hiatus. There he sat, sunk and bent, his hands covering his eyes, so as to shut out all distractions (her distress among them), and enable him to concentrate himself entirely on the unrecorded sentences.

" Kindly read it once more," he said. " At present I have no idea how I phrased the end of that unfinished sentence ! "

The second reading promised better. Before she was through with it he was on his feet and had repossessed himself of Flaubert's paper-knife. When she came to the end of her record, his voice took up the unfinished sentence and completed it. Fragments of the next occurred to him.

" Take another sheet of paper, please," he said, " and jot down exactly what I say, however fragmentary. I think I have a glimpse of the next sentence or two. Ah, there is a hint of it on one of my slips which I have thrown away. Let us search the paper-basket. Yes, that's it : lucky I did not tear it up. Now we are embarked again, I hope."

A dark half-hour, slowly brightening, ensued. Scattered fragments, all carefully recorded, recalled themselves to him and with reading and re-reading they slowly pieced themselves together. Blank places were filled, but in spite of all his efforts of recollection, there was still one passage which eluded him. The session was already prolonged beyond its usual limits, the one game of picquet which marked the arrival of half-past seven was abandoned, and at length he ceased from his walkings, and put down the paper-knife.

"Well, that's the most I can do for the present," he said. "The more I cudgel my brains now, the further off I seem to get from that missing passage. I know just what it was about, but the phrasing, the arrangement entirely escapes me. Let us banish all search for it. Let us have our dinner and force our minds into other channels. Then, perhaps, when we come back fresh to it, we shall find what we want."

She put the written sheets in order, and stood waiting in silence when all was square and tidy again. She had expressed her contrition, and asked his forgiveness, and for her there was nothing more to say. But it seemed to her crucially to matter whether he was going to make any response to that : she found herself hungering for his acknowledgment of her regrets. It did not concern her personally, but it intimately concerned him, that he should recognise how dreadful for her was her lapse of attention. She waited; there was nothing but the trouble of his silence.

"There's the evening paper just come in," she said at length. "Let's switch our minds off on to that, Alan, as you suggest."

"A good idea," said he. "Let's look. Ireland ! Dear me, things seem in a very bad way there. The conference at Genoa. A great deal hinges on that. But things are very critical, it seems. A shilling off the income tax is prophesied. Let us hope that proves true. Well, we have found some topics to occupy and distract us."

Throughout dinner he, with industrious detachment discussed the questions which the evening paper had suggested, and his very strenuousness in keeping his attention fixed on these extraneous matters showed how little they concerned his real mind. Genoa, Ireland, the income-tax twinkled with only the remotest light, but he regarded them steadily, lest his eyes should wander to the dreadful eclipse of the sun itself, over which the shadow was passing. Then followed a quiet half-hour in the drawing-room over coffee, and as its term approached, his glance kept wandering to the table where all lay ready. At last he got up.

"Well, dear, if you are rested and refreshed," he said, "shall we get to work again? I wonder if it would be troubling you too much to read over, just once more, what we have recaptured. It will assist me I think towards further recoveries."

Before long it was manifest that this hope was not to be realized. His face grew drawn and tired with the unprofitable effort, and at length he gave up the search.

"I think we must leave it," he said. "We seem to be doing no good. I had hoped that by absorbing ourselves in other interests we might have disinterred the missing pieces. But it seems not to be so. Leave a blank, please, which to-morrow we must patch in, as best we can. Now I have a little more prepared from my notes made this morning, which is matured enough to be dictated if you are not tired."

"Yes, let us go on," said she.

But in the consciousness of having left a blank behind, his progress was groping and uncertain, and before the usual hour for quitting work he stopped.

"I am unusually fatigued, dear, to-night," he said, "which I suppose is not to be wondered at. Or perhaps that buffeting we got on our walk this afternoon may have been a little too much for me, though, to be sure, I felt fresh enough when we came in. Let us take it that that is the cause. I think I shall be going to bed. And you?"

"I shall follow very soon," she said. "Good-night. Sleep well."

He looked at her with those wonderful brown eyes, that were shadowed with fatigue and worry.

"I hope so," he said. "I daresay I shall."

Agnes sat for a while yet, before the expiring fire, conscious mainly of an unutterable depression, consequent directly, she must suppose, on her lapse of this afternoon. She could not help, absurd though it might seem to anyone else but herself, taking it terribly to heart, for, during all these years, it had been the main business of her life to assist if not inspire Alan. But behind that—here was that which all evening had haunted and menaced her—was the failure in her confidence with regard to Alan's life and her own. There stood the row of glimmering book-backs, which was his harvest. Round and round her head like some persistent gnat a question buzzed and poised and momentarily settled to sting. What was the true result of this labour of years?

To all men alike, strenuous or idle, self-absorbed or laden with bounties for others, there must come, so it inevitably seemed to Agnes, at some such date as that to which she, midway between thirty and forty, had arrived, some visit from the auditor of their life's accounts. He was far from being an unkindly presence. It was as if, while she sat here, watching the clinking and cooling of the fire, he came up invisible behind her, laid quiet finger-tips on her forehead, and by his touch drew out what lay within. She let her books stand open to him, not attempting to conceal anything, and he seemed to say "Yes, yes, I quite see. Your age? Close on thirty-six, are you?"

But where his fingers had touched her forehead, it was not fanciful to suppose that little lines and wrinkles defined themselves, and where his fingers had rested on her hair, that grew low on her brow, there were fadings of its bright auburn into grey. . .

Alan slept in the dressing-room which adjoined her bedroom. Usually he was later in coming up to bed than she, and when he had undressed and was ready for sleep, he opened this door of communication before he quenched his light, and looked in for a moment to bid her good-night. This evening, however, the door was shut, and after she had got into bed she saw a thin line of light on the floor there, and, lying very still, could hear that he was softly walking up and down his room as if still dictating. As clearly as if the door was open she could visualize him, still searching for the lost passage which had made tragedy out of their tranquillity. But now this brought her no emotional impulse. The fault had been hers, and she was sorry for it and had fully said so, and if now he was still agonizing over the loss, it would not assist him in his efforts to remember, that she should reiterate her regrets. Nor indeed had she any desire to do so, the best part of penitence lay in resolve for the future not in regret for the past. But what big words to use, even in thought, over such a thing. How much did it matter if he recaptured that passage or not? But it mattered immensely to him.

. . .

She was drowsy with some dead weight of depression: as she slid downwards into the dimnesses of sleep all that which all evening had vaguely menaced her encompassed her still. Nothing of her own, no sense of personal loss in the vanished years retarded the descent: if the wrinkles and the grey were coming to her smooth skin and the smouldering fire of her hair before they had throbbed beneath passionate hands and eager lips, it was a common fate. She had not lacked, as many women do, all sting and exultation in living. There had dawned splendour on her mind and raptures on her sense of beauty in those days when Alan's books had been to her girlhood the bread of life, and if now the glory had faded, it had once been hers and she owed it to him. It was he who was menaced, and it was for him she feared. For herself she must do all that tenderness and affection prompted, not be lazy, not be self-centred. She, who to-day had been but a hindrance to him, was capable of helping him again.

She had dozed into unconsciousness when with a leap of her heart that set her upright in bed, she heard what seemed a violent crash, repeated and again repeated. To her dazed eyes there came an impression of brutal and blinding blaze. Then, instantaneously, she recovered her waking perceptions, and realized that Alan had knocked once, twice and thrice at her door, and had now opened it, disclosing the light from his dressing-table which shone full in her dazzled eyes. Now, too, she heard him speak her name.

"Ah, you startled me, dear," she said. "What is the matter? You don't feel unwell, do you? You haven't caught cold in that bitter wind this afternoon?"

She turned on the switch that dangled above her pillow as she spoke and encountered a radiant face.

"No, indeed, dearest," he said. "I hope that if I felt unwell I should not have disturbed you. I should have tucked myself up in bed, and waited for the morning. I am not so inconsiderate as that, am I?"

He had sat down, already robed for the night in his brown woollen pyjamas, on the side of the bed, and she saw with sudden surprise how old and lean he was. His scanty grey hair, ruffled by the passage of his shirt, was transparent to the light behind him, and the light in front showed his thin neck, like that of a plucked bird, and the prominent arteries in his forehead. Knee and shoulder were sharp beneath their covering, and his thighs were sapless sticks.

" No, it is no selfish errand on which I have disturbed your sleep, dear," he said. " I knew—ah, don't I know you, Agnes?—I knew that you would wake early and be miserable and toss and turn, unless I brought you my news. I've come to you with such a sleeping draught ! "

Of course she had guessed it by now, and now, wide-awake she must give him the full satisfaction of his impulse. She must make him understand of what transcendant importance his news was. It could only concern one thing.

" Ah, Alan," she said, " how perfectly sweet of you to come to me. I should have had a wretched night if you hadn't."

" Say it then," he said, blinking at her. " Make your guess. You are right, dear, I feel sure."

" But it's no guess," said she. " What could it be but one thing? Of course you have recollected what it was that you could not remember all this miserable evening ! "

" Better than that even," he said. " Guess again."

Agnes could think of nothing better.

" I can't guess anything further," she said. " Tell me : don't tease me."

" Well, not only have I recollected it, but before coming to tell you that, I have written it all down. It shan't escape us again : no fear of that now. It is there on my table in pencil, ready to be copied, in your lovely handwriting, into that blank space we left for it. So you'll sleep well now, dear ? "

" Ever so well," said she. " Thank you, Alan."

He drew his hand over her bed-clothes, down from hip to knee, and knee to ankle.

" I shall sleep well, too," he said. " When a little pleasant excitement has subsided, I shall sleep beautifully."

CHAPTER II

WHEN this first draft of a book was in progress, Agnes's mornings were at her own disposal, for Alan was then occupied in making notes and sketching in the design which the evening's dictation should elaborate. In the mornings, therefore, not only was her co-operation unneeded, but her very presence was undesired, and for two and a half hours, from half-past ten to one, he was in solitary sanctuary in the room where they worked. No interruption of any sort must come to him then, for such might jolt his elbow, so to speak, as it delicately traced and charted the future progress, thus wasting not only the work of the morning hours, but diminishing the material for the dictation in the evening, which was then being matured. So sacred indeed was the morning that it was permissible to be humorous on the subject, and Agnes, in case the house caught fire, was supposed to be under instructions not to warn Alan of the conflagration until the fire-escape was ready at the drawing-room window to rescue him and the notes he had made. . . . At one o'clock he eased off and perhaps glanced at the paper, or played very softly on the piano with one finger, the air of some inevitable little tune, like that with which last night she had beguiled his interval in dictation. But sometimes he was disposed for a stroll in the garden of the square, and liked her companionship, so by one o'clock she was always in the house ready to accompany him.

But for these two hours and a half, he had no need of her; and her first business this morning after her household orderings were done, was to go across to her mother's to take her out, if she felt so inclined, or attend to such small jobs as she might want done for her. The gale and rigour of yesterday were gone : a light warm wind blew from the south, and it seemed that at last the Spring had come. But in spite of these alluring conditions, Mrs. Mowbray decided to spend the morning in bed, so as finally to rid herself of her cold, but Agnes would be helpful if she would examine and add up for her the tradesmen's monthly books, which had come in that morning. . . . When that was done, and her mother, after due complaints as to the total, had signed a cheque as if it was her death warrant, there was nothing more that could detain her here. Her mother clearly preferred reading the paper to conversation, and Agnes walked to her sister's house in Knightsbridge to see Dora, who ought by now to have arranged herself again after the journey from Paris, and to look at the marvellous clothes which she would certainly have brought back with her. Agnes despaired of reforming her own character in this regard, and very wisely made no serious attempt to do so. She adored pretty clothes, though her practise, for want of an appreciative audience, was ascetic enough. Dora had large cedarwood cupboards in which hung rainbows, and Agnes madly envied them and their contents.

Dora Muir, a couple of years older than her sister, led a blameless but hectic existence. Her husband, a man of large fortune, got on excellently with her, but equally well without her, and as the real passion of his life was not Dora but experimental chemistry, they did not see very much of each other, and Dora pursued a pleasant hurricane life, blowing where she listed. She was always in a state of high excitement about something, but never let one thing engross her attention for long. Life therefore consisted for her in a succession of exhilarating climaxes without reactions, for she passed from one to the other without ever leaving peaks. She leaped from one to another, always on the summit of some fad or *dernier cri,* and so little time did she spend on each that when next she alighted on it, it seemed quite new. She was absurd, but to Agnes's view, adorable, and in these days when everybody studied economy, it was exhilarating to see anyone who was so wonderfully wasteful of time, money and energy. She sparkled like a fountain that eternally played and was strictly useless. She had an incisive tongue with which she camouflaged an extremely kind heart, covered her face with powder in order to conceal the freshness of her complexion, and talked a great deal of nonsense in order to hide the shrewdness of her common-sense. In moments of emotion her shrewdness and her kindness sometimes peeped out, just as a high wind would occasionally blow the powder from her face.

Agnes found her in her bedroom, which she seldom entered till dawn or left till lunch-time. She was paying a three-days' visit to her cloistered husband this afternoon, and in order to make a suitable selection from her wardrobe, her maid had been bidden to display the spoil from Paris. The effect was that of a tropical jungle, in the middle of which sat Dora, like the leader of an exploring party, whose business it was to cut a path through these exuberant growths. Her maid was the exploring-party who followed. Dora was eating a green apple.

"Darling Agnes," she said, "how sweet of you to come and see me. I should have rung you up, but I couldn't remember your address. Yes, an unripe apple. It is terribly hard to get them unripe: they are almost always ripe. My wretched digestion: the only thing that keeps me alive is to eat two sour

apples every morning on an empty stomach, and
three more after dinner on a full one. That is all,
Peckham, I will ring for you when I want you
again.".

Her maid laid down something entirely made of
feathers, and slid from the room.

" Yes, that is really her name," said Dora.
" Peckham. Isn't it wonderful? And a treasure.
She's the only human being who has ever understood
me. All my maids have odd names. Do you remember Sassaparrata? I have cause to. Yes,
apples. The second series in the evening gives me
the most marvellous dreams. I send them to a
psychoanalyst, who infers from them extraordinary
sexual experiences which I had before I was old
enough to remember anything. I must have been a
very odd child if he is right. Last night I dreamed
about boiled rabbit, and I fully expect to find that I
had an affair with a hair-dresser at the age of three.
How silly it all is, but you come to see me, darling,
before my brain has made its toilet and is present-
able. . . . Besides I said all the sensible things
years ago, so what's left? What have you come
about? And how is your monstrous Alan?"

Agnes laughed.

" My monstrous Alan is very well," she said.
" One of the reasons why I came to see you is that I
wanted a tonic. I did such a dreadful thing last
night. I forgot to take down what Alan was dictating to me."

Dora took up the second green apple.

" A very good thing too, I wish you would always
forget," she said. " But for goodness sake don't talk
to me about Alan. What a ghastly mistake you
made when you married him. I suppose you disagree with me. That's a comfort, for nothing makes
me feel more wretched than to have people feeling as

I do. It makes me feel so common. And so you go
on still taking down Alan's interminable remarks and
telling him how wonderful he is. Alan's novels!
Indeed they're fiction, as they don't resemble in the
most remote manner anything that was or could be
real. Have you ever seen the reflection of the moon
in a bucket of milk? I can't say I ever have, but I
feel as if I had, and it bears the same resemblance to
the sun as Alan's romances bear to life. So if you
came to tell me about Alan——"

"But I didn't," said Agnes. "I came to see you.
Also I came to see your new gowns. My dear, what
delicious things."

"Now, Agnes, don't be tactful. When you use
your tactful voice, I know you always mean something else. You think, for instance, that I'm too old
for pink and light blue like that little soap-bubble
you're staring at. But you haven't got the slightest
idea of the philosophy of dress. One dresses in a
certain way in order to feel like the people whom that
particular dress suits. Sometimes I want to feel sixteen, and when I do, that frock will assist me. What
does it matter what other people think, as long as one
feels as one wishes to feel? In Paris they understand
that, but in London they never understand anything.
If I wore that frock in Paris, everyone would see
what I was after: they would know I wanted to feel
like sixteen, and would ask me whether it was not
rather late for a *jeune fille* to be still up. If I wore
corduroy trousers and hob-nailed boots, they would
see that I wanted to feel like a market-gardener, and
would ask me how the turnips were getting on. In
England they would only imagine I wanted to be
thought a Dame or some sort of strong-minded
woman. It really was a great mistake when Britain
was commanded to rise from out the azure main.
Yes: what were we talking about? How I drivel!"

Somehow these vivacious absurdities were exactly what Agnes wanted. She had escaped, she was playing truant; it was like being a child again sailing paper boats on the water-butt in the back yard, when she ought to have been practising scales. It would not be for long, it was just refreshing for a minute.

"Paris, you were talking about Paris," she said. "I like hearing about Paris."

"My dear, Paris is heaven to women like me who are forty years old and extremely stout and incapable of two consecutive ideas. The elderly and the obese are the rage in Paris now. Vulgar too. I am incomparably vulgar, and they rave about me. This is the era of hags in France, they have tired of youth and beauty. Indeed I think it was always so. Look at Diane de Poictiers : she was fifty when she became the king's mistress. Perhaps in ten years' time they will have a king of France again; I shall be just fifty then."

She finished her apple, and moved to her dressing-table clad in an apricot satin dressing-gown trimmed with swansdown. Clouds of powder then enveloped her, but her voice sounded firmly and legally out of them, as from Sinai.

"Charades!" she said. "That expresses life in Paris. The French have the wit to see that you must dress in a way totally unsuited to you, and do all sorts of outrageous things, if you want to be fit for the stage of life. It's as indecent to be natural as to be naked, more so indeed, for they are not wearing very much just now. In fact you would have the most wonderful time, dear, if you took your monstrous Alan to Paris and behaved as you do here, writing that appalling book for him, and taking him for walks in the Park, and rubbing his nose with cold cream when he went to bed. They would imagine at once that a beautiful woman like you couldn't behave like that naturally, and would conclude that you were acting the most wonderful charade. All Paris would be absolutely certain that you had got a lover, or probably more than one, and would be all agog to know who he was. If they read Alan's books they would know that you couldn't think he was a heaven-born genius, on whose altar it was an honour to be immolated and dressed in serge. Charades, dear, I tell you, and you can't look me in the face and tell me it isn't. You don't think Alan is a heaven-born genius. You don't: you don't. Do you?"

Here was a disconcerting habit or property of Dora's. She would throw off clouds of nonsense, as thick as the powder in which she was covering herself, and from the middle of it there would suddenly leap out some lambent lightning-flash like this, which startled the listener. No thunder followed: it was innocuous, but it made an illumination. It flashed into that particular dark place, the existence of which Agnes had been denying even to herself. She was prepared to assert that ' she did,' but there was a moment's gasping pause first. Dora, skipping from summit to summit, was perfectly aware of it.

"You needn't trouble to say that you do," she said. "You're trying to convince yourself that you do, but naturally it takes a moment. But why are we talking about Alan? How you keep harking back to him. Tell me about yourself the moment you can get a word in. Really, Agnes, you are a perfect marvel. Your horribly unnatural life seems to preserve and keep you young. You don't look a day more than twenty-five, and you're more beautiful than ever. What a dreadful waste it all is! What shouldn't I have done with your nose and neck! You ought to be making a dozen men desperately miserable, because you turn your lovely nose up at them,

and one man—I don't mean Alan—insanely happy.
But, thank God, I haven't got your beauty. If I had
men would always be making love to me, and I hate
that sort of thing. As it is, I only amuse and amaze
them, and I'm sure I don't wonder. You may talk
now while I'm getting into this frock. It looks like
half-mourning, doesn't it? I wear that sort of thing
when I'm not feeling very well, and then people think
somebody is dead and are gentle to me. What news
is there? But what's the use of asking you? The
only news you know is what chapter Alan has got to.
How inhuman! Why doesn't he fall in love with
some married woman? He might gain experience
about females. And how is mother? Am I to go
and see her? She doesn't want to see me in the
least. It puts an end to her reckoning of how long
it is since she saw me, and she has to begin again.
I am certain she knows exactly the day on which I
saw her last."

Here again was a taste of this uncanny intuition.

" Yes, do go," said Agnes.

" And rob her of a grievance? I'm not sure that
it's kind. Mother doesn't enjoy seeing me. She
doesn't enjoy anything except the fact that she
doesn't enjoy anything. And then there's Alan.
Shall I come to see Alan? He looks upon me as a
freak, and quite right too, and I look on him as a
freak. I'm not Alan's sort. Look at me and tell
me if you can that I'm Alan's sort. But then nobody is. You aren't, though you would die sooner
than admit it. You're the most curious type, Agnes.
The need of your life is to be needed and to make
people comfortable. The need of mother's is to be
uncomfortable and make others so. The need of
mine is to be slightly mad. I wonder which of us is
the happiest?"

She had encased herself in the gown of half-mourning, and put a three-cornered hat with a cockade on her head. Her hair singularly bright red was puffed out over her ears with two large plaits of a slightly different shade. She had sketchily outlined in charcoal a highly curved eyebrow over one eye and a nearly straight one over the other. A final dab of rouge on her cheeks made her lips too pale, and the correction of that with a touch of carmine completed this remarkable toilet.

" I think that is sufficiently weird," she said. " An appalling appearance, darling, isn't it, but it happens to amuse me. And there's a tall ebony cane somewhere—where's Peckham?—with a large sham turquoise for a handle, which should promote a good deal of merriment. And now I'm ready for the calls of family affection. I shall drive you home, Agnes, and look in on Alan for precisely one minute. That will be enough for him and me alike, and then I shall go on to mother's. . . . Being then thoroughly soured I shall motor down to the country and spend three days with my unfortunate Claude. He passes his entire time now in his laboratory weighing salt, and is utterly happy : yes, Peckham, the tall black cane. My dear, why can't Alan be happy without you ? Then you could leave him alone, and I would teach you how to live, and to pass your time in inane pursuits which so absorb you that it is always being next Tuesday before you are aware that it is this Monday. My life is like that, a creeping disease, and I wouldn't be well for anything. How I long to live as you do, entirely devoted to other people. I think that contradicts a good deal of what I have been saying, but who wants to be consistent ? Is my hat crooked ? Yes ? It's meant to be crooked."

Alan was still sequestered in his sanctuary when the sisters arrived at Goring Square, and to Dora's great relief, Agnes discountenanced the idea of dis-

turbing him. A card would indicate Dora's pious
intention.

"But I haven't got a card," she said. "Shall I
leave a lock of my hair, though it's terribly expensive. No? Well, good-bye, dear. I shall be here
again next week, or, if not, next year. What does it
matter? Time! So silly!"

"But you must be here next week," said Agnes.
"It's my birthday on Thursday. Alan and I have a
festival. We walk and we go to the play, and we do
no work, and there is a little party in the evening."

"Very well, then. Next week, not next year.
Apples, dear. Three green apples. Now I shall
walk to the other side of the square with my motor
following immediately behind in case I feel faint.
I've had no proper exercise lately. There are
a million things more I wanted to say to you,
or did I want not to say them? But perhaps I
shall forget them before next week. And now I'll
leave you to your nightmare of a life and go back to
my own foul dreams. You're so wonderfully whole-
some. I wish you would divorce Alan."

It was necessary, of course, when Dora had been
expounding her philosophy of life, to add not a pinch
of salt merely to it, but rather to steep the whole of
her communications in a bath of the strongest brine
procurable, before they could be preserved for human
consumption, or a reasonable estimate of their truth
be arrived at. Dora's mind, as her sister had long
known was just such a jungle as her bedroom had
been this morning, and exotic growths with tropical
colours were rampant in that air. Dora's mind—
Agnes wished that Alan would turn his microscope
on to it, and after study give flawless expression to
his conclusions—was just that sort of hot swoony
place decked in monstrous hypertrophied flowers,
which infected you with its own feverish temperature,

and made the whole of life appear delirious and unreal. If you wanted to profit by Dora's experience
and judgment (for somewhere in the heart of the
jungle there was judgment) you had to hold your
breath while you plucked the flowers which grew in
that miasmic place, for fear of catching its fevers, and
then strongly pickle them in brine till they shrivelled,
and then you could examine them sometime. . . .
Alan, she felt, could have reduced these hot images
to a cool transparent truth, had he brooded and
pondered over them, but unfortunately Alan could
never regard Dora at all as a real phenomenon. He
packed away his lenses on her approach and waited
till she had ceased to cloud and colour the atmosphere.

It was nearly one o'clock, the hour at which he
might wish for her companionship in a stroll before
lunch, and she waited for him with the door open in
the little front room which looked on to the square, so
that she would hear his step on the parquetted floor
if he came out of the room where he worked. . . .
How could Dora's existence and hers be included in
any general definition, even if that definition was so
elastic and comprehensive a one as 'life'? If
Dora's existence was life, her own must surely be
death : if her own was life Dora's must surely be some
lunatic can-can. In any case, if one of them was
using her life, the other must be most incomparably
wasting it. But Dora's philosophy must certainly be
pickled before its nature could be arrived at, and
perhaps her own should be stewed in some emollient
butter.

She stirred the brine and drew, so to speak, to the
top of the vessel the salted specimens of Dora's
jungle-flowers, surprised to find how much solidity
remained after the pickling. Here was a whole mass,
still firm, of genial indulgent enjoyment. That

seemed to be an essential constituent in her jungle-flowers; it was the very stem and fibre that once held up the exuberant flower-heads. Whether its nature was altruistic or selfish did not seem much to matter; it was in itself a laudable thing. Sheer enjoyment needed no apology : it justified itself and wanted no advocate. It was not, in Dora's case, so Agnes infallibly guessed, dependent on wealth, or on the power to do and to buy exactly what she chose. She could easily envisage Dora living in a small tenement flat, sucking an orange with infinite gusto, and, with a draggled feather in her hat dancing in the gutter to the strains of a barrel organ. For the tenement flat, there was the house in Knightsbridge and others, for the orange the food of an exquisite chef, for the draggled feather the gowns from Paris, but Dora would have been just as happy in the other environment. She would have brought to it that which gave it its value, namely her own inexhaustible appreciation of gaiety.

Agnes was not on the track of moral superiority, of altruism or selfishness. She knew, with an instinct that never stirred in the direction of conscious expression that her husband was as wholly selfish as it was possible for a man to be, but she never arraigned him on that, nor did it affect her devotion to him. She was made to be devoted, he to pursue his aims in literature, Dora to be amazing. Those were their respective inclinations. But as with the vote of a jury that does not need to retire for consultation, she condemned herself for the lack of that genial enjoyment which so amply justified Dora. She was not, for instance, enjoying this waiting for Alan, in case he wanted her. She waited, so she freezingly told herself, in some mulish manner out of habit, and because she was harnessed and hobbled. That enjoyment Dora had and she had not. As for what they

missed in common, though Agnes had put this item
on the agenda to be discussed here by herself in the
window seat, she found that now, when it came up,
she did not much like the look of it. There was a
resemblance which she shrank from scrutinizing
between Dora's candid statement that her husband
spent his happiest hours in his laboratory to her own
recognition that Alan spent his on his writing.
Dora and she alike—here was what they both missed
if you look deep enough and honestly enough—were
not essentially concerned in their husbands' pursuits.
She, it is true, was an indefatigable assistant (with
lapses) in what Alan did, whereas Dora took no part
in the weighing of salt. But was there any real difference between them? The thought was disquieting, and she heard with relief the sound of Alan's
door opening, and his step tapping on the parquet of
the passage. She went to meet him. "I must enjoy," she said to herself, "I must recapture the
sense of privilege . . ." He wore a radiant face,
as when last night he had told her of the recollection
of the missing paragraph.

"Ah, my dear," he said. "Are you going to be
very indulgent to me, and be my companion in a
little stroll before lunch? I have had a glorious
morning of work, great clarity of mind, subtle perception, I hope. Though our story gets increasingly
difficult as we near the end, I seem to see the way in
a surprising manner. Difficulties melt as I progress:
they even assist. But I can do no more this morning, and indeed I have more than enough ready for
our dictation after tea. Yesterday I knew no more
than the outline of our next chapter, just the scattered
bones of it. But it is clothed in flesh now: it is
jointed and vigorous. Ezekiel: do you remember
that wonderful chapter?"

"But that's splendid," she said. "We will have

a great evening's work, Alan. How lucky, too, that
I didn't let Dora come in and interrupt you. She
came here with me, but we found your door still
shut."

He put on his hat, a great grey hat that splendidly
set his brow, and hesitated in his choice of coats.

"My Agnes is a wonderful watch-dog," he said.
"I know she will permit no intruder. I work as
securely as if a regiment of guards was round my
room. Dear me, yes. Dora, bright, brilliant Dora
might have wrought havoc. But now, if she were
here, how pleasant it would be to listen to her. What
is your news of her? You must tell me as we are
strolling in the garden. My thicker coat, I think.
But you have been out and know the temperature.
Shall I feel chilly in my lighter coat?"

Agnes threw her whole mind into the decision,
and advocated the thicker coat. You could make a
thick coat cooler by unbuttoning it, and, in extreme
cases taking it off, but no manœuvre, however art-
ful, could make a thin coat, already buttoned up,
warmer. She had to feel zest and interest in the
choice, to feel first-hand authentic enjoyment in his
morning's success.

"Yes, a great bit of work done," he said, as she
unlocked the gate of the garden. "I do not know
when I have felt a greater certainty of vision.
How curious are the ebbs and flows of the mind!
1 had no idea I was to float on so full a tide. But I
hazard an explanation of why my brain was so keen
and imaginative this morning. Now you often
divine me so well: can you guess?"

Agnes pondered the riddle. He had slept well,
but it must be something more involved than that.
He had complimented her on the skill of the new
cook. She could think of nothing else.

"No, dear, tell me," she said.

"I will, and you shall say if you think me fantastic. I could not have told you yesterday, but now the explanation will not hurt your tenderness for me. I think that our dictation yesterday afternoon, interrupted as it was by your strange, your unique little bit of mind-wandering must have proved a stimulus to me. You know how the search for what we had lost agitated me. What if that activity and agitation broke up some little habit of indolence that had been freezing over my mind. A little crust of lazy ice, eh? Our work, you know, up to this point had been moving along with unusual facility, and was I beginning, do you think, to imagine that Art was easy? Then came that sudden check. A shock, a stimulus. I think that is not too fanciful a diagnosis."

He took her arm.

"I do not ask you, my Agnes," he said, "to repeat what may have proved so successful an experiment. If it did not come off a second time, above all, if we were faced with only loss and agitation, we should be left very much in the lurch."

"You needn't have any apprehension about that," she said. "I will take no hand in such experiments again."

He slightly increased the pressure on her arm.

"I can imagine that, dear," he said. "I knew what your self-reproach must be. But I didn't increase the weight of it, did I, by any reproach of mine. I was careful not to do that."

Agnes found herself wondering what would happen if she told him that his silence, when she asked for his forgiveness, had been about the weightiest reproach that he could frame. How would he account for that silence, how, just when he was congratulating himself on his magnanimity, could he explain that? But it occurred to her only as an impossible speculation. Besides, she knew the real answer already: he had not been sorry for her then because he could think of nothing but his own loss.

" No, dear, you were most considerate," she said. Again his finger-tips pressed her arm.

" Thank you, my Agnes," he said. " And I felt sure I was right, even at the risk of awakening you, in coming to tell you as soon as ever I had caught again that paragraph of ours that had played truant so sadly. It has all ended well now, and, as I said, I believe I have you to thank for my wonderful morning of work. . . . How pleasant this calm sunshine is after our gale of yesterday! It is as if Nature was following our moods : stormy weather yesterday and glowing tranquillity now. Perhaps my lighter coat would have been sufficient, though I am sure you were right in recommending me the thicker one. If I had been chilled, Agnes would have reproached herself. And she mustn't do that! We can't have her do that.''

He was speaking, she was aware, not really of the thick coat or the thin : that, at the most, was the text on which he hung his plenary absolution with regard to the great lapse, indicating (under cover of the coat) that she must forget it all. He might have spoken thus to a penitent child, or even to a toy, some clockwork mouse which amused his leisure, whose works had suffered a momentary disarrangement, and which had now been set right again. Just that simile occurred to Agnes, perching on her from without, like a vagrant gnat, but whisked off by her before it could sting. . . .

There were several other strollers in the garden, and the appearance of the great author created its usual mild interest. Agnes heard his name pass in whisper between two women seated at the edge of the broad gravel path, and a little further on they were treated to a pleasant deferential stare. Even when he was not recognised his noble ascetic head and air of detached distinction would provoke alert glances from passers-by, but here in the immediate vicinity of their house Alan's walk in the garden before lunch had long been a limited, local sensation, like that of the passing of a fire-engine. Long, too, had Agnes known that he was neither unconscious of nor disliked this respectful attention. He was aware that wayfarers were interested to see Mr. Graham, in the intervals of his labours, enjoying the sunshine, and Agnes liked that it should be so : it was one of those little human innocent conceits that are proper to all distinguished people. To-day this attention was acutely manifested, for a small girl, evidently propelled by a female partially concealed behind a lilac-bush, darted out with a small album and a fountain pen, and shyly suggested an autograph. Alan beamingly complied, with a charming phrase about Spring, which had occurred in yesterday evening's dictation, and the ' privateer ' so Alan had smilingly called her, with a delightful little curtsy steamed back to her base behind the lilac.

"That was good of you, dear," said Agnes. "How you have pleased that pretty child."

"It's a crime not to make a child smile, if you have it in your power," he said.

Dora, and her points of view were certainly haunting Agnes this morning. Again a vagrant gnat of thought (coming from Dora's jungle) buzzed at her that this observation, characteristic as it was of Alan, as he appeared in his books, was not so clear a reflection of him as he was writing them. If the pretty little privateer with the naïve blue eyes had made her raid in the hours of dictation, and not in the leisure of their stroll, there would not have been much smiling on anybody's part, nor would its absence have constituted a crime. . . . But before the gnat fairly settled Alan spoke again.

"The post, at which I glanced before I settled down to my work, brought me a communication from some firm—Mr. Peake I think was the name—offering to supply me with press-notices. They enclosed a cutting about the forthcoming collected edition."

Agnes laughed.

"I can guess what you said in answer to kind Mr. Peake's letter," she said.

"I doubt it, Agnes. I did not send Mr. Peake our usual formula for newsagents and photographers. It seemed to me that it might be useful, or harmless at any rate, to know what sort of welcome the collected edition is likely to get. That surprises you? I confess that when I came to that conclusion I surprised myself. Hitherto, we have disregarded our readers, have we not? We have been content to do our best, and pay no particular attention to the verdict they pass on us. But I confess I am a little curious to know how our new venture is regarded."

He paused.

"Anyhow I sent a small cheque to our prudent Mr. Peake, who indicated that he liked to be paid in advance for his industrious researches. Ah, the lilac is in bud I see this morning. Our grimy old London renews its youth at lilac-time. We must go in, my dear, it is fully lunch time. And I meant to hear all about Dora and her doings. Wonderful Dora! Your mother, too : I hope she has got the better of her cold. Shall we ascertain if she will come and have tea with us to-day? If she came early, say about four, we could, by curtailing our walk a little, get to work at our usual time."

"But won't you have tea at the club to-day?" asked Agnes. "You have not been there this week."

"True, you clever, remembering Agnes. I should

not like to pass the week without my little outing there, and it is Saturday, is it not? So shall we hope to see your mother to-morrow or some other day? And we're dining out to-morrow night, are we not? Next week too, most important of all—ah, I do not forget that—there comes that double festival, your birthday, and the anniversary of our wedding. That will be a holiday: we shall have one working day less next week. Dear me, how full we are of engagements."

Alan was as regular about his tea once a week at the Athenæum as about all the other routine in which his life was passed. But in this he gave himself the elasticity of choosing and varying the day, provided it occurred once between each pair of Sundays. All this week there had been this flow of inspiration, and the days had gone by without the visit. It was clear then that a break in his custom must ensue unless he went to-day, though Saturday was an unusual day for this particular dissipation, since tea at the Athenæum curtailed the hours of dictation before dinner, and with Sunday, on which no work was done, following on its heels, the break was formidable. Sunday, however, was an inviolable holiday, not from religious scruples in any way, but because a day's rest in the week conduced to keener work on the other six. All this was sifted before he finally chose.

"I think I will not omit my weekly visit," he said, "though with Sunday following, I shall be having quite an exeat. But with so much ready in my head and on my notes for our dictation this evening, it is really difficult to know what to do. Advise me, my dear."

Agnes's advice in favour of the Athenæum was sufficient to determine him, and at three o'clock, according to custom, they drove to the top of Constitution

Hill, from which, for the sake of the daily exercise, they walked across the Green Park and down Pall Mall. There she left him at the club, to return and call for him in an hour and a quarter. Generally she filled up this time with errands of shopping and the like, but to-day being Saturday, she had to make some new employment for her waiting.

There was a diversity of choice. On the one side beckoned the Park, where Alan had recommended her to walk, now radiantly bursting with Spring-time, but to her mood to-day there was something too impersonal about grass and rooted trees, some lack of stir and energy. Or there was the National Gallery close at hand, but pictures . . . she did not want pictures. The streets were more to her mind, there people hurried about on the holiday businesses of pleasure, and she wanted to witness movement. But to-day the streets were comparatively empty : where was there more rush and stir ?

She walked quickly, enjoying the freedom of being alone and unwanted; a certain buoyant restlessness drove her. She hurried over street crossings beneath the bows of hooting omnibuses, rather than wait on midway islands for their passage, dodging in and out of the traffic in some sheer exuberance at being part of the general bustle, and finding in it a nirvana vastly more satisfactory than meditative tranquillity. Tranquillity was just that from which she had made her escape. Yet she desired more stir of movement, more of the preoccupation of strangers and the sinking of herself. . . . Taxicabs, with bags and suit cases strapped on to them, whirled along the street, going for the most part in one direction, and they gave her the hint, so that suddenly, laughing at herself, she made up her mind where to spend this diminishing hour. Charing Cross station was near at hand, and there, even if she took no personal share in the bustle, she could be an entranced spectator of people catching trains. There would be porters wheeling luggage about, there would be boys and girls with tennis racquets and golf clubs, women with Pekinese dogs, men with evening papers hurriedly procured, queues at the booking-office, queues waiting to pass on to the platforms. . .

Agnes took up an advantageous central position, and found it all as she had hoped and pictured. The crowds streamed by, all in a hurry, all alive and eager. How Alan, how her mother would have detested it, how mad they both would have thought her for choosing to embroil herself in this welter, which no journey of her own made inevitable! How utterly they would have failed to understand the mental condition which demanded it! But there she stood, hustled and elbowed and bright-eyed, drinking in the elixir of it with unspeakable refreshment. But she had an eye on the station clock as well. She must allow a clear ten minutes for getting back at the appointed time to the Athenæum.

She was back there a minute or two before the strict hour and a quarter were spent, and there was Alan already on the steps outside the door, looking down the pavement in the direction of the Park, from which quarter he expected her. As she crossed the roadway he saw her.

" Ah, there you are ! " he said. " No, dear, you are not late, not a moment late : it is I who wanted to be ready when you came. Would you mind, Agnes, if we abandoned our walk back across the Park, and took a vehicle from here instead ? I should be glad to gain those extra minutes at our work. Perhaps the porter will kindly get us . . . ah, how sharp of you to see that that one was unoccupied. Something to do with the little red tin flag, has it not ? And what have you done with yourself ? I found the

club rather empty : Saturday afternoon, you know.
But there were several acquaintances willing to indulge me in a pleasant chatter."

" That's good," said she. " You always enjoy
your afternoon at the club."

" Yes, I do. It is frivolous of me, I suppose, and
yet to rub up against other minds is not amiss. And
you? You have not told me yet what you have been
doing."

Agnes laughed.

" I have been doing what you will think was a most
extraordinary way of spending my time," she said.
" I went and stood in the middle of Charing Cross
station and watched all the bustle going on."

" Did you, indeed? That does seem strange. Now
let me think out your reason for that. Consciously or
unconsciously you had a reason. Ah! I have put my
finger on it at once! You wanted, by contrast with
all that bewildering hurry and scurry, to enjoy the
more your return to our sane and quiet evening.
What an Epicurean proceeding! Just the luxury of
contrast! Is it not so?"

Agnes did not hesitate.

" Yes, it was just the luxury of contrast," she said.

CHAPTER III

AGNES woke very early in the morning of that double festival of her birthday and marriage-day; a little light only of the huelessness of the hour before dawn intruded between the edges of the curtain drawn across the open window, and the quality of it was sufficiently indicative, without consultation with her watch, to tell her that she might turn over and sleep again. The silence outside confirmed that: at present only an occasional sound of traffic from the main road at the far end of the square, swelling and dying away again, broke the stillness, whereas a full hour before it was time to get up, the street would be continuously aboom with vehicles. The door, too, between her bedroom and the dressing-room where her husband slept was still open: he, therefore, who always got up at half-past six, waking himself by some unerring and sleepless chronometer in his brain, was not stirring yet, for it was his custom, when he rose, to shut the door with soft precaution so that the movement of his dressing should not disturb her. Dawn would fail to usher in day, and all traffic be mute, before Alan would omit that considerate closing of the door.

Perhaps if she had confined herself to the evidence of the toneless light and the hush of traffic she might have drowsed into sleep again, but this thought of the open door and the inference that her husband had not yet got up, awoke memory, that rummaging and restless imp, and, the wheels of thought making traffic in her mind, she remembered what day it was that would soon be dawning. Then a vague reasoning began also. . . . For on this day, there was no early rising for Alan; from morning to night it was a speckless holiday, and even though, as was indeed the case, a most critical and crucial chapter of his book was in the act of dictation, he never prepared a note, or wrote a slip, or took the Flaubert paper-knife in hand. To-day was a jubilee, a festivity.

They had worked last night to an unusual hour in anticipation of the rest to-day, and it was near midnight when finally the table was tidied and the slips, such as had not been used, slipped into their elastic band. The last ceremony was always the tearing off of the daily leaf from the calendar. "April the thirtieth," he had said, "and that one day we give to idleness, as Wordsworth wrote. Hurrah for a good lie in bed. 'Browsing' we used to call it at school. I shall browse to-morrow till half-an-hour before breakfast time."

Even as he said it, she remembered that exactly one year ago, he had given verbatim the same cheerful little speech.

Agnes's drowsiness was split now like the sheath that envelopes the crumpled petals of a blowing flower; it was no use any longer to try to prevent the expanding process. Thought trod on the heels of thought; her reflections about this day grew firm and outlined. The observance of it was a habit: it was no longer, if it ever had been, any more than a convention. Alan would be far happier spending the day in his usual manner, preparing for his dictation in the morning, taking his walk round the Serpentine in the afternoon, and making further progress with the book which was going so well, after tea. But who could suggest abandoning the conventional idleness, and, by way of observing the festival more congenially, concentrate all efforts on the book? Neither of them surely : not he, who had instituted this yearly repetition of what had been done on the first of these anniversaries, dedicating the day to her 'treat,' nor yet she: it would be unthinkable for her to say 'Let us give up my treat; you would much sooner be at your work, and I——' It was exactly that which she could not possibly give expression to. No: they would certainly go on with the expedition to Kew Gardens in the morning, the visit to the theatre in the afternoon, and the little dinner-party in the evening till the end of their joint lives. And when it was bedtime, she would say, "What a nice birthday I have had, dear," while he saw that the table was in order for the resumption of work next morning, so that he could come down early, and immerse himself in it again. There would be a cordial response to her appreciation. "Yes, what a jolly day, what a jolly day," he would say. "There I think everything is ship-shape for to-morrow. How a holiday, my Agnes (and this holiday above all others) whets the appetite for work!"

Her thoughts slipped the cable which tied them to the immediate and practical present, and drifted away from the quay-side on to the wider seas. Here was another birthday, here was the thirty-sixth of them, and now she had traversed quite half the voyage of probable life. It had been wonderfully serene so far, and she found that if she looked ahead, scrutinizing that which lay between her and the ultimate horizon, she did not augur from the intervening years, anything new, anything which she had not already experienced. Limitations, drawings-in no doubt awaited her, but from no quarter did she expect the expansions of novelty. She quite acquiesced in that: it seemed natural and normal, but even at the moment of her conscious acquiescence it struck her how odd that was, for not so many years ago, she who lay so quietly here expecting nothing, had expected so much. Yet in essentials, she felt she had not changed, no sharp crisis of bereavement or disillusion was responsible for the fading of her eagerness and expectancy : the change had been too gradual for the process to be noticed as it was going on. At the time of her marriage she had been poised on tiptoe, with arms outspread, and figure trembling to clasp and to caress, feeling that the years in front had each its fairy godmother with magic and inestimable gifts. Gifts they had certainly bought, gifts quiet and serene. The fairy godmothers had smiled on her— oh, distinctly they had smiled—and had passed on their way, leaving for her an untroubled voyage on the seas where so many meet storm and shipwreck. For her they had always sent calm weather. For fifteen years they had never forgotten her birthday and the anniversary of her marriage, nor failed to renew their gift. So she had learned to abandon this tiptoe, expectant stance, and now stood firmly on the full measure of her feet, and her arms once raised in welcome of whatever the winds might blow to her, had dropped to her side, for there was no blowing of winds, and her hands were outstretched no longer. Quietly, quietly, as with the slow expiration of a long breath they had drooped. There was nothing sad about it. Besides, if she looked at herself and her environment objectively (how fond Alan was of looking at the world objectively, with a detachment that was seldom ruffled)—she found that she possessed now all that which, in the most expectant days, had formed the summit of her desire. For fifteen years she had realized the dream which then seemed too wonderful for telling. She had asked no more, even when she asked most, than to be his minister and acolyte, and in the casket of every fairy godmother, that gift was present. She had received ' Payment in full ' for her demand-note.

But this morning, in the clarified and ruthless re-

flections which flock to the hour of a sleepless dawn,
when the vital forces are at their lowest, and the sense
of the past most mercilessly awake, she knew that at
the age of twenty she had not ever contemplated the
fact of becoming thirty-six. She had known, when
twenty, less what thirty-six would feel like, than now
at thirty-six she knew about twenty. She had still,
ready to be aroused in her, the sensation of twenty,
whereas then no hint of becoming that which the years
had made her, had ever so faintly seemed possible.
From here, from this childless and comfortable van-
tage-ground, she could imagine what fifty would be
like and sixty, for, in this acquiescence of now expecting nothing new, she could easily imagine the
greyer age. But from the same plateau she could
still see clear-sightedly the wild-rose country of
youth, where miracles were in flower.

Alan . . . it was Alan then even as it was
Alan now round whom she revolved. During that
year before her marriage, it was just he who, as entirely as now (and with what rose of romance!), had
been the core of her life. Indeed the fairy godmother
who presided over her twenty-first year had brought
her the full casket! . . . He had been coming
often to her mother's house that year, in which his
fame had first flowered, though for a decade before
that he had been patiently and perfectly at work,
issuing in that time some five or six introspective
novels which had attracted the attention of no more
than a few hundred readers. But of these her mother
was one, and it had become a habit that he should
'invoke the wizard' (his phrase for the telephone)
and ascertain if she was alone in the evening when
his day's work was done. In those days he had no
amanuensis to take down his dictation, and, tired with
writing, he had often finished with it before dinner.
Sometimes he dined with them, oftener he strolled

across afterwards, and by degrees the further habit was established that he brought with him once or even twice in the week the manuscript of his labours, and read it aloud to them. Sometimes again, work would not be going well, and for a couple of weeks at a time, there was no invocation of the wizard. Then, night after night, Agnes, when she went to bed would peep round the drawn blind of her bedroom, and there in the house opposite would be a light in the window of the room where he still worked, rejecting all that did not come up to the true standard. Well now she knew that room from within, on such evenings as those, when he would dictate and say, "Erase, please," and again dictate, and again consign to the paper-basket. . . .

But in this last year before her marriage his visits had been frequent, and vivid above all in these earlier reminiscences, was the memory of those evenings when he had read to her and her mother the chapters, hot from his pen, of 'The Tyro.' What evenings of enchantment were those : with the modesty of his greatness he would not have it that he was reading to them, he was 'talking over' what he had scribbled, and it would help him (the wonder of it!) to know how these pages struck Mrs. Mowbray and 'this dear Agnes.' He would easily see, so he affirmed, if they found them tiresome and tedious, for yawns, however skilfully masked, were apparent by that lengthening of the chin, corrected almost, if not quite immediately, by the firm clenching of the jaw.

"So sit opposite me, Agnes," he would say, "in the light, and I shall look up now and then, and if I detect those polite suppressions, I shall stop. Really, 'The Tyro' is a very insignificant perform-ance, I expect, but I have the habit of taking my work in a ferociously serious spirit."

Now, in the hour betwixt dawn and day, Agnes had

no inclination to minimize the effect on her of these thrilling recitations, rather she strove to infuse into her memory of them the enchantment which had once been there. And not to her alone had these readings of 'The Tyro' made an epoch, for this was the book which, at a bound, had set his name at the head of contemporary writers. It was a simple enough story, but the charm of it, the spirit, wise and candid and discerning, that it revealed, had gripped the world of readers. He shone large and high in the literary firmament : he came into his own with the accumulated interest of the previous years of neglect. Critics reminded the public of the exquisite tales he had already given them, and bibliophiles sought for first editions (there had never been second editions) of his earlier books, 'December,' 'Sand-banks,' 'Bread of Deceit.' And all this fuss and splendour (and here was the finest miracle of all) did not seem to concern him. For years he had followed where his art had led him, indifferent to the indifference of the world, and now that recogntion, generous and un-stinted, had come, he was equally unaffected.

" But aren't you pleased ? " Agnes had said to him one night when casually, as if speaking of some mild pleasant change in the weather, he had told them that another large edition was exhausted. " Do say you're pleased ! You aren't human if you're not pleased."

He shook his head.

" My dear, 1 suppose I'm not human then," he said, " because the Me—isn't that ungrammatical— which is really Me doesn't care two straws. I'm not any happier—or perhaps you don't quite mean that. But I must be human. I can't stand not being human, so I'll say that I'm pleased though I'm not happier. That is quite true : I'm pleased : I like it : it's fun. But it's not joy."

" Oh, do have some joy," she had said.

How well, in this moment of chirruping sparrows
and brightening dawn she remembered that, for close
on it had come the most wonderful moment in her life.
Her mother, a few minutes before had gone to answer
a telephone call, and she was alone with her idol, sitting on a footstool in front of the fire, her back
propped against his knees as he reclined in the low
chair which he had brought close up to the fender.
The heat of the fire drew out the smell of his homespun. . . . And as she sat there, he leaned forward towards her, and the flames shone on the back
of his hand with the fine long fingers and rather
prominent veins which showed dark through the
white skin. She was utterly happy at that moment,
and would have been content for it to have
lengthened into eternity, with herself alone with him,
propped by his knee, his drooping hand close to hers,
and his delicate high coloured face, with its straight
nose, its kindly mouth, its brown wide-set eyes looking down upon her. She had not wanted more than
that, it was sufficient to surrender herself in homage
to that wonderful mind of his, with no thought of any
reward except the mere permission to be its adorer.
. . . And so, leaning forward he took up her hand.

"Agnes," he said. "Will you accept my devotion? I am old, my dear, ever so much older than
you."

She shifted her position and let her eyes fix themselves again on the chink of light which showed
between the parted curtains waxing and waning as
they stirred in the morning breeze. It was golden
now, for the sun had risen, and there was promise of
a fine morning in Kew Gardens. Well, whatever she
had missed, she had experienced that moment of happiness complete and absolute; not only might she
adore, but in his eyes it was she who was adorable.
Out of all the world he had chosen her to be the

companion of his life.   He was twenty years older
than she, but she found an exquisiteness there, for in
the ripeness of his wisdom, and in no illusion of hot
youth he had sought her.   She knew that it was his
mind, shining like a lighthouse beam over dim seas,
with which she had fallen in love, and it was his
mind, so she was to learn, which had chosen her.
She was still in the sexlessness of girlhood, her
woman's nature was yet unawakened, and to be his
chosen companion and helpmeet was a summit to
which her eyes had never aspired.   At once she had
seen herself with the right to the rôle that since then
she had so devotedly filled, that of keeping far from
him all that could interrupt or disturb him in his
work, so that he dwelt as in some sequestered oasis of
shadow or sunlight, and of co-operating with him
wherever her hand could assist him.   And she had
found that he desired of her just what her girlhood
had been so ecstatically eager to give, companionship
and shelter and tender care.   .   .   .

She heard behind her a noise faint and scarcely
perceptible but so familiar that she had no need to
turn her head to see what it was, for she knew that if
she looked round she would only see that the door
into her husband's dressing-room was closed.   He
had got up, then, earlier than he had intended last
night : perhaps the temptation to get an hour's work
before she came down had been too strong for him.

Alan was standing in the window of the dining-
room, when a couple of hours later, Agnes got down.
He had already opened his letters, and was laboriously untying the string of a parcel.   He could not
bear to cut string : string was a commodity constantly
in request, and to slash your way right and left
through a lovely piece of string which would be sure
to find a use, instead of patiently undoing it, was a
very wanton and wilful waste.   The thick brown

paper in which parcels were wrapped was of an almost equal sanctity, and two drawers of the knee-hole table where she sat for dictation were rich in smoothed-out and refolded brown paper and hanks of string.

"Aha, my dear," he said, "I am down first on our festival. Many happy returns, my Agnes, for you on the one count and for both of us on the other. You have chosen your weather with your usual skill. Glorious sunshine : we shall have a delicious excursion."

"Thanks, ever so many thanks," she said. "But I wasn't so skilful last year. Torrents of rain, do you remember? We spent most of the morning in the glass-houses."

"Ah, you must not recall your occasional lapses. To be sure it was a bad day last year. I had a little cold, too, but you could not make me abandon our festival. Dear me, what strong fingers some people have. The man who tied these knots clearly meant that they should never be unravelled. But I shall outwit him yet."

Agnes busied herself with her tea-making, casting occasional glances at her husband. There was an alacrity, a brisk gaiety about him this morning, which he always assumed on these occasions, as an appropriate mental habiliment for her birthday. He had to be like a school boy on the morning of a holiday, eager for pleasure. That was charming of him, and touching, for he was sacrificing a whole day to her treat. . . . Just then the last knot yielded to the persuasion of his fingers.

"I know you laugh at me," he said, "but it's a beautiful piece of string. And will you allow me to peep at what my parcel contains, without calling me to order for breaking our rule of idleness? We sent a couple of chapters of our book, you know, to the typist, just to see how they would look, though it was only our unrevised manuscript. I should be glad to know that they had come back safely. I will only just glance for mere verification of the contents. Yes, I thought so. See! I put them back in their covering. You must not call that a breaking of our rule. Now for a good breakfast, for there's a long walk before us."

In spite of his alacrity, she could see how his eyes yearned after the contents of the parcel. He would be so much happier spending the morning in his chair looking through the sheets than in walking about Kew Gardens. She determined to risk a possible ungraciousness.

"Are you sure you are up to a long walk?" she said. "There's the theatre this afternoon and our little dinner-party this evening. It would never do for you to overtire yourself, and lose to-morrow as well."

"Indeed I am up to it," said he. "I would not omit our walk for anything. I shall walk with you in Kew Gardens on this anniversary till I am past walking, and then I will have a bath-chair. And the time will not be lost, either, for you remember where we are in our new book. We were just beginning our description of a Spring morning, and we want some hints, some little true and accurate observations of what is in leaf, and what in flower. We can make those, can we not, without breaking our rule, and infringing on our holiday. We need not be blind on your birthday. Now what shall I give you dear, from these dishes? I shall prescribe for you. A little of this . . . yes, fish, and then an egg. I shall have the same: I declare the thought of our walk makes me hungry."

Usually, in spite of his early rising, Alan ate nothing at breakfast beyond a slice of toast and butter, for the morning's work was more acute, the

vision clearer if he abstained from solider victuals.
But to-day was a holiday; there was no need to
abstain, and with a surgical deftness he stripped the
skin from the fish and dissected out the bones. He
had beautiful hands, as Agnes knew long ago, when
she sat on her footstool by the fire, propped by his
knees, and the passage of the years had left them
smooth and white and unwrinkled. Their movements
too, were wonderfully characteristic of him : he dealt
with life, both as lived by himself, and as represented
in his romances, as exquisitely as he dealt with haddock. They made no false or superfluous strokes,
they committed no violence. For the thousandth time
Agnes watched them with fascination, their neatness,
their efficiency, their economy. Just in the same way
he would use the telling word, the swift, dissecting,
precise phrase. . . . And his thought, so now it
struck her, was always concerned with dissection.
The material he dealt with must be cooked and bloodless. He could not deal with raw material in any
form. . . . Some involuntary irony seemed to
have leaked into Agnes's impressions.

Very soon after the hearty breakfast they were on
their way down to Kew, driving there in the hired
motor which would wait for them while they had their
walk, convey them home again, and subsequently
take them to the matinée after lunch, and once more
deposit them in Goring Square. This was all part of
the treat : everything was done in the most convenient manner, so that no walking should take place
except for pleasure. Alan, though extremely well off,
kept no private car, for where was the use of such
expense ? He took his outing round the Serpentine
every afternoon to provide him with exercise, and
when he wanted to go to the Athenæum a taxi to
Hyde Park corner sufficed. But on this day of anniversaries, he had good returns for his prodigality :

it was delightful to be taken softly and swiftly from their door to the gate of the Gardens, and home again from the gate. It was an extravagance, of course, but such a pleasant one. Even with the preposterous income-tax, he never seriously thought of proposing that they should go to Kew by the district railway, or by the tube to the theatre, even though their starting point was so close to a station, and their destination, to-day at least, so close to another.

Spring, so long delayed, had for the last week been flowing in warm tingling tides over the land, and all nature was like a vat full of the new juices, which having lain stored so long, were now bubbling and seething with a sudden belated fermentation. The warmth had quickened into life the earlier growths which had hibernated through the long-continued cold, and encouraged the later to appear before their time, so that April was struck out, and March joined hands with May. The squibs of varnished green which had but recently burst from the tough hawthorn twigs were already crowned with the small buds of blossom, and through the grey of the winter-weary grass, the spear-points of the new velvet were robust and tall. Daffodils were still a-blaze, dancing in the south-westerly breeze which drove the flocks of white-fleeced clouds along the blue, and their shadows over the lawns, but the chalices of the tulips were lit too with the sun that shone through their bright petals, and turned them into flames. Sallows were pendulous with catkins, willows were studded with grey mole-skin buttons, and through the copses and the thickets flitted chirruping and fluting birds, busy with straws and feathers in the call of nesting time. The laggards should have been building long before this, but they recked nothing, so Agnes was bright-eyed to see, of the weeks which the cold had lost to them. It was with the greater merriment and hustle that they made ready for the house to receive and shelter their nurse-lings. Suburban though the surroundings were, authentic Spring, magical in town and in woodland, had flooded glades and house-eaves alike with its seething waters : blackbirds and thrushes in the one, swallows and martins in the other were under the spell of the magic wand, and here in her heart and here in her head it called forth a bewildering and in-toxicating sweetness of delight. Only a few hours ago in the dark of dawn she had told herself that she expected nothing new, nothing fresh, and as if to punish her for her leaden sobriety, she was now forced to drink deep of the new wine of Spring. The blue of her eyes was ensparkled with the amazing rapture of it, she would have liked to walk bare-footed through the shaded grass where the dew still hung on the budding blue-bells. She shook off, as a duck taking to the air shakes the water from its wings, the reflec-tions of maturity which her birthday had inspired, and with them went those of the other anniversary celebrated to-day, so that even Alan was shaken from her wings as she rose through this irridescent ether of youth, which poured over her. . . . Her soul, rising up in the wind made just that one free circle of flight, then came back to Alan's side again with folded wing.

" Haven't I chosen my day well ? " she said. " Surely there was never such a Spring morning ! But we should have gone further into the country. What do we want with a gravel path ? And there's a greenhouse ! How indecent ! "

Just as she spoke, the wind, burrowing under the Inverness cape he was wearing, blew a flap of it across his face. It twitched his soft hat off his head, and sent it trundling gaily across the grass. Instantly Agnes was in pursuit. It was delightful to run : running was an expression and an outlet of this

Spring-frenzy. For all her weight of anniversaries, which a few hours ago had been so ponderous, she sped nimbly in chase of the truant, but nimbly too it bowled before the wind. Now she gained on it, and now, just as she was ready to pounce, a fresh puff took it out of reach again, and she went on in fresh pursuit. When had she last run like this, she wondered; when last had she felt the need of running? . . . Then her quarry grounded on the lee-shore of a bush, and she made the capture of it.

With hair a little disordered and the colour vivid in her cheeks, she went back to where a couple of hundred yards away, her husband stood hatless.

" A thousand thanks, my dear," he said. " This clumsy wind—— But what speed and activity, dear Agnes : you ran like some woodland nymph. Were you wise, I wonder, to race like that ? Won't you sit down and rest for a minute or two after your scamper ? "

"No, indeed. I am quite ready to walk on," she said.

" Quite sure ? Let us go on then. . . . You were saying something when you sped off on your work of rescue. You were regretting that we had not gone further into the country. I cannot, I find, agree with you there. One appreciates the country more I think when one can contrast these wild glades with houses and tidy paths, than when there is no scale to measure their freedom by. A walled garden in a town, for instance, gives no more sense of garden than one surrounded by woods and meadows."

This was a favourite theme of his, this enhancement of effect by contrast.

" In the same way a beautiful house is best set in orchards and lawns, if we want to appreciate its architecture. There are hundreds of fine houses in London which one passes by without perception, because they are flanked by other houses. But how they would shine, if you set them in the country. In dramatic art how true that is! The gravedigger in Hamlet, is an instance which occurs to me. . . ."

Somehow the vernal impulse withered in Agnes as he spoke. He was probably perfectly right, but his very rightness, its subtle academic correctness, hindered rather than helped the untutored joy of instinct. Whatever impression came to him, he, for literary purposes must analyse and classify, must sip and taste rather than gulp it down. He turned it over, deftly dissecting it, even as he had dissected his haddock at breakfast. There was always for him a moral hid in the bosom of the rose, and when you went to smell it, it pricked your nose. So too, when the merest butterfly of a topic (as when she had said she wished they had gone deeper into the country) flitted by, he must catch it and pin it down, and spread its wings out. Doubtless it was then more advantageously displayed, but it could no longer flit by, settle and hover for a moment, and flit away again.

So he had killed that butterfly. . . .

" And besides, dear, this morning would not have been sufficient to make a longer excursion, since we must lunch very punctually at half-past one, if we are to be in good time for our theatre at two-thirty. Perhaps even we should be wise to have our lunch a quarter of an hour earlier; then we shall have time to rest and cool afterwards. I should like to arrive at our play, indeed, a few minutes before the curtain goes up. Then one can grasp the names of the characters, and the scenes in which the play is set. I hate having to guess and grope and try to reconstruct all that would have been quite clear if one had only been punctual. Once, do you remember, we went very late to some play, and missed the first act, and in consequence never clearly understood what

it was about. There were people on a desert island :
a very whimsical idea."

It seemed to Agnes that the daffodils were closing.
She wasn't enjoying this holiday morning any more.
She must enjoy . . .

"Certainly we will get there a little early," she
said. "I quite feel with you. But we have plenty
of time yet to go to the end of the gardens, and stroll
back again."

"Indeed yes, and we must keep an eye open to
note these little characteristics of Spring which so
many miss. We will do it on the sly, for it is holiday . . ."

A space of unmown grass where daffodils danced
and nodded lay near their path, and over these Alan
lingered, trying to find some salient epithet or two
that fitted them aptly, to be polished to-morrow on
one of those little slips of paper, into a perfect phrase.
They grew below a company of great elms, the
blossoms of which were shed thick on the ground,
little round discs . . . ah, they were like sequins :
he must remember that word. The blossom came first
on elms apparently before they were full-fledged with
leaf. Here at any rate, it was lying broadcast,
though on the trees the leaves were not yet fully expanded. He wondered whether Agnes had noted that.

"Now, my dear, I have a Spring-riddle for you ! "
he said. "What plant is there, tree, bush, herb,
whichever you please, on which the flower is full before the leaf ? Not the magnolia which we so enjoyed
looking at : another one."

That was a great success. Agnes, even with the
answer to the Spring-riddle strewn thick on the grass,
had no idea, and was forced to give it up.

"Look round you, dear," he said. "Thousands
of the flowers all over the place. Elm is the answer.
And now examine one : what is it like, what word will

describe it ? But, hush : say it gently below your breath : work comes in here.''

Again she could not think of a similar object, and having teased her a little, he said ' sequins.' She enthusiastically acknowledged the aptness. She tried to be interested and amused, but these little discs that the south-west wind of Spring scattered here, were being pinned down and exhibited.

Alan had put down the package at the contents of which he had strictly and honourably only ' peeped ' this morning, on the closed blotting-book of the work-table, which for to-day was non-existent. Agnes, on their arrival back at Goring Square, had gone to put forward their luncheon by a quarter of an hour, and then having come into the work-room to tell him that it was ready, found him unable to resist a surreptitious glance through the leaves of this tabooed parcel. He had taken it up, and with it open in his hand, was poring over the typewritten sheets. . . . Again with heightened force the farce of this celebration of holiday struck her. How infinitely would he have preferred after this long morning's walk in the wind to spend the afternoon over his work from which, in spite of the sanctity of ritual, he was unable to keep his hands. How infinitely, too, would she have preferred his content to his whipped-up enthusiasm over the play which they were about to witness. He had no taste for drama and action : his passion and his pleasure alike lay in the careful development of thought with backgrounds of minutely-observed material objects to make the setting. Incident repelled him. . . .

Agnes pausing in her step at the doorway, was submerged by some sudden tide of pity for him. He looked old and weary ; what revivified him now, and what only had the power to do so was his work. Apart from it, and from such auxiliaries as her own service in it, or the relaxation of an afternoon at the Club, or a walk round the Serpentine, there was nothing that enthralled or even beguiled him. Outside that oasis, as in a desert, lay both the trivial and delicious pleasure of life, and also its deeper joys and sorrows. Her life, too, had spent itself in such an oasis, she, no less than he, had been cool and quiet there, but, ah, how different were they in their outlook from their pleasant studious retreat. The oasis had been of his choosing, he had taken her there and in congratulation of himself and her, had pointed to the ambient desert, saying ' How tranquil and untroubled shall we be here, I with my work, and you with your delight in it.' Voluntarily, she, in the adoration of her girlhood had been blissful to lay her hands in his, and be conducted to this quiet place, where she would unweariedly serve him. But now in the places he had stigmatized as desert, she saw a peopled and a lovely garden, warm with the scents of human life, and sweet with its needs, and its sting. He had known neither the ecstasy or the anguish of common things : life had never penetrated to his heart, it had only found furnished lodgings in his brain. To observe subtly, and to make a flawless transcription of his observations on the famous slips had been his Paradise. No touch of terror or yearning had inspired him, he had been but a faultless chronicler of symptoms and diseases and joys which he had never experienced but only noted. If that was self-expression, it was a liquor that had never passed through the hot crucible of his heart, or was poured out therefrom in a molten and burning stream : it had only passed through the sieve of his brain and was poured out infinitely fine but cold as powdered snow. She could never have conveyed to him the thrill of the Spring which she had felt this morning : he would never, even at the first anniversaries of the day, have understood what imbecile instinctive joy made her laugh to herself as she ran after his hat. All that he comprehended was her kindness in capturing it for him, and her agility which had effected the capture. And that bitterly defined her relation to him ; she was an admirable, perceptive, affectionate niece or housekeeper, and there not only was his tale told but hers also. How swiftly the years had passed ; if only their passage had left them old together !

The perception of this was a flash, the energy of which had been stored up by the hours of the morning. There was a contact, a sting and a light, and she was empty again. She went back to the rule of the holiday.

" Alan, you're looking at that package," she said. " For shame ! "

Instantly he laid it down.

" I am a wretch," he said, " an abominable industrious wretch. You must forgive me."

" Are you truly sorry ? " said she. " If you are, we will say no more about it. Come downstairs at once, and give me my lunch."

" Aha, I am glad to know lunch is ready. How hungry a holiday makes one ! Really a most charming morning. And our beautiful walk, longer I think than usual, has not tired me at all. I feel quite fresh."

How unreal and how courteous he was ! Courtesy and unreality were invariable guests on the birthday. He had not cared for the walk : he would much sooner have been reading the typed copy that had come back that morning.

" That's good," said she. " And you are right : we went further than we generally do, and we are both unfatigued, although we are a year older. And I ran after your hat too, Alan : don't forget that."

" Indeed, no. I have the clear image of you still

skimming over the grass. Positively skimming. I don't forget that, any more than I forget the elm-flower——"

She made a little ejaculation of impatience.

" Elm-flower ! " she said. " I believe I've forgotten already what you said it was like."

He chuckled.

" I believe my memory's better than yours," he said, " in spite of my age. Think, Agnes, think."

" No, it's gone," she said.

" What you have on that evening gown of yours," he began.

" Ah, I've got it. Sequins. I shan't forget it again."

This was not quite ingenuous on her part for she had not in the least forgotten. But it wonderfully pleased him to think that his memory was still in its prime. That and things like that were all that she could really do for him.

They were back again from the pleasant little play by soon after five, he satisfied that by their early arrival there they had not missed the point of any whimsicality, and now came the most difficult of the birthday hours. Ritual prescribed that they should linger over tea, for to-day there was no fingering of Flaubert's paper-knife, and after that until dressing time came there was nothing to be done but revel in the unusual leisure. On other days she would be in her upright chair by the table with pen poised or busy, while he went to and fro between window and fireplace. But now they must lounge at ease in great arm-chairs, and luxuriously observe how far off yet was the need of any exertion. A little fire had been lit, for though the day had been so warm sun-down grew chilly, and Alan drew his chair close to the fire, and the warmth brought out the smell of the homespun.

BOOK II

BOOK II

CHAPTER I

THERE were, as usual, to be no more than six guests at the anniversary birthday dinner to-night, for the thought of a large number overburdened Alan with a sense of his responsibilities as host. Even so, he had been faintly apprehensive of the festive situation for some days past, as Agnes had deduced from certain scattered ejaculations when the dinner was under discussion. ' Poor Blewitt,' often repeated, had been one of them. ' Mrs. Probyn now,' had been another : a third had been ' Dear Timothy.' The other guests caused him no qualms : he knew exactly what to expect of them. These were Agnes's sister and Professor Arden, the notable physicist, and his wife, who was under the distinct impression that she understood the Einstein theory.

But ' poor Blewitt ' clearly troubled him, though Mr. Blewitt had been present at every one of these anniversaries, since their original institution. He was then, even as he was now, a literary critic; he had been among the first to recognise the quality of ' The Tyro ' and his voice had led the chorus of welcome and acclamation. He wielded an influential pen, but, no more than Mr. Dick could keep the mention of the head of Charles I out of his Memorial, could Mr. Blewitt keep the mention of the late R. L. Stevenson out of his pungent reviews. But on the appearance of ' The Tyro,' a whole column had flowed from him before Stevenson

was mentioned at all, and even then, when in the last
few lines of it, the inevitable occurred, it was but to
announce that the author of ' The Tyro ' was no unworthy successor to him.   (Mr. Blewitt could not have
written ' worthy ' instead of ' not unworthy '; his
sense of style would have choked him before it permitted it.)   Mr. Blewitt saw in this book and,
alas, in no other contemporary work, the divine
instinct of perfection, which was the mark of the
true artist, and thereupon for the next ten years
had constituted himself the interpreter and herald
of Alan to the world.   In addition to being a
powerful critic, he was a very pretty little poet, and
one of his most graceful sonnets was addressed to
Alan, and began ' Spontaneous lark.'   That handsome tribute had, in fact, been recited by the author
at one of the anniversary parties, and Alan had been
much moved, for indifference to the verdict of the
vulgar was quite compatible with appreciation for the
reasoned opinion of so cultured a judge, and Mr.
Blewitt had been ' our dear Blewitt ' in Alan's mouth
for all these years.   But then—was it that the
public, who had so enthusiastically welcomed ' The
Tyro ' was spontaneously cooling off a little, or was it
that Mr. Blewitt, leading not following their judgment, had blown upon their ardour ?—our dear Blewitt
became less fervent, and in Alan's mouth receded into
being ' our good Blewitt,' not without a touch of indulgent indifference, for of late our good Blewitt had
mingled faint praise with his incense which made a
very poor kind of fragrance.   He damped the charge
of powder with which he had been wont to send Alan's
name rocketting among the stars, and the aspiring
firework merely smouldered.   He had asked himself,
so he told the readers of his weekly article on ' literary
news ' in the ' Sunday Magazine ' (a new publication
of high culture and enlightenment)—whether Mr.

Graham's later work did not ever so slightly smell
of the lamp, whether in its obvious polish there was
not a trace, not quite wiped off, of mere emery-powder.
From that it was but a short step to say, on the appearance of Alan's last book, that Mr. Graham had
engagingly given to the world another of his dainty
little cameos, another charming cherry-stone carved
with the industrious finish which his numerous readers
were wont to expect from him, and of which, in the
present instance, they would not be disappointed. It
was a withering little critique; itself a daintily-carved
cherry stone, and soft as the dab of a cat's paw it had
appeared only a few weeks ago, and from that moment
Mr. Blewitt had become ' Poor Blewitt.' And this
growing tepidity was, so Agnes knew, felt by the
public also, who, unable to express themselves with
the neatness of poor Blewitt, testified to their concur-
rence by refraining from buying the book in the way
that they had bought its predecessors. There was
no rush on it; the first two editions had not been
exhausted on the day of publication, and buyers were
no longer exhorted to send in their orders without
delay, for fear of disappointment. Any disappointment that there was, was felt not so much by the public
as by the publisher.

Agnes had felt the unfriendliness of poor Blewitt.
The invitations for the anniversary had not yet been
sent out when his little snarl appeared, and she was
all for omitting him. But Alan, secure in his own
impregnable fortress of having done his best in this
story as in all others, was content with the label of
' poor Blewitt,' and would not hear of such littleness.
It would show a deplorable touchiness to leave out
poor Blewitt, just because in his curious unreadable
column he had talked of emery paper and lamps
instead of spontaneous larks. Certainly let poor
Blewitt come to the dinner : he had a perfect right to
his opinions. Poor Blewitt by all means.

An innovation in the way of guests to-night, and one that prospectively agitated Alan, was the presence of Mrs. Probyn, with whom he and Agnes had dined on the previous Sunday. They had only met her once before, several months ago, on the occasion of a terrible little party given by Mrs. Mowbray, but then and ever since then Pamela Probyn had showered the offer of hospitalities upon them, and eventually, as always happens in the case of importunate widows, she had had her way. Agnes laughed to herself when she remembered Mrs. Probyn's persistency in the cause of her 'salon.' It was Mrs. Probyn's destiny (for it was too elemental to be called a weakness) to make the great moons of the social system revolve round her. Alan had been to her a tremendous moon, the more so that he was so rarely capturable, so seldom let himself shine, otherwise than by his books, on others. But Mrs. Probyn, all glory to her, had gone on and gone on with her bounteous offers of hospitality. . . . And then she had gone on. The effect was that last Sunday they had dined with her, and wonderfully pleasant it had been. Alan had been throned in the middle of a few congenial guests, and had snuffed up homage, which was delicately administered in small strong doses. Mrs. Probyn, handsome and alert, had continually kept his cup brimming, but not brimming over, so as to startle him. She had heard—was not that extraordinary of her, so Alan's subsequent comment ran—about the little anniversary parties : Harry Blewitt, it seemed, had raved about them. It was the event—so said Mrs. Probyn—to which throughout the year he most looked forward, that exquisite birthday party. She had Alan firmly fixed in a corner at the moment when she retailed these handsome expressions of Mr. Blewitt (whom she alluded to as Harry, though his friends called him Henry) and having done that

she pinned on him a firm challenging gaze, against
the influence and import of which Alan felt himself, as
she had intended him to feel, quite defenceless. But
he was gratified and in a pleased preening manner he
looked round for Agnes.

"Agnes, my dear," he said, "Mrs. Probyn has
been so kind as—in fact, can we not persuade Mrs.
Probyn, even at such short notice, to honour us at our
little birthday party? Poor Blewitt—our good
Blewitt, I should say—has been saying much prettier
things about our little party than it deserves. Thursday next: you must help me to persuade Mrs.
Probyn."

Mrs. Probyn's eyes, gleaming with the greed and
gratification of the hunter about to capture his quarry,
closed for a moment as she ran over her engagements
for next week. She kept them all in her head, each
lightly hung, so to speak, on a neat peg and each
detachable in case she wanted to replace it by anything else. There was something on Thursday of
quite second-rate importance compared with this, and
the very shortest deliberation only was necessary.
. . . After that she opened her eyes again, and
ecstatically accepted. . . .

Alan moved his chair a little back from the fire as
they sat there after tea on the afternoon of the birthday. His walk and the theatre had tired him a little,
and still more fatiguing was this ritualistic idleness.
He had perhaps dozed a little, but now was fully
awake again and his mind was clearly occupied by
the thought of the approaching festivity.

"Good Blewitt!" he said, remembering how
pleasurably he had spoken to Mrs. Probyn about the
birthday dinner. "We must be very cordial to good
Blewitt, dear, and not let him think that what he said
in his little article has affected us at all, as indeed it

has not. 'Spontaneous lark,' you know; we must remember that good Blewitt once wrote that very pretty sonnet. And then there's Mrs. Probyn. We must try to justify Blewitt's testimonial, and make her first dinner with us a pleasant one. There will be another new face, too; I wonder what Timothy will be like. It is dreadful that I have not seen my own first cousin for so long, but with his father living in the country, and then the war coming, and then Timothy going up to Cambridge to finish his course, there has really been no opportunity. But now that he has his work in London, we must see him often, if he does not find us too dull and quiet. Before he goes to-night, dear, ask him to come and dine again, but tell him that it will be no dinner party. . . . Let me see—we shall finish the chapter we are engaged on, I hope, to-morrow, and we shall be working very hard, drafting the new chapter next day, but what if Timothy came to dine with us again on Sunday? He must come on other nights too, of course. It would never do to let him feel that he is not always welcome here. I dare-say he will not mind on other nights going away early when we get to our work again after dinner, or if he likes, taking a book and reading while we return to the workroom, and having a little more talk after-wards. Timothy must just drop in, you know, with no ceremony on his side or on ours. Curious to have a first cousin twenty-five years younger than myself; his father is about the same age as I, though he is my uncle."

Agnes, while he dozed, had moved to the work-table, where she was writing out cards with the names of their guests on them, as guides for their positions at the dinner table. Before the end of this gentle soliloquy, she had finished her task, and gave an answering chime on the subject of Timothy.

"He was a charming boy," she said. "He came

here, do you remember, just when he had got his commission in the first month of the war. But that is
eight years ago, isn't it? Why, he'll be twenty-seven
by now. But I remember him quite well. Tall, and
freckled, and brown——"

Alan had left his armchair and was moving backwards and forwards across the room. There was the
Flaubert paper-knife on the table, and as he paused
in his strollings, he took it up and began stroking
and fingering it. Agnes suddenly found her attention switched on to him : the habit of the strolling
and the fingering of the paper-knife had, unconsciously to him, asserted itself in spite of the fact that
to-day was a holiday. And as if dictating he began
to speak.

"We must keep abreast of new tendencies, new
movements," he said. "Of course, nothing, not
even this strong event of the war, can alter the
essentials of human nature, but (dear me, how shall I
say it?) the war has acted on national and individual
expression. I am clumsy to-night. . . . There
is Timothy, who has been through it all—he got some
very fine distinction, did he not? D.S.O. I think it
was, and I confess I am much interested to know what
change the war has made in him. I feel, in fact, dear,
like some doctor who professionally is looking forward
to making a diagnosis and finding out how an intelligent young man, who has come to the age of perception in passing through these troublous times, looks on
the world of to-day, and even more, how he looks on
the world of yesterday. So I hope we shall make dear
Timothy feel at home, and reveal himself. . . ."

He made a turn or two in silence, strolling and
fingering the paper-knife, and began speaking in the
slow distinct voice in which he was accustomed to
enunciate his dictation.

"No external events, perhaps," he said, "even of

the most critical and progressive sort, can change human nature, or even alter the character of the individual, but there must be modification and adjustment in function if not in structure, comma. . . . No, erase that, but kindly read over first from ' no external events.' "

He paused, waiting for Agnes's voice. Then suddenly the eager knotted intensity of his face relaxed.

" My dear, what an extraordinary thing ! " he said. " Upon my word, I quite forgot it was holiday. I thought that I was sketching out one of those general theses that we outline when we are first breaking ground for a new book. Aha, sly Agnes; you wanted, dear, to make me break our rules and scold me for it. Well, I deserve my scolding. I must cry peccavi. But that thought has often been in my mind lately. I have been brooding over the question of the great psychological change that must have come over the young generation who have passed their earliest years of manhood among those inscrutable horrors. You can guess now what will be the root-idea of our next book, when we have finished what now occupies us. But don't betray me, dear. We always are dumb on that subject, are we not ? But to think that I should unconsciously have lapsed into one of our dictations ! I think I am disposed to take that as a favourable omen. It shews, does it not, how already the idea of our next book is beginning to obsess me."

Agnes had the warmest cordiality for this.

" Indeed it does," she said. " You were absolutely lost in your thought. That's always a good sign, and I won't scold you, because I'm pleased. But you forget that you have the revision of your books for the collected edition to do before you begin on any new theme ! "

" True. It will be months before we get to work. And I forgot also about our dinner party. I forget everything. But I must not forget that idea, which came to me with such force. Let me see, how did I put it? Ah, yes: 'modification and adjustment in function if not in structure.' I fancy that will prove a key to unlock many difficulties, dear. But I see it is half-past seven. How short our cosy hour of idleness has seemed."

Mrs. Probyn was not one of those half-hearted warriors who, having gained precarious footing in some fortress reported impregnable, was content to rest on so remarkable an achievement and not to push forward with all speed, by the use of such weapons as seemed to her to promise success, into the very keep itself. She came, indeed, that night terrible as an army with banners and proceeded to demolish more of Alan's defences. In her first successful skirmish, when after the repeated assaults of hospitality she had lured him to dinner, she had scanned his earthworks and trenches with her rapid relentless eye and had made up her mind as to the nature of her next attack. She had seen at once that Alan was guilelessly vulnerable to flatteries on the subject of his work: he appreciated appreciation, if it was of the right kind, and she had in her armoury several species, the first of which she employed without delay. She had intentionally arrived a few minutes before the notified hour, and was shewn into the little front room on the ground floor, where they were to assemble before dinner, to find herself the earliest of the guests. She had brought with her a first edition of 'The Tyro,' which she had taken great pains to procure, and had left it with her wraps on the hall table, strategically accessible should an opportunity for its use occur. Here, with fortune's favour and her own foresight, was an unrivalled occasion.

" I have been so bold, Master," she said (she had tried ' master ' before with success), " that now I am frightened at my own courage. I have brought my precious, my devoured first edition of 'The Tyro' with me, and if—dear Mrs. Graham, add your supplications to mine—if I could induce you to write your name in it. . . . Such a joy it would be, such an unfading honour. May I, might I, would you?''

Alan was a little confused by so unexpected a homage, but he was clearly not displeased. She hurried out (the thoughtful creature had brought a fountain pen as well) and returned with her devoured first edition.

'' But how inestimable of you,'' she said. '' And the date: would you add the date, just the date, which everyone knows is that of the birthday party? Ah, how happy I am!''

Her happiness was rendered even more acute when it appeared that it was she who was to be taken into dinner by her host and placed on his right hand. For the due alternation of the sexes good Blewitt sat opposite Alan flanked by Agnes on the one side and Dora on the other. Then followed Timothy. Professor Arden was next Mrs. Probyn, and his wife on the other side of Alan.

There could be no lack of conversational entertainment when Dora was present. Evidently she intended to be sixteen this evening, for she wore a little pink frock with short sleeves and a string of coral.

'' The country! What a terrible place!'' she said to Mr. Blewitt. '' I have been in the country for three days. If I had stopped there another twenty-four hours I shouldn't be sitting next you now, not because I should still be in the country, but because I should be under the churchyard sod. Cuckoos! All day that foolish bird repeated itself, and all night the nightingales squeaked and whistled. Why are there nightingales? Who wants them? Ah, my green apples! Every green apple takes a year off my

life, or do I mean adds it on? I was always so bad
at arithmetic."

"Dear lady," said Blewitt, "arithmetic and the
country were made for schoolmasters and cows.
Imagine if all the cows and schoolmasters were in
town! They are an abomination, I admit, but what
should we do with our children if it wasn't for schoolmasters, or feed them with if it wasn't for cows? But
this is sacrilege here; I see our dear hostess eyeing us
with most distinguished disapproval, for this baleful
sentiment of ours."

Agnes laughed.

"Oh, you're both incorrigible," she said. "Alan
and I love the country."

"Ah, so do we all," said Blewitt, "if we can take
it in small doses carefully sterilized. A pastel of the
country, heavily framed, in houses, like Hyde Park,
has a great deal of charm."

Alan beat the table softly with his hand.

"Aha, do you hear that, Agnes dear?" he said.
"Blewitt agrees with me: he loves contrasts, do you
not, Blewitt? Values, you know; you only appreciate values by contrast. Ah, what a scolding I got
this morning in our walk in Kew Gardens for saying
—correct me if I mis-state, dear Agnes—that a garden
in a town is more precious, more gardenish, may I
say that? than a garden in the country."

"The only garden for which I have any use is a
kitchen garden," said Dora, "because we eat it. I
prefer that should be in the country because the
vegetables then are less thickly covered with soot."

"Dear urban Dora!" said Alan.

Mr. Blewitt liked addressing the whole table. The
slight pause which had followed Alan's comment gave
him the opportunity.

"Civilization!" he said. "Man's spirited protest against the fatal paralyzing influence of nature.

The whole trend of our evolution as a progressive race is to become emancipated from anything natural. Who in his senses does not prefer a picture to the landscape from which it was painted or the portrait of any dear friend, provided it is sufficiently unlike, to his real presence? Who would not sooner read one of our host's delicate romances, than in actual life follow the fortunes of the persons whom he so felicitously portrays for us? Who would not sooner sleep in a bed than attempt to snatch an uneasy and insectiferous slumber propped on beds of amaranth and moly? I should like to see the whole of our beloved London roofed in, and lighted and warmed with electricity. I am all for Mrs. Muir; I unhesitatingly cast my vote for no gardens except those which supply the kitchen. The sea, too! The unvarnished barbarity of the sea which sends forth insidious tongues of salt water to wet your boots if you attempt to walk by its edge, and produces violent nausea if you attempt to cross it! There shall be no more sea! What a beautiful promise! I would subscribe to any creed which guaranteed that."

This was the type of conversation which Mrs. Probyn longed to hear flowing at her parties. If only Harry Blewitt was a greater figure in the world! Imagine having a Cabinet Minister talking like that at your table.

"Marvellous! You are marvellous," she said. Then she turned her attention to the siege of Alan again. He might not be so amusing as Blewitt, but he was greater.

"I positively insist, dear Mr. Graham," she said, "on your developing to me your doctrine of contrasts. I feel that you know the final secret, the—the ultimate spell. There is something about it in 'The Tyro,' some hint that shews you know. . . ."

Agnes swept her eyes round the table. Professor

Arden had transferred his attention to Alan and Mrs. Probyn : Dora and Mr. Blewitt were both talking to each other simultaneously : opposite, Timothy was listening to Mrs. Arden with a polite but puzzled air, and Agnes was at leisure to look at him. Her remembrance of him, now eight years old, as a charming boy, seemed to justify itself still, for among the older generation he looked boyishly young, especially when he spoke or laughed. Then his upper lip lifted itself into a soft indeterminate curve, adolescent and sensitive. But when his face was in repose, as now at this moment, while he listened to some explanation of Mrs. Arden's which necessitated the posting of two wine glasses and a fan in certain positions, he looked mature and experienced. He was still freckled and brown as with exposure to sun and wind, and a stiff crop of short cut vigorous hair reminded her of the way Alan's hair used to grow before the years had made so plentiful a gleaning. She remembered— how odd that that particular moment should so strongly detach and frame itself—how on the night they were engaged, she had put her hand on his head, and felt the strong spring of its upward growth, and now she was sure Timothy's hair would be resilient like that. His face, too, was shaped like Alan's, and most like of all were his hands. Just now he was helping himself to some dish, and it might have been Alan's hand itself that so delicately grasped the spoon and made so deft a dissection in the sponge-pudding.

" No, really ? " he said to Mrs. Arden. " That's most astounding," and just then he lifted his eyes and happened to catch Agnes's. Some quiet surreptitious smile was lit and hovered there, as if he was inviting her sympathy and co-operation in the understanding of this astounding thing. In response, she lent her ear to Mrs. Arden's exposition with the wine glasses.

" The rays were actually bent," she heard. " Bent

in towards the sun. Light, in fact, showed itself to be affected by a gravitational field."

"Most amazing," said Timothy, in a voice of the deepest interest, and once more his eyes flickered across the table to Agnes, briefly and unmistakably eloquent. Indeed, he was a charming boy, for he was certainly convincing Mrs. Arden that nothing in the world was of such engrossing interest to him as this account of the epoch-making observations of the eclipse. Agnes had quiet applause for one who so delightfully fed Mrs. Arden's flame with the fuel of his own interest.

Alan moved to the empty seat between Blewitt and Professor Arden when the women left the room with strict injunctions from Dora to come and make her a bridge-table before long. He had not forgotten—at least he now remembered—that Blewitt must be made quite comfortable and shewn that his little dabs about emery-paper and lamps, if observed at all, had been observed without the loss of cordiality. But it was with a renewal of recollection that he recalled that, for Mrs. Probyn had quite absorbed his attention. All dinner through she had timed and directed her assaults with the most strategic ability; he had surrendered trench and outpost without the sense that anybody had taken them.

"A most agreeable woman, dear Blewitt," he said. "I am much pleased to have struck up an acquaintanceship with her. Full of perception—is she not?—and a serious student of literature. You would have enjoyed joining in our talk, and we should have enjoyed your adorning of it. Your charming decorative gift."

He turned to Arden.

"Our friend adorns all he touches, does he not?" he said.

"Yes, precisely, quite so," said Professor Arden

very drily.   He wanted port, bridge and bed, and
wondered why that young man opposite did not set
the decanter moving.   So sour a glance did he give
him that Timothy wondered what he had done.   He
could think of nothing, and so wondered what he had
not done, and guessed.

"Shall I send the port round, Cousin Alan?" he
asked.

"Yes, dear Timothy, please do so.   Give Mr.
Blewitt a glass of port.   And cigarettes . . .
dear me, what a shocking host I am.   Ah! there
they are on the sideboard!   Kind Timothy!"

Blewitt took the decanter from Timothy and turned
to Alan.   He was feeling a shade Olympian this evening, and rather vexed that he had not been able to
talk to the whole table throughout dinner.   Mrs.
Probyn, for instance, had determinedly hung on
Alan's lips.   And now there was really no one worth
talking to.   He considered his host a back-number
in the literary world, and for the rest there was his
host's cousin, obviously negligible, and some sort of
Professor.   Then, though Alan's compliments had
been pleasant, he wished to show that he was above
that kind of thing, and mingled vinegar with his oil.

"You quite overwhelm me, my dear friend," he
said.   "You cover me with blushing confusion.   Let
us quickly change our conversation to a more worthy
theme.   What have you been engaged on?   What
charming and graceful pieces of work may we expect
from you next?"

There was an acid flavour about this: he was
rapidly becoming ' poor Blewitt ' again.   But Alan
still wished to make him as honoured a guest as he
had been in the days of the spontaneous lark.   In
his anxiety to give him the full measure of his courtesy
and attention, he let the decanter come to anchor in
front of him.

7

" Ah, it will be a long time before anything fresh of mine is published," he said. " We shall get through just the first draft of my new story and then lay it aside. I shall be engaged on a collected edition of my books."

Blewitt, although he was perfectly aware that this was in contemplation, thought it good for his host that he should seem not to have heard of such a scheme.

" Indeed! You interest me profoundly," he said. " That is a delightful privilege you mean to give us, the opportunity that is, of reading them all over again. How gallant, may I say, of you to challenge and invoke the test of time——"

Professor Arden could tolerate the stagnation of the decanter no longer.

" That is an excellent port of yours, Graham," he exclaimed.

Alan wheeled about, recognised his omission, and, interrupting Blewitt, turned to remedy it.

" My dear fellow," he said, " I am amazingly remiss. And I haven't had a word with you yet all evening. It was good of you to spare us an hour or two, and partake in our little festival."

Blewitt levelled on him a glance of concentrated displeasure and made a complete right-turn towards Timothy.

" I was congratulating your illustrious cousin," he said in a loud lecturing voice, " on his amazing courage in bringing out a collected edition of his works. You, I am sure, Mr. Graham, belonging as you do to the young generation, will agree with me on that, for your generation is convinced, is it not, that all achievements made more than, let us say, ten years ago are rubbishy and obsolete. And what is your profession. Perhaps (I must crave your pardon if this is the case) you are following in the steps of your illustrious cousin, and intending to refresh us by a perennial stream of literary masterpieces."

Timothy gave a short gasp : he was completely unprepared for this violent acerbity.

" No, I'm in the city," he said.

" I am glad to hear it. You relieve me indescribably. I should discourage any young man from treading the thorny road of letters."

" Quite," said Timothy pleasantly. . . . There really seemed nothing better to say.

Alan caught the last words, and guessed that good Blewitt was being Olympian.

" Thorny indeed," he said. " Old stagers like you and me, my dear Blewitt, know that well enough. Your admirable Stevenson gave just such advice, did he not, to a young man in one of his pleasant essays ? Now I must not forget my sister-in-law's injunctions. I must lead you upstairs."

Blewitt's good temper, as usual, had been completely restored by being disagreeable, and he had had the additional gratification of making himself felt (or so he hoped) by a member of that younger generation, whose very existence was so detestable to him. They seemed to him without reverence or respect, but in reality the chief cause of their offence was the fact that *en masse* at any rate, they would be alive and vigorous after he was dead; this incurred his just and unwavering resentment. The sight of the prepared bridge-table completed his convalescence, for, in the general convention of silence that prevailed, he could talk without ceasing. Alan himself did not play, and it was clear that Mrs. Probyn meant to engage in no pursuit which did not include him, while Timothy, blind with fear at the thought of opposing or, even worse, partnering the savage Blewitt, denied that he knew the rudiments of the game. The four, therefore, who were trembling with anxiety to begin, sat down without preliminary competition. The others assembled in a loose group.

Mrs. Probyn meant that the group should be looser yet as a whole, though perhaps tighter in one of the component parts into which she was firmly determined to split it.

"And is this where the Master works?" she asked Agnes. "This beautiful room! And which is the table? *The* table."

"No, this is not the workroom," said Agnes.

"Ah, I am disappointed! I hoped we should see *the* room."

Alan was alert at this: he had certainly found something strongly to his taste in Mrs. Probyn's appreciation. Just now she had addressed her enquiry to Agnes, but it was he who answered.

"But what is easier?" he said. "It is—our modest little workroom—just through these double doors. But they are closed. They are even, as you see, blockaded by a sofa. Another door, however, on the landing outside: a pleasure to show you."

Agnes and Timothy were thus thrown together. She had by no means planned it, but she was delighted it had happened so, for, among other reasons, it gave her the opportunity to work at the footing of intimacy which Alan had desired should be established.

"Now sit down, Timothy," she said. "I've not had a word with you yet. I only heard you being wonderfully intelligent at dinner."

Timothy glanced up at the absorbed players.

"You heard some bubbling cries as I sank," he said. "But I believe you would have come to my rescue if you could have. Einstein, you know, Cousin Agnes."

She laughed.

"But I can't swim either in Einstein," she said.

" We should have drowned together. Did you get ashore after we left you ? "

" Yes, ashore," said Timothy. " Oh yes, ashore. But it was even more frightening ashore. I was told that my generation thought everything achieved ten years ago rubbishy and—and obsolete."

Agnes raised her eyes also to the bridge-table, clearly indicating Mr. Blewitt, who had risen to get a cigarette.

" Yes, quite so," said Timothy with that boyish smile. " And I was nearly in the most awful hole, for he asked me if I intended following Cousin Alan's vocation. Luckily I could say I was in the city, which he thought far more suitable."

" But why luckily ? " she asked. " Why an awful hole ? "

They seemed, so she fleetingly reflected, to have shovelled away, without effort, the sticky snow of first acquaintanceship, and to be standing firm and solid. Even that perception escaped Timothy ; he did not spare a second's surprise for it.

" Oh, because I'm dead keen on writing," he said. " I want to write a good story more than anything in the world. I thought that Mr. Blewitt would have got that out of me, by putting his question some other way round. Lucky he didn't think of it."

" And do you write ? " she asked.

" Oh, I'm always scribbling, I'm always trying," he said. " Just short stories. I think I would sooner write a first-rate short story than a long one. But it's silly for me to talk about it. Boring."

" But why boring ? You must tell me all about yourself," said Agnes. " We've got to know each other. You're making a splendid beginning, Timothy. Keep it up. When I find you boring I shall yawn."

He laughed.

"Now you have made it impossible, Cousin Agnes," he said. "How could I tell you about my silly affairs, if I was always watching to see if you yawned?"

"I shall ask questions, then," said she. "Have you had any story published? Have you sent any to magazines?"

"How did you guess? I sent one this morning. Just a yarn, you know. About the war."

"Oh, but I want to see it," she said.

"You shall as soon as it is returned with or without thanks. Now I want to ask you about Cousin Alan. Do tell me how he writes his stories. What happens? Does he plan them very carefully first? Or does he get just a general idea and go ahead? And when it comes to the actual writing?"

Agnes gave in outline 'what happened.' . . . Somehow it was difficult to speak of the incorporation of the slips without making the process seem a niggling and stippling one. Until she came to describe it, she had no idea what it would sound like when described. Timothy was evidently trying to enter into sympathetic comprehension, and she felt she explained it awkwardly. What certainly was conveyed to his mind was the patient unwearied labour; his ejaculation at the mention of the second manuscript copy, and the second typewritten copy, showed this. Then, without pause, she went on with welcome of him.

"Alan and I both want you to feel ever so much at home here," she said. "Come, anyhow, on Sunday; there's no work going on that evening. I warn you that we shall be quite alone."

"But I should love to," he said. "Just you and Cousin Alan and me."

"That's fixed then. It's dear of you to come and

brisken us up. You must know that all the week we work very hard, but Sunday is a day off. Are you still living at your club?"

" Yes, worse luck. Everybody sits in armchairs and blots himself out behind the evening paper. I'm looking for a small flat, bedroom, bathroom, sitting-room, where I can shut my door and be undisturbed, but apparently there aren't any. Agents send me notices of immense houses in Berkeley Square with garages and ballrooms, and highly recommend them as being great bargains. So I daresay are ropes of pearls and diamond tiaras, but what's the good of them to me?"

A thought passed at long range through Agnes's mind, small and distant. But it did not completely vanish : it hovered there. Of course, before utterance could be given to it, she must look at it more closely, and primarily Alan must be consulted. Yet even if he approved, what was a boy to do in the evening on his return from the city, when night after night the dictation went on in the work-room. Timothy, if the suggestion took shape, must certainly be made to realize what a hermitage the house was, and in such a way that he might without un-graciousness prefer the club until he found himself a nest of his own. She would not, anyhow, speak of it to Alan till after Sunday evening; then she would have seen in the course of the quiet hours whether Timothy's presence at dinner every night and at breakfast in the morning, was likely to suit him. For herself she gave the notion a cordial welcome. Between the two evening periods of dictation, Alan often brooded silently from soup to savoury : it would be very pleasant, if another presence was not distract-ing to him, to have this nice friendly boy (provided he did not find it appallingly dull) briskening and brightening the interval. And if he was so keen about writing himself, perhaps he could find his own employment when the silence of the workroom closed over Alan and herself. It was natural, too, that his cousin should give him a temporary refuge. . . . But all this hovered quite distantly : it seemed somehow improbable that it should come nearer and perch. She imagined it without any sense of realization, for it seemed, trivial and temporary though his sojourn would be, so tremendous a change from the unvaried habits of fifteen years. She just got the momentary glimpse of it, and it was without pause that she answered him.

" Ah, do get a tiara and live in a house in Berkeley Square, Timothy," she said. " It would be delightfully original. No one has ever yet written stories in a tiara."

He got up as the door opened, and Mrs. Probyn and Alan came in.

" How you laugh at me ! " he said. " But not a word about my stories, Cousin Agnes."

She gave him the promise with a nod and a smile, and was instantly involved in Mrs. Probyn. She, the sound tactician, addressed the remarks intended for Alan to her.

" You lucky woman," she said, laying her fan gently on Agnes's wrist. " How I envy you ! I am madly jealous. Oh, I have heard all about it, how it is your privilege to take down every word as it comes forth fresh and wonderful in that first draft, while the Master walks up and down with the Flaubert paper-knife. And then to have it read to you again with his fresh thoughts and corrections and additions ! And then to read it yourself to him, and all this before we wretched outsiders know a single sentence of it all ! If you weren't so utterly charming and so worthy of it, I should think it an outrage that you should have all this. But I am to have something, too. He has promised me—can you guess?"

Agnes made no effort whatever to guess: it would clearly take the gilt off Mrs. Probyn's wonderful gingerbread, if she did not disclose this promise herself.

"How can I guess?" she said. "How can I know what you and he have been talking about this last hour?"

Mrs. Probyn gave a glance at Alan, who was standing there with an air benignantly mysterious, and came closer to Agnes.

"Some day next week," she whispered, "when he feels that he has made good progress in the morning, so that the dictation will go easily and fluently, and I shall not be bored—bored, you know—by his silent walkings up and down and his hesitations and erasures, he is going to get you to telephone to me, and I am to come and have tea with you, and sit in the workroom afterwards while he dictates. You have to give your permission as well, but I know you won't be so cruel as to refuse that."

Agnes was suitably amazed. Here was a fine antidote to poor Mr. Blewitt's acidities, for nothing could be more genuine than Mrs. Probyn's rapture. Her homage clearly delighted Alan.

"I do call that a nice plan," she said. "And you will be the first person in the last fifteen years who has ever been present when Alan is at work."

"When we are at work, my dear," said he. "Our work: I told Mrs. Probyn so."

"Yes, indeed," said she. "Without your permission I am not allowed to put the end of my nose into the workroom. Please, dear Mrs. Graham! I shall go home in floods of tears if you don't give it me."

Agnes was unfeignedly glad to give it. Perhaps

her mother was right: perhaps this hermetical existence was not good for him. The intrusion, it is true, was a very slight one; Mrs. Probyn, it appeared, was to do no more than sit there while the work proceeded. Still, the fact of any innovation in the habit of fifteen years could not be called insignificant.

Ten minutes later the party had dispersed, and she waited in the drawing-room for Alan, who was seeing them off, to come upstairs. To-night his step was most brisk.

" A charming birthday party, my dear," he said. " I do not know when I have enjoyed one more. Timothy, I thought Timothy a very pleasant young man. I am glad that he is coming to dine with us again on Sunday. How amusing, too, were our dear Dora and poor Blewitt about civilization and the country. Such spirits, such pleasant little paradoxes! They reminded me of kittens whisking round after their own tails in the sunshine. But after you had left us in the dining-room, something I am afraid worried poor Blewitt for a few moments. He was quite worried."

Alan took a turn or two up and down the room, and his thoughts came in to roost. It was time for them to get home again after this flutter abroad.

" You do not, I hope, dear," he said, " object to the presence of Mrs. Probyn at our work some afternoon. I do not believe I shall find Mrs. Probyn's presence at all disturbing: you need not, I think, fear that. She is so very receptive, so eagerly appreciative. Indeed, I should not be surprised if we found a certain stimulus. We shall want to do our best— though we always try—to produce something worthy of a really brilliant auditor. But it is late: I must be at work betimes after the refreshment of our party."

CHAPTER II

TIMOTHY proved so marked a success at the dinner *en famille* on Sunday night that it was Alan himself who suggested that, pending the discovery of a suitable flat, he should occupy a spare room in the house. Though he set considerable store by his weekly tea at the Club, his imagination shrank appalled from the contemplation of Timothy's lot of dining most evenings at a Club, and sitting till bedtime in that uncloistered publicity. When, therefore, as he and Timothy sat over a cigarette after dinner, he learned that such was his cousin's mode of life, the suggestion was made without any consultation of Agnes at all, though he was careful to tell Timothy that social life was extinct in the house in Goring Square from after tea till dressing-time, and for an hour or so after dinner. Timothy gave a grateful acceptance, provided that his presence would not be a nuisance, and Alan introduced him to Agnes afterwards in the character of the new inmate. So tremendous a revolution in the household as an occupant of the best spare-bedroom could not, he expected, be effected in a moment. Still, if they all ' buckled to,' the best spare bedroom ought to be habitable by Tuesday, and it was arranged that on that day Timothy should be installed.

After Timothy had gone, Alan and Agnes played the usual Sunday evening game of piquet before going to bed, but he was so strongly pre-occupied with the excitements and innovations which were imminent, that he could devote but the most wandering attention to the game.

" That was a happy thought of mine, dear, was it not," he said, " to propose that dear Timothy should quarter himself on us. To be sure I did it without reflection, but even now—yes, I take only three cards —I am far from repenting of having spoken without due consideration. It is certainly a great experiment, for I cannot remember that we ever had a guest staying with us. Guests in the house demand more leisure from their hosts than busy folk like you and me have at our disposal. . . . For the third time I have nothing but a point of four to tell you of : one is almost tempted at times to believe in luck, and its corresponding absence."

It was his deal at the end of this contemptible hand, but instead of presenting the cards to be cut, he leaned back in his chair.

" I was, of course, careful to tell Timothy that from teatime till dinner we are completely invisible, and again for an hour after dinner. But he appeared to be confident that he could amuse himself in solitude, and I daresay, as a matter of fact, he will be dining out with his friends not infrequently. I am not wishing him to feel himself bound in any way. I do not, however, anticipate any distracting influence from his presence at dinner when he is here ; indeed, sometimes I think that I am not always the gainer by letting my thoughts dwell uninterruptedly on our work between the two dictations. And if the experiment does not succeed, you will be able, dear, to hint, ever so delicately with all your tact, to the boy that I seem somewhat disturbed and distracted, and I have no doubt that he will make his conclusions and offer to withdraw. But I do not anticipate that at all : indeed, I feel that I shall experience quite the contrary effect from his sojourning with us. I hope indeed that he will not prosecute his search for a flat very sedulously, if we all suit each other."

He got up, still leaving the cards disregarded.

" And dear Timothy's advent is not the only fresh excitement that we are to experience this week," he said, rambling quietly up and down the room. " Some day very soon our pleasant Mrs. Probyn is to be installed in the workroom while we are at our dictation. To-morrow certainly will be out of the question, for I foresee certain shoals and shallows immediately ahead, but these I hope we shall push over to-morrow and find ourselves floating on the full tide again. So if my preparation goes as I hope it will on Tuesday morning, I should not wonder, dear, if before lunch I asked you to be so kind as to telephone to her and bid her to tea that day. To be sure that is the same day as Timothy arrives, but I do not see that the one scheme will interfere with the other. He knows that he will see nothing of us till dinner time. Mrs. Probyn ! More and more do I anticipate a stimulus from her presence."

" I hope you will be right," said Agnes, projecting herself as always, into his point of view. " If she proves to be a drag upon your dictation, it will mean the loss of a couple of hours."

" I had thought of that : indeed, I thought of it before I gave her the invitation to come, but it seemed to me worth risking. To lose two hours is a small thing compared with a gain in quality. Well, I think that it is time for us toilers to get to bed."

Agnes gathered up the cards without calling attention to the unfinished game.

" You, too, will have much on your hands," he said, " with providing for our new inmate. But I knew you would give a welcome to my scheme and not grudge the extra trouble. I think I would put Timothy, dear, in that sunny room above mine. There should be an inkstand there and writing materials and some books : that I know I can leave to you. There is a bathroom on that floor, I believe, which he can consider his own. He will not disturb me getting up in the morning, for I warrant that I am an earlier riser than he. Off to bed, dear? I shall follow you very soon. These busy pleasant days!"

Agnes woke next morning to a sense of anticipation that was somehow surprisingly pleasant; that new conditions and experiments should occur in a life that for fifteen years had flowed in so even a passage gave her the sense that comes to a voyager who, after long and tranquil drifting down a quiet stream, sees that the current is quickening into eddies and ripples. She continued, and no doubt would continue, to pull her slow rhythmical oar, but he, the helmsman who gave her his orders, was looking ahead now with quickened interest, and it was his interest, so she convincingly told herself, which inspired her own. Probably these eddies and ripples portended nothing fresh: very soon, when their boat had traversed but a little of the journey, the stream would reassume its sedate going again. Indeed, Alan had stipulated that if this brisker movement interfered in any way with his own steady progress, that if the ripples rocked or agitated the even level, they would pursue the adventure no further but get back into the quiet waters again. If Mrs. Probyn, for instance, at the dictation proved a disturbing presence, she would be allowed there no more: if Timothy proved distracting, he would be sent back to the club again until he found a suitable flat. But Alan clearly expected stimulus without disturbance from these intrusions, and that was sufficient to give Agnes the quickened sense in sympathy with him. But she was conscious that she personally, and not in relation to him, was also looking forward to new and changed conditions. There was a bubble in her own private spring. . . . She went across the square next morning, when Alan was settled at his work, to see her mother. Mrs. Mowbray, as regularly as birds build nests in spring time, always started in the month of May a piece of *petit point* needlework, which in the course of the ensuing year blossomed into a covering for a sofa seat, or, under glass, the top of a table. To-day the inception of this work of art was announced in the usual manner.

"I am thinking of beginning—I daresay it will be no more than that—a piece of work for the sofa in the dining-room," she said, "for it is sadly shabby. Very likely I shall not get far with it, for it tries my eyes terribly, but I find that in my solitary life I am the better for some such employment to occupy me in the long holiday evenings when I am alone in the Isle of Wight."

"That will look lovely, mother," said Agnes. "Your work is so beautiful."

Mrs. Mowbray sighed.

"I feel that it is more than I shall be able to manage," she said, "but I shall try to make a beginning. I wonder if it would be too much trouble to you to draw out the design for me on my canvas. Just a basket of flowers, I thought, in the centre, with perhaps a border of leaves round it. Daffodils, do you think, in the basket? A brown ground: the yellow will shew up well against it."

The canvas was ready, and a design of flowers in a basket from some book of prints. Agnes propped this up in front of her, and with due enlargement, began to outline with hard etching strokes, the design her mother wanted. Her hand was nimble, she felt, and her eye keen : everything was a pleasure this morning.

"Any news?" asked Mrs. Mowbray, when she had got well started. That was a constant question : she liked asking it because there never was any news; this gave her a pleasant sense of disappointment.

Agnes looked up with a flush and a smile. The pleasure came bubbling to the surface.

" Yes, indeed, there is great news," she said. " Timothy, Alan's cousin, is coming to stay with us till he finds a flat that suits him. It was only settled last night : he comes to-morrow. Such a nice fellow : he dined with us."

" Indeed : that is something very new. Poor Alan ! He will find it most disturbing to have a guest in the house."

" Oh, but he doesn't think so," said Agnes. " He invited Timothy himself, without even consulting me. But, of course, I was delighted."

" Age ? " asked Mrs. Mowbray.

" Twenty-seven or twenty-eight, I suppose. And full of jolly spirits. Alan liked him immensely."

Mrs. Mowbray looked round to find some dark side to this plan. She was completely and immediately successful.

" These sudden fancies ! " she said. " I should not wonder if Alan's work was not utterly upset by it. You cannot break the habit of many years without grave risks. And I suppose that both he and I must expect to see much less of you now that you have got somebody else to look after."

" But not in the least," said she. " Besides, dear, only the other day you were saying that I ought to get Alan out of his isolation. Now he is beginning to do it himself. I hoped you would have approved."

Mrs. Mowbray spoke with energy.

" If you want to shift the responsibility of the step on to me," she said, " I must totally demur. When I said (if I said) that Alan lived too isolated a life, I did not contemplate the taking of so hazardous a course. But I don't suppose that my approval or disapproval makes any difference to anybody. Any other news ? "

It was part of Agnes's attitude in these visits neither to resent nor remember her mother's acidities. Acidity was her self-expression, just as much as Agnes's own was geniality. Above all, anything that concerned Alan called forth this self-expression. What was the cause of that Agnes had no idea : familiarity with it had only served hitherto to deepen the mystery of its origin. To-day, though the fact struck her with unusual force, she let it be, and passed on to her other news.

" Yes," she said. " Alan, I think, is on the way to make great friends with Mrs. Probyn, whom he met here for the first time. We have dined with her, and she with us, and some day soon she is coming to sit with us while Alan dictates."

" Indeed ! Dear me ! Great changes ! " said her mother.

" Naturally it was Alan's suggestion," said Agnes. " No one was more surprised than I when he made it. But I was very glad of it. He thinks that he may receive some stimulus from her presence. She adores Alan's work."

" And you ? " asked Mrs. Mowbray. " What do you think of the plan personally ? "

Agnes laughed.

" Really, where Alan is concerned I don't think of anything personally," she said. " I want Alan to have just what he believes will suit him."

" I see. You absolve yourself of all responsibility with regard to him."

Agnes looked up. Mrs. Mowbray's eyes were regarding her with some smouldering animosity that seemed ready to burst into flame. Just that one glance she had of it, and with it there came into her mind distant and fleeting as a remote lightning-flash that revealed a horizon which she had never seen before, some guess at this perennial fierceness of criticism in points where Alan was concerned. She blinked at that light, but in a moment it was gone : only before her eyes there still swam the phantom of what she thought she had seen. Whether it was real or not she hardly knew, but for that second's illumination it had appeared real.

She bent over the canvas on which she was tracing the basket of flowers.

" I don't think that is quite fair, mother," she said. " Alan must know best what conditions suit his work. I have plenty of responsibility in securing them for him."

Once more the distant lightning gleamed as her mother spoke.

" You have never understood Alan at all," she said. " All along he has wanted somebody who would help him not only by yielding to him. But it's no business of mine. It long ago became your business when you married Alan."

She paused a moment, as if making asterisks at the end of a topic.

" And the new book still gets on well ? " she asked.

An hour's work, plied in silence, was sufficient for Agnes to outline the details of the basket of flowers, and, even as when Alan was dictating to her, the mechanical occupation of her hand seemed to give a special liberty to her thoughts. . . . That gleam, that blink of illumination had shewn her something, she felt sure, which her mother had never meant her to see, and the glimpse of it smote her with the heart-ache of compassion. It explained much that had hitherto been incomprehensible, it explained that veiled hostility with which her mother had always regarded her and Alan, her watchfulness of them, her disapproval of all they did, her alacrity in auguring the worst for the future and in detecting the worst in the past and present. Its illumination reached further back, too : it revealed in a new light her mother's stunned surprise when she was told that he had proposed to her, and that she had accepted him, the freezing that had come over her then, the bitterness that had never since been sweetened. . . . It was all wounding, all pitiful, but it was one of the irremediable things which had better never be contemplated. . . .

The work was done at last, and Agnes got up.

" There you are, mother," she said.   " It makes quite a good design.   And now I must be going home to get Timothy's room ready for him."

" It will be pleasant for you to have an inmate more of your own age than Alan is," said Mrs. Mowbray.

Alan was still immured over the negotiation of the difficult shallows, which when surmounted would lead to the full stream again, and Agnes went softly by his room and up two further flights of stairs to the floor where Timothy would be lodged.   Though this was within the walls of the house where she had lived for fifteen years, it was quite strange to her : his room struck her with a sense of novelty, it might have been the flat which he had found for himself, and she had been invited to have a look at it, and suggest comfortable details. Though it had all the usual requirements of a bedroom, it wore the frozen lifelessness of a room long unlived in, and she set herself to imagine it as occupied and to adjust it to the needs of habitation. It had two windows, in one of which must stand his dressing-table with a good light for shaving, and an electric lamp for illumination in the evening.   In the other window at present stood a chest of drawers, but that must find other anchorage, since the writing-table with inkstand and paper must stand there, and she must remember to put a waste-paper basket beside it. There was a big easy-chair now mournfully marooned in a corner where nobody could sit : the proper place for that was in connection with the fire-place, for though it was summer now, the habitable thing was to have an arm-chair there. Then the bed : she tested that by lying on it, and found it somnolently springy but the posi-tion of it was wrong. With the head of it turned round against the side wall, it would not face the light. At the bottom of it there was a reasonable place for the tall screen which now stood ineffectually between the windows, but at the foot of the bed it would mask the door. Then, very conveniently, in this new posi-tion for the bed, a small hanging bookcase came into play close to the right hand of the occupier, so that Timothy could lift a hand after he got into bed and drowse or interest himself over what he plucked from it. At present its two shelves stood empty, but from this house of books it would be easy to fill them with a reasonable little library. Of his literary taste she had no notion, but in this house of Alan's there must be in the room a set of Alan's books : these would fill the lower shelf. In the other spare room next door she knew there were several sets of these, sent him, six at a time on publication, and she filled the lower shelf with them.

She moved the armchair into sociable connection with the fireplace, and sat there a minute, meaning to call her housemaid to help her in re-arranging the rest of the furniture. Then suddenly she changed her mind : it was a small matter to wheel the bed round, to move the chest of drawers to a position which would leave the second window free for a writing-table, to fold and carry the large screen to its place at the foot of the bed, and in ten minutes more she had adjusted the room, without other assistance, to her notion of comfort for the occupier. It looked habitable now; Timothy could read or write or sleep: there was a light over his bed, a screen at its foot, a half-filled bookcase at its side. She began to envisage him here, turning into bed perhaps, but not yet ready for sleep, and he would find the light apt for the reading of a book he could recumbently select. Or dressing in the morning, the window would illuminate his toilet, and the washstand stood near so that he could lather his chin and with a half turn find himself in range of the looking-glass. And there, in the other window, was his writing-table, at which, when she and Alan were at dictation in the workroom, he could do those ' scribblings ' which he had made into a secret between herself and him. But that table still needed its appurtenances, and she tiptoed downstairs again and brought up ink and pens and a sheaf of paper and envelopes. But for his ' scribblings ' he must have just such a writing pad as she used when Alan dictated; you stripped off the filled leaves, or turned them back, making a book or a pile of loose sheets. . . . An ash-tray, too, for perhaps he smoked when he was writing: that and the paper-basket for waste products made a set arena for an author.

Once more she sat herself down in the armchair, projecting herself into Timothy's comfort. She could imagine him here now; she could hear a sort of home-like purring as he quartered himself. Even if his flat was not immediately discoverable, he would not find that the search for it had to be too eagerly prosecuted. Surely he could settle down without any spur of the need of independence. This floor would be like a flat to him: he could always find a comfortable solitude here. . . .

There was a bathroom next door, and on inspection that proved to be ' well-appointed.' A large porcelain bath filled the long side of it; there was a hot rail for towels, and her housemaid had already decked the room with soap and cork mat and wire. cage for sponges and soap. The door into it was just outside the bedroom door; he could pad in and out as if it was part of his bedroom. Really, as far as his hostess was concerned, there was no need for further questionings. But once more minutely and imaginatively she scrutinized her arrangements: nothing must be omitted or misplaced: he must feel that the room had expected and understood him. To-morrow morning she would bring up a vase of flowers to give brightness to his writing-table: they would be fresher than if she made his nosegay to-day. . . .

Just then she heard the opening of the workroom door, and she ran down to see if he wanted her companionship in a stroll. His face was a barometer clear to read for indications as to how the work was going, and there was no need really for a spoken report.

" The tangled twisted thing," he said, " its knots and ravelment eluded me a long time and I began to fear that we should not be able to have the audience for Mrs. Probyn to-morrow. But only ten minutes ago it loosened itself, and I think, dear, I may confidently say that we have left all snags and shallows behind us. No more grating keel, I hope, no weary puntings. . . ."

His letters, still unopened, lay on the table, and he inserted the Flaubert paper-knife into the flap of a big envelope. He took out a little bundle of press-notices.

" Ah, our good Mr. Peake," he said. " I will just glance at them. Yes, an announcement of the collected edition, another, and yet another. Good Mr. Peake is determined that I shall know I am about to bring out a collected edition. Ah, here is something more substantial."

He smoothed out a folded column of printed matter

and began to read, and Agnes, watching his face, saw
the alacrity die out of it. A frown deepened, the
corners of his mouth grew grim.

" Upon my word ! " he said. " Blewitt—he makes
no secret of that—Blewitt expresses himself in very
doubtful taste. Just read that: I call it a very unkindly bit of work. It is not as if Blewitt were criti-
cizing some new production of mine, which he could
not view with his distinguished approval. These are
the books on which when they first appeared he
lavished appreciation."

Agnes took the cutting from him. It commented
on the approaching collected edition with unconcealed
hostility. " Mr. Alan Graham was revising the books
which had given pleasure to so many readers, but were
we to understand that this revision was to embrace all
those pleasant little stories which the industrious
author had already published ? . . . Collected
editions seemed to imply some sort of permanence
. . . these graceful ephemeralities . . . only
perhaps the greatest writers like Robert Louis
Stevenson . . . the author would do well to con-
fer with his publishers before he risked his reputation
and their money . . ." Agnes just ran her eye
down the captious carping sentences, and crimpling
up the slip threw it into the waste-paper basket.

" But, my dear, how can it matter to you what Mr.
Blewitt says? " she asked. " If he is ill-natured
and ludicrous he only hurts himself. I am surprised
that you give a thought to it."

She spoke gaily and lightly enough, but it was an
effort. Alan, who once had been so indifferent to
praise and blame, so well satisfied to do his conscien-
tious best—she above all others knew how conscien-
tious that was—had lately shewed himself to be of far
more vulnerable stuff. His isolation, his independence of others' opinions, was breaking down, and if

on the one hand his delight in praise was stimulating to his energies, criticism such as this discouraged and upset him. It had been a surprise to Agnes that he had taken in these press-notices at all; it dismayed her to see the effect they produced.

He hardly heard her. He was glancing through the rest of the bundle, and by degrees his face cleared again.

" I am glad to say that others do not seem to take the same view as poor Blewitt," he said. " There are several, which you will like to see, giving a very cordial welcome. Dear me! I am afraid I allowed myself to be agitated over poor Blewitt's unfriendliness. We must remember that he once tried his hand at romance himself, but found it easier and no doubt more profitable to pick holes in the work of others. Ah, I see you have thrown his little yappings away. That is wise. We will not think of them again."

It was clear, however, during the day that Alan was thinking of little else. Their longer walk round the Serpentine that afternoon was more silent than usual, and the silences were broken by allusions to troublesome things. They weighed and preyed on him: whatever he saw translated itself into their terms. Even the birds on the lake which Agnes fed suggested to him some aspect of them.

" There are fewer recipients of your bounty, dear," he said, " than there were a week or two ago. Your gulls have gone: there are only a few of them left. They go off to their breeding-grounds, I believe, in the Spring. The new generation . . . Mallards also; Spring-time, of course. Just a few old birds. . . . I wonder if the libraries have any books by young authors which would repay perusal. One should spare a glance sometimes, however busy one is, to see if there is anything which suggests fresh points of view. However, we need not bother ourselves about that. Timothy comes to us to-morrow, does he not? he will give us new impressions. Poor Blewitt: soured, I am afraid, by the advancing tide of the years, which ought to bring freshness! You have finished your bag, dear? Let us walk on; I feel disposed for the longer walk to-day, if that is agreeable to you."

"By all means," said she. "And shall I go to the library to-morrow to see if they recommend anything? I expect they will recommend me something of yours, in case I have not read it."

He pushed a crumb of bread into the water with the end of his stick.

"Aha! That would be a good joke against poor Blewitt," he said. "Dear me, why does Blewitt run in my head like this? We must step out, dear, if we are going on our longer walk."

They passed along the north edge of the lake, but when they came to the bridge he hesitated.

"I feel inclined to make a compromise," he said, "between our two walks. If it is not disagreeable to you, I think we will not go round the long water. I should like to get an extra half hour at our dictation to-day, for I have some new matter, which may want clarification. I should like to know that we have left all difficult passages behind us before we give our public performance to-morrow. Mrs. Probyn! Well, she does not appear to share poor Blewitt's views as regards my work."

The dictation was fluent this evening, and the waste-paper basket, after an hour's work, had not been fed with any discarded or erased sheets. Crumpled up there was Blewitt's diatribe—Alan had already christened it a diatribe, a yapping diatribe —and as he hesitated for a word, he bent down and picked out the crumpled record.

"Aha," he said. "Blewitt, poor Blewitt, will find

himself my inspirer instead of my destroyer.   There
was   a   phrase   of   Blewitt's—yes,   I   have   it   . . .
' these graceful ephemeralities ' : we will hoist Blewitt
on his own petard.   Blewitt will find he has but presented   me   with   just   the   phrase   I   wanted.   Full
stop,   dear,   and   fresh   sentence.   ' These   graceful
ephemeralities   . . .' "

All was ready for Mrs. Probyn the next afternoon.
Alan was wonderfully elated at her advent, which, so
Agnes augured, was to him an emollient of the wound
which he repudiated and winced at.   She would hear
best, would she not, if she sat between the windows :
a comfortable chair for her there.   What fun to make
poor Blewitt attend one of these séances, to bind him
hand and foot so that he could not stir, and force him
for a couple of hours to listen to these graceful
ephemeralities !

There was not much explanation necessary for the
comprehension of the story, but such as there was,
was sketched out, over their tea, to the guest, just the
elusive subtle lines concerned with the play of temperament on temperament which was the framework
of the book.   A problem, easily indicated, and certainly insoluble, unless the rude presence of some
natural law, like death, intervened, was already
apparent, and nothing remained to be done in these
last chapters, except to record the faint expiring
fragrance of spoiled and inhuman existences.   Grey
shapes, getting gradually older and fuller of subtleties,
would be conducted in shadowy procession towards
the dusk of the last page.   Alan could be trusted not
to cut knots by death in order to secure a possible
future for the grey shapes, for anything definite and
determining was alien to his methods.   People contrived to live and had nothing to live for.   The after-

glow of what might have been and what certainly was not to be, alone illuminated them.

How new and wonderful had these wan pilgrimages once been to Agnes, how beautiful the unembittered acceptance of nothingness by these unreal shadows which so subtly confused themselves and everybody else among the mists of their own making! They had no physical, scarcely even an intellectual, existence: their sole mission was to analyze themselves completely away, or at the most to be left in some sort of dim resignation. She found herself envying the reverential excitement of Mrs. Probyn, who now for the first time was to be witness of the practise of his skill. To see his delicate creations unfold themselves like the fronds of some exquisite fern had once been to her just such a rapture of the spirit. And that was not all that this next hour had in store for Mrs. Probyn, for scarcely less sacred to her than this intellectual initiation itself was the prestige that admission to this audience would dower her with. Few but she had ever induced the great man to accept a hospitality, and none except her had been permitted to enter the sanctuary of the workroom. She would make the most afterwards of the *cachet* it gave her, and bake innumerable loaves from this rare and splendid grist for her social mill, and it was evident that she was making the most of it now, for Agnes saw her bright intelligent eye noting the appointments of the workroom, as, after tea, they moved there in sacerdotal procession. First came the two acolytes, herself and Mrs. Probyn, swinging censers, and behind them, presently possessing himself of the Flaubert paper-knife, the priest.

Alan's anticipation of stimulus was abundantly justified: Blewitt was forgotten in the flattery of this tense listener, and never had Agnes heard him so fluent and so sure. She sat at the table besprinkled

with the phrase-bearing slips, and there was scarcely
a pause in his even, distinct voice, when he pounced
on one or another, and embodied it in his sentence.
Her hand had to be nimble to keep pace with him,
and it was but seldom that he desired her to ' read,
please, from the beginning of the paragraph,' or to
' erase, please.' Once she had to discard an ill-flow-
ing pen, saying ' Wait a moment, Alan,' and Mrs.
Probyn, rapt and ecstatic, whispered, ' Hush, dear ! '
as if she was in charge of this wonderful business,
and Agnes some sort of hired secretary not yet quite
used to her job.

At length Alan paused.

" Let us give ourselves a moment's rest," he said,
" me from my talking, Agnes from her writing, and
our dear friend from her listening. We owe her our
grateful thanks, dear Agnes, do we not, for I cannot
remember when I have dictated with greater illumination, and I attribute that to her sympathetic presence.
Perhaps, dear, you would read what we have done.
I shall be ready, I think, then for a further bout."

As she read, Agnes caught some subdued murmur
of movement in the house. There were discreet steps
on the stairs, the muffled sound of mounting luggage,
and she guessed that Timothy had arrived. But no
disturbance came to the working party; clearly he
remembered that this was the sequestered hour, and
presently the house was silent again. When she had
finished, Alan got up and without pause continued
for another half hour. Then suddenly, as with the
turning off of a tap, he ceased.

" That is as far as we shall get for the present without rest and refreshment," he said. " And yet I feel
quite unfatigued : may I hope that our guest has found
the tedium of listening not intolerable ? "

Mrs. Probyn leaned forward in her chair, her chin
on her hand with upward reverent gaze at him.

" Ah, what a privilege it has been, Master," she said. " Wonderful. A revelation ! "

Then dexterously, she included Agnes.

" Happy woman ! " she said. " You have it all ! How I shall think of you at my dull little party this evening, coming back here and hearing what further miracles the Master makes. And now I've got to tear myself away, but what delicious memories I shall carry with me ! "

Agnes felt sure she could venture on a suggestion without consulting Alan.

" But you must come again," she said. " Alan has found your appreciative listening most inspiring. I think when we get to a difficult place we shall have to send for you."

" Surely, if dear Mrs. Probyn is so good as to wish to hear more of our puppets' adventures," said he.

" Ah, will I not come whenever I am allowed ! " she said. " I shall spring to the telephone to-morrow whenever it rings, hoping it will bring a message from here."

" But there is no need of that," said he. " If seriously, dear lady, you feel one tithe of the pleasure you have so generously expressed, will you be present at our séance to-morrow ? We will read over first whatever progress we have made this evening."

Mrs. Probyn floated downstairs with Alan on the full tide of her own gratification, while Agnes went into the drawing-room next door, where she found Timothy sitting mouse-like till the work-hour was passed. He jumped up on her entry, and his plain, pleasant vigour made, by no volition of hers, but from its own simplicity, a wonderful contrast with the effusiveness, the elaborate ecstasy, all genuine no doubt, but all effective of the other visitor.

" Ah, that's nice," she said. " Welcome, my dear.

I knew you had come : I heard just the echo of your arrival. You entered with burglarious softness."

" Oh, I'm not a burglar," said he.

" I know you're not. We're just out from our dictation. It went so well. Alan will be up here in a moment : he is seeing Mrs. Probyn off. She—ah, here he is."

Alan made a beaming entrance.

" Dear fellow," he said. " How inhospitable you must think me ! But these hours after tea. . . . I remember telling you. We have had a great evening of work, unusually prolonged, for I see that it is already half-past seven. I must take you and shew you your room, where I hope you will find everything comfortable."

" But I've seen it," said Timothy. " Writing table, armchair, books, everything."

" That's good. Agnes and I put our heads together, and tried to think of what a guest wanted. Yes, a great evening's work. No pause, no fumbling, immense progress. Indeed, I am not so sure that I shall dictate again this evening. How would it be, Agnes, to take an evening's holiday ? Perhaps I might look through some slips, and jot down a few little *obiter dicta* which presented themselves to me as we worked this afternoon, . . ."

He took up the evening paper, turned a page and laid it down again. There was nothing there to interest him.

" Then there will be no recapitulation for Mrs. Probyn when she comes to-morrow," he said. " We shall be able to go straight on, after you have perhaps read over to us the concluding paragraphs of to-day. Yes, dressing-time. A holiday this evening ! Yes, I come to you, dear, like a school-boy, and ask you to give me a holiday, because I have worked so well to-day. There was not a single sheet, I

think, cast into the waste-paper basket this evening,
Agnes. Poor Blewitt's yappings are the only
tenant of the place of our failures. You will find a
bathroom next door to your little lodging, Timothy."

Agnes had received that morning an exciting box,
accompanied with a note, from Dora, which began
like most of Dora's communications, in the middle
of a sentence, of which the first part, presumably, had
been present in her mind when she started to write.
" But I know it would make me feel like a magpie,"
she had scribbled, " and I should hate that. But
somehow I see *you* in it without looking like a magpie,
so do let me unload it on to you. It's quite terribly
smart, and I can't think why I am so generous except
that I know I don't want it. Darling, even Alan will
notice that for once you are decently dressed. Tea-
gown, just black and white. . . ."
The exciting box supplied the necessary com-
mentary. Now, when she went upstairs, Agnes took
the sumptuous shimmering thing out of her cupboard.
Admirably it suited her warm colouring. Why not,
as Dora said, be decently dressed for once, and see if
Alan would notice?

CHAPTER III

AGNES was sitting in the drawing-room one afternoon, some ten days later, waiting to give Timothy his tea when he came back from the City. Her right arm was in a sling, for coming downstairs that morning, she had slipped on a rug that lay treacherously loose on the parquetted floor, and had fallen, spraining her forefinger. Alan, already in the dining-room had hurried out to help her up, condoling and commiserating, but she made light of it, and gaily got through a clumsy left-handed breakfast. Timothy, more practically helpful, had fetched lint and iodine, and after proving himself wonderfully dexterous with bandaging, went off for his day's work. Ten minutes sufficed for Alan's frugal meal, but at the end of that he remained, visibly troubled, and looking at her anxiously.

"But indeed, it's nothing," she said. "Just an ordinary sprain. It will hurt a little, it will swell a little, and then it will cease hurting and subside."

"You must take care of it," he said. "I doubt, dear, if it would be wise of you to use your hand to-day. We will wait on you, Timothy and I, we will cut up your food for you, do whatever you are incapable of. I hope you are not in pain."

"It's nothing at all," she said. And then a sudden thought struck her, and she waited for him to speak. Up and down the room he moved, struggling, so it seemed to her, with some impulse of speech which he still checked. At last it came.

"Terribly inopportune," he said. "That unkind

rug to slip under your foot like that! I hope it will not mean a long incapacity for you. Even to-day— let us look forward only to to-day and not anticipate a continuance of calamity—what shall we do about our dictation this afternoon? I certainly shall not permit you to martyr yourself with writing, if your hand is painful. A sprain always needs rest."

She knew that would come. It was that, the difficulty about the dictation, which had worried him. Once stated, it made a clearance of his trouble; the trouble anyhow was being talked about, and perhaps they could hit on something which would relieve it. Agnes had her suggestion ready.

" I am sure Mrs.—I mean Pamela—would take my place this evening," she said. She could not manage ' Pamela ' quite easily yet, though it was now nearly a week since, at Pamela's request, all prefixes had been dropped. Alan, Pamela and Agnes : these were Pamela's wishes.

Alan was evidently pleased that the suggestion had come from her.

"Ah, our kind Pamela," he said. " That is a brilliant idea of yours, dear. Shall we see—perhaps you would be so good as to invoke the wizard for me —shall we see if Pamela will throw herself into the breach? It would be a wonderful relief to me to go on now with our book, and have no intermission. A week's steady work, as we conjectured yesterday, would see us at the final page, and I must confess I should be glad to sweep on in this fair gale that is carrying us so felicitously into port. Yes : let us lose no time in invoking the wizard. Dear Pamela is seldom at home in the morning after ten. Not for anything must you use your poor disabled hand, but if I hold that black stand while you invoke and give ear to the wizard, we should be able to employ him successfully."

Pamela therefore, all ecstasy and condolence, had duly appeared at tea-time. Since Timothy's advent tea had taken place in the drawing-room, so that he, arriving perhaps late, would not intrude into the workroom, and now Alan, getting restless as five o'clock approached, had clearly indicated that the time for work had arrived.

"And is our kind vicarious scribe ready?" he said. "If so, Agnes will excuse us. Nurse your poor hand, dear. Sling comfortable?"

There had been no suggestion made that she should listen to the progress of the work. The scribe was what he wanted, and it was for her that he held the door open.

"Ah, how terrible if I make a blot," said Pamela. "Your sacred beautiful sheaf of manuscript, dear Agnes. . . ."

Agnes heard the door of the workroom shut behind the workers, and presently the low murmur of Alan's voice sounded through the partition of the communicating door. Not once in all these years, when Alan was closetted in the workroom after tea, had she not been closetted there with him, and now the first prevailing impression was a sense of jubilant holiday. Had her disablement been, in the smallest degree, impedimental to him, she would have regretted and bewailed it; as it was, she acquiesced in it with surprising welcome. Pamela, she was sure, would be as efficient an amanuensis as herself, and Pamela's enthusiasm, her intelligent adoration of Alan's work, supplied him, as the last ten days had testified, with a stimulus which she was quite powerless to give him. No touch of jealousy spoiled her pleasure in abdication; if Alan had been dictating with closed door, to Cleopatra herself, she would have only hoped that Cleopatra would commit no such lapse as that of which she herself had been once guilty. He would only want Cleopatra to have a ready pen, and when bidden to erase or to read. . . . As for Pamela herself, it was surely a matter for gratification that just when a scribe was so urgently needed, so enthusiastic a one should be at hand.

She heard the soft quick footfall on the stairs which had already grown familiar and Timothy, with a stealthily turned door-handle, slipped into the room. He had evidently not expected to find her here, for his face lit up with surprise and pleasure, then swiftly softened into sympathy. But his first instinct was gladness. He carried in his hand two long slips of paper, the general form of which she knew well.

" Hullo, Cousin Agnes," he said. " Is the hand still bad ? I am sorry. It just occurred to me that I might be of assistance and take your place if it was, but I heard dictation going on as I came upstairs. What's happening ? "

" Pamela has taken my place," she said. " But it was good of you to think of that, Tim."

Timothy gave a little stifled explosion of laughter. To these two Pamela had her humorous side, unshared either by her or Alan.

" She'll like that," he said. " Glory for Pamela. She'll have a dinner-party over that, and tell everyone what a wonderful afternoon she and Alan—Alan Graham, you know—had together. Ha ! "

" But isn't she a blessing ? " said Agnes. " Alan was tremendously relieved when I suggested we should try to get her. . . . Tim, I'm going to be inquisitive. What are those long slips ? I know they are proofs. Galley proofs, Tim. I can tell one a mile off. Oh, I believe the story you sent to a magazine has been accepted. My dear, how lovely ! Let me look at once."

" You've guessed ! " he said. " And of course you shall read it if you want. But when you're alone. I should burst with self-consciousness to see you sitting reading my rot, while I had tea; I should choke."

"Tim, you're not sincere," she said. "When you say 'your rot,' you don't mean 'your rot.' You think it's wonderfully good."

He nodded.

"I know I do," he said. "I think it's the most marvellous story ever written. Nobody could write a line unless he thought he was embarked on a work of genius. Lord, what fun! And the kind gent wants to know if I haven't some more for him to look at."

"And you have?"

"Why of course I have. Haven't I been writing away in my beautiful room every evening when you and Cousin Alan were at dictation? Any more indeed! He shall be sorry he said that! Ten pounds, too, for this first story."

"I want to know when I may read it," said Agnes.

"Whenever I'm not there. You may take it to bed with you to-night, but how shall I be able to prevent myself from tapping at your door after you've had time to read it, and asking you if it'll do?"

"Can't you go away now?" asked Agnes.

"Not just yet, please. I want to know about you first. What have you been doing? A sling, too."

"Yes, I went round to the doctor this afternoon instead of going for a walk with Alan. But he made it comfortable."

"And you haven't been out otherwise?" he asked.

"Only to see my mother. I really didn't feel up to walking; otherwise, as you may guess I shouldn't have sent Alan round the Serpentine alone. What a hot day! Wasn't it awful in the City? I want to sit under a tree near a lake."

Timothy glanced at the clock, and then jumped up.

" I shan't be a couple of minutes," he said. " I must just give a message."

" What is it ? Ring the bell, Tim," said she.

" No, I'll go myself."

He was back again before the couple of minutes were up.

" Now there's another thing I want to talk about," he said. " I've been here ten days. You know Cousin Alan was kind enough to tell me a few nights ago, not to be in any hurry to find my flat."

" Well, don't be in any hurry then."

" I haven't been. In fact I haven't looked for it at all since I came here. But to-day I did hear of some-thing that sounded likely. And I can't stop on here indefinitely, can I ? You're much too kind both of you to say you've had enough of me, but it would be dreadful to find that I'd outstayed my welcome."

For a fleeting moment Agnes pictured to herself the evenings as she had known them for so long without Tim, the silent dinners, the sense of being perpetually in harness. She smiled at his anxious face.

" You needn't worry about that," she said. " Alan and I both find you a delightful guest : I meant to tell you so before. So dismiss that from your mind. The only possible reason for your taking this flat which sounds likely, would be if you found it dull and cheerless here. I promise you that that's true. So, if we give satisfaction, Tim——"

" You know how I like being here," he said. " Or if you don't I'll inform you of that fact now."

" Thanks, my dear. Oh, what pretty speeches we are making to each other. As for indefinitely, let's be definite instead, and put the matter out of our minds for another fortnight. Now no more pretty speeches. There really isn't any need for them."

She had got up with some restless instinct, and had

strolled across to the wide-open window. As she looked out a motor-car slid up to the door.

"But is that Pamela's car already?" she asked. "It's not half-past five yet."

Timothy had followed her.

"No, I don't suppose that's Pamela's car," he said. "I expect it's mine. I'm going to take you for a drive, did you guess? We're going to find a tree and a lake. We shall find them quickest in Richmond Park."

"Oh, Tim, how wicked of you!" she said. "And how delightful of you to think of it. But supposing Alan wants me? I don't think I can come."

"Well, he'll get you at half-past seven. And what are the chances of his wanting you before? One in a million. And if the millionth turns up, what then? We'll leave word."

Agnes still hesitated.

"If you won't come I shall go alone," said he. "I shall drive round and round Richmond Park, which would be rather silly. But you may go alone if you don't want me. Which is it to be? I don't think there are any other alternatives."

"Tim, you're a bully," she said.

"I know. You'd better give in."

"And it's dreadfully extravagant."

"Not to a man who is making a superb income with his pen."

"Ah, take the story with you and read it me," she said.

"Anything you like, provided you'll come."

"Of course I'm coming. Oh, my dear, what fun. I'm pining for my lake and my tree."

They left the drought and the dust behind them, and were soon strolling across the tussocky grass towards the Penn Ponds. The hawthorns, each with its round shadow below it, were in the full cream of their whiteness, elms were in thick foliage, and the later oaks yet tawny with their more youthful leaves. There were a couple of grebes, yes, those birds with smart orange whiskers, on the pond, there was a red-start flitting through the branches, and there, coming down with wings spread like a parachute, and a chromatic descending scale of notes, a tree-pipit. There was a reed-warbler in those rushes, that cheerful aimless piping. . . .

"There were lots of them," said he, "in some reed-beds near Ypres, and they went on chirping away quite regardless of shells and machine guns. If I had been a reed-warbler I shouldn't have stopped in that hellish place another minute."

And all these things were matter of casual observation to him, so Agnes perceived. They were just the ordinary jolly sights and sounds of the country, not interesting phenomena to be noticed and noted for future use, like the sequins of the elms in Kew Gardens. Alan turned his observations into little gems of literary art, for Tim they were gems already, not to be facetted and set, but left precisely as they were. She could not help drawing the contrast between them, though without disparagement or preference.

"But indeed you must take Alan out with you one day," she said. "You would point out to him no end of sights and sounds which he would make use of. Such beautiful use, too," she added.

"I know : I have his books by my bed," said he.

"And do you read them, Tim?" she asked.

"Yes, I read something of them every night. What workmanship, you know. I love noticing that : I love trying to find out how it's done. There's an exquisiteness——"

Agnes found herself immensely interested in the question of how Alan's books struck him. To find

that out was part of that study of the younger generation which Alan had promised himself.

"Don't I know that?" she said. "And what else
do you find? Go on, Tim."

He wrinkled up his forehead.

"You must remember I'm a barbarian," he said.
"You'll see that when it comes to my story. All
that I did from the time I was nineteen to twenty-
three, was to be in terror of my life and put other
people, as I hoped, in terror of theirs, and somehow
to enjoy it, though I loathed it. I was out to kill,
and the others were out to kill me. It gave me a
violent mind, I expect. See?"

"Quite. And I sympathize," she said.

"I don't know why you should do that. The effect
is that now I'm always wanting excitement in whatever I do. If I read a book I want to be gripped by
it : not melodrama, nothing of that kind, but some
. . . some reality at the bottom of it. The reed-
warbler will do all right, because he's in deadly
earnest. I think that's it. The things I'm interested
in are those that feel. I don't mind whether they
chirp or howl with anguish, or commit murder, so
long as it's sincere——"

Agnes was at once up in arms for Alan.

"But, my dear, did you ever come across such
sincerity as Alan's?" she said. "Why, his writing
is an overwhelming passion with him! What's
wrong there?"

"I didn't say anything was wrong with Cousin
Alan," he said. "But are they real, the people he
writes about? Real to him, of course. And ever so
graceful and unhappy. But what about? There
isn't anything so real as a toothache among the lot of
them. Why don't they ache sometimes? Why
aren't they sick? Why don't they get drunk? Or

fall in love? That would do all right. . . . Of course I'm wrong. But you asked me."

Tim was expressing, she knew, just all that she would not allow herself to feel. But she did not clasp hands with it when it was thus presented to her, she whisked away from it, giving a dead cut to the phantom whose every gesture and habit she knew so well. Loyalty to her own consciousness was light in the scale compared with loyalty to Alan.

" Yes, I think you are wrong," she said. " At least Alan is right. You see. . . . It's like this : he sees temperaments clashing and acting on each other : he sees subtle play of nerves and affection, all that makes psychology. Whereas you see fists and faces clashing, and . . . and people kicking each other. At least that's your account of yourself : I don't know what account your story will give of you."

She felt herself to be ingeniously wriggling away from what beckoned her. She was sick to death—this she would never admit though she knew it—of fine shades and barely perceptible points of view, of dissection as opposed to demonstration, and of demonstration, as opposed to deeds. How like Tim it was that he should have ordered this sumptuous motor and then have confronted her with the deed done, and how like Alan it would have been to have suggested a drive in Richmond Park and at once to have yielded to her demur, and let her take a chair for herself out into the garden in the square.

Her own life, after all, was spent in practical ways, however small their service might be, and it was little wonder, so she said to herself not in excuse but in the sensible facing of facts, that such was her habit. Fine shades, and oh, how fine they were, subtle perceptions, and oh, their subtlety, seemed now to have been grafted on her, but the sap which fed them was from some wild briar-root, which had been cut out from a hedgerow, and transplanted to the sheltered garden-bed. How wonderful at first had the pale blossom-ings which surrounded her seemed, how rare their fragrance! What more had she desired than to breathe that atmosphere, and be grafted with the most exquisite of its roses? She, her sap, the very life of her, had borne so many of them. Now, in close proximity to her, was another wild root, not yet grafted, not yet tamed to the garden. Let her see at any rate what sort of roses it bore.

"So out with the story, Tim," she said. "Here's a lovely tree for shade, and there's the lake, and you are giving me a nice time."

Tim stretched himself on the grass beside her, rest-ing on an elbow. He had been hatless since they left London behind, and once again Agnes noticed that thick brown mat of hair and the hands which were so like Alan's. But anything more deliciously unlike Alan's than his story it was impossible to conceive. A grim, violent vivid little sketch it was, the scene laid in a front-line trench. Two boys who had been at school together and had enlisted in the same regiment were now dozing, now talking as the night wore on, for there was to be an attack at dawn next day. Neither of them seemed much to care; whatever damned horror was in front of them, it was so inevitable that it was not worth thinking about, and they talked chiefly about a particular school cricket match on the details of which they sharply dis-agreed. And then, emerging very slowly, came the sense of the abysmal terror which lay just below. . . . Drop by drop it embittered every word, and you knew that essentially they quaked and cowered. For an hour or two before dawn they lay side by side and slept, one with his head resting on the other's shoulder. Then in the last paragraph of the story came the word passed down the line to stand ready, and drearily and sullenly they laced their mud-smothered boots and buttoned their tunics.

"I tell you it wasn't in that match at all that old Joyce made his fifty," said one. And that was all.

From beginning to end there was scarcely a line which Alan would have allowed to go even as far as the second dictation; narrative and speech alike were conveyed in barked out, snapped out sentences. There was no fine constructed framework, no development in intensity, no leading up by due preparation to the climax. Indeed there was no climax. Timothy gave no picture of the two climbing over the parapet into a rain of machine-gun fire, and the boy who uttered the words of conclusion had said precisely the same thing when first their futile argument began. And what of the psychology, the dissection and laying bare of character which alone could have excused a narrative in which there was no incident whatever? The two boys seemed exactly alike, both seething with terror and talking about cricket. . . . And yet Agnes, trained in the intricacies and arts of story-telling, felt that the quarter of an hour in which she had listened to Tim's voice passed in a flash of agonized tenseness. The tale was a gem, a master-piece, a blood-sweat.

"Oh, my dear!" she said. "My dear Tim, how atrociously good! The pity of it, the reality. Don't talk to me just yet. I'm all to pieces."

Agnes wiped her eyes with the back of her hand.

"Poor little devils!" she said. "Just thinking about their cricket match. . . . Thanks ever so much for reading it to me."

Tim folded the slips together, and sat up.

"But do you mean it?" he said. "Will it do?"

"Of course it will do. It's heartbreaking, which I suppose is what you meant it to be. How did you manage it?"

" I didn't. It managed itself. But it took me no end of trouble to find out what it wanted to do. I began by putting in a lot of beautiful reflections, and then it didn't want those, so I cut them out. I even moralized a little about War, and I cut that out. I cut out everything that didn't seem to be wanted. I daresay a lot more ought to go."

" No, leave it alone," said Agnes. " In fact let me have it. I want to read it over again to-night. And you will show me your other stories, Tim ? "

" Why, of course I will. I am pleased you like it."

" I don't. I can't bear it : it's terrible. I see what you mean by saying you've got a violent mind."

She got up.

" We must go, my dear, if we're to finish our circle round the Park," she said. " I want to be back before the dictation is over. . . . And what about Alan ? Does he know you're writing stories ? "

" No. I haven't told him. In fact, I didn't mean to. He might ask me to read one, and I can't—can you ?—imagine anything less in his line."

Agnes cast a sideways look at him, and saw that his mouth was twitching with some suppressed merriment. That made her laugh outright, and he checked himself no more.

" Frankly, I can't," she said, and turned more directly towards him, so that she should see him laughing. Tim's laugh was one of the most delightful things about him : his mouth a little grim at the corners when he was grave, relaxed itself with the lifting of his lip into curves of abandoned gaiety. She had noticed that the first day he dined with them, and since then had never ceased to notice it. He looked not a day over twenty when he laughed like that, and so far from that making her feel old, it made her feel as young as he. That, up till now, was the

supreme gift which he had brought, as far as she was
concerned, to the house in Goring Square. His
presence with that laugh which the most minute gaiety
could evoke, made her feel young. He postponed for
her the dawning of the grey unknown days which on
the morning of her birthday party, scarcely a fortnight ago, she had settled were all that the future
march of the years would bring to her. He flashed
a signal of halt to that advancing march; and it
seemed that the years were retracing their steps again,
and, instead of advancing upon her in firm procession,
were receding.

The fact that they had not decided whether Alan
should be told about Tim's first raid into authorship,
meant that the decision had been made, and that he
was not to be informed of it, and this, on their return,
made a secret knowledge between them which, just in
proportion as it drew them together, caused Alan to
glide off into some sort of remoteness. Nothing of
the sort had been contemplated by either of them; it
was not for that, but only for the story not being, as
Tim said, ' in his line,' that the concealment had been
connived at. But the secret, however trivial, was
there, and the knowledge of its existence had all the
flavour of an innocent conspiracy. About their other
doings they were voluble. Tim took it on himself to
say what they had done while the dictation was in
progress, and Alan was cordial and self-derogatory.

" Your stupid old husband," he said to Agnes,
" wrapt up in his own affairs ! It was the very thing
for you, after your evil and tedious day, to get a
breath of fresh air. Look at our dear miscreant, who
thought so quickly of what my muddled old brain
never lighted on ! He has—what is that expression ?
—he has wiped my eye. I left you, dear Agnes, so
cool and comfortable, I thought, when good Pamela

and I retired to the work-room, and then, after that, we got absorbed!"

Agnes recollected her own duties. . . .

"And you've never told us yet how the dictation went, dear," she said.

She knew quite well how the dictation must have gone, for Alan was alert and beaming. That could only mean that the dictation had gone very well: there was no need to ask. He looked at the decanter of port, and then took half a glass. That, too, was an infallible symptom. He always abstained from anything alcoholic when the dictation had gone badly.

"A wonderful couple of hours," he said. "Not a pause, so I think Pamela would tell you. An extraordinary clarity. And we made a plot, to be revealed to you, and to obtain, so we ventured to hope, your sanction. But whether with your sanction or not we are going to be very autocratic about it. Guess, my dear."

"Ah, you and your Pamela and your plots!" said Agnes, with an air of singular absence of annoyance. "Go on, Alan: I believe you're meaning to elope with her."

"Yes, we're going to elope," said Alan, "we're going to run away from you, my dear, exactly at five o'clock to-morrow afternoon. Our elopement will last for two hours. You shan't take any risk of using your hand before you can safely do so. For the period of another dictation, I elope with Pamela."

"You wretches!" she said, "as if I shouldn't be quite well to-morrow! And I can ask awkward questions about your plans: you were two very drowsy conspirators. There's the dictation to-night. You never thought of that."

Alan gave a little squeal of exultation.

"Not so drowsy as you think, dear," he said.

" We thought of that. Indeed that was the first thing we thought of. Guess again ! "

" Ah, I know," she said. " She's coming back here at half-past nine for an hour. But how inhospitable of you, Alan. Why didn't you make her stop for dinner ? "

" Wrong ! " said Alan. " Now, Timothy, your turn."

Timothy assumed a rapt conjectural aspect.

" You're going to take your manuscript round to her house, Cousin Alan," he said. " And you're going to dictate there."

The thing had become a game. . . . Agnes pressed a finger to her forehead.

" No," she said. " You're going to Hyde Park Corner, and dictate to the policeman." . . . Really that did not seem more ludicrously improbable than the notion of Alan's going out after dinner.

And then it all came out. Timothy was right. Pamela was dining out, but was to feel unwell at a quarter past nine. By the half-hour she would be at home again, and ten minutes later, picked up by her motor, Alan would arrive at her house.

Agnes saw Tim's mouth a-twitch, and steadily forebore to look at him. If she did, she would laugh, and Timothy would laugh too, and she would feel exactly twenty years old again. Yet there was Alan visibly rejuvenated with his plans and his Pamela and his glass of port. He was quite excited at this daring excursion, and Agnes had to draw out the full honey of it for him.

" I never heard of such rushings about," she said. " Tim, you and I are to be left at home like discarded chaperones, while Alan has assignations with his Pamela. That's quite the modern style."

" Tush, my dear," said Alan, with a broad grin.

They had sat late over the dinner-table, and even

as he spoke, Mrs. Probyn's motor was announced. Alan hurried upstairs and presently came down with a sheaf of slips, the book into which the dictation was written, and the Flaubert paper-knife.

" Equipped ! " he said. " And it is not cold, dear, is it ? I think my lighter overcoat will be sufficient."

" And don't forget your latch-key," said Agnes, " in case everyone is in bed before you come back."

He drove off with a salute on the paper-knife, and now Agnes could refrain no longer from looking straight at Tim.

" It's the most daring thing I ever heard of," said he, and she let the years peal off her at his laugh. There was no faintest shade of irony there, else she would have detected and resented it. Tim joyously and unerringly took exactly Alan's own view of his adventure.

They sat down again opposite each other at the table, for Tim had not yet had his invariable second cup of coffee.

" And what wonderful luck," said she. " All to-day and to-morrow would have been lost for dictation, if his Pamela hadn't salved them. O, Tim, how she'll talk about Alan's dropping in after dinner. It *will* make her happy. I'm not sure if I can bear that. . . . Now it's your business to keep me amused. How do you propose to do it ? "

" I'll go out of the room while you think of a word, and then I'll come in and guess it," suggested Tim.

" I don't think I should care about that. But you may go out of the room and fetch a quantity of the words you've thought of and read them to me. . . ."

Pamela's large circle of intimate acquaintances, to whom she was so invincibly hospitable, was sumptuously regaled with these experiences during the next few days. In fact most of them, and in particular Mr. Blewitt, grew rather tired of hearing about the marvellous new story of Alan's for which she was the amanuensis. In her vivid allusive manner she let it be understood, without actually stating it, that she had long been engaged in this employment, and that Alan's visits to her house for after-dinner dictation were no unusual occurrences. The fact that the sprain to Agnes's finger had alone (and that so lately) caused her promotion to the post of scribe naturally formed no part of her narrative, for it was really a side-issue altogether and away from the point.

" I must scold you," she said to Mr. Blewitt, whom she was entertaining on one of these days, " for your horrid article about Alan a couple of weeks ago. So brilliant, too, which made it all the worse."

" Nothing is the worse for a little brilliance, dear lady," interpolated Mr. Blewitt.

" Now listen to me and take some more asparagus and your scolding. How could you say such dreadful things about Alan's collected edition ? But you will be forced to eat your own words when his new book comes out."

" A terrible diet," began Blewitt. " A grammatical diet, one may hope, but none the less——"

Mrs. Probyn saw the opportunity of addressing her remarks to a larger audience, for two or three people opposite her at her round table happened to be silent. She forgot about the scolding.

" I was speaking about Alan Graham's new book," she said. " He has been dictating it to me : we have got to the last chapter but one. Sometimes when we have been going on with it late after dinner I can't sleep a wink. It's the most wonderful, the most perfect thing he has ever done. I am glad to be alive when such a book was written. And to hear it come out, fresh as a stream from under a rock, in that wonderful silvery voice of his ! He walks up and down always when he dictates, stroking Flaubert's paper-knife. I declare I'm beginning to believe in magic. Sentence after sentence comes welling out, every word a gem. . . ."

She was really very ridiculous, thought Blewitt, as he waited alert for the smallest pause, in order to chip in himself. It was so like her too, to exploit some-body who for the last ten years had ceased to matter at all. But she was always doing that : she never saw new merit or captured young and promising lions with all their roaring in front of them, but collected about her in the cause of her salon obsolete and out-worn old specimens, who could not ever jump through hoops any more. For himself, as keen a discoverer as she, he was always on the hunt for fresh voices and budding talent, for new movements and violent yeasty modes. In order to draw attention to these, it was his habit to go on iconoclastic raids among the old idols, crashing, so he would put it to himself, their dusty effigies off the shelves, and generally demolishing them. . . . At this moment Mrs. Probyn com-mitted the tactical error of pausing to sip her wine, and he plunged into the opening.

" Dear lady, you interest me indescribably," he said. " It will indeed be a marvel, a miracle, if our revered old friend is indeed plucking fresh music out of his antique lyre, and I shall be the first with my garlands and my applause. But string after string of his graceful instrument has been for years mouldering away and snapping, and when I read his last book, I found myself involuntarily picturing the image of a charming and delightful old man thrumming the empty air, and, I suppose, imagining that he is ravishing us with his music, whereas no sound of any sort comes forth. Profoundly distressed, I turned to his earlier books again, hoping to recapture the glamour which once we attributed to him. But my distress, instead of being relieved, became vastly more acute. I could hardly believe that once we had read betwixt smiles and tears such works as 'The Tyro,' and 'Bread of Deceit.' Where had the fragrance gone? They reminded me of little muslin bags, such as careful housewives fill with lavender and dispose among under-clothing. All the aroma had departed, they rustled and were scentless. Then, hearing that our old friend was contemplating a collected edition of his lavender bags, I felt myself compelled to issue in my modest little column, a word of the friendliest warning, for which now you brand me with unmerited obloquy.''

Dora Muir was one of those who had been silenced by these protagonists of talk, but here she pounced on a silence which a less vigilant ear might have never noticed. To-day her costume resembled a Union Jack, probably because she had that morning received some remarkably large bills from Paris.

'' Alan is infinitely the happiest man I know,'' she said, '' for he has never wavered in his belief that nothing in the world is half so important as his books. The fact that I find them totally unreadable only fills him with a wondering pity for me. For fifteen years my poor dear sister's life has been one long martyrdom : every day of it has been mapped out to suit Alan's terrible fecundity. Isn't there some animal, a spider I think, of which the female, as soon as the marriage has taken place, proceeds to eat up the male? Alan has made things even now. He has slowly been eating Agnes up ever since they were married. And now he appears to have got hold of Pamela. Escape while you can, dear Pamela. Come to Paris with me to-morrow. This terrible England! The domestic affections, you know! Such rot! We're the lucky ones, dear Pamela : you're a widow, and my husband has eloped with salt. He spends the whole day in weighing it, exactly as if he was the mother of salt, and wanted to have evidence of its thriving. I wish you would elope with Alan."

Dora's conversation was like the chalking of rude remarks on the wall by an intelligent street boy. She wrote there ' Pamela and Alan '; she wrote there ' Alan is an ass ' : she wrote there ' Martyred Agnes.' Any passer-by was invited to elaborate these sugges- tions, or to put in a ' not.' Pamela on this occasion put in a ' not.' ' Alan is not an ass,' was the gist of her comments.

" You will all see," she said. " And as for eloping with Alan, I might as well try to elope with the moon. There is he, swung high and glorious above all our heads, yours particularly, Henry, (she had just grasped the fact that nobody ever called Mr. Blewitt ' Harry ') and you are jealous of his rays, and say there is going to be an eclipse. Wait for his next book."

" I am charmed to wait for ever," said Blewitt. " But you seem to imply that it will not be so long."

She got up.

" I shall have to scold you again," she said.

Pamela was amanuensis for the fourth day in suc- cession this afternoon and these depreciations, as she proceeded on her way, only inflamed her own en- thusiasm. Her taste for fine literature had, in case of its existence, nothing whatever to do with her de- votion to dictation. Alan Graham had the distinction of success and seclusion, and having penetrated his seclusion, she was bound to foster his success, which implied her own. Not half-a-dozen people in London had enticed Alan to their houses, and she had had difficulty enough, God knew, in enticing him to hers. But when once he had ventured in, the trap had closed

behind him, and now she had him in her hand, and
was feeding him with the sugar which had been his
bait. She had no intention of ' hedging ' : of beginning to wonder if now, as on several other disastrous
occasions, she had been making a very mild animal
into a lion, but in the after-chill from Blewitt's remarks, she began to wonder whether it would not be
wise to make Alan so special a lion that very few were
ever allowed to come near him. It might easily be
the most distinguished thing of all to hedge him about
like that : to invite only the few and the fragrant when
he was with her, and to deny him so ruthlessly to the
general, that the general would be wild for admittance.
Yes : tiny dinners when Alan was there, and the
cancelling of engagements already made—' I am
desolated,' she would write, ' but Alan has proposed
himself to dine with me that night, and I must beg
you to let me off and not be angry with me. You will
understand, darling.' . . .

There were further plans. She had a charming
little house in Sussex, and when this book was
finished, she was determined to get the Master down
there for a week's rest. She could write no end of
interesting little notes from there, saying that she
would be out of town, and giving reasons. She did
not quite see Agnes there as well. It would be really
more interesting to wangle the Master down there
without the mistress. . . . It would be wonderfully daring and delightful to spend a week down
there alone with Alan. Frankly, she felt she could
trust him as perfectly as she could trust herself not to
let the smallest touch of sentiment cloud the clear
pool of their intellectual partnership.

Of course all these bright dreams depended on one
firm condition, namely, that Alan should continue to
be sought for by others (and only obtained in small
quantities from her). Just for a little during lunch

when Blewitt on her right and Dora opposite to her
had been so very malicious about him, the firmness
of that condition seemed to waver. She realized that
to certain minds, the ' smart ' but wholly illiterate on
the one side, as unconsciously typified by Dora, and
the professionally literate on the other, as consciously
typified by Blewitt, Alan cut no figure at all, and it
was clearly desirable and even necessary that either
the new book should be a triumphant success and renew the great days of the Tyro, or that the collected
edition should bring him to the front again. Naturally she would not continue copying out the prose
works of any author, unless that laborious and lengthy
task brought her high dividends of honour and distinction : she would not have copied out the Odes of
Keats from the poet's lips, unless she had been quite
convinced that the world would madly envy her for so
doing. But she allowed no thought of Alan's possible
eclipse to darken her. She was ' all out ' for him
and it should not be her fault if he (and she) were
not in the lime-light. By his own confession, he
found a stimulus in her help and presence, and she
would with all her time and energy continue to inspire him. How lucky that dear Agnes had sprained
her finger ! How careful she must be of it !

It still wanted twenty minutes of the hour at which
she was due at Alan's house, when she arrived at the
bottom of Goring Square, and she might well spend
them with Mrs. Mowbray. She found her at home,
and fiercely employed in the *petit point* which Agnes
had laid out for her.

" Ah, how fortunate I am, dear Mrs. Mowbray, to
find you," she said. " I am due in a quarter of an
hour at the house opposite. Daffodils ! What a delicious pattern ! Alan delights in daffodils."

Mrs. Mowbray laid down her work.

" I have heard how good you have been to my sonin-law," she said, "while Agnes was incapacitated. It is wonderful how with your many engagements you find time to take down his dictation."

"Ah, that is the first call on my time," said Pamela effusively. "There is no engagement which would not have to give way to that. Such a privilege!"

"Most unselfish of you. You are a great admirer of his work then."

"He is surpassing himself," said Pamela. "The new book is the masterpiece of all his masterpieces."

"That is good news. One had been afraid that he was no longer at his best. A sad falling off in his work," said Mrs. Mowbray. "But your assurance is most gratifying. Who should know, dear Mrs. Probyn, better than you? Indeed who except you can form any estimate about the new book? My Agnes, of course, is naturally biassed, but a clear, cool cultivated judgment like yours. . . . Most welcome news indeed."

It struck Pamela that Mrs. Mowbray's voice gave the most joyless rendering of Alleluias which she had ever heard : there seemed more gusto in her fear that there had been a sad falling off in his work. It was curious though she would not allow it to be disquieting that there was this general sense abroad that Alan was a waning moon. Was there, too, some faintly ironic inflection in these tributes to her own judgment?

CHAPTER IV

IT invariably happened that when, as now, one of Alan's stories was approaching its close, his absorption in it rose like a fever-temperature till the crisis was past and the last word written. But never before, so thought Agnes, had this concentration of his been so strained and so troubled. His step would pad about his dressing-room long after he should have been asleep, the door of communication was shut again in the morning at unheard of hours, and at breakfast, weary-eyed, he would confess to having put in three hours of preparation already for the evening's dictation. All the morning, without a restorative stroll in the garden before lunch, he remained closetted in the work-room, and afterwards, in the hour for exercise, he could not spare time even for the shorter of the walks in the Park.

"I think, dear, if we went perhaps half way along the Serpentine," he said, when they started next day, "that will be sufficient to freshen me up for our evening's work. There are half-a-dozen slips on which I have jotted down no more than the embryo of some point which will be valuable to me, and I should be glad to get a little time to myself before tea in order to outline the scope of these more definitely. Sometimes, you know, if there is no more than a mere jotted heading, I find I cannot always recall the full suggestion, the full . . . the full significance. Yes, I express myself awkwardly to-day : I confess that I am much preoccupied with our final pages."

"But that's all to the good, dear," said Agnes encouragingly. "The more your finale preoccupies you, the better and sharper is the expression of your thought. So at least, you have always found. You're satisfied, aren't you, that you've got your threads firmly knitted?"

He looked very tired to-day, his steps were more than ever short and shuffling, and, whether the impression took its rise from the contrast now so familiar to Agnes between Tim's alert and careless vigour and the effort which activity, whether of the mind or body, caused Alan, he struck her suddenly and newly as a man old beyond his years. Yet often before at such stages in production, she had seen how the climax of his work aged and strained him, and there was nothing novel or disquieting in that. A few days more, and the last chapter would be finished, and the bent bow relaxed. . . .

"Yes, I'm satisfied, as far as I can be," he said. "'Ars longa,' you know; there is no such thing as perfection and indeed, dear, you must be tired of that eternal parrot-cry of mine. We have always been content to do our best, and leave it at that. But this time, somehow, I need to do better than my best. Is it, do you think, our dear Pamela's encouragement and appreciation that has strung me up to some unheard-of pitch? She is so certain that we have never reached these levels before. Wonderfully stimulating, a mental oxygen. . . ."

He stopped, and poked with the end of his stick at some half-loosened pebbles in the roadway.

"Mental oxygen," he muttered, "making effort possible in rarefied air. Ah, now, what was it exactly?"

The pebble would not yield to his prodding ferule, and he moved on again.

"The exact terms of the simile have slipped my memory," he said. "Very tiresome. I had just put down the heading 'mental oxygen' and the expression of the thought was taking form in my head, when you came for me to go our walk. Perhaps, dear, for the next day or two, it would be wiser if after lunch you did not come to tell me it was half-past two, but waited till I was ready. I should have thought of that sooner. . . . Let me see now. There was something about the weight of the oxygen apparatus requiring more effort to carry than was compensated for to the climber by the extra power of effort which the oxygen gave him. I am on its track, I think."

Agnes took her usual practical line over such per-plexities as these. It was generally successful, and a hundred times it had received his sanction.

"Now, my dear, you're to dismiss all that from your mind for another half hour," she said. "You and I came out for our walk, in order to make you leave behind you all thought of your work. We've got to freshen ourselves up for our evening dictation, and how are we to do that, if you bring your work along with you? Look, here we are at our bird-corner of the Serpentine, and all the gulls have gone off to their building places, and the mallards too, and there's not one left for us to feed! What am I to do? with our crusts and crumbs? Shall we share them, dear?"

He paid no attention to her, continuing with down-cast eye to prod at the pebbles on the path.

"Ah, I was close on its heels, then," he said. "My hand was on it, but it basely eluded me."

"And it will continue to elude you," she said, "if you go prodding at it. Turn you mind to my per-plexity. What am I to do with these crumbs? Attend to me, dear!"

He interrupted her with a gesture of impatience.

"There! It has gone again!" he said. "It was scarcely judicious of you, my Agnes, to head me off when I was so hot on the track of what I am hunting. I am not, I grieve to realize, a lively and vivacious companion for you to-day, as our Timothy would have been, but you should make allowance for me, and realize on your side, that however trivial the world might think my preoccupation, it is not every day that I arrive at the last pages of one of my poor little stories. At such times the minutest detail which I search for, is a pearl of great price to me."

Agnes could easily divine the real cause of his impatience. The loss of this unfortunate little simile (or whatever the oxygen-business served for) was no more than the chance spark that had blown into the heap of that nervous inflammable stuff with which his mind was charged : anything would have set it on fire. Up it went now in a flame of censure and ill-temper.

It produced in her nothing but a tender and wise commiseration. It but roused in her the eager hope that his nervous tension would be justified by its fruits. She put her hand inside his arm.

" Ah, my dear, you mustn't talk to me like that," she said. "We've often proved, ever so successfully, that the best way to recall something which we've mislaid in our minds, is not to grub about in the mind, but to open its doors and windows and let in the air. I was acting quite sensibly in trying to divert your attention. You needn't apologise for speaking hastily to me. I rather like it. And you shall guess why, if you can't help me in advising me what to do with our crumbs."

The petulant creases in his forehead did not quite smooth themselves out : he still resented the loss of his simile. But he could go a little way to meet her.

" Yes, you are right," he said. " Certainly we often have found that to divert the attention is successful. But these last pages, dear, the strain of them must be my excuse. . . . And as regards what you ask me to guess, you must tell it me. I have no spare energy for conundrums. Why did you, so amiably, not mind my impatience just now?"

"There can only be one reason," she said. "I find in it an excellent augury for the book."

His egoism sprang to meet her now.

"Ah, I see, I see," he said. "You mean that it has gripped me so that just now I forgot my manners, and that to be gripped like that augurs well for the force and vitality of it. I hope, indeed I trust that is true. It is not on my own judgment alone that I rely, you know—our dear Pamela's certainty about it, I confess, inspires me with a confidence I should not allow myself to entertain, if I depended only on my own estimate."

Agnes had her own idea of what Pamela's opinion was worth. It was not that Pamela was unintelligent or that her judgment was valueless, but it was impossible not to remember that Pamela had an axe to grind. She had in fact been grinding that axe with characteristic assiduity for the last week: Pamela's axe must be supposed now to have the keenest of edges. She had 'collected' this recluse: she had stamped him with her own die, she was voluble over the wonder of the new book, and the raptures of the hours of dictation. It had been of course most kind of Pamela to take up the duties of the amanuensis when she herself was incapacitated, but as Timothy said, it had been 'glory for Pamela,' and glory could not but infuse her estimate of the book. She was feeding her private and wonderful lion with the juicy chops of her appreciation. . . . Agnes herself had not yet seen the chapters which had been inscribed by Pamela: it might be that they were amazing.

"Yes, Pamela is wild about your work," she said. "I am longing to see it."

Alan had now completely recovered his chagrin at the loss of the simile.

"You shall, dear," he said. "In fact I meant to suggest that, before you resume your writing for me this afternoon, if your hand is really its nimble self again, you should glance through the chapters that have been written in your absence. You will be more in sympathy with me if you do that : you will be better able to appreciate the absorption which my work is being to me just now. Let us turn then. We must give you time to read what we have done these last four or five days. Dear me ! Is it no more than that ? I feel as if my Agnes had been absent from the work-room for a far more protracted period. I attribute that to the fact that so much has taken place since then in that world which, as you know, is at such times more real to me than the material realms in which I actually exist."

"Pamela and her appreciation have been inspiring you," said Agnes. "You found her presence stimulating from the first day she came to listen to the dictation. How easily and surely it went."

"Day after day it has continued like that," said he. "I feel, dear, like the climber confronted now by the last slope that leads to the peak never before scaled. The route is open : only the rarity of the air. . . . Ah, I have it ! The way being open, if only the limbs and sinews can be stimulated for that final effort : that was the missing link, that the way is open. How right, my dear, you were to divert my attention from what my mind was seeking ! How doubly wrong was your grumpy old husband to feel even a momentary impatience at your interruption which was so wise, so well-warranted."

She laughed.

"I knew you would recapture it, if you thought of

something different," she said. " I inspired you that time."

Alan pressed her arm.

" Dear Agnes," he said, " as if you are not always my inspiration ! "

How radically untrue that was, so she told herself, and how radically ignorant Alan was of its graceful falsity. She knew in her own self that she had never inspired a line or an epithet in all the books he had written. All that she had done, all that she had attempted since the days when she had realized that she was nothing to him in that regard, was to secure him, zealously and unremittingly, the conditions for his work that suited him best. All day and every day she had been intelligently at his disposal, ready to walk with him for his freshening-up, to write to his dictation, and play him little soothing tunes when things went heavily, and, generally and wholly, to efface herself or be herself for his convenience and comfort. That was the work to which she had eagerly surrendered herself, and that was real enough : but that she should be accounted his inspirer was part of some interminable charade, like those of which Dora had spoken, to which also belonged such rites as the annual jubilations and idleness of the birthday cele-bration. It was a habit, and a meaningless one, but Alan called her his inspirer with no more sense of falsity than if, absent-mindedly, without thinking what he was saying, he wished her good-night.

Yet now, as he made his small compliment, it was something of a shock to her to find how little she cared whether she was his inspirer, or whether, as had certainly been the case since she had sprained her finger, Pamela had filled the office with more reality than she had ever done. Emotionally (here was the shock) Agnes found that she was quite indifferent who it was who inspired him, provided only that inspiration was on tap. She cared immensely for securing, either personally or vicariously, his perfect conditions: she cared for that, so she truly believed, as much as he himself cared, but she cared as little as he who his minister was. Pamela might permanently occupy the seat by the writing-table, she might dig herself in there, with Agnes's eager approval, if only her possession of it secured Alan the stimulus he needed.

That stimulus for him was the idol to which (how willingly!) she had sacrificed the sex and splendour of her own youth; she wondered now whether she had sacrificed her individuality as well on that bloodless altar. To-day that was a difficult question to answer, though a month ago it would never have occurred to her to ask it. A month ago her individuality was drugged with habit, it existed in a dozing drowsiness. Only the night before her birthday party, she had told herself that she looked for nothing more from life beyond what she had already experienced; there was the drowsiness. And as if in swift punishment for her indifference, the very day that followed had brought into it those first faint stirrings, sweetly disquieting, those mysterious messages from the air, wordless and all but incomprehensible. Just those dots and dashes behind which lurked a code that systematized and interpreted.

She found nothing direct to say in answer to his little compliment. What was there to say which could in itself be true, and yet not admit the inherent falsity of his speech? She equivocated.

" I should love to think that I inspired you, dear," she said.

But she spoke to the empty air. Alan was deep already, she supposed, in fashioning and trimming the recovered simile. Once again she had served his turn.

Presently, as they arrived home, he emerged.

"That will not escape me again," he said. "And now, dear, I think I will just go and brood and ruminate in the work-room till tea is ready. It will be delightful to see you in your place again afterwards. What luck, was it not, that dear Pamela could fill the vacancy. We should otherwise have lost four days over your injury."

"Is she coming to sit with us while we're at work?" asked Agnes. . . . So little did she care who inspired Alan, that the question had not occurred to her before.

He smiled.

"Aha, we had a little joke about that," he said. "Dear Pamela, ever so playfully, said that she would feel terribly jealous to see you back in her place— her place, you know, dear!—that she would not come in at all to-day, neither this afternoon or this evening. By to-morrow, she hoped, she would get over her wickedness. Amusing of Pamela, was it not?"

Agnes was aware that it needed an effort to summon her careless geniality and make a suitable reply. What Alan appreciated in Pamela's 'little joke,' what he hugged to himself was not the humorous side of it but the serious side, her sense of the privilege in being dictated to, the preciousness of which was such that she could not bear (without a struggle) to see her place tenanted by its normal occupant. This was a tribute to his magic, it was for this he valued her joke. Therein lay Agnes's sense of misgiving that he who had once been so royally independent of praise or comment, so content to have done his best, finding the only reward that was of value in his devotion to his art, should at this moment, when in the belief of many his star was on the wane, be becoming susceptible to external verdicts. Just as his aloof serenity had been darkened by poor Blewitt's depreciation, so now Pamela's less subtle flatteries brightened it again. But Agnes had to adapt herself to his more vulnerable mood; she must hilariously abound in humour similar to Pamela's.

" I suspect you and Pamela are making jokes half the time you are supposed to be at your dictation," she said. " I shall like to think of the poor dear's jealousy when we get to work after tea. I shall ring her up at dressing-time to tell her what a splendid hour we have had."

" No, no, no," said Alan quite seriously. " That would never do! Poor Pamela!"

Agnes went with him to the work-room, and leaving him there with his slips round him, took away with her the dictation book, in order to read up what she had missed during their last days. Indeed the dictation had been fluent, page after page of Pamela's firm and most legible hand, ran from first line to last with scarcely an erasure. Clearly too, there had been but little hesitation on the part of the dictator, for twenty pages had been added to the manuscript since last she held the pen, and this gave an average of five pages for each day's output. No wonder Alan was pleased at his facility, for he reckoned that three pages of manuscript was a good shewing for a day's work. Prosperous indeed in point of quantity had her absence proved, and as for the quality, she knew that he would never permit a single line to stand which did not fulfil his demands on himself.

It was with an eager tenderness of longing to find here the old magic that she sat down to read. Perhaps her co-operation with him, her daily witness of his endless toil in making every phrase perfect, every paragraph a shining slab the more in his building, accounted for the lack of freshness in his work which she had so long been conscious of; but now coming new to it, without having assisted at the labour and the erasures perhaps the spell would enthrall her again. She had been, all these years, so she told herself, like the conjuror's assistant, who had always seen him at practice, perfecting the cunning and the skill on which the finished illusion depended. She had been the accompanist who had heard the great singer learn his melodies, bar by bar, acquiring with infinite pains that effortless spontaneity, which was distilled drop by drop from those hours of labour, that marshalling of slips, the trudge up and down the room, the strokings of Flaubert's paper-knife. Little wonder was it that she failed to find freshness in his work when in the long matter of its preparation she had been at his elbow in the work-room, and had seen the chisellings and the hammerings and the polishings. Now for the first time since he had read the ' Tyro ' to her and her mother, she was going to be one of his audience again, not his assistant, nor his accompanist.

She turned back to the beginning of the chapter on which he had been engaged when she surrendered her place to Pamela, and reading with all her faculties alert for appreciation came to these new pages. And as she read her heart sank. New though they were to her in the sense that she had never actually perused them before, each line, each perfectly phrased sentence was not only familiar but already stale. There was all his exquisite workmanship there, his beautiful simplicity of style, those fine etched strokes, infinitely delicate, the skilled handling of faint topics, the subtle alliterations, all the dodges and devices of his finished art. But not one gleam of fire leaped out, not one breath of live breeze stirred the stagnation. Exquisite dissection of something dead . . . it was that which inspiration had come to mean to him, just the faultless handling of his tool, the graver that never slipped, the hammer which, despite the eagerness of its plying, never made a false stroke. In vain she felt for some pulse which should show that life still flickered in his dissected pieces, in these motion-less semblances of humanity, some sign that should proclaim their existence and snatch them from the Morgue. . . . But there to her mind they lay, behind glass, so to speak, the glass of Alan's cold and crystal mind.

They had no life, these exquisite dolls : they had never been alive. As she recalled the earlier chapters of the book, she realized that they had come still-born into an arctic world. They had not been conceived in any womb of the imagination, but in the cells of the brain. Their whole record did not contain one such twitch of energy and vitality as a single sentence in that short story which Timothy had read to her beside the Penn ponds, or in that other which she had heard the same evening when Alan took the dic-tation book and the Flaubert paper-knife to Pamela's house after dinner and returned elated with the triumphant march of his story. With the book be-fore her, she could see what pages there were which had so satisfied him, and once more she read them. Even as he had been dictating them, Timothy had been reading to her that second story of his, that blurted ecstasy of mere escape from the trenches, and a forty-eight hours' leave in Paris. . . . Alan would have repudiated every word of it, and every word of it contained all that Alan lacked. Timothy had gone up to bed that night with the avowed inten-tion of wrestling with another tale, the germ of which was yeasty in his brain, and what a delightful con-fession it was which he made the next morning.

"A most awful thing happened, Cousin Agnes," he had said. "I worked on till after two, and the damned thing wouldn't go right, so I gave it up. I found I was frightfully sleepy the moment I stopped, and I just tumbled into bed, and went to sleep with my light burning, that light just over my head."

"Terrible of you, Tim," she said. " All that good light wasted ! "

" Oh, that's not it. I woke again—I had put the story on the table by my bed—and a sudden idea came to me. I fetched a pen and an inkpot, and began writing again. And I forgot that the sheet was not my blotting paper, and I'm blowed if I didn't blot the page on my sheet where it was turned down over the blanket. A most awful mess : I can't tell you how sorry I am."

" Oh, Tim, I congratulate you ! " she said laughing.

She smiled again now, as she thought of his radiant penitence. But if only Alan could awake at some similar hour in such an authentic ecstasy ! He had slept so well that night, she remembered his telling her, after the splendid evening of work.

She put the dictation book aside with its polished little statuettes that Alan pushed about like pawns on his chess-board. There in contrast was Tim, exultant and perspiring, hewing away in shirt sleeves at the quarry in the cliff of human life. He was scarcely in shirt sleeves : he was stripped to the waist, and the young supple muscles rose and fell with his strokes. Out came the rough blocks, toppling over each other as they rolled to the foot of the slope, and there was Tim at them again with impatient imperious chisel, and the chipped fragments flying about him. The tasks to which he was so unaccustomed raised blisters on his fingers, great bleeding blisters, and his strokes were often random and illtimed. But the sun beat on his shoulders, and the wind of life blew there, and the stains of crude soil blackened him and his hewings. Those rough fashionings were hugely alive. . . . For a moment she turned this flash-light of impressions on to herself. She saw herself dusting the chessboard for the ordered movements of Alan's pieces, and she saw herself, bright-eyed and eager, in the brushwood that fringed the foot of Tim's quarry, watching, surely, not him, and the splendour of his naked vigour, but just the fruit of it, the hewn stones which he had tumbled out of the shining cliff. How it shone for her, who had never scaled it. . . .

The smallest stir of movement behind the folded doors which separated the work-room from the drawing-room where she sat, sufficed to whirl her back from some infinite distance of dream to the actual moment and the actual place. The tea-table was already laid, and the signal of Alan's opening of the work-room door, which indicated that his half-hour's rumination was over, caused her automatically to ring the bell, which would signalize the call for the tea-kettle. That was mere routine : her parlour-maid would answer the bell by bringing up the kettle, for round about half-past four, the ringing of the drawing-room bell could mean nothing else, any more than the opening of the work-room door could mean anything else than that Alan was coming in for tea. Once a week the bell was not rung at half-past four : that was because he had tea at the Athenæum. . . .

Alan entered.

" A half-hour well spent, dear Agnes," he said. " We are all in order now. Things have been moving so quickly these last few days that I was almost afraid I was not keeping sufficiently ahead in my preparation. But it was faint-hearted of me to have any doubts about that. I anticipate a glorious evening's work."

" That's good," she said. " That's a splendid hearing."

" Yes. I can't help being pleased. I see my way

now right to the end. And your verdict, dear, about the pages that were new to you? No: I don't think I need ask for it. I know that your critical eye has detected nothing slovenly or hasty in spite of our speed. The rapids, you know. The swifter motion that precedes. . . . Ah, I shall keep it from you, yet. There is a further bend coming which I fancy you have not anticipated. But I won't tease you! You will see as quickly as my voice can lead you there."

He took his cup of tea from her, stirred it and sipped.

"Would it be too dramatic of us, dear," he said, "to arrange a grand finale for to-morrow? What is that fox-hunting phrase? Ah, yes. I should like our Pamela to be in at the death. Her little joke, you know, jealousy. What if we fell in with her humour, and to-morrow afternoon had a long sitting, and wrote all that remains right up to the last half page? Yes: I knew I should surprise you over that. But that's the case with my little story. If we have a good spell of it this evening, and work again to-morrow afternoon, I feel sure we shall get to the last word to-morrow night. What then, if we had Pamela to dinner to-morrow, and let her be in at the death?"

He hesitated a moment.

"You must negative my proposition at once, dear," he said, "if you do not give a cordial, an instinctive consent to it. But it had occurred to me that our dear Pamela would be hugely and, of course, irrationally gratified if we let her be the scribe for that last page. She hinted as much, though I am sure she never meant the hint to be taken. It was just an ejaculation that escaped her."

"Yes: what was the ejaculation?" asked Agnes, as he paused again.

"Just that. 'Ah, the last word!' she said. 'Fancy

writing the last word!' But I saw what she meant,
though I gave no promise of course. This book, like
all others of mine, is yours. Now I say nothing on
behalf of or against Pamela, but I thought I would
just put it before you, and if you negative it, how
completely I shall understand."

Agnes's cordiality convinced him. As they went
into the work-room it was settled that the wizard
should be invoked as soon as the end was absolutely
imminent and announce the scheduled time for the
last page. Glory for Pamela! . . . She settled
herself down in the accustomed place, and Alan, with
Flaubert's paper-knife in hand, listened to the last two
pages which she read out to him.

" Her acquiescence had the fragrance of hawthorn," so ran the final words, "and all the promise
of summer was there. Yet the risk of late frosts made
a limitation. . . ."

Agnes sat with poised pen.

" Once more, please," he said, and she repeated it.

" Late frosts," he said. " Ah, I have it."

Her pen slid forward over the paper as he began
the dictation, and simultaneously she heard a quick
and stealthy foot on the landing outside. There was
the opening and closing of the drawing-room door,
and she knew that Tim had come in. He was having
his tea, mouselike in solitary silence, and presently the
drawing-room door would quietly open and close
again, and there would be the faint sound of his foot
on the stairs as he went up, hotly eager, to his room,
to dive into the unfinished tale which was bubbling
inside him. He had given her the bare outline of it,
and she longed to know how it was turning out. How
crude and violent the dénouement was . . . what
a smash. But when youth takes the bit in its mouth
and bolts, those who loiter on the road are apt to be
run over. This quiet work-room presented itself to

her like some green shady paddock, safe behind tall
hedges, adjoining the road where these galloping
hooves rattled by. The quiet creatures that grazed
there cropping the lush grass, just raised their heads
for a moment as the tumult swelled and crashed on its
way, and before it died into silence they were grazing
again. Just so, the grey leisurely personages with
which, in that vellum-backed row of Alan's books the
room was peopled, would incuriously raise their mild
eyes as Tim's hot-blooded youngster bolted by. Not
otherwise, too, would their creator regard Tim and
his impetuous scribblings. . . . And she? She
was struggling somewhere in the hedge that separated
the dusty dangerous road from the secure pasturage,
where she belonged and where so long her home had
been. She could not get through it, for the years had
made its growth high and thick, but even if she could
not penetrate it, she could push the stubborn twigs
aside and see what was going on there, where the dust
rose high and the hooves struck fire from the road.
. . . How long ago it was, how young she was,
when she had ever so eagerly come in through the
open gate into this sunny pasture-place! But her
heart sent the blood pulsing through her arteries still,
when she looked through the hedge and saw Tim
whirling by, plying his pen like a whip on the back
of his runaways.

The twigs of this sundering hedge sprang back into
their place again as Alan's voice recalled her to the
quiet paddock.

"We can allow ourselves, I think, dear, just that
paragraph or two about this river-edge without being
accused of describing for description's sake. In an
earlier chapter, as you remember, we dwelt more fully
on it. But a short recapitulation is not out of place,
I think. How does it strike you?"

Agnes had one moment's desperate panic. She

had no notion of what Alan had been saying : her hand had but followed his voice. What if again she had lost herself in her own musings? Then with unutterable relief she saw that the ink in which she had taken down the last few words was still wet, though the sentence was unfinished. Hurriedly she ran her eye through the last page. It was a charming description of a meadow bordered on the one side by a stream, on the other by a tall hedge beyond which lay a dusty riband of a road. That perhaps had suggested the images in her own thoughts which had been so vivid to her.

Alan sat down in the chair beside her.

" Perhaps you would just read it through, dear," he said.

She did this, down to the unfinished sentence which ended ' the pink spires of——'

" Yes, pink spires of willow-herb and loosestrife," said Alan, unconsciously filling in the missing words. Then he glanced at her with that sideways look and his voice took on a sharper note.

" Have you not got down ' willow herb and loosestrife ' ? " he said.

" No," said she. " You stopped very abruptly, did you not, and immediately asked me my opinion about the last paragraph."

" True. But still, my dear, you should have put down those last words. That terrible lapse of yours not so long ago, you know. I could ill afford again to lose a page or more because your thoughts were elsewhere. In the present tension of mind which I am in over this ending, I should despair of recapturing any such omission. But let us say no more about it. There is no harm done luckily."

Agnes was too much relieved at not having missed more than this couple of words to question the generosity of Alan's reminder. A few weeks ago it

would have seemed incredible to her that she would
have failed to inscribe every word he dictated in these
sessions, to be other than braced and ready to receive
and record all directions, to follow his syllables, to
' erase, please,' or ' read, please,' with instant speech.
. . . She was somehow imperceptibly drifting
away : once her own intense interest in his work had
been the cable that moored her to his quay whatever
current swept by her; following that, her own conscious devotion to his interests had moored her there.
Now the cable seemed to have lost its tautness, a space
of water, swiftly bubbling by, had swung her out into
a stream which she must constantly resist by sheer
force. She must make efforts to preserve a habit that
had long been effortless. . . .

He lifted himself out of his chair, and took up the
paper-knife again.

" Well, dear, if you are ready," he said. " I think
we will go on. That little description seems to me
justified, though it is a recapitulation. We wanted
the scene laid afresh. Now for the action. Difficult
though the excogitation of it was, I think you will
agree that I have pierced to the heart of the matter.
Now ! "

He flowed along fluently enough for a few lines,
but constantly interrupted himself to ask whether she
had put down his last words, and she could divine
that he was uneasy about her missing something.
This, she knew, was wholly unnecessary and she reassured him.

" I am all attention, dear," she said. " There is
not the slightest chance of my——"

" Ah, pray be silent," he said. " There was the
phrase I wanted then on the tip of my tongue."

He frowned and muttered to himself.

" Read, please, from ' willow-herb,' " he said.

That failed to evoke what he sought, and he peered among the slips on the table.

" I have found a note which belongs to our description of the meadow," he said. "'Solid comfrey.' Let us dispose of that first. Please read that paragraph again, and make the insertion on the blank page opposite when I stop you."

But even the suitable setting for the solid comfrey would not come easily now. The insertion was made, and he found it unbalanced his sentence, and another place must be provided for it. . . . The thought of Tim, and his rough-hewn efficiency compared to this delicate filagree-work flashed across her. . . .

" You have erased ' solid comfrey ' from that sentence ? " he asked sharply. It was clear that his distrust of her reliability was disturbing him.

" Yes, dear," she said. " Shall I read the paragraph again ? "

" No. Well perhaps you might."

She read it.

" Yes. I notice, Agnes," he said, " that you have given me no word of commendation for my little picture of the meadow. Ah, I think I have it. No : that won't do. . . . Perhaps you do not like it."

" But I do," she said. " I think it is charming."

" I am glad. These last few days, you see, I have been accustomed to a word or two of approbation, of delight from my scribe. I found it encouraging, dear. But no matter. Let us dispose of our comfrey and get on. I really do not see where to insert it. But I should be sorry to omit it. It is a just piece of descriptive observation.

The thing was unduly worrying him. Agnes knew well that he would be less than ever able to cope with what was coming, if he expended himself over this **detail.**

"I think I would leave it out," she said. "Your description is very charming and complete as it stands."

He crumpled up the note and tossed it into the waste-paper basket.

"Perhaps you are right. . . . No, I think I will not sacrifice that yet. We will leave it for the time. I shall find a place for it by and bye."

He picked up the crumpled slip, uncreased it, and laid it again on the table.

"Now let us get on," he said. "Dear me, it is six o'clock already. I hoped we should be bowling along under full sail by this time."

For another half hour he desperately struggled to get forward with his narrative. But he made no progress, and a dozen sentences, ragged and incomplete and erased, was the entire harvest of his efforts. Then occurred a catastrophe regrettable in itself, and to him in his growing agitation, infinitely ominous. Flaubert's paper-knife slipped from his hand, and was broken in half against the sharp edge of the fender.

"Terrible, terrible!" he cried. "There is no material possession in the world I valued more than this. The breakage seems to symbolize my powerlessness to get on with my story. Well, well: that is a foolish thought! Let us get back to our work. I must have a fresh blade put on to the handle, and I do not know where that can be done. I am all at sea: my brain is just a riot of glimpsed ideas that drive each other out before they attain coherence. Go back, please, without wasting more of these precious minutes, and read over our first description of the meadow once more. Read it slowly: I have yet to settle where to put in the insertion about the comfrey."

Again and once again, like the recitation of some impotent spell, Agnes read about the meadow.

Finally Alan, with a gesture of despair, threw himself down in his chair.

"I cannot conceive what we are to do!" he said. "I am at my wits' end."

Agnes hesitated a moment. Though, a little while ago, she had told herself that she cared not at all where Alan got his stimulus, provided only that it came to him, she found it very difficult to make the suggestion which had entered her mind. It symbolized the giving up of all that she had done for him for fifteen years. Little enough, so she had often told herself, it had been, but it was all there was. . . . And then she scorned herself for her smallness. How could she hesitate, if Alan's work and well-being meant anything to her? She got up.

"Oh, Alan, I've guessed what's the matter with us this afternoon," she said. (She was careful to include herself in these disasters.) "You've been accustomed to dictate these chapters to Pamela. You've subconsciously planned them out in your head with the notion of dictating them to her. You associate the crisis your story has got to with her. One's mind often acts in those curious ways. . . . Let's invoke the wizard at once, and see if Pamela can't come to the rescue."

She saw his face brighten.

"1 wonder if that would do any good," he said.

"My dear, we won't waste time in wondering," she said. "We'll try. Come to the telephone with me, and give an S.O.S. to Pamela yourself."

"It's a good idea," said he. "It's worth trying."

Once more an involuntary bitterness, instantly suppressed, surged up in Agnes. It was not only that she herself was a failure with regard to Alan's work: it was that he admitted that someone else possibly was indispensable to it, and that now in the prospect of his own rescue, no thought of what he jettisoned so much as entered his head. He had been gracefully considerate of her over that question of the writing of the last words of the story, because it did not matter to him who wrote them. But when there was the question of arriving at the last words of the story, of getting out of this impotent stagnation, nobody mattered. . . .

As she waited for Pamela to answer, he spoke again.

" I should not be surprised if you're right, dear," he said. " I can fancy myself going along swimmingly if our dear Pamela was taking my dictation down. A very subtle, wise notion of yours, my Agnes, I think——"

Agnes interrupted him.

" Oh, Pamela," she said. " Yes : it's Agnes and Alan. We can't get on without you. We've quite stuck. Can you be a perfect angel and come round here at once, and be Alan's secretary again ? . . . Ah, how lovely of you ! And you'll dine with us, won't you, and work on with Alan afterwards ? That is good of you. Now Alan's going to speak to you."

Scarcely a couple of minutes had elapsed before the epiphany of Pamela in a taxi, for realizing the urgency of the situation she had not waited to send to the garage for her car, and hardly had she crossed the pavement when Alan in person had the door open for her. Agnes, waiting in the drawing-room, heard them come upstairs, but they went straight into the work-room without entering here. That was quite right, so she told herself : Pamela had come to inspire Alan, and the sooner they got to work to retrieve this tragically wasted hour the better.

Through the folding door of communication between the work-room and the drawing-room, it was easy to hear any sound of stir or of speech, and Agnes waited and listened. First came the high incisive tones of Pamela reading : no doubt she was repeating once more the description of the meadow. Occasional words were audible, and now came Alan's voice and she caught the word ' comfrey.' In reply there was Pamela again. " O, Master, how lovely, how perfectly delicious ! " she said. . . . For a little while more Pamela read, and there was silence. But the silence only lasted a moment : Alan's voice almost instantly begun. He spoke, as usual, slowly, but there was no further pause.

There was a note or two Agnes wanted to write, one to Alan's typist, another to his publisher, and there was the message to be sent that there would be four of them at dinner. She despatched these little businesses, and listened again. His voice was still flowing evenly on ; her idea of calling Pamela to the rescue had evidently met with marvellous success. . . .

So she was free till dinner-time, she could amuse herself without compunction. Alan did not want her, for he had found the assistant who could really help him, and upstairs Timothy was hewing away at his refractory quarry-stones, as absorbed no doubt as Alan. She had spent the morning with her mother, conscious of not being the least wanted there, Dora had gone back to Paris, and it seemed as if in a moment, that, whereas she had not long ago told herself that she had no life of her own, for her time and her energies were always claimed by others, the whole situation had been reversed, and that nobody had the smallest use for her. After dinner, Pamela and Alan would pursue their prosperous course again, and only yesterday Timothy had been loud in praise of these quiet evenings, when, since everybody else was employed, he could sit down to his stories without a suspicion of unsociability. No doubt, to-night, when he found that she was unemployed, he would offer to keep her company, but she must not permit that and take him away from his tales. To-morrow . . . well it was abundantly clear that until Alan's story was done, Pamela's co-operation (Agnes felt sure she would willingly give it) must be secured. It was she who held the key which unlocked Alan's brain and made accessible the treasures there. For another day at least Pamela would hold the pen.

And after that? Pamela's enthusiasm (whether or not it took its rise from the *cachet* that this intimacy with Alan seemed to hold for her made no difference to its efficacy), Pamela's outspoken adoration of the Master, gave Alan a stimulus which Agnes could not. In a few days now he would be engaged on the revision of his books for the collected edition, and it seemed much more than likely that he would crave her co-operation. Many passages were to be rewritten, so Agnes had learned, and these would be dictated. . . . Indeed, had not the second spare room better be got ready for Pamela?

She pulled herself up: there was no good in these revolutionary anticipations, and yet her own unemployment in the hours of dictation showed that red flags were flying. But they were Pamela's flags, the flags of the friendly ship which had rescued Alan in this desert island of his impotence to compose, and had taken him off. But the rescuer had left Agnes marooned, and she had not the smallest idea what to do with herself. How very odd it all seemed! In the last few days of her enforced idleness she had rather enjoyed the liberty and leisure: now, there was a different quality in them.

CHAPTER V

THE great event took place two evenings later, and was the occasion of playfulness. . . . There had been something secret and wonderful on hand, so Agnes conjectured, when for the third night in succession Alan took Pamela into dinner. Little smiles and signals passed between them, when Agnes asked how the work had been progressing. " Not badly, I think : Pamela and I are not dissatisfied with our afternoon's session," said he, and catching her eye he did not quite wink, but he nearly winked. Also Alan took a glass of port. . . . But Agnes did not state the suspicion which verged on certainty : if, as she guessed was the case, the book was within a touch of completion, and Alan wanted to surprise and hugely delight her, it would never do to spoil the plot. Afterwards, when the workers had gone back to their task, she and Timothy grinned over the discovery.

Agnes had not been so utterly unwanted these last two days, for Timothy scouted the idea of literary composition of an evening, if her society was to be had. His stories would wait; it was far more enjoyable talking to her. And, if it really did not weary her, might he read a third tale that had been completed, when Alan and Pamela had gone to their work.

" Why shouldn't you and I have our secret, too ? " he asked to-night. " Besides, I can't tell you how it helps me to read you my rot. Oh, I mustn't say that : it was insincere, wasn't it ? "

" Yes, Tim. Most insincere."

" Right. Well, my masterpieces, if capable of improvement at all, are improved by reading them to you, and talking them over. You put your finger so infallibly on weak spots. By the way, the first story is coming out in 'The Bookshop,' to-morrow. I shall see myself in print. I shall swoon."

" O, Tim, how exciting. But begin reading to me at once. It's my belief that we shan't have more than half an hour to ourselves to-night."

" Then I'll put out the draught-board," said he, " so that if we're interrupted they'll not guess what we've been doing."

Agnes made a place for her on the sofa, for his voice must not be raised for fear of interrupting the session next door. Little did Tim know, she thought, what balm it was to her that he should want her. Indeed, it surprised herself, she had not realized how strong was her need of being needed. With Alan, Pamela could take her place far more successfully than she could fill it, but she was tremendously aware that Tim wanted her companionship and counsel personally and individually, and that Pamela would have been no sort of substitute. And from her side she admitted that it was with no automatic mechanism of the mind that she listened to him : had she been his amanuensis, her hand would not, out of habit, have just followed his words, leaving her thoughts free to roam : her hand, she knew, would have been poised, like a hawk, over the paper, eagerly darting to record. Not for years had she given such quality of co-operation to Alan's dictation : it was not hers to give, and in truth he did not require it. Her task with him was to set down just what he said, and be careful not to disturb the line of his thought. When he wanted her criticism—and how rarely that was—he asked for it. But Tim sought her and snatched at her. He was all alert for any expression of her approval or her criticism, and if she but stirred, he would look up from his page, eager for her interruption. He wanted her mind : Alan wanted her beautiful handwriting. Sometimes Tim deferred to her judgment, and scrawled a cross in his margin with a word that would recall to him the gist of her objection. Sometimes again he would ponder her suggestion and shake his head. " No, I don't think so," he said. " You'll see why."

These suggestions and criticisms that she offered him were often merely verbal, sometimes to secure a sentence that balanced itself to swing forward, sometimes they embodied some mere telling technicality, a dodge, a device for keeping a climax suspended a little longer, a hint to cut out a reflection on the author's part. This was the case just now.

" Oh Tim, you're making them tell the story quite nicely," she said once. " Don't interrupt them to explain. Keep yourself out of it."

She spoke low, in order not to interrupt by the faintest noise the smooth dictation going on next door. She was not quite sure, indeed, that Tim had caught what she said and turned to him. He was looking directly at her, she found, wide-eyed with the smile ready to break on his mouth. But, for once, he did not immediately reply, not because he was weighing the value to him of what she said, but because he was thinking of something else. Such at any rate was her impression.

" Or don't you agree ? " she asked.

He clearly had to recall himself.

" Yes, I see," he said. " I must let them do it. I—I mustn't butt in. Keep myself out of it."

Then the smile broke through.

" It's angelic of you to take so much trouble," he said. " Let's see, where was I ? "

The just audible murmur of Alan's voice next door ceased. Pamela spoke : Alan answered her, and immediately there was the sound of the door on to the landing being opened.

"Hell, they're coming," said Tim, and crammed his manuscript into his pocket. He jumped up and faced her at the draught board.

"I begin this time," he said. "You shan't huff me again."

Pamela was followed by Alan. He sat down with an air of weariness, wonderfully unconvincing.

"We are early," he said. "But I can't dictate another word, dear Agnes. Not another word."

How obvious it all was. Charades.

Pamela gave a rather hopeful kind of sigh.

"But we've got through something to-night," she said. "Think of what you've done, Alan. It didn't go so badly."

"I doubt if I shall ever dictate another word of my poor story," he said. "My dear Timothy, it's a dreadful life."

Timothy looked wonderfully solemn.

"But you'll have a good time at it to-morrow, perhaps, Cousin Alan," he said.

"No, Timothy," he said.

It seemed to be Agnes's turn.

"But you've often had checks before, dear," she said, firmly removing one of Tim's pieces. Alan was playing with her and Tim, making a game for the children.

"I've never had such a check in this story," said he.

"Oh, I'm so sorry, dear," she said.

He spread himself in his chair again with chuckling alacrity.

"It's too bad of us. We must tell them, Pamela," he said. "Agnes, my dear, great news. It's finished!"

She jumped up.

" But how splendid. How perfectly splendid ! "
she said. " You two wretches to make Tim and me
think that you were in despair about it ! What fibs,
Alan ! "

" Not a single fib, dear," he said. " I told you
I should never dictate another word of it. I told you
I had never had such a check. Isn't that scrupulously
true ? "

" Certainly not," she said. " You will dictate it
all over again. This is only the first dictation. I've
caught you."

He was delighted at this : there was yet another
surprise in store.

" I slip out," he said. " I have been lectured
this evening. I have been told by one who has read
it all that I am not to touch the story again, but send
it straight to the typist's. A new plan, I know, but
our Pamela was wonderfully autocratic about it. We
shall secure, she thinks, a greater freshness, a more
vivid spontaneity . . . at any rate, it is going
straight to the typist's, and when it comes back we
can consider the question afresh."

He got up out of his chair, and moved over to
where Pamela stood close to his wife. He put himself between them, taking an arm of each.

" My dear assisters and fellow-workers," he said,
" where, indeed, should I be without your wonderful
help ? "

At that, though his hand threaded her arm, Agnes
saw, as in a bird's eye glance, how far she and Alan
had travelled from each other. She did not know
whether it was she who had moved away from him,
or he from her, nor exactly how and when that
estranging distance had intervened. The result,
whatever the process, was the same ; they were
separated now by a broad and shining channel, and
as on a map, its name was legibly inscribed. Pamela

had come in between them; she warmly and sunnily lapped their sundered coasts. . . . There they stood, the three of them, Tim still sitting at the draught-board, and in Agnes's hand was the draughtsman of his which she had captured five minutes before. Did that also symbolize the sundering, she asked herself?

Before Pamela left, she took the opportunity of a quiet word with Agnes and used it to make an appointment with her next morning for a quarter of an hour's talk. This she suggested should take place at half-past eleven in the little front room on the ground floor, so that Alan in his workroom should know nothing of the interview. This was all slightly mysterious, and not less so was Pamela's manner next morning.

" I left my motor at the bottom of the square, dear Agnes," she said. " So important that Alan should not know I was here. How is he, by the way? Did he sleep well? "

" As far as I know," said Agnes. She certainly would have known if he hadn't.

" I am deeply thankful. Deeply," said Pamela. She was silent and fixed her eyes on Agnes with an eager intentness that seemed to demand rather than invite a question.

" Is it about Alan you want to talk to me? " asked Agnes. She knew that she was doing just what Pamela wanted, and rather despised herself for her obedience.

" Dear Agnes, I see you have noticed it too," she said, laying a sympathetic hand on her arm. " I can speak freely, then. Of course, we mustn't allow ourselves to be anxious, but certainly he is terribly overdone. The end of the book has been a tremendous strain on him."

Agnes found herself wondering what Pamela was ' up to.' It needed no perspicacity to guess that she

was up to something, for she was never otherwise.
But what exactly was it? Certainly it concerned
Alan.

"I think he is very well," she said. "The end of
a book always tells on him. But I am not the least
anxious about him."

"Ah, if he would only rest!" exclaimed Pamela.
"But I think the Master can't rest. Like radium:
always throwing off light. He told me he was going
to begin his revision for the collected edition at once.
What a blessing that you and I are such friends, and
have this great bond between us of looking after him.
We can put our heads together and make plans for
him. . . ."

It would never do to resent this for a meddlesome
interference, for whatever was the object of her inter-
fering (glory for Pamela broadly covered it, perhaps),
the care of Alan was the subject of it, and if the object
of it deserved a snubbing assurance that Agnes had
looked after him for fifteen years and was perfectly
capable of doing so now, she could not quite dismiss
Pamela with this squirt of coolness. On the top of
that came the reflection that Pamela, with all her
glory, had undoubtedly come to Alan's aid, when
she herself was powerless to minister to him, and it
was Agnes who had suggested that S.O.S. appeal.
In spite of this there was something to be swallowed
(her own pride, was it, her sense of property?) before
she could put heads together.

"But Alan is quite determined to begin work on
the collected edition," she said. "He will revise his
first two books, 'December' and 'Sand Banks,'
before we take our holiday. They will appear, he
hopes, in the autumn."

"I know. I wasn't dreaming of trying to dissuade
him from working at that," said Pamela. "All we
can do is to insure for him the best conditions for it."

" Surely the conditions which he has always chosen for himself," said Agnes. " He will go through the books first, marking passages, chapters perhaps, which he means to rewrite. He will prepare them and dictate them to me as he always does."

Pamela gave the impression of taking a plunge.

" He needs a change," she said. " He ought to get out of London altogether in this hot weather, and get refreshed in the country. Of course he will take his work with him, and I am sure that not only he but the work of revision will benefit by the change."

" Where do you propose we should go ? " asked Agnes.

Pamela had taken the plunge : now she struck out.

" I want him to come down to my little house near Rye," she said. " The coolness, the greenness ! Change, you know. The change should be as complete as possible. He should get away from all that reminds him of the strain and struggle he has been through. Yes, dear, I want your leave to carry him off there. I would look after him, as you can guess, so diligently, and I think with promise of success. My whole time will be his. I shall permit no interruptions."

Agnes decided to help her out with the statement of a somewhat important detail.

" You mean without me," she said.

" Yes, dear Agnes. You need a rest, too, you know. I can see that. The strain of seeing him unable to get on with his work, and of being unable to help him, has told on you as well."

Agnes laughed.

" You won't get Alan to consent to that," she said.

Pamela said nothing but looked wistful. It struck Agnes that her silence was pregnant.

" Or have you already asked him ? " she said. The

moment she had said it, she was sorry. It sounded so ludicrous when stated, a sarcasm, a bit of unwarranted irony.

" I can hardly say I asked him," said Pamela, very carefully.

" I see," said Agnes. " You mean that somehow the suggestion got made. There was talk between you of his getting away for a little, and of going on with his revision somewhere in the country. And no doubt he wondered if he would ever dictate to you again. His book had gone so well when you took it down. Something of that sort ? "

Pamela beamed : she clasped her hands and beamed.

" Really, I don't know which of you two is the more wonderful," she said. " What intuition you have, dear Agnes ! How beautifully you expressed it ! All shades and hints, and your lovely perception ! I shall begin to wonder whether Alan does not owe his insight, that subtle exquisite insight, to you. You react on each other : you chime each other's golden bells."

There flashed into Agnes's mind the thought, " Oh, I must tell Tim that. How he'd yell ! " The idea still seemed ludicrous. . . .

" My dear, you and Alan seem to have been chiming," she said. " You've been wonderful with him. I don't know what we should have done without you. Tell me all about it."

It was strange to her how instantaneously the notion, which had been just now so ludicrous, had become feasible and sensible. All these years it had been so instinctive a habit with her to accomplish, with the whole energy of her mind and her heart, whatever Alan wished, that there was no difficulty in ranging herself with any proposition to which he had scribbled his signature. Whatever he wanted was an order, sent down to her for execution. Hitherto she had always carried his dispositions into effect. . . . Meantime Pamela was in ecstasy again.

"You wonderful people!" she exclaimed. "Why the first thing that Alan said when our idea took shape was, ' You won't get Agnes to consent to that,' and you said precisely the same. You are not two: you are the most marvellous one. I feel myself like a sort of housemaid who dusts your room for you, just makes it neat and tidy."

As surely as if she now witnessed Alan's getting into Pamela's motor, with his luggage a-top, Agnes knew that this scheme was destined to be carried out. Alan, subject to her consent, had approved it and desired it, and that was sufficient to ensure her co-operation. It had always been so : it would be strange indeed if she set up her will against his wish or his benefit. But no such quality of decision had ever been presented to her before : no other human being, man or woman, had ever attempted to arrange their affairs for them, nor, till now, had she ever imagined that any disposition of them would entail Alan's being in other hands than hers. Probably his most prolonged absence from her immediate proximity during the last fifteen years had been his weekly teas at the Athenæum.

But she had no difficulty in visualizing him and Pamela together : there was no kind of obstacle that stood in the way, provided that she and her pride or sense of property did not. Probably Pamela was quite right : a change as complete as possible would do Alan good, and Agnes knew that she could leave the arrangements of all that concerned Alan's physical and intellectual comfort completely in her hands : she would be Martha and Mary rolled into one, full of catering cares, and orders to her chauffeur, ready to take down his dictation, and him for a stroll, and at the same time sitting at his feet with that eager humility and appreciation which suited the Master so well, and wonderfully stimulated him. As for any conventional wifely objection to granting him a *tête-à-tête* in the country (apparently that was Pamela's plan) with this attractive woman, such an idea did not even come up for rejection. It would have been like the introduction of farce into a quiet comedy.

All this was a flashlight impression, and in the darkness that followed, Agnes gave a moment's thought to see how the plan appeared to affect herself. She would be perfectly free : from morning to night nobody would want her, for her mother within a few days would be off on her holiday to the Isle of Wight, and she would just have herself alone to please and beguile. The gate out of that secure paddock in which she had grazed so long would be open : she need no longer peer through the hedge, but wander out, if so she chose, on to the dusty busy highway, where was movement and swift wheels. . . . And at that came the thought of Tim, for in the first flashed survey she had seen herself alone in this house in Goring Square, rather doubtful how she should amuse herself, what she would do with the hours. But why, after all, should she be alone ? There was no more reason for Tim to pack up and leave her, than for Alan not to pack up and go to Pamela.

She could not help, and she did not try to help a flush of more eager cordiality flooding her consideration of the scheme.

" I think it's you who are wonderful," she said to Pamela. " It's amazingly good of you to devote yourself like this. It's a brilliant idea to give Alan a complete change. It may be just what he wants."

" You too, dear Agnes," said Pamela. " And as for my devotion such as it is, it is a pure joy, a pure delight to have the privilege. . . . Ah, surely that's the Master's foot on the stairs. What am I to do? He doesn't know I'm here."

Agnes got up.

" Why, tell him what we're going to do with him," she said. " Pass his delightful sentence on him. Come in, Alan," she called, as his step sounded on the parquet outside.

Alan entered. He held in his hand a copy of his first book, ' December,' with many slips of paper thrust into the leaves. In spite of Pamela's secrecies, he was quite aware that she intended to have a talk with Agnes, and so the discovery of her was not unbalancing.

" Aha," he said. " Why, here's our dear Pamela. What's this? It looks like a conspiracy."

" It is," said Agnes. " And who are the prime conspirators, dear? You two. But I've been admitted. I've taken the oath, Alan."

He looked from one to the other, his egoism unconsciously sunning itself in the knowledge that they were all thinking about him, and making plans for him. He did not put it like that.

" You watchful Agnes ! " he said, " and this dear Pamela ! I protest against, I deprecate all this conspiring and plotting. I know what it's all about, and enough time and lovely energy has been spent on it already. As if I couldn't go on with my work here quite comfortably, quite prosperously ! We had a little anxious time, but that's over. Look, I've begun on ' December ' already. Most of it, I am afraid, is slack stuff : it wants careful revision and re-writing."

Pamela clapped her hands.

" Master, you shan't change the subject like that," she cried. " We're busy conspiring. You shall listen to Agnes and me, if you like, but if you interrupt us, we shall turn you out. You're coming to

Playden with me: that's already settled, and what we've got to fix now is the day."

" You dear bullies," he said.

" Yes, we're bullies, though we like to hear that we are dear. Now Agnes, I can't see why the Master shouldn't begin his country-cure on Saturday. That will give me two full days for getting the house ready, and on Saturday I will motor up and carry him off. What objection has anyone to make to that ? "

" Saturday ?   Saturday ? " asked Alan.   " Impetuous Pamela, I shall never be ready by Saturday."

" But you will. With Agnes at one end and me at the other, you will be perfectly ready. Oh, please, be good ! "

It was quite clear that Alan was fully as delighted with the plan as was Pamela herself, and in consequence no very strenuous persuasion was necessary.

" And this morning's work ? " she asked. " Now that we have settled these little details, tell us what is so vastly more important. How have you sped ? "

Alan turned over the leaves of the book.

" Sadly crude, sadly awkward in places," he said.

Pamela pointed to him, and spoke to Agnes.

" Just listen to him ! " she said. " He is talking of ' December.' It has been reserved for him to find it crude and awkward. We shall see about that."

" But it is so," said he. " Indeed, I am pleased to find it so, for it shows that I have gained rather than lost in fastidiousness since the days when I wrote it. There is a whole chapter, for instance, which must be rewritten. I think, if the dear arbiters of my destinies are determined that I shall leave town on Saturday, I shall devote these two days merely to reading and marking the passages which fail to satisfy me. It occurred to me, too, to write perhaps a little preface to each of the books, describing how I came to write them, and what circumstances surrounded their inception and accomplishment.''

'' Ah, lovely, lovely ! '' said Pamela.

'' It might conceivably be of interest,'' said Alan. He laid his hand on Agnes's arm.

'' There will be one reader, dear, will there not ? '' he said, '' who will find time to skim through my account of how ' The Tyro ' was written, to whom first it was read, and what marvel of happiness dawned for the solitary author soon after its publication. It must be to you, dear, that I dedicate that preface. Not even our dear Pamela must be allowed to hold the pen for that.''

Pamela was quick in response here. She did exactly the right thing, and laid her hand on Agnes's other arm.

'' And is your poor Pamela quite so idiotic as to think she would be ? '' she asked.

The duration of Alan's visit had not been definitely fixed, but the conspirators, into whose hands he so willingly placed himself, had fixed on a week as the minimum likely to benefit him solidly, with a possible extension; and during the two days before his departure it was clear that he looked forward to it with excited anticipation. It was frequently on his lips that he could not imagine how he would get on at all without Agnes, but not less frequently did he succeed in imagining it and that with no sense of difficulties ahead. Above all, it was with no anticipation of loss but, on the contrary, of gain that he faced the un-imaginable. Pamela had proved herself to be oil in his mechanism : she had been indeed more than the oil for its smooth working; she had been the key which wound up the immobile wheels again. He had been very diligent in a careful re-reading of ' December,' and by dinner-time on the evening before his departure this was finished and he had a sheaf of notes ready with reference to marked pages, and key-words to suggest to him the lines on which his corrections would be laid. To-night Tim was dining out, and since Alan's work of preparation was over, the two sat in the drawing-room, leaving the work-room, as Alan whimsically said, to go to bed early.

" Dear me, yes, how strange it seems," he said, " that to-morrow at this time Pamela and I will be getting to our work while you and Timothy keep holiday up here. There will be no grumpy old author haling you to the work-room. A holiday, dear, will do you good. I consider it very fortunate that Timothy is still with us. Indeed, I should have quite refused to fall in with the conspirators' plan if that implied leaving you alone here. To be sure, there is your mother close at hand; perhaps the determination of the conspirators might have overcome my opposition."

" The conspirators would have overcome all opposition, dear," she said.

" Aha! You think that, do you? Perhaps you are right, though indeed how I shall get on at all without you I do not know. However, with dear Timothy to beguile your evenings, you will not miss our evening dictation. It has been very pleasant to me to see what friends you and Timothy have become. I hope he will be with us till we go for our holiday in September. By then I should have two volumes ready for the collected edition. . . . Let me think if there are any further arrangements to be made before my departure. Dear Pamela will be here by half-past eleven. We shall lunch on the way, and I hope to feel quite settled in before dinner. Indeed, I should not wonder if we had an hour's work before dinner. She or I, you may be sure, dear, will send you a line every day to say how the work progresses.

. . . Ah yes, the Flaubert paper-knife! Dear Pamela knew of a shop where they repaired such injuries. She took it there, I think, this morning, before she came in to conspire with you. She says it is a very simple fracture which they will mend in an hour or two. Still, if it does not come back before I leave to-morrow, please send it to me, care of our Pamela, registered.''

Agnes found herself listening, during this ambulatory speech, for any indication that she was in his mind. She did not intend to listen for it : she only found herself doing so, even as, if Alan was working, she would have found herself listening for the sound of his footfall on the stairs, which showed that his morning's preparation was over and that he might want a stroll. But there was no such signal. She was in his mind, it is true, but only as a minister to himself : she was not there for a moment independently or individually. He was glad, for instance, that her evenings would be beguiled by Tim, for otherwise he might have had some remote twinges, unsettling to his work, at having left her alone in town. Otherwise she was of moment to him just as the possible forwarder of the Flaubert paper-knife. He did not need her. . . .

" That reminds me of letters that will come for me here," he continued. " Perhaps, dear, you would just open them, and use your own wise judgment as to what you will send on to me, when you think I should wish to give such my personal consideration. I want to be without needless distraction, or else I shall not be acting in obedience to the real designs of the dear conspirators. So perhaps you, as the conspirator working in London, would ever so shortly deal with all other letters. Ah, here is the last post of the evening. I wonder if it brings my paper-knife.

I hope so : it will save you further trouble, dear, if it does."

This hope was not gratified : Alan's share in the delivery was one letter only from his publisher, which he held balanced in his hand, not at once opening it.

" I am tempted to be naughty about my letter," he said, " and to pretend I have forgotten it in the bustle of departure, and then you will open it after I am gone to-morrow.   But we must be honest, and I daresay Mr. Bristowe's communication will require no answer.   Perhaps, dear, you would drop a line to good Bristowe to-morrow, and say that I will send him all corrections and additions and omissions which I want made in ' December,' as soon as they are ready.   Doubtless good Bristowe wants to get on with the fresh printing so as to be in good time for his autumn season of publication.   Odd that books should have a season like vegetables or fruit, as if, periodically, the human mind put forth its little globes of ripeness. . . .   But I will not let myself be hurried.   I will not, especially now that we are seeking to attain the—what was poor Blewitt's phrase ?— the immortality of a collected edition, no, not immortality : Permanence, was it ? some not very felicitous phrase, so it struck me."

He had paused with his letter now open under the lamp, and the slow tranquillity of his voice gave place to agitation and shrillness.

" What does this all mean ? " he said.   " This is a very singular communication !   ' In consequence of the very disappointing subscription to the collected edition '—Bristowe writes an abominable hand— ' we do not propose to issue ' . . . ' start with one of your better known ' . . . where are my glasses ? My reading-glasses, dear : surely you know that I do not read with these.   Ah, thank you.   Let us get to the bottom of this piece of impertinence at once.   Perhaps you would read it for me, and then I can attend more closely to what poor Bristowe means to convey."

The bottom of this piece of impertinence was soon reached.   The order forms for the collected edition had now been in circulation for over a month, but the response had been so meagre, amounting only to a few hundred copies, that the author must expect but a miserable return of royalties for all the work of his revision and of the writing of the proposed prefaces, while the firm of publishers would without doubt find themselves faced with a very heavy financial loss.   To bring out a complete edition which was evidently to meet with so chilling a reception was a humiliation for author and publisher alike, and Mr. Bristowe proposed that without completely abandoning the idea of it, they should, instead of starting with ' December ' followed by ' Sandbanks,' first re-issue Mr. Graham's best known book, ' The Tyro.'   The demand for that (with its interesting preface) would no doubt be satisfactory, and if so, they might then, after this whet to the public's appetite, proceed with others. The firm no doubt was bound by its contract, should Mr. Graham insist on it, to adhere to the original scheme, but in their opinion it would only result in financial loss for them and a disagreeable situation for him. . . . There was an amiable doxology with regard to the poor reception which often awaited such exquisite work as his, in these days when every young man and girl dashed off a huddle of ill-digested impressions and considered it literature.

Agnes's heart sank as she read, and she felt herself traitorous in that it did so.   But she had known for years that at heart she no longer believed in his wizardry, and she could not with any ring of conviction urge him to raise an unsurrendering banner and march forward on his course undeterred by these

menaces and mutterings. What concerned her more
closely than the justice of Mr. Bristowe's advice was
the effect it would have on Alan personally, and on
her relation to him. Often she had wondered (and
feared to wonder) how he would take it, when first he
began to realize that his name and repute no longer
basked in the sunshine of popular favour and in the
high fine air of critical approval. His last book had
not been a success in either regard, but Alan had been
stalwart enough (or blind enough) to shrug his
shoulders alike at the public and poor Blewitt. Since
then he had shewn himself more vulnerable : Blewitt's
attack on the collected edition had stung him, while
the very fact that Pamela's ointments had been so
healing, only confirmed the loss of his aloof independence. Now came this more telling thrust : here
was a question of fact and figures, not of the opinion
of a soured author turned critic, and she saw how it
staggered him.

"And what is to be done now ? " he said when she
came to the end of the letter. "Already I have given
a couple of hard-working days to the revision of
'December,' and now this fellow. . . . Upon my
word I have a good mind to make them abide by their
contract and prove how utterly wrong they are. What
does Bristowe know of the extraordinarily interesting
matter which I have ready in my notes for the prefaces ? My early devotion to writing ! My resolve
to learn and practise my art in a manner not un-
befitting the traditions of English fiction ! My
failures at first to find a publisher, the impossibility,
so few years later, of accepting the offers which those
who had rejected my earlier work were so eager to
press on me ! Is that all quite outside interest and
significance ? " In his agitation she saw how deeply
and stingingly the thing affected him. She was to
learn now how she stood to him. . . .

"My dear, of course it is interesting and significant," she said. "But, if as Mr. Bristowe says, the subscription for the whole collected edition has not been satisfactory, may there not be something in his suggestion of beginning with 'The Tyro,' and seeing whether that does not help?"

He turned sharply on her with interruption.

"Ah! So you agree with this fellow in thinking that my collected edition is likely to prove an expensive and disastrous experiment!" he said. "I have been long aware that you do not find my work as admirable as you used. Your thoughts when I have been dictating to you have before now so wandered that you have failed altogether to hear or to record what I was saying."

It was more for his sake than her own that she could not let this pass.

"That is not a generous speech," she said, "and though it is true it is not fair. How many pages of yours, Alan, have I written for you, and how many times have I failed you?"

That reached him but only superficially. He was back again at once on the only thing that really affected him.

"Yes, dear, I should not have said that," he conceded. "Though it was true, as you say, it was not fair. You must allow me to withdraw that, and then ask your attention again for this letter. I gather that you agree with Bristowe?"

"It's a matter not of your worth," she said, "but of business. He is as anxious from that point of view as you are, that the collected edition should be a success. His knowledge of business, which neither you nor I share, suggests to him that the most promising course is to issue 'The Tyro' first. His last words show how he appreciates your work."

"Yes, I see. There is something in what you say. He contrasts, does he not, my work with the huddle of ill-digested impressions, which now passes for literature. And this is a matter of business : I must give that its due weight. I shall be anxious to know to-morrow what Pamela's view is. In any case, I must add to my luggage a copy of 'The Tyro' as well —perhaps, dear, you would see to that—in case I decide to follow Bristowe's counsel. Let us then postpone any further consideration of it till I have ascertained Pamela's view. . . . Do I not hear Timothy's step? Yes : here he is."

For the last couple of nights at this hour Alan had been at his revision in the work-room, and Timothy expected to find Agnes alone. He had in his hand a copy of 'The Bookshop,' which contained his first story.

"Ah, my dear Timothy," said Alan, "you have entered most opportunely to divert our minds from the topic that we have been discussing."

Timothy paused in the doorway; a swift telegraphy of eyes showed him that Agnes had seen that he carried 'The Bookshop,' and guessed its significance.

"But are you sure I'm not interrupting you?" he asked. "Shan't I leave you?"

Alan recovered his serenity.

"I am sure you are interrupting us, my dear fellow," he said, "and that is precisely why you shall not leave us. A magazine? Dear me, it is a long time since I glanced at any of these—what was Blewitt's phrase with regard to me? I remember I used it myself subsequently?—ah, yes, these 'graceful ephemeralities' which nowadays seem to satisfy the public taste for literature. . . . Stories, I suppose : short stories in prodigal abundance. A short story is probably the most difficult form of literary art, There has never yet been written in English a short story even passably readable. I, at least, have always despaired of my ability to write one which would satisfy my own sense of form, such as it is. Yet every week the book-stalls are gay with many magazines containing the work of more able artists than me, who are perfectly satisfied with their own productions. Really I should like to glance at the sort of thing. One gets out of touch. . . . Let me have a look, Timothy, at your collection of masterpieces, and try to learn the trick from what our severe Mr. Bristowe calls 'the huddle of ill-digested impressions.' "

Timothy raised an eyebrow as his glance swept to Agnes's face, and saw his question answered by an almost imperceptible little nod. Alan, it is true, had heavily committed himself with regard to short stories, but it was impossible to withhold the magazine, and clearly wiser to tell him what he would find there. On the first page (the pride of it) he would find ' Cricket ' with the name of the author in full. . . .

" I shall sink into the earth if you read the first story, Cousin Alan," he said. " Because it's by me. And Mr. Bristowe's expression describes it excellently."

Quick, as a lizard out of some dark crevice, and back again, there popped out into Alan's face some darting hostility, some whisking malevolence. It disappeared as soon as it was seen.

" How very interesting, my dear Timothy," he said. " An author ! Dear me, I had no notion that you had fallen victim to the taste for writing. Agnes, dear : is not this a great event ? But as to minding my reading your story, Timothy, you will soon find that what we authors really mind is that people do not read our stories. Dear me, yes ! I see yours is the first story in the magazine. A very distinguished position. Why did you not tell me, Timothy, that you were a budding, I should say now a blooming author ? "

There was a studied cordiality in his voice : there was also a suppressed ring of ironical indulgence.

" I felt so certain my story could not interest you, Cousin Alan," said Tim.

" We must not be so sure about that. ' Cricket '? About a cricket match, is it ? "

" Yes, in a way," said Tim.

Agnes laughed.

" Tim, you will have to get used to people reading your stories," she said. " But I'll have a game of draughts with you to take off the edge of your self-consciousness. It's an excellent story, Alan. Most trenchant and vivid."

Alan put on his reading-glasses.

" Ah ! You have read it then, dear," he said. There was just a touch of resentful surprise in his voice.

The two settled down to their draughts, and Alan to his reading. Tim cast an occasional glance at the reader, but Alan's face betrayed no sign of enjoyment or boredom, nor did he make any comment whatever. At the end he closed the magazine, took off his glasses, and got up.

" Have you finished it, Alan ? " asked Agnes, as she meditated her move.

" Yes, dear. I have finished it. Very terse. Very vigorously written, Timothy. But I am not competent to criticize, nor, I imagine, do you want my criticism."

Timothy put in an eager interruption.

" But I should value it immensely," he said, " if you would be so good as to give me any hints. Of course it's crammed full of faults : I am quite certain of that. But the fact that they are there shows that I don't know what they are."

His sincerity clearly mollified that dislike and distrust with which Alan had clearly received the fact that Tim had ventured to write anything at all.

"A very sound observation," he said. "The faults we writers"—surely irony peeped out again—"are unconscious of are the deadliest. But again, my dear Timothy, I must repeat that I am not competent to criticize. I am such a fanatic myself on the subject of form, style, the evidence of intention and design, of chiselling and hammering and polishing that I could find no foundation in your very vigorous little story, for the setting up of my views. Style, you know : it is by style we are saved. Generally speaking, I should say I did not find your tale so ferociously literary as my ideal. Construction again : a short story should lead up from first page to last to one climax, an act, a sentence, a word even, which is the key to it all. I do not detect that building up, that pull, that spring, unreleased till the very end, in your tale. You end, in fact, with some remark about a cricket match, which I think has occurred verbally identical before. I was expecting, I must confess, some shattering explosion, some shell that wiped out for all time these pleasant boyish prattlers. But, again I repeat this, I am not competent to criticize. I can appreciate, however, your great vigour and your accurate observation. There was a sentence about a reed-warbler, or some bird, unknown to me, which clearly showed you had used your eyes."

His mind had quite lost grip on Tim's story, as if it had been a smooth slippery object of which he could not catch hold. But clearly his intention now was to be cordial and encouraging.

"Cultivate your observation," he said, "for that gives you the rough material on which you have to work. Agnes could tell you what store I set by observation. Only the other day we spent a morning in Kew Gardens, and those hours were rich in reward for me, apart from the pleasure they afforded, because I noticed just one tiny detail in all the loveliness of the spring. The elm-trees were in flower, and the flowers were scattered on the grass. They were like—— "

He turned to Agnes.

" What were they like, dear ? " he said. " Ah, I see you have not forgotten. They were like sequins, Timothy, and it was worth while to spend a morning in Kew Gardens, instead of toiling with my notes, to observe that. There was a tiny bit of rough material."

" I see," said Tim. " Yes, that's got them : they're just like sequins."

" Well, you will remember that, if you ever try your hand at a story again, as no doubt you will, and are inclined to daub in some general impression, instead of etching it in with a definite certain stroke. What years, my dear Timothy, of patient work has it taken me to assimilate that ! But now I know it ; I can give you my bond on that. Then, having got his stores of accurate observation, psychical as well as physical, the real work of the story-teller begins. He composes, he arranges, he files and hammers and polishes. And that, my dear Timothy, you have got to learn. We have all had to learn it. *Ars longa !* We can never get away from that. . . . Dear me, it is close on midnight, and with my journey before me, too. . . ."

Alan looked into his wife's room after they came upstairs for a goodnight word.

" I shall feel strange and lonely to-morrow night, dear," he said, " at the thought that you are not near. But we are agreed, are we not, on the wisdom of our plan. You may be sure that dear Pamela will be taking the utmost care of me. I shall, I feel certain, want for nothing. There are one or two little commissions which I will ask you to execute for me in the morning, but those will wait. And you must not allow yourself to miss me. I am glad you will have Timothy here. Ah, poor Timothy and his story! I trust I was not unduly severe on him."

It struck Agnes with certainty that this topic of Timothy, casually introduced, supplied the true reason for Alan's entrance.

"No, you were very kind," she said. "I am sure you made him feel you were interested in his desire to write."

"I introduced those hints on the importance of observation for that very reason. But it was difficult not to show how I really felt about his work. Indeed I was strictly truthful when I said I could not criticize. There was nothing to criticize. From a literary point of view his story did not exist. And that it should be the plum, the feature in that magazine!"

"You think as poorly of it as that?" asked Agnes.

"I do not think of it at all," he said. "I wonder, dear, if in these next days you could manage, with all your tact and friendliness, to convey something of that to poor Timothy. He has not in him the germ, the protoplasm of the story-teller. It would be kind of you to do that. It would save him wasted hours and disappointment. His story shews no promise."

Agnes was divided between her long habit of ministry to Alan, and the sincerity of her feeling about Tim's story. The latter prevailed, and she wondered at it.

"Oh, but Alan, I don't really agree with you," she said. "When Tim read me the story—it was the first day that Pamela took my place—I was thrilled with it. I found it vivid and picturesque and moving. I told him so, too; I could not now pretend to think it worthless."

Once again that whisking lizard popped in and out.
. . . He made a gesture as of dismissal of the
topic.

" Poor dear Timothy and his story ! " he said. " I
do not know that it concerns either of us very closely."

CHAPTER VI

AGNES was sitting close beside the window in the little front room which looked out on to the garden of the square. There had been a couple of hot cloudy days with soft thick showers, which, like a magnet, had drawn up out of the earth the new midsummer grass, and washed the soot from the trees. She had really never noticed till last night that there were any elements of beauty at all about the garden : probably, indeed she had never actually looked at it, for it was just the ' square garden ' where sometimes she strolled with Alan before lunch, and heard how the work had progressed during the morning, while all her conscious thought was occupied with him. But yesterday evening after dinner, finding the house close and airless, she and Tim had brought deck chairs out, and sat for an hour there as the last light died. A little breeze was obtainable there, the air was lucent with the ' clear shining after rain ' and the smell of the damp earth was delicious in the dusk. Above all she was free to notice these things; she had a holiday-sense of irresponsibility, and she and Tim had sat there chatting or silent till lights began to twinkle from the houses, and above them the rain-clouds gathered again. She had gone to bed soon after, and had awoke once or twice to hear the rain softly hissing again on the lime-tree just outside her window, and drowsily to smell again the fragrance of the wet earth. . . . Just now she was awaiting Tim's arrival with some eagerness to know what they should do this evening, for he was to procure tickets for ' Siegfried ' at the opera if they were obtainable : if not they would stay quietly at home, and, most likely, sit out in the garden again. From her seat here in the projecting window she would see him coming up the pavement while he was still a hundred yards away. Probably when he came close she would pretend not to see him and be immersed in her book again, and listen with some secret thrill of pleasure to the rattle of his latch-key in the front door, his crisp step, and then look up as he entered. Why she would behave like that she did not trouble to ask herself, but she thought that she would. . . .

To-day was the fourth of Alan's absence, and the postman who was even now drawing nearer with pauses and raps at the intervening doors would probably bring her the daily letter which he had promised that he or Pamela would send her. Hitherto Pamela had been the punctual scribe, and she had not yet had a word direct from Alan. But Pamela reiterated a joyful explanation of that. He had dived into the revision of ' The Tyro ' (for so it had been settled in accordance with ' ridiculous ' Bristowe's famous letter) and he was so immersed in it that he knew dearest Agnes would be content to receive all cheerful assur-ances from her. He was nearly through with this immersion now and would then take a morning off work to write her a long, long letter. . . .

The postman paused on her doorstep, and hearing his rap and the dump of his insertion into the post-box, Agnes went to the door. There was one letter for her, again in Pamela's writing, and she took it back to her seat in the window, from which she could see up the pavement. It would contain probably, as well as its budget of news as to how the work was going, an intimation of when he was coming back. A week had been fixed on as the minimum, and Agnes thought it would not be exceeded, since, if his work was going on so well, he would soon be engaged on

the preface to ' The Tyro.' For this, he had said that
she must be his amanuensis, as it dealt with the friend-
ship that culminated in their marriage. Pamela, dear
Pamela, must not put pen to that. Probably then,
from what Agnes knew of his speed of writing when
all went well, he would be back on Saturday. . . .

She glanced down the pavement outside, opened the
letter and read.

" Another wonderful day of work, dear Agnes:
even you, who have known all the marvellousness of
him so long would be surprised at . . . at his
illumination. He is like a great serene light shining
and never dimmed for a moment. Glorious!

" He is busy now with his preparation for our afternoon's dictation, and I have time to write you a good
letter instead of the scraps I have sent you before.
Each day, just in its mere skeleton of events, is like
every other, but who knows better than you what
various feasts the Master spreads as he walks up and
down with his paper-knife? (Ever so many thanks:
it arrived quite safely.) For the work-room we have
a little parlour that opens on to the garden, and before he came I had the furniture arranged like that
in his work-room at home: piano in one corner, big
writing table between fireplace and window, arm-chair
close by it: I need not tell *you* how I arranged it.
You should have seen his face when I took him into
it. He looked this way and that, and then broke out
into his lovely laugh. ' Why, it's the replica of the
work-room at home,' he said. ' You cunning
Pamela: I believe you arranged it all on purpose.'
How I treasured those words!

" The Master prepares all the morning for our dictation, and just before lunch he usually comes out
for a stroll in the garden. Afterwards we walk: we
have a longer walk out into the marsh (no, dear, he
will not get his feet wet, for the marsh consists of big
fields with dykes in between) and a shorter walk if he

does not feel inclined to go so far, just round Rye and home again. Then we have dictation till dinner, and again afterwards for an hour. In a day or two, very likely by Saturday, we shall have finished the re-writing in ' The Tyro '; that includes a whole new chapter to take the place of the seventh, which does not satisfy his exquisite taste, and a dozen other pages dotted about the book.''

Agnes paused a moment in the perusal of this lucid epistle. Not only was the work-room a replica of the one at home, but the manner of the day also. The only difference was that it was Pamela who walked and strolled with him and was dictated to, instead of herself. That substitution seemed to suit Alan excellently, and surely that was all to the good, for his work uniquely prospered. . . . Something flickered at the back of Agnes's mind, and she went on with the letter.

'' And now, dear, I want to conspire again with you, and we shall need great delicateness about our new plan. The Master, I feel sure, intends to come back to London on Saturday, for by then (or thereabouts) he will have finished his revision of ' The Tyro,' and has to write the preface. (What an exquisite thing that will be!) But I feel sure also, that this place suits him extremely well, and he is so enjoying the quiet and the country air. Now there is only one person who can persuade him to stop a little longer, and that is you, for as you know, it is you, not I, to whom he has given the lovely privilege of writing *that* dictation. I feel sure, too, that he will not stop here in idleness, boring himself with poor Pamela : unless he can get on with his work (which must be the preface) back he will come. But a word from you would do it, if you could only tell him that you permit him to dictate the preface to me. After all, dear Agnes, does it signify who actually writes it ? The preface is all yours, just as all the

work he ever does is yours. It is you, who inspire
it. I know he wants to stop here (so often he says
'This delicious place : how well it suits me!') but I
feel he won't without your permission to go on with
his work. Of course it would be lovely if you would
join us here, but I know how impossible it is for you
to leave Mr. Timothy while he is your guest. My
dear, what a trouble men are, and how nice it is to
make them comfortable. . . . So if you can write
just that little word to the Master, how that will solve
all our difficulties, but if you can't how well I shall
understand! And now I must be ready for the
Master coming for his stroll in the garden. Much
love : such a joy it is to me that you and I have in
common our care for him. How close together it
brings us. . . ."

The flicker at the back of Agnes's mind flamed up,
and shed a great illumination. Pamela was perfectly
right in her main point : it was a matter of no significance at all who held the pen for the preface.
Alan, in spite of his beautiful promise that Agnes
and no other could, for memory's sake, be en-
trusted with that task, would clearly prefer to stay
on in the country and dictate to anybody, and Agnes,
for her part, could utterly repudiate the unreasonable
claim that he should come back and dictate to her.
To do so would be insisting on a ritual as meaningless as the habit of holiday-rejoicing on the anniversary of her birthday. It was the easiest thing in the
world for her to write a little letter to Alan, in the
style of the determined conspirator for whom he had
already cast her. As for Pamela's suggestion that
it would be 'lovely' if Agnes joined them there, that
was purely conventional. When Pamela said it
would be 'lovely,' she did not in the least mean that
anybody concerned would find it 'lovely.' It might
be 'lovely' theoretically. . . .

The little roll, which the prophet devoured, was ' sweet to the mouth but bitter to the belly.' So to Agnes was the note which she now immediately wrote to Alan in the approved style of the conspirator. It tasted sweet for the sake of the work which was going so well, and of the benefit which the country air was bestowing on him, that she should tell him that if he came back on Saturday, she would instantly leave the house. (There!) It tasted pleasant too— she did not seek to conceal it—that for a few days more she should enjoy her freedom and irresponsibility, and her comradeship with Tim. But close upon that there welled up from within her an overpowering bitterness that not Alan alone but she herself should find the extension of his absence so agreeable. After her fifteen years' service and devotion to him another woman, a late acquaintance, could fill her place not only as well but better than her, while she, if she let herself know the truth, was delighted, not for the sake of his work and well-being alone, but for the gratification of her own personal inclination, that he should be in no hurry to come back. He did not need her, nor she him. It was no altruism which made it so easy to spare him.

She had gone back to her sideways seat in the projecting window when she had written to Alan, and saw Tim straw-hatted and swift coming up the pavement. She had known what she would do when she caught sight of his return, and now took up her book again and bent her eyes on it. She asked herself why she did that, and got an inkling of an answer, namely that in some stupid fashion she wished to conceal from him the fact that she was really watching for his return. It would never do to stand at the window and smile and wave to him.

The step, crisp and rapid, which she knew so well

from hearing it haunt the house, came nearer. It was on the threshold now, and she listened for the scratch of his latch-key at the door. But no such token of his entry came, and she glanced up. Tim was standing on the threshold, looking at her through the window. His face was eager and alert, and when their eyes met the smile which made him seem such a boy still, broke through. But it did not leap to his mouth as usual : he had a moment of grave gazing first.

He only gave her a glimpse of it, and next moment came round the corner of the door with latch-key still in hand, and a small pink envelope which he waved at her.

" I've got the tickets," he said, " and it begins at the unearthly hour of half-past six. Now it's most important to get Food right. Art means nothing at all if you are hungry. May we have eggs with tea and—why are you laughing ? "

" Yes, my dear, you may have whatever you like," she said. " And I think I was laughing from re-action."

" Reaction ? I hope that doesn't mean you've been crying ? " he asked.

Agnes felt a momentary impulse to tell him exactly what she did mean. Tim was human and normal, and she longed for just such plain common sympathy and comprehension as she knew he would give her. Her life had been spent in unwearying service, which, she had told herself, no one but she could undertake. But now Pamela was undertaking it beautifully, indeed Pamela had come to the rescue when her own ministry was a wreck on the water, and had floated Alan off. And—was it the worst of it all or the best of it ?—she herself was so content that it should be so, even while the bitter tide flowed over her. She saw it all in this moment with the

clearness of a flashed picture, and in the same flash
she remembered Tim's face as he looked in on her
just now, his eager gravity, his retarded smile. That
look of his was not quite new : she had seen, anyhow, the semblance of it before on his face more than
once in these four days since Alan had gone, and
the question which she had only faintly whispered
to herself as to its meaning, sounded a little more
distinctly. . . .

She answered him now, not as her first impulse
had suggested, but with an irony known to herself,
which might mean nothing to him. Whether it
would or not she had no certain idea. Sometimes
it had occurred to her that he understood what her
relations with Alan were.

" I think it does mean that I've been crying," she
said. " Pamela tells me that she is sure Alan wants
to stop in the country a little longer, and with my
permission would do so. So I've written to tell him
that he mustn't think of coming back on Saturday."

She looked directly at him as she spoke, and saw
the brightness leap to his face. It was not in his
power to veil that, nor yet the joyful tone in which
he commiserated.

" Oh, how——" he paused and clearly substituted
another word for that which was on his tongue's tip
—" Oh, how disappointing for you, Agnes," he said.
" And you were hoping he would be back on Saturday. I think it's awfully good of you to suggest his
staying on there. But if it suits him and his work
I know that matters more than anything to you. And
so the work's going well. That's splendid. You
must cling on to the knowledge of that, when you
miss him. But I am sorry for you."

Tim turned to get a match for his cigarette, but
even through his pursed lips the gaiety of his voice
was undiminished.

" I think I shall take you out into the country on Sunday," he said, " to distract you. Where shall we go? You must make a plan. And when will Cousin Alan come back? "

" There's no date fixed," said she.

Tim gave a great cackle of laughter.

" But Pamela never had such glory," he said. " She's put paragraphs in the papers already that Mr. Alan Graham is at work on his collected edition at her house in Sussex. I can't bear to think of Pamela's glory when she returns and recounts it all to her wonderful luncheon-parties. It makes me feel perfectly ill."

" I'm jealous of Pamela all the same," said Agnes, going a little further. " She comes along, seizes my pen, and does it so much better than I have been doing it lately. She certainly came to the rescue last week, when Alan was hopelessly stuck."

Tim gave her a quick look, and again seemed to withdraw whatever it was that so nearly reached his lips.

" Well, I'm not jealous of Cousin Alan," he said. " If Pamela wanted—she has shewn no sign of it— to take down my stories, there wouldn't be any more stories. They would freeze on my tongue."

Agnes laughed.

" Oh, Tim, I can imagine you dictating to Pamela! " she said. " By the way, what about the second story. Ring the bell and we'll order tea and eggs—when is it coming out? "

Tim drew a letter from his pocket.

" Ha! I want to consult you," he said. " The second one comes out next week, and the third the week after, and so on till they've published the six which they already have. That's what the obliging publisher proposes, and far, ever so far, am I from thwarting him."

" O, Tim, how splendid ! " said she. " It means
that they think awfully well of them."

" But that's not all," said Tim. " Oh, I blush !
Apparently the first story, ' Cricket,' you know,
has caught on. It has been noticed in ' Literary
Columns,' and the Editor-man thinks equally well
of the rest. So he wants to commission me to
write half-a-dozen more, and at the end proposes
to publish them in volume form, or rather—he's
cautious—to get me to give him the refusal of
them. He wants to enter into negotiation about it—
there's elegance for you—and wonders if I would
lunch with him some day. What a pleasant man
Mr. Bristowe must be."

" Mr. Bristowe ?" asked Agnes.

" Yes. He's the Editor of the Bookshop : it's the
property of his firm. He's all right, isn't he ? Oh,
yes, he says he has had the privilege of publishing
for Cousin Alan for many years. So I want you to
coach me about the negotiations. Shall I ask for a
royalty or what ? I know nothing about it."

So the firm which had announced the meagre response to Alan's collected edition, was eager to secure
Tim's stories. Stars had their setting, and others
rose. For herself, she felt no doubt about the quality
of Tim's work, but she wished that it had been any
firm sooner than Bristowe's who wanted the publication of it. Yet it was impossible to dissuade Tim
from welcoming these advances because Mr. Bristowe
had not secured a promising subscription for Alan.
And she could not fail to associate herself with Tim's
delight. It was not only that she must not damp that,
but that she could not damp her own joy in it.

" Tim, how glorious ! " she said. " You are
lucky, and I don't wonder. But it's luck too. There
was Alan, for instance, writing beautiful stuff, and
for a long time no one would publish it. And then

you come slap-dashing along, and there's Mr. Bristowe running after you instead of running away from you. . . ."

She stopped : then recollected with relief that Tim knew nothing about the letter which (after consultation with Pamela) had set Alan to work on 'The Tyro' instead of 'December.' Tim had interrupted that discussion, and she certainly had not spoken of it to him. He must suppose that she alluded to the early difficulties Alan had experienced over publication. His next words shewed her that he did.

"They know better than to run away from Cousin Alan now," he said. "In luck? Why of course I'm in luck! What luck in my name to begin with! Bristowe must have made a pile of money out of it!"

Agnes wondered if unconscious irony could go further than that.

She chose for her toilet that night the sumptuous affair in black and white which Dora had given her, and wore over it a lace-trimmed cloak of orange-coloured silk, and saw Timothy positively blink at her splendour when she joined him. She had once been to Baireuth in her girlhood, and as they drove she ran over in her mind the general lines of the great tetralogy, which she still found vivid enough. Best of all she remembered the maiden Brunnhilde being put to sleep on the fire-ringed mountain top, and the finding and awakening of her, goddess no longer but human maid, by Siegfried. She had seen it then with wonder and delight at the colossal romance of it, but she had seen it wholly from outside, like some melodious picture hung in front of her, of which the centre and focussing point was the dawn and the fading of the ring of fire, Siegfried's kiss, and the awakening, when Brunnhilde, in the splendour of the morning, hailed the light and the sun before she saw

Siegfried. But to-night the romance touched not her senses alone, but her heart : the music of the awakening seemed to dive into her soul, and in some strange fashion mirrored her to herself. Thus, only lately, had she hailed the world, the blossoming Spring, the crowds at Charing Cross Station on the day she waited for Alan at tea in the Athenaeum. She, too, seemed to have had an awakening. . . .

Beside her sat Tim, and since the beginning of the act she had been quite unconscious of his presence; now, with a slight sense of interruption she noticed that his shirt creaked as he breathed. She gave a hasty impatient glance at him, and saw that his eyes were a-light as with experience, and his mouth was breaking into a smile. Instantly she turned her face to the stage again (it would spoil his ecstasy of looking if she said ‘ don’t creak ’ !) but knew that he had turned also and had glanced at her with her own swiftness. So the romance was gripping him too, and now she could not refrain from one tiny communication of herself to him. Just for a second she let her finger-tips rest on his arm, but without looking at him, and at that contact she felt as if his sleeve had sparkled electrically at her touch on it. She had only wanted to give a token of her comradeship, and an answer had come. Had he given it, or had she imagined it for herself? It was utterly unexpected, and now with deliberate effort, as on the stage Brunnhilde turned and saw Siegfried, Agnes shut the door of her heart which had already hailed the sun. The spring and the sun were locked in there now, and . . . and had Timothy’s sleeve just caught in the door as she banged it ?

She forced herself, as in the days of her girlhood, to look at and listen to the final scene as something external to herself, not as on herself as mirrored there, and this was her deliberate pose, her conscious attitude when, as at the end the hushed theatre blazed into sound and light. Timothy lifted the orange-coloured cloak on to her shoulder. His sleeve-link caught for a moment in the lace and she sat motionless and without speech as he disentangled it.

"Thanks, Tim," she said. "What an admirable performance. I am glad you could get tickets. Now let us go out before the crush and walk a little to pick up a taxi. We shall get on quicker than by waiting."

"So glad you enjoyed it," said he in a voice as conventional as hers. "But I'll fetch a taxi for you. Why should you walk?"

Tim had his way and she waited for him in the porch. . . . She could not help remembering, though instantly she daubed some other impression over the memory, that when last she went to the theatre with Alan on her birthday, a little drizzle was falling as they came out, and she, fearing the wet for him, ran out into the street and returned with a taxi. . . . Then, as she stood waiting, she heard her name shrilly called with a squeal of recognition, and there was Dora at her elbow. Another reaction, she must suppose, made her burst into sudden laughter.

"You, Dora?" she said. "I thought you were in Paris. How delightful!"

Apparently Dora felt to-night like a bird of Paradise which had casually perched itself on a rainbow, for her dress was composed of prismatic colours and long plumes.

"Yes, dear," said she volubly. "But what is more delightful is that that hideous caterwauling is now over. The last act resembled Victoria Station on a bank holiday, when everybody screams. Why does one ever go to the opera? I was in Paris till this morning, but there was a day of tedious engagements in front of me so I fled. I lost my passport, and expect any moment to be arrested and deported as an undesirable alien. I suppose they will take me back as far as French soil without my having to buy a ticket. But why are you here? Why are you not writing with both hands as Alan pours out his interminable effusions? What monstrous irregularity is this? Or is Alan here, and has he heard what I said? My dear, what a charming gown! Ah, I remember now I gave it you in a fit of generosity because I saw that I could never wear it. And a decent cloak! Agnes explain to me at once how you dare to appear in public properly dressed? Here is my motor. Get in at once and explain on the way home."

"I can't, dear," said she. "I'm here with Tim, Alan's cousin, you know. He's looking for a taxi."

"And you've left Alan to dictate his weary work alone?" asked Dora, in a voice of high congratulation. "The only sensible thing you've done, darling, for fifteen years. Dear me, I seem to be stopping all the traffic. But I'm delighted. I hope you'll go and sup at the Savoy now. Do I know Tim? I believe I met him at your house on that terrible birthday party. Yes. Send him to see me. Perhaps I had better go on. It is outrageous the way one is not permitted in England to exchange a word with anyone. Probably I shall look round to-morrow morning. Where am I going? I am sure I don't know. Perhaps I had better go home and find out. Home!"

As she drove off there moved up behind a taxi with Tim standing on the step. Agnes felt that a short comic interlude was over which should never have been inserted.

And yet it was not that which made restraint and awkwardness between them, as they drove home; for that, the moment when, rightly or wrongly, Agnes had seemed to herself to shut the door of her heart, was responsible. There was the spring inside it, and Tim outside had his sleeve caught in the door. The simile, rough and ill-hewn as it was, which had occurred to her then, fitted its place : she could even elaborate it, and picture herself standing outside her own heart, back to the door but with the key in her hands. It was not that as far as words went they talked otherwise than they were accustomed to : they spoke of the opera they had seen, of Dora's bewildering and tropical epiphany, of the letter Tim had received from Mr. Bristowe. It was rather the silences which were unusual. . . . If, ordinarily, a silence fell between them, they were at no pains to break it, thoroughly happy with each other, a silence was as natural as speech. But now if a topic failed both were swift with a new one; it was as if silence was dark and formidable and must be banished with the light of talk. Agnes knew well enough the cause of it, for it had been she who shut up her heart like that, and now stood barricading it. With amazement and bewildered sense of sweetness she knew that the door had swung open just now to him who had long stood close to it, and she must keep him out. . . . But to Tim the changed atmosphere was inexplicable. Without cause Agnes had shut herself up. He was sure, at any rate, that he had not betrayed himself.

All through their drive home and through the supper that was ready for them on their return this embarrassment lasted, and presently they were upstairs again in the work-room where they often sat in Alan's absence. On the conclusion of the last book, all his notes and slips had as usual been cleared away, and now the table where she sat for dictation was occupied by galley-proofs of Tim's stories, and a pile of scribbled manuscript. To-night she had seated herself in her chair there, and beside her, where Alan sat when, in the intervals of his perambulations, the last paragraph was read aloud to him, was Tim. As he sat himself there, she felt the breath catch in her throat, it was all she could do to prevent herself telling him to sit in any other chair but that. Something rose and rebelled and was insurgent within her, and she left the sentence that was on her lips unfinished.

Tim got up.

"You're tired, Agnes," he said quietly. "Five hours or nearly of opera, you know. I shan't be sorry to go to bed either."

She had never felt less tired; she had never known herself so alert and vigorous. And suddenly she became aware that she could not let Tim go like this. She must open a chink of that closed door, not thus woodenly and ungraciously give him blank walls and windows. What was there which she could show him of her real self, which would yet not reveal what had so lately only revealed itself to her? . . .

He leaned over the table for a moment.

"Or does anything worry you?" he asked.

She saw here an opening for making herself real again. She could tell him, though she had put him off before, of that bitterness which had invaded her just before he came in this afternoon. That was part of herself, truer, at any rate, than the closed door and the clutched key, by which at present she knew that she was parodying herself.

"Yes, my dear, I have been rather bothered," she said. "And I know it's only my stupid egoistic self that bothers me. Pamela's letter you know, and my answer to Alan. Of course I'm delighted that his work goes so well, and that he shouldn't interrupt the spell of it by coming back. But it's rather a heart-ache, Tim, that after all these years it should be an interruption to him to come back and do his work here with me at the table. But that's the fact, and I've got to digest it not . . . not, well, be sick about it. Pamela as an amanuensis, with her little gasps of admiration, and her 'Master' suits him, just now anyhow, better than I do. She stimulates him, and I'm sure that is quite natural. But it wounds my pride. Just a scratch."

He nodded.

" I knew that," he said. " I felt it must be so."

The mere putting her feeling into words emphasized and defined it for Agnes. She had repressed it, but she could say to Tim what she had tried to conceal from herself. He stood there close to her, and she felt the tide of his sympathy rising round her, floating her off the shallows on which she had grounded. . . . Or, it was as if he had struck the rock, and the water flowed out.

The spring which his comprehension had released did not come from the deep places, for these were not to be revealed yet. But she could go deeper than this without getting near them. At present these were mere surface waters.

" It's so feeble of one to mind at all," she said. " The whole purpose of my life since I married him has been to help him in all possible ways, and when I find that when I fail, he can get help elsewhere, I ought only to rejoice at it. It's my own fault too, that I fail."

The mere relief of speaking to someone who understood more than counterbalanced all other considerations. Neither Dora nor her mother could have understood as Tim was understanding. Dora would have given opera-bouffe solutions, her mother would have gleamed with hostility. And she was talking after all about nothing more than intellectual companionship, and it was on these lines she continued.

"It's my fault, Tim," she said, "because I am out of sympathy with his work. I take it down for him as a task; my heart isn't the least in it. Once I so lost myself in my own thoughts that I stopped writing altogether. But never mind that. But Pamela —let's say Glory to Pamela—Pamela brings enthusiasm and admiration, and it warms him. He is never sure I shan't forget again to go on writing. What her enthusiasm is worth doesn't matter. Alan is her 'stunt' anyhow: she likes it to be known that 'she works with him.' She's running him . . . There's nothing whatever, though I needn't tell you that, to make me jealous."

Tim permitted himself to smile, and she had a laugh for answer.

"Oh, dear me," she said. "Imagine my thinking that Alan was fond of Pamela, like, like that, or she of him. Don't make me laugh, Tim."

Tim had seated himself on the arm of Alan's chair, and she with elbows on the table leaned towards him.

"There's much worse to come," she said, "and here it is. Though my pride and egoism smart at it all, I know I don't really care. If I am hurt with Alan for not needing me, I ought to be far more hurt at myself for not needing him. I don't want him to want me really. I find it fearfully tedious to write and erase and read. I tried to tell myself that I minded his stopping down in the country now to dictate to her the preface to 'The Tyro,' but I didn't care to whom he dictated it. You see that preface concerns the time of our marriage, when he used to read the chapters, as he wrote them, to my mother and me. Then it came out and very soon after we were engaged. Alan had said so very emphatically that it must only be I to whom he dictated that, and Pamela agreed. But they will begin on it, Pamela thinks, on Saturday, when he was to have returned

here. I ought to have minded that dreadfully,
oughtn't I? But I don't. There are lots of things
that would mortally hurt me, but that doesn't. For
instance——"

Agnes stopped suddenly. She was aware that,
even as she had lost herself over her own thoughts,
when they should have been with Alan's dictation,
she had lost herself now over Tim, when it was this
matter of the preface that she was speaking of. She,
with his brown eager eyes that so frankly and fully
gave away his secret looking with steady light into
hers, had so nearly given some instance of a matter
which would have hurt her, in which he was involved.
Just so had he looked at her through the window
when she seemed intent on her book : now his eyes
met hers.

She drew back as from a sheer edge. She had
already done what she set out to do : had given him
in this confidence something of herself that was real.

" Ah, we won't talk about me any more," she said.
" I'm perfectly sick of the subject, and so, I'm sure,
are you. But you've been a dear to me, Tim, as you
always are. You've let me blow off my . . . my
rancid steam, and I'm so much better. And in spite
of this dismal pow-wow of mine, I'm not without a
certain self-respect. I shan't croak any more, and I
assure you, there's Spring in my heart as well as
these dripping autumn rains."

Tim got up, holding out both hands.

" Thanks ever so much for telling me," he said.
" I'm proud. It's a decoration to be trusted. I
can't say anything to help you, you know. All
you've told me is . . . is like that. But keep
Spring in your heart. There is nothing which
Spring doesn't heal."

He stood holding both her hands.

" You're happy in spite of it all," he said.

She did not withdraw her hands : she could not interrupt that swift tingling flow of sympathy and love which poured into her. It drowned the sense of perplexity and failure which attached to the past, it even swallowed up the difficulties and repressions, more acute than any she had yet experienced, which she knew confronted her in the future. And though her reply came from some stratum very near to the sealed waters, she did not attempt to check it. She owed him the acknowledgment.

" Yes, my dear, I am happy," she said, and as she spoke she took a step back from him, bursting the contact of their hands. The contact of his steady smiling gaze had to be broken also, and, with a greater effort, she looked away from him to the clock on the mantelpiece.

" What an hour ! " she said. " I am a brute for keeping you up when, ever so long ago, you said you wouldn't be sorry to go to bed. What a lovely evening we've had, Tim. Oh, and I've never paid you for my ticket for the opera. How much is it ? "

" Five hundred pounds," said Tim, " plus the entertainment tax."

She laughed.

" I had no idea it was so cheap," she said. " Seriously, though."

" I am serious," he said. " Don't be silly."

It was like that they parted. Timothy went downstairs to put out lights and Agnes went up to her bedroom. She shut the door, and standing stock-still close to it, waited there till she heard his step go softly by and up to the storey above. Just outside his room there was a loose board on the landing : she had often heard it creak as he passed over it. It creaked now, and immediately after came the muffled sound of his door closing.

CHAPTER VII

AGNES was returning one afternoon early in the next week from seeing her mother off for her annual ' holiday ' in the Isle of Wight, where she owned a stark stucco villa obliquely set in a windy garden. According to immemorial custom she had spent the day with Mrs. Mowbray in order to superintend her packing. This did not require much surveillance, for Mrs. Mowbray always took precisely the same trunks every year, in each of which was stowed in precisely the same places just what years of experience had told her she would need, and her maid could have probably packed everything in her sleep. The most important item in the luggage was the Emergency bag, which in case everything else was delayed or lost, would be found to contain everything necessary for desperate and immediate needs, and travelled in the carriage with her. It comprised the needle-work which beguiled the journey and vast quantities of worsted, for during her holiday she got through more work than it was possible to do in London. The last strap was buckled, the last label affixed a full hour before it was time to start for the station early enough to be sure of securing a corner-seat, and Mrs. Mowbray with her hat and cloak on, so as to be ready to go the moment the luggage was on the taxi, had leisure to take the most censorious view of the matters concerning her daughter and Alan. . .

Agnes had an errand or two in Oxford Street and she strolled back across the Park remorseful in mind at her unnaturalness in not being able to help being glad that her mother had gone. But though the

224

bitterness of that last hour's talk still wrung her heart, she knew that below it her soul basked in a wonderful sunshine. . . . Mrs. Mowbray, in obedience to her duties as a mother had felt it incumbent on her to say what she thought of Alan's continued absence, and she had done so with a gusto which kept oozing or spouting out of her grimness. The length of Alan's absence she understood was still indeterminate; she understood that Agnes was perfectly willing that he should remain at Mrs. Probyn's till this revision of ' The Tyro ' and its preface was complete. So, from this sense of duty she pointed out what the world would say. As a corollary she pointed out what the world would say about the other half of the situation. If Agnes had any spark of proper feeling, she should either summon Alan back to London, or instantly join him there. . . .

Agnes, probing herself, had simple unadulterated pity for anyone who could ' feel ' as it was clear her mother felt. It was the relish with which she regarded her view of the situation which was so utterly pathetic. It sprang not from duty but from that unwinking hostility which lurked in the shadow of her mind, a thing not to be brought out except masked and dressed up in these trappings of duty. Mrs. Mowbray did not wish them well, neither Alan nor herself : she watched in no guardian fashion, but like a neutral, strictly proper in the conduct of her neutrality, but with a malevolent heart. She hugged her conception of the view which the world would take, of Alan's *villegiatura* with Pamela. Agnes could easily laugh at the notion (she had already, in fact, done so with Tim), but what she could not laugh at, what stabbed her with pity was that her mother should hold it. It was no laughing matter when Mrs. Mowbray, as a final benediction before starting on her holiday, should descend in this shower of bitter hail, congealed and hoarded from those far-off days when Alan had declared his choice. . . . Had she been in love with him, Agnes wondered now, or had she merely wanted to exchange her widowhood for service and companionship, such as had been her own? Certainly she had contemplated marriage with Alan, but he had not chosen her. . . . If there had been love there, could it possibly have turned rancid like this, so that now, though she covered and cloaked herself in motherhood, she danced this jig of gratification? Day after day now, since Alan's departure up till this culmination of Mrs. Mowbray's last hour in London, Agnes had known herself to be silently and malevolently watched.

Now her mother was gone, and as, leaving the path, she walked across the grass towards the Serpentine, she knew that her heart was light, and that in its lightness this departure of her mother had its share. She had gone, even as Alan had gone, and the sense of holiday was complete. Presently Agnes would come to the Serpentine, and at a trysted corner Tim would be waiting. They meant to take the longer walk.

There still remained the second half of the situation. Her mother's sense of duty had not quite permitted her to say that she and Tim were in love with each other, but had impelled her to indicate what view might be taken of their solitary companionship. And never had a conclusion been so literally true in its premises, so portentously false in its deductions. She was as conscious of her love for Tim, as she was of Tim's for her, and the knowledge filled her with sunrise, cool and radiant. She did not, in these moments of earliest day, feel the slightest desire to anticipate or deduce; the actual present moment stupefied her with sweetness. No word of any sort conveying the knowledge forth and back had been spoken : it seemed to her that she and Tim had slid into it as a boat launched from the slips, slides on an even keel into the water. She could still give Alan all she had ever given him, but she gave it now of herself no longer, but borrowing it from Tim. She had nothing of her own now, and was rich beyond compare. How odd it seemed, and how inevitable ! She could not ' think back ' to the days when it had not been so. There was no hunger yet, nor any thirst. Just the fact, and no more than that, was complete in itself.

He was standing at the corner where she had so often fed the gulls in winter, while Alan watched their poisings and dartings and assimilated little facts and observations for use. Neither gulls were there now nor Alan, but if the birds had been wheeling there, and if she had seen Alan's caped figure, a little bent and round-shouldered, standing by Tim's straw-hatted slimness, there would have been sincerity in her word of welcome. All that mattered was that Tim should be there. She was some minutes ahead of the time they had appointed for their walk, for she had hurried over her errands in order not to keep him waiting, and he was before the time also, and was evidently not expecting her yet, but was watching a spaniel retrieving a stick thrown into the water. His back was towards her, but as she approached, he turned quickly as if she had called to him.

" I knew you were there," he said. " I felt it. You're early, and so am I. So much the better. Oh, I went home first, and found a telegram for you. So I brought it along."

She loved his saying ' home ' like that : her heart swelled with delicious pride, as she tore open the orange envelope. . . . The telegram was from Alan, and announced his immediate arrival. He gave no reason for it. And though, a couple of minutes ago, she had told herself that if by some queer juggle Alan had been standing here with Tim, she would have cordially welcomed his presence, she knew now that something stood still. . . . But she crumpled up the pink sheet, and dropped it into a wire-cage for waste-paper.

"Now for our walk," she said.

Tim gave her a quick glance, that penetrated and divined.

"Nothing . . . nothing wrong?" he asked.

She had wanted to get a little more of Tim as he had been all these days while Alan's return was still unfixed. But it was no use trying to do that: the fact that she knew he was coming back to-day had altered everything already. Tim might as well know at once.

"Nothing wrong at all," she said. "Alan has telegraphed to say that he's coming back immediately. He must be all right, therefore, for surely he would have given some reason if he was ill or anything of that sort."

They looked at each other in the full light and focus of their mutual consciousness.

"Certainly he would," said Tim. "You needn't fear anything of that kind. That's . . . that's capital."

His voice rang false as a cracked bell, and sweet to her was the falsity of it.

"But we'll have our walk, Tim," she said. "I promised Alan, you know, that I would walk every day. We shall be home by six. Come along. We settled to take the longer walk."

Once again Tim looked at her and then stepped out by her side.

"And how has everything gone?" he asked.

" Did your mother get off comfortably ? Corner seat and emergency bag ? "

" Yes, that was all right," said Agnes. " And you ? "

" Very stuffy in the city," said he. " I half made a plan, but that doesn't matter."

Agnes did not ask him what the half-made plan was. She guessed that it concerned some drive out into the country after dinner that evening, or some similar expedition next day. But that was no longer possible, and, as Tim said, it did not matter now. For the rest, acutely conscious of him, she was as acutely aware of superficial impressions, keenly noted the crackle of fresh gravel under their feet, the persistent chirping of sparrows, the faint odour of the flowering limes along the edge of the road. She was perhaps more conscious of the silence that had fallen between them than of anything else. But unlike that which had descended on them after the performance of Siegfried a week ago, there was no quality of restraint or embarrassment about it. They both knew the reason for it, in mute and complete agreement. He understood as well as she what could be said, and what must remain unspoken.

Suddenly Tim stopped.

" There are all my papers lying about on the table in the work-room," he said. " Hadn't we better . . ."

Before he finished his sentence she had turned.

" Yes, we must go back and tidy up," she said. " I'm glad you thought of that."

She laughed.

" Oh, Tim, the sacred table ! " she said. " By the way, what about telling Alan that Bristowe's are to publish the book of your stories in the autumn ? We never settled that. What's your feeling about it ? "

"I'll tell him, I think," said Tim. "After all, there's no material for a mystery. Even if there was, it would be solved in the autumn. But I'll wait for a decent opportunity."

"Do, and then tell him. But not about the work-table. It was harmless enough and natural enough for you to work there, but . . ." She broke off.

"Oh, my dear, we're being schemers and conspirators when there's nothing to conspire about," she said. "That's a dreadful state of mind to get into. We're talking as if in some way we had been doing wrong. Why shouldn't you write and publish stories, and why shouldn't you scribble at his table? It's all absurd. Let's put the attitude away. It's the attitude that's so silly."

They still hurried, as if, in spite of the clear common sense of Agnes's view, there was still something in her exclamation of 'the sacred table,' and presently they came to the entry of the square, where a hundred yards up the pavement the bow-window at which she sat waiting for Tim's return, projected from the flat perspective of the houses. But below these little worries and mysteries, there still gleamed for each the great tranquil lake of happiness. Just as they came to the house Tim spoke once more without turning his head.

"It has been absolutely delightful," he said. "I have never been so happy."

As he fumbled with the latch-key their eyes met.

"Thanks, Tim," she said.

She went in, he following. There was Alan's hat and coat on a table in the hall.

"He has come," she said, and ran upstairs. Alan was back then, and in her mind was some clash of readjustment, as she clicked a lever over which would set the familiar machinery at work again. It was stiff : it required the full force of her mental energy to tug it into its place. It grated and shrieked as she got into the old gear. . . .

The door of the work-room was open and she looked in to see whether he was there. He was seated at the work-table which was littered with scribbled sheets and proofs belonging to Tim.

"Welcome, Alan," she said. "I was out when your telegram came. Tim brought it to me when he joined me after business hours for a walk. We turned almost immediately, but you have got here before us."

He rose and kissed her, putting down the proofs which he had taken from the table and was reading.

"I arrived a quarter of an hour ago," said he. "I hope you experienced no anxiety at my telegram."

"No: I knew that if you had been ill, you would have said something about it. And you look splendidly well. Tell me about the work: tell me about everything."

He sat down in his usual chair.

"A sad misfortune," he said. "We were sailing along with full canvas and favouring winds when our poor Pamela was stricken with influenza. So swift and easy had been my progress that I found an hour's preparation in the morning was enough to furnish me with material to begin dictation at once, so that for the last three days we have started on our joint work soon after eleven. But she looked so ill this morning that I insisted on sending for the doctor."

"Very sensible," said Agnes.

"I think so, for our poor Pamela felt feverish, and I feared influenza for her, while in addition there was no use in my exposing myself to possible infection. You remember how terribly pulled down I was the last time I had that dreadful plague. . . . Well, a very intelligent man came, who packed her off, protesting, to bed, and agreed with me that I had better go away; so poor Pamela most kindly made arrangements for me to be motored up to town at once. She would not hear of any further risk for me, and, as she pointed out, her disablement implied that my work would be at a standstill. It was all a dreadful calamity, for a couple of days would have seen the preface finished. Pamela, poor soul, felt that more than her own sufferings : she could not bear the thought that her illness should interrupt my progress. But I feel so well and fit from my out-door country life that I do not seriously fear that I shall be a victim. It is just the interruption——"

"Ah, but we mustn't have any," she said. "We must get to work at once."

"The same idea was in my mind," he said, with a glance at the littered table, "and in fact, I was intending to arrange notes and dictation book on the table, so that we might resume our work immediately. But it was profusely occupied. I found abundant and unmistakable signs that literary activity had been going on in my absence. I gather that poor Tim so far from being discouraged at the advice I thought bound to give him has been industriously disregarding it. I had just picked up a proof I found there and read a few lines. I do not know that I was tempted to proceed. Another story, I suppose, for some magazine. Would it, dear, do you think, incommode Tim if I resumed possession of my table?"

There was something icy and ironical in his words. He seemed to resent, thought Agnes, the very idea that Tim should write or publish anything at all. His egoism like some sensitive plant; even while it shrank from intrusion, it was thorny in the attack of self-defence. Though the mechanical habit of life was at work again now, she could not help being conscious of the strain and creak of it, compared to . . . but she nipped off the bud of comparison.

" But we'll have your table clear in two minutes,"
she said. " I wonder where Tim is. He came in
with me."

Tim, under pretext of a couple of letters waiting
for him, had deliberately stopped downstairs to give
them time for the first salutations. Now he came in,
and the sight of him seemed to Agnes to stiffen Alan's
thorns.

" Ah, dear fellow," said he, " I am very glad to
see you. We were just talking, Agnes and I . . .
we were wondering if perhaps—just a corner, you
know. Some work of mine which demands a little
space. . . . You have been busy I see, Timothy."

Tim swept his papers together.

" I'm dreadfully ashamed of my litter," he said,
" but one sweep removes it. There, Cousin Alan."

Alan got up.

" The impetuous fellow ! " he said. " Your proofs,
your delightful manuscript. . . . You have
jumbled everything up into a salad of disorder. Have
you been so impetuous, Timothy, over your writing?
I just glanced at a galley proof : is it not a galley
proof, that long strip of interminable print ? Galley
proof, yes, galley proof. More stories yet, Timothy,
just thrown off at white heat ? Enriching the magazines. Some day you must collect them and give us
a little volume. Aha, Timothy, I believe I have
divined you. There is some such idea in your head."

Agnes found herself waiting with suspended
breath for Tim's answer. He had said that
he would tell Alan about this volume when a fit
opportunity presented itself, and here, if ever, was
the occasion. But by some interior sense she knew
how unsuitable this seeming occasion was. She
knew Alan's mood : his silken address covered something as grating as a file. But Tim was unaware

of these subtleties.   He only saw the ready opportunity.

" Yes, I'm getting near the end of twelve short
stories," he said.   " When they are finished they
will come out in volume form."

Agnes saw the hostility gather in Alan's face. He
was busy now with groping in a suit-case which was
on the floor : a copy of ' The Tyro ' came out of it
and the dictation book.

" Dear me, that is a famous beginning," he said.
" To write a volume of short stories . . . the
most difficult medium . . . twelve short stories.
And have you secured a publisher ? Or is this
volume form just an aspiration ? No doubt, no
doubt !   That is your design : twelve short stories in
a volume ! ²'

" No : it's arranged," said Tim.   " I've a contract.
" Bristowe's——"

Alan paused with the sheaf of slips in his hand.

" Bristowe ? " he asked.   " Has Bristowe offered
to publish your stories ? He must indeed think highly
of them.   Well, dear Agnes, I think if you are
disposed, we will put in an hour's work before dinner.
I have my material all ready."

This seemed a sufficiently direct hint to Tim that
he should disembarrass the work-room of his work
and himself, and the door closed behind him. Agnes
established herself at the work-table, and opened the
book where Pamela had broken off in the middle of
a sentence.

" Shall I read the last paragraph or two ? " she
asked.   Alan did not at once reply, and in the silence
she heard the tap of the creaking board outside
Timothy's room.

" Before we begin," he said, " I should just like
to make one small comment.   I was a little surprised,
dear, to find that Timothy had been working at our

table, and that you had permitted it. I should have thought that you would have regarded just this one table out of all others in the house as dedicated to me and my work, not poor Timothy's trash. I should even have thought that you regarded the room itself in the same light."

" I am sorry you feel like that, Alan," she began.

" Enough, dear; I only pointed out that I was surprised you did not feel like that. I do not think we need discuss our difference of feeling in the matter. I should like to ask also whether you already knew that Timothy's stories were to be published by Bristowe?"

" Certainly I did. Tim told me about it a few days ago. Mr. Bristowe owns the magazine in which they are appearing serially. It was perfectly natural that, if he liked them, as he appeared to do, he should be the first to make an offer for them."

In spite of Alan's contemptuous comment on Tim's work, there was clearly some vague nucleus of jealousy forming in his mind, due no doubt to the fact that the firm which had wished to publish these stories had not secured an adequate subscription for his own collected edition. Agnes felt that he was ranging her on Tim's side.

" And you share that liking?" he asked.

" Yes, dear. I am no judge, you know, and, as you told Tim, they are not what you called ferociously literary. But I think they are full of vigour and observation. I think they are true and vivid."

" Has he been dictating to you?" asked Alan suddenly. The question came out as from a squirt.

" No, my dear," she said. " He has read them to me, and I have often criticized. Now will you not dictate to me?"

He took the Flaubert paper-knife out of the suit-case.

"I thought you might perhaps care to read over such poor pages of my preface as I have written," he said.

"Indeed I should," she replied. "Shan't I take the opportunity to do that some time when you do not want me to write for you? You said you had material ready now."

He had looked at her as through some gauze of suspicion, but now that cleared. Her answer, perfectly genuine, seemed satisfactory.

"Let us begin then," he said. "Such was the scrimmage and upset owing to the doctor's arrival this morning, that Pamela stopped in the middle of a sentence."

He leaned over her, and turned backwards through a couple of pages of Pamela's manuscript.

"Will you begin reading from there?" he said, pointing to the first line of a paragraph. "A little offering to you: I hope you will not find it unworthy."

Agnes read, and the beautiful, balanced sentences, each hewn and polished and perfectly fitting, dripped cold and crystal-clear upon her heart. Never till she was confronted with this flawless presentation of his emotions about her in the days that preceded his proposal of marriage to her, had she realized just how he had regarded her then. With delicate vivid touches he had etched those readings of 'The Tyro'; she could feel herself back in her mother's drawing-room, sitting on the footstool by the fire, intent and wonderstruck, while the story's enchantment unfolded itself to her. With infinite dexterity had he conjured up the scene, the lamplight shining on her head, her mother with the eternal needlework on her lap, sitting on the shadowed sofa, with eyes now bent on her work, now watchful and intent on the reader.

All this was exquisitely rendered: the utmost wizardry of his art inspired it.

And when that was all admitted and admired, so thought Agnes now, as, with him bending over her, she read these pages, she came to the essential, the vital part of it. Her heart grew like lead within her. He had seen her as a beautiful girl with the intelligence to revere him. He saw himself as the great artist willing, even eager as out of a rosy cloud, to reach down and take her to be his wife, for the sake of her adoration of his gifts. He had never seen her as an individual with needs and longings of her own: the utmost need that he had perceived in her was filled with the honour that he had done her. He described and acknowledged her wonderful devotion to him; in that pure and limpid style of his he told of the unbroken harmony of their joint lives, the perfect happiness which had made halcyon weather of these years. He had imagined that her undeveloped bud of girlhood had never burst its sheath, that her task of honoured housekeeper and amanuensis was her reward as well as her service. He had never looked at her life or contemplated the possibility of an identity of hers which was not rapturously merged in his, so long as he strolled and walked with her for his refreshment, and dictated to her for her exceeding recompense. That was the point of view from which he had spoken the preface which Pamela had indited.

Her eyes in their travel over the lines had come to the last paragraph which ended, owing to Pamela's sudden indisposition, in an unfinished sentence, and cudgelling her brain as to what she should say when it was finished, she read the more slowly. And, as she read, not rebellion nor ridicule rose within her, but again pity and the sense of the pathos of his existence. . . . It ran thus.

" The advancing years bring no sadness of remembrance, no remorse for wasted hours, nor any uneasy scrutiny of the years that remain to my dear one and to me. We have been and are still fellow-labourers in this building of the great temple of Art, we hew and chisel our humble stones, and the reward of our work is the work itself. Many years have now passed since first to her ardent ear I read these chapters of the book of which my maturer craft to-day is not wholly ashamed, and her companionship and sweet co-operation is now, as it has always been, a ' lantern unto my feet and a light unto my path.' Without her, without the unfailing solace of her eager devotion I could never . . ."

That was the end : all this had Pamela taken down in her neat hand, and Agnes's eyes left the paper and looked up at him. The habit of years inevitably reasserted itself, she had to please and encourage and minister to him. In the ways of the heart he was such a child for all his grey and thinning hair. He had no experience : he did not know what love meant. If she had tried to tell him all or any of that which, as she read, so chilled her with its sense of husk and emptiness, he would never have understood her : he would only have been hurt and disappointed : his face now glowing with pride at the splendour of his own tribute to her, would have crinkled into ashes.

" Ah, my dear ! " she said. " What lovely news for me. And how beautifully phrased and built up, Alan. You have never been more sure and firm in your touch. But you are too generous in your praise : you make me out to have really helped you. I think I shall have to add a footnote to say that all I have done is just the manual part."

Not one inch did he penetrate into her deeper feeling : all that was outside his comprehension.

" No, dear Agnes," he said. " I have not said a

word too much. You are worthy of the fullest tribute that I have paid you. And your Mother? The little etching I made of her sitting at her work and listening? You find that justly observed?"

Agnes did not attempt a perfectly direct answer to this.

" But how it brought back to me the sense of those evenings!" she said. "I could hear you reading again, and see the glow of the firelight."

He patted her shoulder.

" It is well, then," he said. " Pamela, too, thought that my hand had not quite lost its cunning, nor my mind its perception. Pamela, in fact, was quite enthusiastic about all I said concerning you. Poor Pamela, I hope she is better this evening! She said that the thought of dictation going on in spite of her foolishness—was not that like Pamela?—would do her more good than any of the doctor's remedies. . . . And if you are satisfied, too, I am content. . . . Well, dear, shall we get to our work? I want particularly to finish the preface in one swoop now. Three days more I think should complete it, if the gale of inspiration blows benignly on us. Aha, dear, this is a change, is it not, for you from evenings when poor Timothy has been sitting at your table, inscribing his violent little snapping sentences."

He took up the Flaubert paper-knife which the repairer recommended by Pamela had restored so marvellously.

" The last paragraph once more, dear," he said. " Your modesty must allow you just to read it aloud."

For ten minutes the dictation prospered: Pamela's unfinished sentence was completed from memory, and the paragraph built to its apex. But then the benign gale began to blow less favourably: there were erasures and re-readings, consultations of notes, all the signs of stagnation and lack of progress. Alan began to mutter to himself.

"Very odd, very odd indeed," he said. "I did not foresee any difficulty. . . . Ah, write, please. 'This delicate and comprehending partnership, this unity of purpose.' . . . No, erase—what can be the matter with me this evening? All these last ten days there has scarcely been an erasure, and to-night we have nothing but them. The change from the country to town again? The long motor-drive perhaps? . . . Ah, I think I see my way."

He progressed a little but with innumerable haltings and creakings, and the lines of worry and fatigue began to rule themselves on his forehead.

"We will pause a moment," he said. "Curiously and fancifully I seem to feel the presence of some distracting influence. My mind keeps forming the image of Timothy sitting where you are, dear, and scrawling away. I hope I am not inhospitable in wishing that he had not used our work-room. By the way, dear, has Timothy succeeded in finding a flat for himself yet? He has been here, let me see, he has been a month or more with us now. A charming inmate, of course, but still not a permanent one."

Agnes looked up at him.

"Just lately he has not been enquiring for a flat," she said. "When you went down to Pamela's, if you remember, you told him that you insisted on his stopping here to take care of me till your return. We did not know till an hour or two ago when you were coming back."

"Quite so; quite so: that is very reasonable. Naturally I should not wish to hurry Timothy's departure. But I think, dear, that unless he makes some spontaneous suggestion in the next few days, the

time has almost come, has it not, when you might
ask him, quite lightly and casually, whether he has
got his eyes on quarters which are likely to suit him.
No hurry, of course, no hurry. Now let us get back
to our task again.''

During the days that immediately followed, Agnes
found herself watching with a sort of detached intuition the circumstances of the two with whom she lived.
She seemed to have no part in that life herself : she
stayed passive but alert, and now she felt herself seeing through Alan's eyes and now through Tim's, but
never through her own. No ease returned to Alan's
inspiration and the work that should have been accomplished in half-a-dozen dictations dragged stiffly and
laboriously on. He seemed quite unable to bring the
full pressure of his energy to bear on it. His mind
that should have discharged its stream whole and
powerful through the nozzle, leaked and spouted
through fissures in the hose that conveyed it. A touch
of catarrh worried him, and he feared that he might,
in spite of his prudent precautions, have already been
infected with Pamela's complaint, and his anxiety for
her speedy recovery was transformed into anxiety for
himself. But this little ailment soon yielded to treat-
ment, and again he was distracted by conjecture as to
when Pamela would be able to travel. Though he
made no intimation of what Pamela would do then, it
dawned on Agnes, as these fruitless sessions of dictation were interrupted by little periods of resting,
that he longed for Pamela to take her place at
the dictation table again. Whoever might be
the subject of this weary preface, it was she who
was associated with its successful progress, and
instinctively Agnes knew that on the earliest possible
opportunity she herself would be asked to resign the
pen to an apter co-operator.

And not less than with Pamela's convalescence he was frowningly pre-occupied with Timothy's stories and Timothy's presence in the house. The idea that there was a taint in the work-room, owing to his having scribbled his stories here, which had at first presented itself as a fanciful notion to Alan's mind, began to take root there. Timothy's lively presence at dinner and at breakfast in the morning no longer diverted and refreshed him : he looked at the young man with sidelong glances, and a dry " Very humorous, I am sure," was all his response to some little story that had set Agnes laughing. . . . Then seeing through Tim's eyes, and perceiving through Tim's perception, she noticed that this altered attitude on Alan's part was not escaping him. Agnes and he never met alone now, or, so she fancied, Tim would have had some communication to make to her, but in the morning Alan would be down to breakfast before herself, and in the evening, when Tim returned, she would be closeted with her husband in the work-room, and soon after dinner returned there again till bedtime. Three or four times, perhaps, in the course of the evening her eyes and Tim's would meet, and some conjectured question flashed to and fro between them. It was hardly perhaps a question : it was more the mutual asseveration of the existence of each to the other. That alone came forth clear and radiant out of the lowering cloud that seemed to have settled down on them all, so that they moved separately and unseen of each other about the house, each girt about with sundering mists.

Three or four days went by like this, and then one evening while they sat, all three of them, in the drawing-room with coffee and cigarettes, the end of the situation came. There had been a silence in the room, which Agnes expected that Alan would soon break, by asking whether she was ready to resume

their work. Tim was sitting balancing his spoon on
the edge of his coffee-cup, quite intent apparently on
the feat. Then he raised his eyes, gave that one
radiant glance at Agnes, and spoke to Alan.

" I have found to-day just the rooms which suit me,
Cousin Alan," he said, " and I have taken them from
to-morrow. You and Agnes have been absolutely
delightful to me : I never knew that there were such
kind and hospitable people. I have enjoyed myself
immensely here : you have both made me feel so completely at home. I hate going, but it has got to be
done, and so to-morrow morning I shall pack up my
trunks and settle into my new quarters. They suit me
so well that I mustn't risk losing them, and they would
certainly have been snapped up if I hadn't engaged
them."

Alan quenched the end of his cigarette.

" My dear Timothy," he said. " This is all very
sudden. But I know, I know : naturally you want a
little corner of your own. We have enjoyed having
you so much : the month that you have been here
seems to have passed like a flash. Yes . . .
Agnes, dear, I know you feel with me. Timothy
has been a most welcome and delightful guest."

Agnes knew that this must come soon, and she had
thought she was prepared for it. But when it came,
she was aware that no amount of anticipation had
made it real to her. The announcement of it,
the sudden mental picture of what the house would
be without him, though for those last days each had
been so withdrawn from the other, was like some bewildering blow. She turned to Alan to answer him,
but Alan seemed unreal and phantasmal. There was
nothing she could say to him, for he would not understand. . . . In a sort of desperation she turned in
her chair and looked at Tim. He was real enough :
nothing else perhaps was real.

"O Tim," she said, "I am sorry you are going. . . ."

Surely this was one of the charades of which Dora had spoken. His reply, too, was a speech not of his own at all, but put into his mouth for the purpose of the play.

"Indeed I am, too," he said. "It has been delightful here. You have both been so enormously kind."

"And your rooms?" she asked. "Where are they? You must let me come and see them some time."

"Ah do! You and Cousin Alan must come and have tea with me as soon as the preface is done, and he will grant himself an afternoon off."

Agnes laughed.

"I never heard such a cautious invitation," she said. "He is careful, is he not, Alan, not to tell us where we are to come to."

"Oh, I forgot. St. James's Place. 3A."

"That will be nearer your work," she said. "You can have an extra ten minutes in bed. That appeals to you, Tim: that's why you want to leave us."

"You've hit it," said Tim.

Alan raised himself from the low chair where he had been sitting.

"I see there is no persuading Timothy to put off his departure," he said. "There is an alacrity about Timothy to-night, consequent on his determination. Ah, my dear Timothy, I am only joking. But it is half-past nine, I see, and if you are ready for a short spell of work, dear Agnes, I am ready also. I have just one note to answer, a reply to poor Bristowe, who wants to know when 'The Tyro' and its little preface will be finished. I will write it downstairs, and thus I shall not disturb our work-table with extraneous matter. It will be an affair of three minutes. I will be with you directly."

With his exit the curtain came down on the charade, and the two who were left stood side by side, on the hearthrug ; Agnes leaned an arm on the mantelpiece : Tim put straight a small bronze statuette that was out of place. Over the fireplace was a broad strip of mirror, and thus, though neither of them looked at the other, their eyes met in their reflection there.

" I had to go," said Tim, turning round towards her. "We both felt that, didn't we ? I went to see the rooms this afternoon, and took them straight away from to-morrow. We all knew that Cousin Alan didn't want me any more."

Agnes's reticence gave way. It was not as if she was telling him anything new : she but felt the imperative need of expressing herself, of putting in definite words what he and she were aware of to the exclusion of all else.

" But I did, Tim," she said.

" Bless you for it. Good Lord ! to-morrow evening, when you won't be there ! What's to be done ? "

The reticence, the repression had slid from her face like a mask removed, and she shewed him the radiant youth of it. The years of habit and service dropped from it like a patina consumed by sudden incandescence. The ardent presence of a girl was by him, in whose eyes had lately dawned the sense of womanhood.

" What's to be done ? " he repeated. His voice was harsh and peremptory, but all the fierceness of it slid over her, like a wind in the tree-tops, whispering there but not touching her.

" Nothing's to be done," she said quietly. " We've got to endure. . . . No, not endure quite. . . . We've got to be kind, Tim, to be decent . . . to give thanks, Tim."

" What for ? Give thanks ? "

" Yes. I for you, and you for me. We're here :
we're living."

His face softened at that. " When will you come
and see me ? " he asked.

" O Tim, not yet," she said. " And don't come
here just yet. Leave me alone a little. . . .
Siegfried : do you remember that night ? The
wonder : the joy. . . ."

That made his eyes dance : next moment they were
stricken into a listening immobility again.

" There's Cousin Alan coming upstairs," he said.

" Yes, Tim. Look at me once. . . . Yes, like
that."

She laid her hand on his arm, and without turning
again went to the door.

" I'm ready for you, Alan," she said.

BOOK III

BOOK III

CHAPTER I

IT was the morning after the return of Alan and Agnes to London from their holiday at Littlestone, and, according to immemorial usage he had gone directly after breakfast to the work-room, there to sort and set in order the sheaves of notes and observations with which these weeks had furnished him. They had intended not to come back until quite the end of September, but the continued atrocity of the weather had caused them to forego their last week of seaside residence. Day after day a gale from the south-west had driven cold aspersions of rain against the windows, all night the house on the exposed sea-front had quaked and shuddered at the blasts, and Alan's observations on natural objects had mainly been confined to the effects of squalls streaking across the grey sea, and the tattoo of showers against ill-fitting panes and sashes. Besides, he had in his head the scheme for a new book, and for the making of that he wanted the familiar environment. Usually he was content, except for these gleanings of notes, to lie fallow during the weeks of his holidays: this year, however, there was some goading restlessness in his brain that made him eager to be at work again. He was conscious, as he often told Agnes, of a seething of material there, which must be drawn off. A further cause for his unsettled, unholiday mood might perhaps be found in the fact that two publications of his were imminent, the new book over the end of which Pamela had been so useful, and the revised and prefaced edition of ' The

Tyro,' which Alan had begun to dictate to her when
the influenza laid her low. Hardly any progress had
been made with it, when once more she slid into
Agnes's place again in the work-room.

They had stayed in London till nearly the end of
August, for an unprecedented procedure had been
adopted over this new book. Instead of a second
dictation of it, followed by the double revision of it in
typewritten manuscript, Alan had sent the first
version straight to the printers, and all the month,
after the preface to ' The Tyro ' was finished, he had
been passing the proofs for press. The innovation
was wholly due to Pamela : she had convinced him
that this first draft was a gem, flawless and faceted :
that further work on it could only mar its freshness
and dim instead of polishing it. Her enthusiasm had
infected him, and he believed that in ' Ages Past ' he
had risen at last to his high-water mark. Pamela
had revalued that ' Your high-water mark, Master ? '
she had said ' *The* high-water mark I Agnes, dear,
can we never convince the Master what he has
achieved ? Oh . . ." and she gave a beatific sigh.

Without convicting herself of malice Agnes could
not avoid finding another cause for Pamela's eagerness that ' Ages Past ' should appear now instead of
(in the ordinary course of procedure) some six months
later. ' Glory for Pamela ' was at the root of it, for
she had, without any figure of speech, annexed Alan.
She controlled and inspired him, and it would be a
triumph complete and decisive if under the new constitution he put forth without delay this supreme
flower. Ever since she had been admitted to the
work-room on the night of the birthday party she had
trumpetted forth the splendour of Alan's genius;
many were the luncheon and dinner-parties on which
she had proclaimed both it and the fact that the privilege of taking down the sentences of the new book,

as they fell from his lips, was hers, and without doubt
it was she who had supplied to the press a series of
little paragraphs telling the world how ' Ages Past '
was getting on, and noting that he had been very hard
at work over the revision of ' The Tyro ' at Mrs.
Probyn's country cottage at Playden.   But the world
would not go on indefinitely being interested in these
preliminary puffs.   Her incessant declarations of
faith demanded the justifying works, and the narration of her own part in it might, if continued for six
months more, conceivably become tedious.   It was,
therefore, the part of wisdom not to try the patience
of the world too severely.   So, as soon as she had
recovered from her indisposition, she had flown back
to London and day after day throughout August had
read his proofs to him, taking down at the dictation-
table his corrections and insertions.   The preface to
' The Tyro ' which had gone so haltingly was speeded
up and finished, and according to the arrangements
suggested by her and accepted by Mr. Bristowe, the
two books would appear on the same day.   Not till
everything was settled, and the last batch of proofs
gone to the printer, had the indefatigable one suffered
them to go for their holiday, and she had seen them
off at the station.

Agnes wondered at her own emotional indifference
to Pamela's intrusion in affairs which had so long
been in her own province.   She grudged her none of
those arduous hours which she spent in the work-
room, nor yet the triumphant visage which emerged
when the day's work was done, nor the sense of great
things accomplished with which she inspired Alan.
Nor did she grudge her the future triumph which
would be hers, if under her stimulus and appreciation
Alan should have proved to have written something
of first-rate quality, which should restore him to
that eminence in the world of letters which had

once been his. Whatever social splendour and prestige might come to Pamela, she had certainly deserved it all, and if only Alan was satisfied with the reception of his work, nothing else mattered. Agnes's own office with regard to him through all these years had been to secure him the environment he needed, and if this environment implied the effacing of herself and the permission to another to take her place, she effaced and permitted now without a single emotional reservation. But this period of waiting for the publication of the books, whole-heartedly as she hoped for their success, had not the quality of suspense about it. What she waited for with suspense was the appearance not of Alan's work but of Tim's.

She had been making a housewife's tour this morning, and had lingered in the room which had been his. Just outside it the board had creaked, and she let herself imagine that he had entered the room with her. She had not seen it since the day she had arranged it for his occupation. Then it had been dead, waiting for the life of its tenant to be breathed into it; now that life was there, even though he had been gone so long, but it was in some trance of suspended animation, partaking exactly of the quality of her own emotion. It was no ghost which haunted it, but someone very much alive, though entranced and not to be communicated with. Tim haunted the whole house like this: he had slipped into his empty chair at dinner last night; he had been perched on the arm of the sofa behind her afterwards; the whole place was continually instinct with him. To-morrow, no doubt, he would be here in corporal presence, for at Alan's bidding she had written to him, asking him to dine with them, for it would be Sunday, and no work would be in progress afterwards. But he could hardly be more real than he was now in his empty room. . . .

There was Alan's step on the landing outside the work-room, and she ran down to see if he was inclined for a garden-stroll before lunch.   He had that air of alacrity which betokened a good morning's work.

"A brisk stroll, dear?" he said.   "Are you prepared to accompany me on a brisk stroll?   Really, I think the continued rough weather at Littlestone was a benign device, instead of being, as we thought, a mere piece of malignity designed to wreck our holiday.   It drove us, did it not, back to our work again, and though that seemed naughty of it . . . aha, I see you have pierced my secret, dear."

It was not very hard.

"You have had a good morning's work," she said. "If the weather had not been so bad, we should still be idling at Littlestone."

"You have divined me, dear," he said.   "But I doubt"—he fitted his gloves neatly to his fingers— "but I doubt whether you have divined the utmost of my news.   What"—the gloves were fitted now and the coat-collar adjusted—"what would you say was my utmost achievement in these first days of the conception of a new story?   Guess high, my Agnes."

"Half is planned already," she ventured.

"Guess higher yet," he said.

"Three-quarters——"

"It is wicked of me to keep you in suspense," he said.   "I must have you without pause a sharer in my felicity.   All!!   I see my story from beginning to end.   I shall at once begin to plot the chapters. It came to me with a miraculous clearness; Pamela will have told you how I had a similar visitation, vastly inferior in scope, about our preface.   But now (a thing which, as you can testify, has never happened before to us) I saw as I meditated and pondered this morning, the whole lucid perspective of my tale.   I am not sure, indeed, that I shall not want you to be at

the dictation-table this evening to take down the first
few pages. Miraculous, is it not, that I should have
had already the vision for which sometimes I grope
for weeks, clear and unshadowed. But my dear, I
must not raise your hopes too high. It may easily be
that I shall find myself not sufficiently prepared to
dictate to-day. We will, anyhow, take our shorter
walk this afternoon, which will give me time for a
little more preparation before tea, and if you find me
silent and *distrait,* you must know that the brew, the
yeast, is rising. . . . Now let us talk on other
subjects. I feel that a complete distraction will benefit
me most. Pamela now or Timothy. . . . Let us
speak of Pamela or Timothy. Poor Blewitt, too!
We must be very magnanimous about poor Blewitt
and his little carpings; we must ask poor Blewitt to
come and dine some Sunday soon. Poor Blewitt's
face will be a fine study when he hears that ' Ages
Past ' and the revised ' Tyro ' appear on the same
day, and that I am already deep in a new plot. There
is a little spirit left in the old horse which he would
fain have seen turned out to grass.''

Some goose-flesh of misgiving shivered over Agnes.
Alan had never been so jovially optimistic about his
work. It might be—she prayed that it would prove
so—that his elation would be justified, but she recognised that it sprang not from his own cool estimate
but from Pamela's asseverations and enthusiasms, and
that these in turn sprang not from her literary appreciation but from the vigorous stock of ' glory for
Pamela.' What would be the effect on Alan if these
high hopes and splendours were not realized ? How
would his growing eagerness for recognition take it ?
But there was no use in indulging in speculations of
disaster : she must screw herself up to his level.

" You have never been so full of ideas and vigour,"
she said.

" No : I think I can fairly join with you in that,"
he said. " I owe it, largely at any rate, to you two
dear conspirators. Pamela has been a wonderful tonic
to my powers. You have noticed that, dear, yourself,
have you not ? That is not news to you ? "

Agnes had no need to call on her cordiality. It was
all ready.

" Indeed it is not," she said. " I shall never forget
how Pamela came to the rescue over the end of ' Ages
Past.' I was as grateful to her as you."

This seemed to make it easier for him to say what
she half guessed was in his mind.

" You dear, unselfish Agnes ! " he said. " I am
glad to hear that from your own lips. In the future,
I take it that you will have no sense of being out in the
cold, if kind Pamela often scribbles away for me at
the new dictation which I hope may begin this very
evening. I find rare stimulus in her enthusiasm for
my work."

He paused a moment.

" Besides, dear, have I the right, as I sometimes ask
myself, to usurp your life in the way I am only too
prone to do ? Out of your exquisite unselfishness you
are ready—do I not know it ?—to devote your whole
time and energies to me, but that does not free me
from the responsibility of allowing such a sacrifice.
Pamela rejoices to take part of that burden off you, to
give you more freedom for living your own life."

It flashed through Agnes's mind as a certainty that
Pamela had suggested to him that he should make
some sort of speech like that. Coming from Alan, it
reeked of insincerity : he would not after fifteen years
of not allowing only, but of taking for granted the said
sacrifice, have suddenly remitted and forbidden it, if
Pamela had not put it to him like that, nor would he
have accepted the suggestion if, when he gave her

this tardy manumission, he had not got another to perform her service with greater stimulus to him.

She could not quite let this insincerity pass. She was quite willing to give place to Pamela, but she could not, like a child, be served with this unconvincing sugar-plum.

"My dear, we must look at it a little straighter than that," she said. "You find that Pamela's co-operation makes your work go more prosperously : that is why you want it. I accept that, Alan. I accept and welcome it. But we must be clear about the reason. It is what I have stated."

This seemed to trouble him : his voice rose to that shriller quavering pitch which indicated agitation.

"You contrive to put me in an odiously ungrateful light," he said.

"No, dear. I do nothing of the kind. It would be I who was odious if I made you out to be ungrateful. There is no such thought in my head."

It was clear that he was thinking not of her at all : what occupied him was the justification of himself.

"You must make allowance for the sensibilities of an artist," he said. "I cannot help feeling the difference of atmosphere, while I am dictating to her. She is alert and appreciative, and that encourages me. But of late and increasingly, Agnes, I have felt that my work is not of that unique and supreme importance to you."

"But it is," she said. "It is for that reason that I welcome and delight in the fact that she suits you so well. It would be very wrong of me to do otherwise. I quite realize that to do work like yours, you must be exquisitely sensitive to atmosphere. For instance, it irritated you to know that Tim had been writing in your work-room. I saw that, and I regretted that I had allowed it. His presence grew unsettling to you also. Oh, my dear, I am not quite blind."

He saw a tribute to his personality in this. His voice resumed its ordinary tones.

"Yes, that is so," he said. "One cannot escape the defects of one's quality. One cannot be robust and sensitive. . . . You understand me so well, dear. . . . You have quite reassured and comforted me."

"That's good. Now, tell me what plans you have made for the dictation of the new book. Remember that I am one of the conspirators, and have a right to know them."

He slipped his arm into hers, symbolizing their unity.

"Well, dear, it was Pamela's intention to come up to London again at the end of the month," he said. "She expected that we should be back then, and meant to hold herself in readiness to help me, and relieve you of some of the burden I lay on you. But I sent her a little line this morning to say that the wretched weather had sent us scuttling home again, and I shall not be surprised if she arrives earlier than she originally proposed—"

Agnes laughed.

"Nor shall I," she said. "I shall be very much surprised if she doesn't."

"Well, we shall see. In any case, dear, there will be a surprise for Pamela, when she finds that we have made a beginning already on our new book. She will rejoice at that. . . . But we must finish our stroll, and get home."

There was a postal delivery of parcels going on, as they walked back, and Agnes saw that a package was left at their door a few moments before they re-entered. It lay on the hall table, a book clearly, and she guessed what it might be, for Tim had told her that his stories would be published to-day, and that a copy should be sent her. Alan was in advance of her, and he took it up.

"A parcel from Bristowe, I see," he said, looking at the label. "An advance copy, no doubt, of 'The Tyro' or 'Ages Past.' Ah, it is for you, dear. Good Bristowe. He has been very nimble about getting it bound, but I wonder why he has not sent both books: this packet clearly contains only one. Give me the pleasure of undoing it for you, and writing your dear name in it. You, I know, would cut the string in your impatience! Which do you guess it is, Agnes? Which would you prefer it to be? 'The Tyro' or 'Ages Past'? I shall tease you."

Already he was busy unravelling the knot, so that he might preserve this precious morsel of string for his store. She felt that she must prepare him for finding neither 'The Tyro' nor 'Ages Past' inside.

"I think it may be another book altogether," she said. "Tim's book of stories is out to-day; he said he was sending me a copy."

The knot yielded, and he folded back the brown-paper covering.

"Yes, I see you are right," he said. "'Cricket and other stories, by Timothy Graham.' . . . Cricket and other stories. . . ."

He opened it and paused at the title-page.

"Dedicated I see to you," he said. "You had not told me that."

"But I didn't know it myself," said she, looking over his shoulder. "How dear of Tim."

"You do not find it an impertinence that he should dedicate his little stories to you without consulting you?" he asked.

"Indeed, no. Tim couldn't be impertinent. It is charming of him."

He handed the book to her.

" I will not keep it from you," he said.   " You
will be anxious to read it, I am sure."

Agnes determined that any attitude of Alan's
towards Tim's book should not spoil her own pride
and pleasure in it. She had always stood between his
sensitiveness and the jars of human existence, but she
had no intention of sacrificing her own honesty to
what was sensitiveness gone sour. It was sweet to
her that Tim should have dedicated to her the work
for which she had so keen an appreciation, and she
meant to preserve that sweetness and that appreciation
from all taint. Had these stories, as the work of an
unknown author, been casually brought to her notice
she would still have reserved to herself the right to
admire them, but Tim was the author. . . . She
did not want to discuss them with Alan, or uphold
them, but she took him at his ironic word, and showed
herself anxious to read them. It was clear, too, that
he had an uneasy curiosity about them : he turned
over a page or two after lunch, and again, when they
returned from their walk, she found him dipping into
them, and though he put the book down with a shrug
and the comment, " Poor Tim : not a sign of workmanship or literary taste," it was evident that there
was something in his mind beyond condemnation for
their lack of quality. To merely incompetent work he
would have been indifferent : there was something
here which made him seek for cause of disapproval :
something which made him anxious to decry.

" It is curious to me, dear," he said, " that you
should think highly of poor Tim's first effort.   I
should have thought your sense of style, your knowledge of right construction would have led you to
agree with me.   I am puzzled."

" But, Alan, why think about it at all ? " she said ;
" why should we expect to agree ?   What does it
matter ? "

He got up.

"It seems to throw a light on certain things," he said. "I cannot, for instance, help remembering that you once failed to follow my dictation altogether. It was clear it did not interest you. Supposing I had been dictating to you one of these little tales, would you have had a similar lapse of attention?"

"My dear, that is an unfair argument," she said. "You cannot compare Tim's work with yours at all. They have nothing to do with each other. But if you choose to remind me of that, for how many hours all told, against one inattention, have I been alert and accurate? It is not fair."

He pondered this a moment.

"We will think no more about it," he said. "I must dismiss it from my mind, or I shall not be able to concentrate on the new task. Now, dear, are you ready for our dictation?"

She forced herself away from the thought of his ungenerosity. "Ever so ready," she said. "And what an event, Alan, that you should be prepared to dictate so soon."

Agnes was prepared to keep her mind on the curb, not trusting to the habit of her hand to follow him, for surely it would tug at her, eager to bolt with her. She was environed and occupied with all that symbolized to her the shackled existence enclosed within the impregnable walls of Alan's egoism. He resented her peeping through the grated square of window: he resented above all the light which Tim flashed on her from it. Alan saw but little of it; was blind to its intenser beam, for that, love, was outside his spectrum. But what he saw of it he resented. . . . Once, years ago, her mind had fallen in love with his, but that was the height of her full tide for him, and far down had it ebbed: now once again her mind had found its home in Tim's, but that was the

low tide, just beginning to flow. Up it crept over
long stretches of dry sand, vivifying and bracing her,
so that the trivial round which now encircled her
again, with its service of ministration, was somehow
ennobled. So fine a thing could not but infiltrate
the drynesses and tediums with pity and tenderness. . . . She might let her mind run on
a loose rein, after all : there was no need to
check or hold it well in hand, for very willingly,
with eagerness for the success of Alan's work, it
let itself be harnessed to the familiar burden, which
now ran lightly behind her, and now was mired
in difficulties. She saw herself no longer as mounted
on some fiery steed, which she must ever control, for
of its own accord it backed and was buckled into the
shafts. For all its fire, there was its task. . . .

The work did not go well : there were innumerable
erasures of sentences begun and cancelled again.
Alan had planned to open his first chapter in an
environment of squally weather, such as they had
experienced at Littlestone, and there was a fat sheaf
of notes and observations about the grey sea and the
sharp-flung showers and the boisterous wind.
Generally, his handling of such material was deft and
easy : he painted such pictures with a swift, unerring
touch. But now he made stumbling and uncertain
strokes, and she could guess what ailed him. No
doubt their disagreement about Tim's stories con-
tributed to his unsettlement, but it was chiefly, so she
felt, that the Pamela-tonic was absent. She tried to
compound a similar elixir : she made appreciative
comments on his phrases, she held herself alert and
appreciative, but without doubt she had not got
Pamela's recipe.

" We are making no progress at all," he said at
length, " and, if you will excuse my saying so, your
comments and encouragements only interrupt my train

of thought. If you will just confine yourself, dear, as you are accustomed to do, to taking down what I dictate, you will serve me best."

But her silence was no more efficacious than her applause, and soon he laid the paper-knife down.

"Perhaps I expected too much of myself," he said, "in thinking that one day's meditation would enable me to make a beginning. We will abandon the dictation, and I shall devote the rest of my evening to a further digestion and assimilation. Perhaps a little quiet tune on the piano would assist me. If it would not weary you, will you indulge me?"

This proved equally effectless, and after one more trial he gave up the attempt.

"I really do not know what is wrong," he said. "I do not feel ill: my brain appears to me to be perfectly active. Indeed, it is unusually so: the thoughts crowd into it, but before I can take firm hold of one, another twitches me away. There are outside disturbances, too. I find myself wondering what reception will await our 'Ages Past' and the revised 'Tyro.' As you know, such considerations are wholly alien to me. Let me see, to-morrow is Sunday: perhaps if I felt in the mood we might make an exception and have an evening of work."

"Tim is dining with us," she said.

"Ah, yes. I forgot. Dear me, Timothy seems to crop up at every turn. First it is his stories, then it is his dining with us. I will see how I feel to-morrow, and if I can reasonably anticipate a fruitful evening, I daresay it would suit Timothy just as well to dine with us the Sunday after instead."

"It is putting him off at rather short notice," said Agnes.

"I do not think we can weigh so small a readjustment of Timothy's plans against the prospect of my making a start on my new book. But we will settle that to-morrow. It is seven o'clock already. Would you kindly see if the post has arrived, dear ? "

This restlessness of mind was unlike Alan : usually when his work went ill, he would tranquillize himself and concentrate upon it instead of darting about to distracting topics, and Agnes found herself pondering this as a physician might ponder some symptom, new but not necessarily disquieting, in his patient. . . . There were two letters for him, which she brought him, and one for herself, evidently from Tim. She lingered below to read this.

" You will have received the silly book by me," he wrote, "and I hope you don't mind the dedication. I had to dedicate it to you, you see, because it's yours. . . . Looking forward frightfully to to-morrow. I have persuaded myself that you told me dinner was at 7.30 not 8, so I shall come then. So if you happen to dress rather earlier than usual, why——
"Yours,
"T."

One glance, as at a picture, gave her the contents of those few scratched lines, but she could not throw the sheet away. Upstairs Alan was seated at his table, frowning over the couple of pages of erasures that represented their evening's work.

" Not half a dozen sentences left," he said. " I do not remember so barren an evening. . . . Ah, thank you. One, I see, from Bristowe. . . . Let me see what Bristowe says. Yes : both of my books will appear on Monday. Advance copies have already been sent out, and your's, dear, your special copies will reach us then. And—and now what has our Pamela got for us ? That is good news again : she is coming up to town on Monday. She purposes to fly round—is that not like her ?—to fly round in the afternoon to see if she can make herself useful.

. . . I think, dear Agnes, we will play a little trick
on Pamela. We will tear out our two pages of
erasures, just copying in the few sentences which we
have passed, and conceal this afternoon's failure from
her. Who knows? By Monday we may have something worth her perusal. We must concentrate : we
must not let our thoughts grow slippery. We must
get fast hold of them. . . . And advance copies
of my two books, Bristowe says, have already been
sent out. Perhaps we shall have a few words from
Blewitt to-morrow in his column of literary talk.
Considering what enthusiastic welcome poor Blewitt
gave to 'The Tyro,' on its first appearance, he can
hardly fail to sound a genial 'salve' at its re-entry."

"Surely he will," said Agnes.

"I think we may count on it," he said. "Then
there is work in 'Ages Past' which I feel sure Blewitt
will appreciate. It would be pleasant to convert poor
Blewitt again after his very naughty apostacy. I
confess that such a conversion would gratify me. And
I cherish high hopes of it."

Agnes felt a qualm of anxiety. There was nothing,
she thought, less likely than that Mr. Blewitt should
see the error of his naughty apostacy, and she figured
herself as peering into a doubtful if not a dangerous
darkness, when she imagined the result on Alan of
his unrepentance.

"But it won't matter to you what Mr. Blewitt
happens to say," she said.

Alan laughed without gaiety or conviction.

"Assuredly not, dear," he said. "I hope our
status is not determined in poor Blewitt's little
analytical laboratory. Ultimately, of course, Blewitt's
appreciation and disdain have no more stability than
thistledown, but for the immediate present one would
never deny that his word has weight. However, I
do not think we need occupy ourselves with such

speculations. Our Olympian will declare himself to-morrow.''

Agnes was first in the breakfast-room next morning, and hastily opened the copy of the 'Sunday Magazine.' There in its accustomed place was Blewitt's signed article, entitled 'The Mantle of Elijah,' and extending as she saw at her first skimming glance to half-a-dozen pages. . . . Then there flitted across her eyes the name 'Mr. Graham' and again and again 'Mr. Graham.' Still in this first impression she was arrested by a word here and a phrase there, 'a masterpiece of subtle observation,' 'firm, true touch,' 'exquisite . . .' 'agonizing.' . . . Simultaneously she saw also near the beginning of the first paragraph 'a new star in our literary firmament,' and found herself wondering what 'The Mantle of Elijah' meant.

And then in a blink of perception she saw and understood. The whole article was devoted to Tim's book of stories. Blewitt had let himself go, and poured out a torrent of unstinted admiration. There was, of course, the usual allusion to Robert Louis Stevenson, but now it was to say that the Mantle of Elijah, of him who alone of English authors was perfect master of the art of the *Conte,* had fallen on the shoulders of Mr. Graham. Indeed, Blewitt was guilty of a new apostacy, for he permitted himself to wonder whether even R.L.S. could have written so masterly and original a tale as 'Cricket' after which the volume was named. R.L.S. confessedly had played 'the sedulous ape' to others, but here was a star that owed not one flicker of its light to any external sun. 'Long have our eyes wearied themselves with scrutiny,' wrote Mr. Blewitt, 'to see whether the agony of war would prove the birth-pangs of any splendid artistic achievement, and to-day unto us a child is born . . .'

Agnes's eyes travelled swiftly down the pages of panegyric: she had completely forgotten about Alan, for there was no room in her heart for anything beyond exultant rapture on behalf of Tim. They leaped up again to the head of each new page and skimmed on their joyful way, when suddenly they stumbled on Alan's name. "We believe that Mr. Timothy Graham is a cousin of Mr. Alan Graham," so wrote Blewitt, "whose gracefully-conceived tales have in their time diverted the leisure of so many readers. By the same post that brought us the first-fruit of Mr. T. Graham's work, we received a copy of Mr. Alan Graham's 'The Tyro' (a book that long ago attracted some attention), embellished with a voluminous preface, and also a copy of a new work of his of which the title, appropriately enough, is 'Ages Past.' The space at our disposal to-day is not sufficient, nor yet has been the time at our disposal sufficient to do more than note the titles. To-day a superb, an unrivalled Tyro . . ."

There was Alan's step on the floor outside, and an aching pity stabbed deep into her. He entered.

"Aha, dear Agnes," he said. "You are ahead of me, I see: You are first on the trail of our good Blewitt. Is he apostate still, or has he dipped his spoon in the old incense? Ha! 'The Mantle of Elijah' . . . 'Mr. Graham' . . ."

Agnes was conscious only of a complete emotional blank as Alan took up the paper. She felt herself only watching as he read.

"He does not write about 'The Tyro' and 'Ages Past,'" she heard herself saying. "He—— "

He interrupted her.

"I see," he said. "That little book of

Timothy's . . ." and he took the magazine across
to the window.

Agnes made tea, numbly acquiescent in this
emotional blank, wondering, also numbly, what would
break it, and what had become of her exultant rapture
for Tim's sake and her aching pity for Alan. She
heard the rustle of the page as he turned it, and the
rustle of the boiling water in the silver tea-kettle. The
silence of that interminable pause sang in her ears.
Then from behind her came the creak of his step, and
he sat down at the table.

" A morning such as we had no example of at Littlestone," he said. " Real September weather at last.
If it will not tire you, I think we must take our longer
walk this afternoon."

" That will be nice," said she. " Your tea, Alan."

" Thank you. Now about our arrangements
to-day. I feel much refreshed and braced by this
change, and, for exception, I shall go on with my
preparation this morning, and we will hope for a
good bout of work to-night. You mentioned, I think,
that Timothy was dining with us, but I shall be
obliged to you if, when you have finished breakfast,
you would invoke the wizard, and suggest that he
gives us the pleasure of seeing him some other day."

Agnes had nothing but assent for this. Nothing
seemed so inconceivable as that Tim and Alan should
meet to-day.

" I have finished," she said. " I will do it now."

Alan stopped her.

" Yet I hardly know," he said. " We shall get
our first dictation before he comes, and after dinner,
if I am in the mood, Timothy will not mind our
shutting ourselves up again. We have often done that
before, when he was staying with us. We must not
make a stranger of Timothy. Why, after all, should
we put him off ? "

She could read his mind now. The pride which would not allow him to say a word about Blewitt's article would not permit him to show any sign of recognition of its existence. To put Timothy off could be construed into such a sign. Last night it was she who demurred to this being done : now she supported it.

"Tim will understand," she said, "that you want an evening of quiet work. Another Sunday, no doubt, will suit him equally well."

"No, dear, on consideration I cannot see why dear Timothy should not come to-night," he said. "Let the wizard remain uninvoked."

Throughout the day he made not the faintest allusion to Blewitt's article, but his silence, so far from reassuring Agnes, disquieted her, for by it, as by nothing else, she could estimate his sense of outrage. Had he been annoyed merely or moderately disturbed, she knew that it would have been continually on his lips, but so profoundly did he feel it, that nothing except a complete ignoring of it could meet the case. All morning he shut himself into the work-room, but when she called him to lunch, his packet of notes was still untouched. But he had taken the 'Sunday Magazine' in with him, and she heard him lay it down as she entered. Had he been reading and re-reading it since breakfast? The nimbleness with which on her entry he threw it aside and took up one of his little sheaves of notes convinced her that it was so, and her heart ached for him. But he still desired to. say nothing of it; indeed, he spoke at once of something else. . . . She felt that in the ingredients that went to the analysis of his silence, there was his knowledge of her admiration for Tim's work : her sympathy therefore was no use to him : he did not want it.

Tim came at the earlier hour which he had named,

but they had only a few minutes together, for Alan had kept her at work till it was nearly time to dress. As if Blewitt's article had acted on him as a challenge, he had been unusually fluent to-night, and there would certainly be a fine surprise for Pamela next day. He had lingered behind her for a little, and when she came down to the drawing-room there lay on the table the ' Sunday Magazine ' open at the page on which was printed ' The Mantle of Elijah.' She did not see it at once, for there was Tim to be greeted. Once again, as when first she had read that, she was oblivious to all but him.

" Ah, my dear, how delightful to see you," she said. " And the book, Tim, and your dear dedication, and, oh Tim, the mantle of Elijah ! But the dedication pleased me most. Have you seen the ' Mantle of Elijah ' ? "

Tim pointed to the magazine that lay there.

" Haven't I ? " he said. " It's a delirious dream, and I'm terrified of awaking. But the dedication pleased me most."

" Ah, but we mustn't leave that about," she said. " Did you bring it to shew me in case I hadn't seen it ? Put it away somewhere."

" I didn't bring it," he said. " I found it there."

She frowned, puzzled.

" Leave it there, then," she said. " Alan must have put it there. I think I see why."

" Tell me," he said.

" Yes, in a moment," she said. " But I must speak of you and the book first. Tim, it's utterly glorious. I gasped with pleasure. You've vaulted on to a platform which it might have taken years of perseverance to climb. I've been right about your stories all along : I knew I was right, and I've never been so proud. It's you, you—— "

She still held his hand in hers, but it was not of the

book that either thought now. Their eyes sought and found each other, lingering and breaking away and returning. The fire of her youth long choked and huddled broke into flame.

" I thank God for you, my dear," she said.

Then she dropped his hand.

" We must get back to earth," she said. " The book, you know, and Alan."

" I know, I wondered if I had better send an excuse. But—but I couldn't."

" He read it," she said, " and he has not said a single word about it. That's how he takes it. He minds it too much to speak of it. I don't suppose he will say a word about it to you. He, too, was thinking of putting you off, but that would have shewn he took some notice of it. He is ignoring it more completely this way. But I'm not easy about him. Can it be good to repress like that ? It's out of pride : it's a supreme egoism."

" Has he been working to-day ? " asked Tim.

" Yes, quite a good spell. My dear, forgive me if we have a dreadful evening."

He smiled.

" Why are you to be forgiven ? " he asked. " What have you done ? "

" I don't know. That's the worst of it. I am so absolutely helpless. I can do nothing for him, and that's so horribly sad. Pamela is the only one who can ; and thank goodness, she will be here to-morrow."

That amazing comprehension of Tim filled the space between them. It surrounded her with its loving tenderness that healed because it understood.

" I wish I hadn't written those yarns," he said. " The fact of them makes it more difficult for you."

" But they're part of you," she said. " We can't spare them."

" They're yours," he said, and paused.
" Like the rest of me," he added.
She looked at him with radiant candour.
" I know, my dear," she said.

Those little clipped unemotional sentences did their
work. They brought the two together again above
instead of below the whole problem of Alan. Agnes
felt herself no longer in the gloom of its shadow : she
looked upon it as from some sunlit perch, where,
warmed and invigorated instead of being numbed and
chilled, she could study it and contrive for its mitiga-
tion and dispersal. Tim's presence gave her that sunlight, and she must use this evening well, so that in
the days of shadow and cold which most surely
awaited her, she could use the memory of this truer
vision. . . . She was eagerly at Alan's disposal
for all such service as he required of her : Tim's love
seemed to have kindled her tenderness for her
husband.

A few minutes only passed before he joined them.
In his hand he carried a copy of Tim's book, which
he still held as he greeted him, so that it should be
seen by both of them.

" Charming to see you, my dear Timothy," he said.
" We are lucky to find you so soon after our return.
It is a very quiet evening to which you have come,
but we thought, dear Agnes and I thought, that you
used not to find our quiet evenings so intolerable.
Eh, dear Agnes ? "

" I was delighted to come, Cousin Alan," said he,
" and all the better for there being no-one else here."

Alan gently deposited the book beside the copy of
the magazine which contained ' The Mantle of Elijah.'
Even if there had been any doubt as to the intention

of his policy before, there could be none now. He ignored, he assumed a glaring oblivion. . . .

"Aha, I wonder if I can take that literally," he said. "I suspect that a gay party would have been more to your mind. But you must make the best of us, and you must perhaps even allow Agnes and me to spend an hour at our dictation after dinner. You will find some book, no doubt; you might even care to glance at the last duplicate proof of my preface to 'The Tyro.' It comes out to-morrow: good Bristowe ushers it into the world to-morrow."

Throughout dinner Alan abounded in neutral trivialities, and every moment the whole situation grew more tensely unnatural.

"Our dear Pamela returns to-morrow," he said. "So kind and amiable. She has quite associated herself with my dictations, and Agnes—eh, dear?—will have a little relief from her incessant bondage."

Tim's glance flickered across Agnes's face. She caught it and held it.

"Tim, I shall appeal to you," she said. "Is it wise of me, do you think, to let those two spend hours and hours together daily alone? He goes and stops with her in the country, as you know: he might be there still if it hadn't been for her influenza. And no sooner have we got back from our holiday than up she comes. What would you say, Alan, if I spent hours daily with Tim in his flat taking down his dictation—— "

She had spoken with all lightness, meaning only to keep up this equable flow of twaddle. But here was the forbidden topic, and with a gesture of impatience at herself she looked at Alan, who was inscrutably regarding her. Something secret and unspoken looked out quick as a lizard and back again from his wide set eyes.

Tim saw it all. He had to take his part in the unreal situation which Alan had created.

"You wouldn't stand my dictation for long," he said. "It consists of interminable rows of figures ending in eighths and sixteenths. Ledger accounts, too."

Alan took a sip of the barley-water which was his beverage when dinner preceded work.

"We have not yet told Timothy about our holiday at Littlestone," he said. "The rain and wind were incessant: it was seldom that we returned from our walk other than drenched. But I made my gleanings, little observations about squalls and gleams of sunlight and a grey sea. We cut it short by a week or more, and I was not ill pleased to get to work again."

They had coffee upstairs, and very soon Alan intimated that he was ready for an hour's dictation.

"But do not dream of going away, Timothy," he said, "if you can divert yourself in the meantime. There are the proofs of my preface for ' The Tyro,' if you should care to glance at them. You will find an account there of the early days when I read the original manuscript to our dear Agnes. A not unworthy tribute, I trust you will think. Come, my dear, if Timothy will be so kind as to excuse us."

Agnes settled herself in the writer's seat.

"Before we begin," said he, "I should like your definite assurance that you have never acted as amanuensis for Tim. And if you can give me that, you will then kindly read over the last paragraph. . . ."

CHAPTER II

PAMELA duly presented herself, all briskness and enthusiasm, at the appointed hour next day, and found conspicuously placed on the hall table a parcel addressed to her and marked ' To await arrival.' It contained, needless to say, copies of ' The Tyro ' and ' Ages Past,' with a pleasant little inscription in each from ' her tiresome old dictator.' She gasped for joy, and hardly pausing to fold the string again into just such a neat coil as Alan delighted in, ran swiftly upstairs, and was shewn into the drawing-room.

" Oh, Master," she cried, " I could hardly believe it. Too, too lovely! Tiresome! How delicious of you. Look, I have folded up the string again for you. I can hardly believe it yet. . . . Dear Agnes! Look what the Master has given me. Tea? I'm not sure if I can spare time from my gloating to have tea."

She was like some warm spring wind on frozen ground. Agnes could feel him thawing under the Favonian air.

" But I insist, dear Pamela," he said, " on your having a good tea. Your tiresome dictator hopes to prove a perfect slave-driver this evening, and he will not have his slave languish at her work. Give me these two little rubbishes. You shall not have them back till you have had your tea."

" What ? " she cried. " You've planned a new book ? You're going to dictate to me this afternoon ? "

" Aha! I knew it would be a surprise to you," said he.

" Oh, it's too much ! " she said. " First there's
that lovely surprise of the parcel, and now there's this.
I'm longing to begin. Let us go to the work-room
at once."

" Not before you've had your tea."

Pamela tossed her head in her high-nettled manner.

" Bully ! " she said. " I'm afraid the Master is a
bully. But on my side I insist that you shall tell
me, while I obey you, all about your dear selves since
I saw you last. How I thought of you at Littlestone
in that atrocious weather ! I nearly drove over to
see if you were taking good care of yourselves. Tell
me about it."

" Well, Shakespeare was right. ' The rain it
rainèd every day,' said he." (Pamela emitted
a babble of laughter at this misquotation.) " And at
last I could see that our dear Agnes could stand it no
longer, and we came up here two days ago. And
there's a little more surprise yet."

" I can't guess," said she. " Tell me."

" Several pages of the new book dictated already."

Pamela rolled her eyes heavenwards.

" You marvel ! You eighth wonder of the world !
I feel as if I ought to scold you for beginning work
again before you had had the clear month's holiday
you promised me you would take. I'm going to have
a confidential word with Agnes, and you mustn't
listen. Agnes dear, is he rested ? Shall we allow
him to work again ? "

Charades. . . . Agnes had to be quick on her
cue.

" I think so," she said. " He seems quite rested.
But keep an eye on him and report to me if you aren't
satisfied."

Pamela nodded, and then cast a melodramatic eye
at Alan.

" Hush ! We are observed," she said in a loud

whisper. "We must dissemble! Now, Mr. Graham, sir, you promised to show me your pretty room next door."

"You'll dine here?" asked Agnes.

"Yes, I should love to. If my bully keeps me working till close on dinner-time, you must allow me to dine in my overalls," and she indicated her very smart gown.

The two breadwinners, so Alan now termed them, presently left Agnes to earn the money to pay for dinner, in the work-room. . . . There had appeared that morning in the 'Times' a long but rather languid appreciation of 'Ages Past,' and of the revised 'Tyro,' which Pamela had not seen, and Alan's first business before dictation began was to show her this. As in the case of the 'Mantle of Elijah,' he had not spoken of it at all to Agnes, but he wanted the ointment and tonic which he knew Pamela would give him. She read it with pishes and pshaws and little laughters, and threw it gaily aside.

"Delicious!" she said. "How can people be such fools? I wonder what the author of that priceless rubbish will say when he finds that nobody can talk about anything else than 'Ages Past' and the preface to 'The Tyro.'"

"I confess that a warmer word of commendation——" began Alan.

"Dear Master, you are trying to take me in, to make me imagine that you can possibly care one atom what some nameless scribbler thinks. I should like to cut out some tit-bits from that, and get your publisher to quote them when he announces the twentieth or thirtieth edition of 'Ages Past.' Wouldn't that be delightful?"

"Aha, that would be a very pretty little answer," said he.

"Yes, if it were not beneath you," said she. "But I can't seriously allow you to take these little gentlemen seriously."

He expanded and thawed under this genial adulation. It was just what he wanted, that unreserved faith in his splendour, and he found himself eager to tell her of the affair about which his lips had been so sternly sealed.

"Quite so, quite so," he said. "Blewitt, for instance, poor Blewitt. You must know that my young cousin Timothy has just published a book of little stories . . . let me see, what is the title?—ah, yes, 'Cricket.' 'Cricket' is the name of the first of them. Crude little gasping violences, without form, without construction, not within measurable distance of being readable. . . . They came out on Saturday, and what must poor Blewitt do but go into six pages of ecstasy over them in his Sunday lucubration? Really I do not know whether the appreciation or the subject was the more unreadable. Timothy used to be a nice simple young man, without perceptions or subtleties. He stayed with us for many weeks, and I liked his cheery, light-hearted companionship. But I am afraid his head is being turned by these preposterous nonsensical eulogies. I glanced at them, but I have not opened my lips on the subject either to him—he dined with us last night—or to Agnes. Inexplicably, dear Agnes finds something to admire in the stories. It passes my comprehension altogether, and what is worse, it puts me out of my perfect sympathy with her. It jars on me that one who has been so closely associated with my work . . . it is as if she preferred some tawdry tinsel ornament to decorous jewels finely set. But I ignore it: I have not said a syllable on the subject. That is wise, is it not, dear Pamela, just to ignore it, to forget it? I mean, in fact, to ask poor Blewitt to dine here some

Sunday soon, to shew him I ignore it. Aha, poor
Blewitt! He used once to have a charming taste, but
it has been ruined by all the trash that his profession
obliged him to read!"

Alan did not deliver himself of these reflections in
the manner of a soliloquist who holds the stage.
He dropped the sentences about, as if watering
the room with them. Now he addressed the
sheaf of notes which he carried, now he confided
in the fire-place, now he sprinkled, as with a
disinfectant, the table where some of these stories
had been scribbled, but ever and again, as if orientat-
ing and establishing himself, he spoke direct to
Pamela. She, on her side, was grateful for the intermission, for she, when by reason of his averted face,
she did not need for herself an expression of the
vividest interest, cudgelled her memory to recall
what she knew already about some book called
'Cricket.' Before Alan had finished, she had landed
her fish, for the 'Evening Standard' of to-day, at
which she had glanced before she came here, contained a very tepid appreciation of 'Ages Past,' preceded by a column-long panegyric of 'Cricket and
other stories,' in which the reviewer hailed the work
of this débutant author as the first true literary trophy
of the years of war. She had not read half-a-dozen
lines of it, for then her eye had fallen on the sub-
ordinate review which followed it, but no doubt this was
the same book as that which Mr. Blewitt had eulogized
the day before, and which Alan declared was unreadable. She therefore now made up her mind to be
among the first to read it. Already it was attracting
great attention. 'Ages Past,' on the other hand, was
attracting but little. Faintly she wondered . . .

Alan faced her again, and she clapped her hands
in applause.

"That would be lovely," she said. "Ask poor

Henry to dine, do, do . . . and let me dress up as a parlour-maid, to see how wonderfully and ignoringly you deal with him. But now, let us get to more serious and lovely things. We are the bread-winners, as you so deliciously said, and I want to work. Give me five minutes, Master, and let me read what you have already dictated, and then I'll be ready. There's your Flaubert : I know how you want to wave it for a few minutes before the glorious words begin. Oh, how happy I am to be back in my old place ! "

She commented and ejaculated as she read. . . . " I can see the squall, oh, the rain, the pitiless rain . . . wonderful wind . . . the dreariness of the down-beaten garden. . . . Littlestone : I know you got this from your holiday. . . . Ah, marvellous, marvellous. . . . Now I shall read you the last two sentences."

She had not yet Agnes's gift of automatically recording what his voice enunciated, while her thoughts were free, but in the pauses she was actively engaged in her own reflections. She put the worst case before herself : she imagined ' Ages Past ' exciting no interest, and the preface to ' The Tyro ' satisfying no curiosity. She had so often said of the latter, ' Such a unique revelation : at last we are to be admitted into Alan's own life. He has been such a figure of mystery till now, but no mystery can be so beautiful as his revelation of it. My heart used to beat to suffocation as he dictated : yes, down at my cottage at Pleyden. . . .'' With the same propagandist enthusiasm she had spoken of ' Ages Past.' . . . " Nothing that he has done yet comes up to it at all : I read it in manuscript, and indeed he dictated much of it to me. Yes: I don't think he goes out to any house but mine, but one day you shall come and meet him. Just a little party, and we will sit round, just we *intimes* : he is at his best then." . . .

To face the worst then, all the time she had devoted to dictation, all the zeal with which she had preached and prophesied him would be scrapped energy. But it was better to cut the loss than lose more.

Alan had just said, 'Read, please,' and she read. . .

"That goes well, I think," he said. "That begins to give the vague trouble of her life. I am pleased with that. I do not think I have been quite unsuccessful there."

"No one but you could have written that," she said. "Oh . . . go on : go on."

"Give me a moment. Ah . . . that little packet of gleanings. Thank you. There is something there I know. . . ."

As he turned them over, she pursued her frank facing of it all. She had pictured the worst, but it would not come to that. Yet, if it did? . . . The great shy lion's place would be vacant, for where was the use of granting little intimate evenings to a favoured few if they were not thrilled with them, and did not spread broadcast the news of their felicity, coupled with the fact that the lion could only be seen at dear Pamela's? In fact, if he was sadly ceasing to be a lion at all, he should not be seen at dear Pamela's at all, for a bogus lion was no good. But the lion's place must not be vacant. There must be another lion : there was always a knife and fork for a lion. . . . She wondered whether Mr. Blewitt (for all his spoiled taste that had once been so exquisite) had discovered the authentic spoor of a new and magnificent creature. With her wonderful memory for faces she remembered Tim on the only occasion when she had met him, here on the birthday party, with great distinctness. A charming young lion with a boyish mouth and a great gaiety. She must certainly get a copy of yesterday's paper to see what Blewitt said, and, if

that was sufficiently promising, a copy of ' Cricket.'
. . . And if that was sufficiently promising, she
must get Tim. Perhaps he would write her name
in her copy of ' Cricket.' . . . The task of making the best out of the worst began to occupy her.

Alan was fluent. Dismissing the whole case of
' the worst ' from her mind, she was herself again in
those exclamations and gasps which so richly
nourished him. But the thought of the worst had
left just this residue in her mind that she found herself wondering whether his narration was not much
in the same mould as moulds that were already
familiar. Were not these sweeping squalls reminis-
cent of a chapter in ' Ages Past '? Was not this sad
damp pilgrimage down the lime-avenue, when the
dusk of silent estrangement was gathering in the
air, like that dim chapter in ' The Tyro,' in which it
was impossible to tell (Alan had meant it so) exactly
what was happening? " I want to produce the
atmosphere," he had said, " the uneasy setting.
. . . The hint of the *lacrimæ rerum*." That had
seemed so wonderful at the time, but she was not so
sure now that it contained an arresting quality.

Throughout the evening the impression grew.
Pamela had thought Agnes so sweet in abdicating her
rights at the dictation table, but now she could, in
certain circumstances, imagine herself being just as
sweet as Agnes. It was far from certain yet that she
would feel called upon to evince such honey, but,
when it came to a late ' good-night ' after a long industry, she felt that her hives were capable of it. But
she promised, she even rapturously volunteered, to
be at the desk again to-morrow afternoon. It would
be very short-sighted, until it definitely appeared that
she had been throwing good money away, not to put
a little more good money into the investment. There
was a ' call,' so to speak, a small ' call.' If she did

not take it up, she would indubitably sacrifice all that she had already put into the concern.

Throughout the week the papers were unusually occupied with literary affairs, eager to claim the kudos of having discovered this shining star, which had suddenly made its rising. It was a superb orb, so declared the majority, a planet of pure and beneficent beam, audibly hymning to the bright-eyed Seraphim. Out of the parted thunderclouds of war had appeared its effulgence; at last and at last had a supreme flower of art blossomed from the ruins of devastated soil. . . . Others, a small minority, proclaimed it to be a star of evil origin and maleficent influence, or no true star indeed at all, but some phantasmal marsh-fire of miasmic origin, while a minority smaller yet assured their readers that they had examined that quarter of the heavens where the star was supposed to have appeared with eyes of the keenest experience through unexceptional telescopes, and could confidently assert that there was no star of any description visible there. As to the claims of the various Galileos with regard to the credit of the discovery, poor Blewitt wrote a slightly waspish note to all the leading journals referring them to his article in the 'Sunday Magazine.'

Hardly less violent were the controversaries about the author. The Pure-Planet party was unanimous that he was some young man who had certainly been through the fiery furnace of experience: none else could have written such authentic stuff. The Miasmists were equally clear that it was the work of some ripe and experienced author—they admitted he could write—who in safe seclusion had concocted these tales, and adopted the pseudonym of Timothy Graham to conceal his identity. The tales rang false: it was patent that they were the mere literary product of some well-known writer who perhaps had outlived his popularity and made a fresh bid for it in a new province. Those who denied the existence of any star at all were sure that this feeble little volume about which others made such a fuss was the pseudonymous work of some nasty-minded old maid. . . . A few of the more careless of the fraternity, in an excusable state of mental confusion owing to the fact that they had on their table two volumes by Alan Graham, were under the impression that ' Cricket ' was a work of his and reviewed it as such. They praised the vigour of the veteran, but bade him beware of the dangers of his fatal facility. There were signs of haste in his usually careful writing. . . .

A similar carelessness was exhibited by the press cutting agency to which Alan subscribed, and morning by morning a bulky packet compounded of notices of ' Cricket ' and of his own books awaited him. About his there was no controversy at all : the critics were at one in their short and gentle appreciation of ' Ages Past.' It was just another thoughtful and graceful addition to the author's work : ' his numerous circle of readers would be sure to welcome it, and they would not be disappointed.' About the re-issue of ' The Tyro ' there was more divergence of opinion, but no voice was raised in eagerness concerning it. Some found it pleasant to glance again at a book which had once been so popular, and to admire again its careful workmanship. But perhaps it was unnecessary to write so voluminous a preface about matters purely personal and trivial. Others could not understand in whose interest it was to republish a piece of such old-fashioned tissue, or above all to give so elaborate an account of its original manufacture. The book itself being so frankly obsolete, it was a mere piece of senile egoism to imagine that the circumstances which surrounded its remote and forgotten birth could be of the smallest import.

Of less concern to Alan but of infinitely more to Pamela was the fact that in all this the critics only followed the lead of the talkers, and echoed the excited babble that frothed along in circles which had no claim to be even remotely literary. Wherever Pamela went (and where did she not go?) 'Cricket' was the salient topic: whoever went to her house (and who did not go there?) was sure to ask about Tim. Quite early in the week she recognised his potential lion-hood, and before the week was out he had attained his full growth. She bombarded him with offers of the richest hospitality, reminding him (quite untruly) that when they had met at that lovely birthday party of dear Agnes's, he had promised to come and see her. . . . If he could dine with her on Friday he would meet the most distinguished of Arctic explorers, and by the same post she wrote to the distinguished Arctic explorer saying that he would meet Tim. By dint of an unceasing storm of invitation, she got him to promise to dine on Sunday, and with that bait she at once angled for two or three very notable folk, who had not previously availed themselves of their numerous opportunities to dine with her. She proposed to have an evening party afterwards, and her telephone grew quite hot with the eager breathings of her multitudinous messages.

The same week which witnessed the tumultuous rising of the new star, witnessed the setting of the other, as far as 'Glory for Pamela' was concerned. Alan's two books, her association with which had occupied so many speculative hours, had done nothing whatever for her, and her investment must be written off as a dead loss. But meantime she had been committed to a further considerable investment in the same bankrupt concern, for tacitly and implicitly, if not verbally, it was understood that she was to be sole scribe of the new volume only just begun. As that agreement was nominally based on the altruistic grounds of giving dear Agnes more liberty, more time to herself, it was difficult to see how, without a semblance of failure in altruism, it was possible to cancel it. The real grounds of it, as she knew very well, were not so altruistic as they appeared. From her side she had sidled into the dictation chair and there firmly established herself for the sake of social glory, while Alan had helped to consolidate her there because her ejaculations of admiring wonder had proved themselves a stimulus which Agnes could not supply. But where was the use of spending time in stimulating still-born births, or where the glory of being associated with indifferent failure ? Alan's next book, too, was designed to be of great magnitude, not in quality alone. " We must employ a much larger canvas than usual, dear fellow-worker," he had said. " I see this book on a scale which I have never yet attempted." Worse than all he experienced great difficulty in his task : the two sessions of Tuesday produced an immense crop of erasures but little other fruit, and she could not quite echo the robustness of his artistic instinct when he said, ' These blackened pages of erasures ! I take them as evidence that we will not admit careless and slovenly stuff into our work. Nothing done without an infinity of trouble is worth doing at all.'

She marvelled at his robustness. Though not one syllable regarding the tepidity with which his own two books had been launched, and the rainbowed flags and shouting multitudes through which Tim had taken the water, passed his lips when he was with Agnes, he preserved no such reticence when he was closetted in the work-room with Pamela and her ardencies. Morning by morning the press-notices

poured in, and when his preparation for the afternoon's sittings was done, he read them and under-
lined the more magnificent absurdities.

"Some screamers, dear Pamela!" he would say
when she joined him. "Here is poor Timothy compared to Michael Angelo, hewing his statue straight
out of the block. Aha! I thought you would like
that. And here is poor Alan playing in his *démodé*
dolls' house and making his puppets dance their
antique minuets. Dear me, such plums. . . .
But let us get back to our puppets. I think you will
like the dance I have arranged for them to-day."

But for Agnes there were no such jests and
mockeries of the amazing critics, for she admired this
Michael Angelo of theirs, and her perverted tastes
must not be ridiculed. She must not be laughed at
for things she could not help. . . . Dear Agnes,
for all her long association with the work-room, had
not acquired that 'ferociously literary' eye. She
never omitted to enquire at the end of any of their
sessions how the work had progressed, but she was
beginning to enquire now from the outside: she
tapped at the door, so to speak, to ask after it. The
very fact that she found merit where these absurd
critics found it was enough to put up a barrier which
admitted Pamela, but left her outside.

Pamela, during this week which saw Tim now
blazing high in the zenith, and Alan sunk low in the
misty West, gave a great deal of concentrated
thought to the manner in which she should emanci-
pate herself from this unguerdoned slavery. The
solution when she arrived there seemed so simple that
she wondered how she had not lit on it at once.
Altruism would play its shining part again. . . .

She was gathering up, at the end of the Saturday
evening session, those slips with notes and phrases
on them, which had not yet been used, and putting

them back into their elastic band, ready to be spread abroad again on Monday. The dictation had gone fluently to-night, and Alan was brisk with satisfaction.

" It's full speed ahead now, I think," he said. " We've left the shoal-water behind. How many pages is it to-day, Pamela ? "

She counted them.

" Eight," she said. " Eight precious pages. You were wonderful to-night, Master. There'll be no grounding now. I seem to see you positively rushing along. Oh what a lovely book it will be ! The best of all, I think. Perfectly perfect ! Exquisite handling ! How delighted Agnes will be to hear how you have got on with it."

He paused a moment in his strolling, and put down the paper-knife which he still carried. Some sort of constraint came over his ease.

" Yes . . . yes . . ." he said. " No doubt Agnes will be pleased to hear that we have got on. My work I know makes no very special personal appeal to her. . . . I noticed that before dinner to-night she made no enquiries whatever as to what progress we had made."

Pamela supported her chin on her hands, and looked at him with pensive intentness.

" I'm going to be very bold, Master," she said. " I've got something really serious to say. Will you let me ? "

" Surely."

Pamela had rehearsed very carefully what she meant to say. She had done even better : she had kneaded the reasoning that prompted it into her mind, so that it now quite permeated it.

" I have to accuse us both of selfishness, dear Master," she said. " We meant to be, oh, so unselfish and thoughtful for dear Agnes, but we didn't think deep enough. Now, I've been trying to put myself more truly into Agnes's place, and I see we've been selfish. These lovely hours of dictation have absorbed us: we've only been thinking of our joy in them, and we haven't considered that dear Agnes is feeling left out and neglected."

He had not comprehended her purpose yet. But the notion that Agnes missed these dictations somehow fed his egoism.

"Dear me, do you think that is indeed so?" he asked. "If it is we must certainly do something to remove that impression. It would never do to let poor Agnes feel left out. Another night—it is too late to-day—we must finish our work a little earlier, and read her what we have done. Or she might perhaps sits in here while we were at work. That would be a hazardous experiment though. To dictate—to be sure I did do it once, but then she was scribe and you were audience—to dictate with two people in the room might prove disturbing. And where would she sit? Perhaps if we read our work aloud to her afterwards——"

Pamela put her chin more forward yet, and gazed more steadily.

"We must do more than that," she said. "More even than having her in the room while we work. Oh, I know that we thought we were being wise and kind in giving her more time to herself but it has been a failure. When I put myself in Agnes's place I understand. . . . And now I have got to be much, much more self-sacrificing than I was when I took her place. That was no self-sacrifice: that was a pure privilege and delight. But now I have to give up something lovely and cherished. I mustn't sit in Agnes's place any more. She must come back to it."

Alan was much perturbed by this time. He had
seen the final proposition coming, and its approach
hardly less than its advent had profoundly disturbed
him. His egoism enveloped him like a cloak from
head to foot; it was a hood over his head, and swept
the ground. From that impenetrable shelter he spoke.

"But, dear Pamela, the matter is not so easy and
straightforward as that," he said. "You are so good
as to say that you have enjoyed your hours here——"

Pamela made great eyes and dropped them again.

"Enjoyed!" she exclaimed.

He relented over that.

"Well, let us say that they have been, as you put
it, a privilege and a joy. Joy is more than enjoyment is it not? And you are willing in your little
prick of conscience to give those pleasures up for
Agnes's sake. You are wrong, dear Pamela, I who
know Agnes so well can reassure you. She admires,
strongly admires, for she has told me so, work such
as poor Timothy's. It is impossible therefore, that
she should rate that which is a privilege and a joy
to you, as anything higher than a tedious duty. It
is impossible for her—I am not arguing with you, I
am telling you—to enjoy my work if she enjoys
his . . ."

Pamela in her rehearsals, had foreseen some such
argument or 'telling' as this.

"Ah, but she does," she said. "There is the
wonderfulness of her."

Alan put up a deprecating hand.

"Excuse me, dear Pamela," he said. "You have
not permitted me to finish the outline of my thought.
I must make my complete sketch before you dispute
its accuracy. I tell you that she cannot admire my
work and Timothy's. You are not therefore depriving her when you are so good as to take down my
dictation, of any privilege that ranks with yours—I

am but quoting your words when I use 'privilege' in connection with my poor imaginings—you are not, I say, depriving her to the extent that you deprive yourself. And have you considered me? I feel you have not : your sweet sympathy with dear Agnes has usurped your whole horizon. . . ."

He had picked up the paper-knife again, and was moving up and down the room in a state of agitated concentration on himself.

"My work is at stake also," he said. "Your appreciation has been my inspirer. You have, just now, told me that we are engaged in the most perfectly perfect (again I quote you), the most perfectly perfect piece of work that this poor brain has ever conceived. I do not affect to disagree with you about that : I have never felt myself more consciously rejoicing in the full exercise of my powers. But if now you are determined to dissociate your presence and your admiration from me altogether, you will make yourself like a May-frost for apple-blossom. You will nip the bloom : it will not come to fruition. . . ."

There was no mistaking his seriousness, for she had often before seen how he and his work were to him an interest beside which all others were immeasurable : they did not come into that scale at all. And he rose higher yet.

"I have thought sometimes that if years ago I had met you, dear Pamela," he began.

She looked hastily towards the big folded door which separated them from the room where, since dinner, Agnes had been waiting for their emergence. This was completely a new note, a scrannel unmeaning note. It meant, she realized, no more to him than it did to her. It was just an argument of unbridled egoism.

"Hush, hush!" she said. "There is no use, dear Master, in imagining what might have been.

. . . You said something just now which I have
to protest against. You spoke of my dissociating my
presence and my admiration from you altogether. I
protest : I deny : I disclaim. And I had no intention—unless you wished it—of dissociating from you
my presence or my profound admiration. We shall
have many happy hours of dictation yet. But I must
not exclusively usurp them."

Some sort of compromise was clearly necessary.
She knew she had not the force of character to say
bluntly, "When I go away to-night, I shall not return." General kindliness, in part, prevented that, in
part a certain sense of fairness. She realized that,
intellectually (from the point of view of his own in-
tellect) he had fallen in love with her to the extent of
finding her indispensable. When he was at work, he
could not do without her : he claimed her presence.
She was responsible for that, because she had for the
sake of ' glory for Pamela,' professed herself intellectually in love with his work. She wanted to be
his intellectual mate, so long as he had a coronet to
give her. But the coronet had crumbled, or was it
more true to say that Tim had whisked it away ?—
Compromise then was indicated.

She went on without pause.

"As to dissociating my presence from you," she
said, "nothing was further from my mind. I want
often, often, dear Master, to be your humble
amanuensis. But not always. It wouldn't be fair.
I should feel mean."

Her eye lit up with the splendour of a sudden
thought, and she turned back the leaves of the dictation-book.

"I say that so clumsily," she said, "but now you
shall hear it beautifully said by yourself. Listen,
dear Master : it is Eva who is talking. . . . ' The
one unforgivable sin is the sin against oneself. What-

ever achievement or adventitious glory may be the fruit of it, that fruit is the dust of apples from Gomorrah. It burns with the fire that God rains on it. . . .' Oh! You would not have my joy and privilege turned into dust. I know you too well for that."

It was stupendous: it was admirable. Probably nothing less than a quotation from himself would have so smoothed out the wrinkled perplexity.

" I am hoist on my own petard, dear Pamela," he said. " *You* are not arguing with me, *you* are telling me."

She was very careful not to exhibit the smallest sign of relief.

" Oh, we are so much at one! " she said. " I knew you would see it all as I did, when I showed you what I saw. And I see further yet."

She adopted his trick.

" Guess, dear Master," she said. " Guess what difficulty still faces us, and how I have solved it. Beautifully solved it. . . . You cannot? Ah, I have picked up some little thread then of your subtleties, which you have passed by unnoticed. I will tell you the difficulty. How are we to explain to Agnes about our new plan? We have steadily told her that my bad-halfpenny presence here (always turning up) is to give her more liberty——"

" But she realizes," said Alan, " that you bring me a greater stimulus than she could. Partly true, dear Pamela, you know, I could not contradict it."

She tossed her head, quite free now from the curb.

" My solution is as good as ever then," she said. " I take it all on myself. I will tell her that I am so busy with fussiness and entertaining, that I cannot spare time to be always here. It will make me seem selfish, but I must put up with that. She will not guess our true reason, that we are doing it for her sake. She is such a marvel of unselfishness that she would certainly refuse our boon, if she knew it was for her that we had devised it."

Pamela went next door to have a private word with Agnes, explaining how selfish she was, and presently Alan followed. He received the news that Pamela could not, owing to other engagements, be dictated to on Monday or Tuesday with perfect equanimity.

" I shall tingle to know what has happened in the story, when I come back on Wednesday," she said. " But all these tiresome engagements! I shall begin being jealous of dear Agnes again. Oh, you happy people! But just for to-morrow I shan't be jealous, for I know that the dictation-book is shut on Sunday. Have a good rest to-morrow, Master. That darling Eva : Agnes has to learn about Eva. Oh, so wise and wonderful! Perfect! "

She went off, full of self-congratulation at her dexterity. She had made the first step, and though for the present she would go back every now and then to the work-room, and gasp and ejaculate with joy, she had broken the fetters now, and standing free, had snapped them back on to Agnes. A few times more she would wear them again, but not often : she would have a very unexpected and peremptory engagement one day when she was pledged to secretarial work : she would be called out of London on another, and before long she would be wholly emancipated. After all, it was Agnes's business, not hers (unless she chose to make it so), to minister to Alan and write his stories for him, and with the fiasco and bankruptcy of the last two publications, it was not likely that she would so choose. Time was precious : time was given you to " get on " in, and there was no progress to be made in that backwater. Most of all had she been dexterous in the asseveration of the motives owing to which she secured her freedom. She had been prepared, if necessary, to be firm, to tell him that she could no longer find leisure for so great a sacrifice of her hours, but so far from having had to put forward a selfish claim to him on her own time, she had contrived this very flower and felicity of altruism, and by quoting the noble sentiments of his own Eva, had associated herself with the soul of a heroine. Afterwards, according to plan, she had given Agnes the authentic reason for her withdrawal, and Agnes seemed to have no difficulty whatever in accepting it. She had thanked Pamela with all sincerity for the time she had already spent on Alan, and told her how much she had helped him. If anything, indeed, Agnes seemed to understand too well about it all. That candid gaze perhaps penetrated a little deeper than Pamela had meant. But there was always something a little mysterious about candid people. One could not help wondering what their candour concealed. It was not natural to be so natural.

She had a sense of holiday with a great treat, a shining glory in the immediate future. It was only just a week since the book which had set all London a-gabble had appeared, and to-morrow the author about whom so much was conjectured and so little known would appear at her house. There would be dinner for a chosen few, among whom was Mr. Blewitt, in order to reward him for having, so to speak, set light to the blaze, and quite a quantity of people were coming in afterwards for a little music, and would find not only a charming string quartette, but Timothy, already, she hoped, quite at home, as if he was there as constantly as Alan had been. It was well known that she was intimate with the Grahams: the Christian names of Alan and Agnes had been always on her lips, and she thought that

she could at once embark on " Mr. Tim." She
would engage him for a theatre party or two,
and a week-end down at Playden, where he should
have Alan's work-room at his disposal. . . . She
foresaw that a little dissimulation might possibly be
necessary, for Alan, of course, had a permanent invitation to invite himself whenever he chose, and it
would never do to have him and Tim together. She
had no intention of dropping Alan completely, for
there were still a few old-fashioned folk who liked to
paddle in the backwater. But all that would arrange
itself : what mattered was that to-morrow night had
arranged itself, and she would give a private view of
Tim.

Sunday, as usual, was a day of rest for the workers
in Goring Square, and during the morning Agnes
went across to see her mother. All this last week,
with Pamela coming every day for dictation she had
spent much time there, going in after tea as soon as
the dictation had begun, and to-day she had to tell
Mrs. Mowbray that these visits must be discontinued,
since she would again be occupied in Alan's service.
She knew that her mother did not in the least enjoy
her visits, except in so far as they fed, by the sight of
her, that secret hostility which Mrs. Mowbray
cherished for her, though she would certainly find
cause for complaint in their abandonment. But Alan
had the first call on her : in Pamela's withdrawal she
must be at his disposal again.

She told her mother this, as soon as she was seated,
and saw some secret gleam in her eye. All the week
she had been aware that there was something sim-
mering and stewing in her mother's mind, which had
not yet disclosed itself. Now a bubble burst on the
surface.

" Ah," she said, " your Pamela has had enough of

it, I suppose. I have often wondered when that would happen. And the world generally, the reading public, seem to have had enough of it too."

She speared her needlework.

"Alan is finished," she said. "I have read half-a-dozen reviews of this new book of his in various papers, and they all are agreed. No one who had waded through the mud-flats of 'Ages Past' could possibly come to any other conclusion. And then there is 'The Tyro,' the re-issue of the 'Tyro' with its new preface. How does that strike you, Agnes? I should like to know what you think of Alan's picture of you and me; you a doll on a footstool in the fire-light, me a shadow in the shadows, and between us Alan, the divine genius."

Agnes made a call on her sinking heart . . . her mother had the gift of putting articulately before her all that she herself stifled at the birth of thought.

"I think it is a wonderful piece of writing, mother," she said. "It brought back those evenings to me with extraordinary vividness."

"Ah! You grasped then at the time just how much or how little you were to him? You knew when you accepted him that you were only that to him?"

Again she held fast to her loyalty.

"It was enough for me to know how fond I was of him," she said. "I was honoured and overjoyed at his choice of me. That is all I can tell you. Let us speak of something else."

"By all means. Let us speak of to-day and not of fifteen years ago. It must warm your heart to know that his feeling for you has never altered. The new preface written so lately testifies to that."

Never had her mother's hostility gleamed so savagely. There was in it, too, a light as of gratified revenge, something triumphantly and bitterly exulting. . . . Agnes faced it, and refused to see it. Heavy of heart, she put a certain lightness into the tone of her answer.

" Ah, but I don't accept your description of me as sitting doll-like in the fire-light," she said. " You may have thought I was doll-like, dear : I daresay great admiration and affection like that I had for Alan makes a girl constrained and silent. But I accept the other, I rejoice to think that you too recognise that Alan's affection for me has never faltered. That is quite true. He often treats me like a girl still."

This was fencing and she knew it. Mrs. Mowbray shifted her attack.

" And what does Alan make of Timothy's immense success ? " she asked.

" He has not said a single word to me about it," said Agnes.

" Indeed. Does he not know of it then ? "

" Yes, he knows of it," said Agnes. " But he has read some of Tim's stories, and thinks them unreadable rubbish. I imagine that is why he does not speak to me about them, for he knows I admire them very much. Have you read them, mother ? "

" All of them. And the dedication to you."

Again Agnes felt that she was defending herself.

" Was it not charming of Tim ? " she said. " He never told me he was dedicating them to me. I felt wonderfully proud."

She was being stalked : it was exactly that she felt. The stalker crept ever nearer to her, concealed in cover of these perfectly ordinary enquiries. It was not precisely her mother who was the stalker, but some thwarted and unsatisfied desire of hers, long passed, long cold, of which the emptiness rather than the hunger remained. It had been starved into extinction, but there was some deadly wraith of it here, which wished ill to Alan and herself.

"You are great friends with Timothy, are you not?" went on the inexorable voice. "That makes a trying situation for you, for Alan, I imagine, does not care about seeing Timothy now. It is different from the days when Timothy made his home with you, and when you and Timothy were alone together. You miss him very much, no doubt. It is sad for you."

Then, with a vengeance, were the twigs snapping under the silent foot of the concealed stalker. That instinct of her mother, terrible and unseen, hungry once and empty now, saw in Agnes something that suffered as it had once suffered. Agnes could bear the pursuit no longer. She came right out into the open, with her next words. She dropped her rapier, and stood an undefended target.

"You speak as if I were in love with Tim," she said.

There was no reply, and looking at her mother she saw in her eyes an unmistakable assent. It was just that which she had meant. She had suffered, and the cruelty which is so often in hard harsh natures the result of suffering, looked gleefully on another victim. There was no need for answer, it feasted itself on its own silence, which neither affirmed nor denied.

The blackening moment passed, and Mrs. Mowbray, with the air of dismissing a distasteful subject, took up a copy of 'Ages Past' which lay on the table by her.

"I have read Alan's book," she said. "It makes me very unhappy, for it seems to confirm what I have always feared. We talked about it all once, Agnes; I remember that I blamed you for allowing him to make himself so isolated and self-centred. But now you tell me he is very busy at work again.

I hope you can give me some good news about the new book, something to reassure me about the loss of grip and vitality that I feared."

Quite suddenly Agnes found that she could bear no more of it. All that had fought and fenced, all that with a supreme bravery had let itself stand target, collapsed. What remained to her beyond sheer helplessness was pity. It wasn't her mother who made this nightmare, but some bitter denizen of the spirit which poisonously diseased her. Her spirit was sick with the deadly germ. . . .

" I don't know much about the new book, mother," she began. "He has been dictating it to Pamela. But now I shall begin to know more of it."

She broke. What was the use of continuing to take these ironies at their smooth face-value ? . . . She knelt down by her mother's side.

"You have been very terrible," she said. "You have not been saying what you mean. You don't want good news about the new book. You don't want reassurance about Alan. . . . My dear, don't answer me. It is as I say. I wish you would feel more kindly to Alan and me. I am trying to do my best, so you mustn't discourage me. If . . . if things have been hard for you, why should you make them harder for me ? I want to forget all you have said this morning, and all that you've left unsaid. I can't talk any more. But always remember how awfully sorry I am for you. . . ."

She turned as she spoke, and left the room without waiting for any reply, for she had seen that no semblance of softening came over her mother's face. And that was the most pitiful of all.

As she went downstairs, the tears brimmed and blinded her, so that she had to grope for the door latch through the haze of them. She paused a moment, wiping and scolding them away, for it was the hour when Alan might be needing her for the usual small stroll before lunch, and she could not bear that he should guess that there had been anything amiss between her mother and her. A thing of that kind must be studiously kept from him, for in these days, it was impossible to tell what might unsettle and agitate him, and make him unable to concentrate his mind in tranquillity upon his work. But she would have given anything just then for ten minutes with Tim, for the tonic of his presence and the succour of him.

Alan's preparation had been most fruitful that morning, and he was half inclined to make another exception, and though it was Sunday dictate to her in the evening. But careful consideration led him to abandon the idea : it would be more prudent to ' get the steam up ' still further and prepare for a glorious time to-morrow. She read through, at his suggestion, all that Pamela had written for him, in order to bring herself into touch with the new story, for since, owing to the lovely little plot of not allowing her to feel out of it, she was to resume the work of amanuensis, it was well that she should bring sympathy and knowledge to her task. She threw herself with all possible eagerness into the task, for she must fit herself to fill Pamela's place, and commended and wondered, and discussed. She had her reward too, for she knew that Alan was beginning to melt towards her, to put away her offence in having admired Tim's work, and to find her worthy of initiation into the new projects of his imagination, and she did not despair of becoming an adequate substitute in Pamela's absence. Of course there were hints unconsciously dropped by Alan that reminded her that she was only an understudy. . . .

" Pamela found the last three pages particularly successful," he said. " She had a happy suggestion that would indicate, very subtly, what Eva's train of unconscious thought was during the last conversation. . . . It struck me as very felicitous, but somehow I allowed it to slip from my memory, and I can find no record of it in my notes. Just a hint, you know, which I meant to develop. I have tried a dozen times to-day to recollect it."

They had dined and were now up again in the drawing-room, where they would sit and beguile the hours till bedtime with a game of piquet, and perhaps a little reading. But the search for Pamela's hint was clearly making Alan restless.

"A thousand pities that I did not note it at the time," he said, "for to-morrow morning I shall certainly need it."

"It may come to you during the night," said she. "Very likely you will wake up to-morrow with the full recollection of it."

"That is possible, but what shall I do if it is still an absentee? We shall have to invoke the wizard and get hold of Pamela to see if she remembers it. Of course she is sure to, but the matter will be difficult to explain through the wizard's agency. I shall perhaps have to get her to come here, or go round myself to see her, and that will mean a loss of time."

He rose from his chair with alacrity, and laid down the hand which had just been dealt him.

"An idea!" he said. "Why should not we go round to Pamela's now and get her help? We have an hour of leisure, and we may as well use it. Let us then drop in on Pamela, as we have several times done before without warning on a Sunday evening."

"Shan't I ring her up first and see if she is in?" asked Agnes.

"No, dear; we will just get a taxi and pop in on

Pamela. If she is there the matter can be cleared up at once. If she is not I will leave a note for her explaining the point which I have forgotten. We shall get an answer from her before I begin my work tomorrow."

"Shall I come with you?" asked Agnes.

"Please do, my dear. I am so stupid about taxifares, and to my old eyes that little enamelled face with the bill on it is illegible. They charge me what they like."

CHAPTER III

PAMELA'S little dinner-party, only eight in all, was being a brilliant success. Her guests, the distinguished few, selected with great care for the dinner, were all delighted to meet the literary lion of the moment, and delighted with her for having given them the opportunity : while to judge by the distinguished many who had accepted the minor honour of forming the party with music that was to follow, that was likely to be as great a success as the dinner. . . . An association with Alan and his analytical mind had perhaps quickened her powers of self-dissection, and though she liked Tim well enough personally, she found herself noting that it was not for lions—*qua leones*—that she cared so much as for the honour and glory which their presence and exhibition conferred on the hostess. She would not—here was the discovery—have cared to be feeding all the great ones of the earth, securely caged, if nobody else knew about it. And she paused to laugh at something which Mr. Blewitt had said, which was clearly very amusing, though she had no idea what it was.

She had never known him in so admirable a temper, and, in consequence, so conversationally entertaining. Indeed he had good cause for enjoyment, since he was sitting between two women who were stars of considerable social magnitude, and he promised himself other equally desirable auditors afterwards. Socially, then, all was well, and professionally all was even better, for had he not, a whole week ago, before a single word had appeared in the press about 'Cricket,' hoisted all the flags, and cheered himself hoarse through six pages of the 'Mantle of Elijah.' Since then not only had the large majority of his critical colleagues endorsed his acumen, but the book had been hailed by the public with a roar of welcome. . . .

Pamela could not help contrasting this evening with the half-dozen immediately preceding it, on which, every night, she had sandwiched a dinner with Agnes and Alan between two spells of dictation. Each had been more irksome than the last, as the fact grew more luminously clear that she was wasting her time and her ejaculations and her energy on that which profited not. She had no kind of reproach for Alan on the score of these unremunerative labours : she had backed him entirely of her own initiative, and if in this last event his two steeds had come in unplaced and unnoticed, she blamed nobody but herself. She had even been induced to back him again before the result of this race was known, in his new venture, but she had not precisely named the sum which she was prepared to pay, so to speak, for the training of his horse, and she was even now whittling it down in her mind. . . . A fragment of Wednesday evening had been definitely promised, and no doubt she would manage others occasionally. . . .

"'The Fashion!' my dear lady," exclaimed Blewitt to his literary Marchioness. "How little we can say what we really mean by that very common word! Let us, with your kind indulgence, leave out all considerations of dress from it, or my male mind, confused and confounded by your talk of ruches and herring-bones and toques and gussets, will but 'weep its burden to the ground,' as our late laureate remarked, and subside into a bewildered silence. Do not, I beg you, condemn me to silence, for I feel, as you have already no doubt

shudderingly conjectured, peculiarly talkative to-
night. The very word 'Repression' appals me; I
might figure in a text-book by the interminable
Freud."

This sort of thing was popular just now. . . .
Blewitt had once been described as a dinner pill : he
promoted digestion by stimulating the mental liver.
You were not obliged to think, or to exert yourself :
you just swallowed what he gave you.

"But let us get back to our fascinating explora-
tion," he said. "There is something admittedly
ephemeral about the Fashion. We hail it as the last
and final word, and all the time we know it isn't. It
has never the stability of greatness or of true illumination. It is the glitter of sunshine on the reflecting
surface of water and the merest breeze will break it
up. . . . I abound in metaphors, none of which
will stand close examination. So let us take some con-
crete instance; the sight of our gifted young friend
opposite suggests one to me. . . . There were
days, dear lady, known as the nineties (I allude to the
last century which you remember not at all, and I,
alas, only too well). The nineties were crammed with
fashions in the world of art and literature, and we
talked glibly of the return of the Golden Age, and
tried to believe that we were basking in its effulgent
beams. Masterpiece after masterpiece made its
shining appearance; our libraries of contemporary
literature were bursting with them. But those books,
those forgotten volumes, were only the fashion, and
we half suspected that after our golden morning there
would follow a long inclement afternoon. Most of
all do I remember—again our young friend opposite
is the spur to my memory—most of all do I remember
the appearance of certain early works of his venerable
relative Alan Graham. Chief among them was 'The
Tyro,' and I among many others hailed it as a revela-

20

tion of supreme art, and publicly announced my conviction. . . ."

He saw that he had got the ear of Pamela, and
though the meat of Pamela's admirable dinner was
yet in his mouth, he could not resist a small feline
dab.

" That book was republished only a few days ago,"
he went on, " and certain of us anticipated the renewal of its magical spell. But what did we find?
There was no spell at all, and there never had been.
An amiable conjurer had been juggling with words :
it was a trick of the most puerile kind. We wondered
how it could have taken us in for a moment. Kind
good man, he has been diligently producing similar
tricks ever since ! Indeed I cannot call them similar :
they are all the same trick, performed in different
corners of the same room which thus provides slightly
novel backgrounds."

Blewitt was enjoying himself immensely. He was
revenging himself on Alan for having induced him
years ago to believe that ' The Tyro ' and others were
true artistic achievements, he was making himself interesting to his desirable neighbours, and now he was
leading up to a well-conceived climax.

" Those little conjuring tricks are Fashion," he
said. " At first sight their glitter and dexterity de-
ceives us, but there is nothing behind their dexterity.
There is a rabbit and a gold-watch and a knotted
handkerchief. What we devotees of Art look for even
as weary sufferers look for the morning which ends
the black night is the deep underlying humanity of
eyes that truly see and hearts that feel. All the dexterity, which by itself is but a tinkling cymbal, must
be there as well, for that is what we call ' form.' And
for twenty years, dear lady, since the epoch of the
exciting nineties closed, have I looked, at first with
unaided vision, and then with an ever-increasing

power of spectacles, for the Real Thing. Till last
week I looked in vain, and then sudden and un-
trumpetted it appeared. It was my privilege to be
the first to hail it."

The party to follow was not bidden till ten o'clock,
but the diners passed straight into the big music-room
for the further entertainment, with a quarter of an
hour before them yet. Blewitt was again to the fore
and soon, to Tim's great embarrassment, made it
impossible for him not to consent to read aloud to
them the first story of his collection. His audience
disposed themselves in a loose semi-circle while Tim
stood by the fireplace facing the door. But embar-
rassing though it was, it was idle for him to pretend
that the situation did not teem with enjoyment. He
loved the sudden leap into fame, the inundating offers
for more stories, the requests of photographers for
gratuitous sittings, with two copies of the ' approved
position ' as bonus, the paragraphs, the autograph
collectors, all the bubble of the boom. One thing
alone was dreadfully lacking for its completeness : he
longed to share the extravagancies of it with Agnes.

The reading was nearing its end, a couple of pages
alone remained, when a servant entered holding the
door open. He would have announced names, supposing that these were the earliest guests of the ensuing party to arrive, but saw that something demand-
ing silence was in progress. Close behind him came
Agnes : Alan apparently had lingered for a moment
over the bestowal of his coat and hat. Precisely then,
Tim looked up at the interruption and saw her. Why
she was there alone he did not trouble to enquire of
himself. The flashed message of her presence sped
between his eyes and hers : he saw the smile that
answered him spring to her face, and he bent
his eyes on to his book again. The signal had

passed between them; they had greeted each other, and now he would read on to the end without another glance at her. . . . Pamela had been conscious of the interruption, for she looked half round, without however seeing who had entered, and resumed her little jerks and sighs of admiration. At the end Tim closed his book, and looked towards Agnes again. She was seated now in a chair near the door and beside her was Alan.

Pamela rose.

" Ah, too wonderful, Mr. Tim," she said. " Quite, quite marvellous ! Those delightful boys talking about cricket ! And what wonderful art to leave it just there, instead of telling us that one was killed and the other got the Victoria Cross. Perfectly perfect ! Exquisite handling ! "

She turned and saw what Tim had already seen; she remembered also that only yesterday she had said ' perfectly perfect. Exquisite handling ! ' to this unexpected guest. Something had to be done immediately, though she had not the slightest notion what it was. Or rather nothing could possibly be done except the usual thing. . . .

" Agnes and Alan ! " she exclaimed. " Why, how delicious of you to have looked in. To spare me your evening of holiday ! All old friends here, I expect. Here is Mr. Blewitt and Lady Sanderson and Tim. You know everybody I am sure."

Blewitt had been warmly congratulating Tim : on the sound of his name he turned.

" Dear Mrs. Graham," he said, speaking with loud elaboration, " and you my dear friend. I commiserate, I condole with you. You have come just too late. Your gifted young relative was induced to lay aside his charming modesty, and read us that gem of a story, which has set us all wild with delight. You, dear Graham, with your intimate and veteran knowledge of the craft, will appreciate better than any of us its wonderful technique, learned we must suppose in the cradle or at latest the nursery. And you, too, have been delighting your numerous admirers again. We envy you your industry. How many times already you have charmed and diverted us!"

Alan had listened to Blewitt's ripe period, up to this point with polite attention. Now, quite dignified and courteous, he made him a little bow and turned to Pamela.

"I see you have friends," he said. "Agnes and I would not have dreamed of looking in if we had known. I thought you might be alone. I had a question to ask you about some point you suggested to me at our last dictation. . . . But it is of no consequence: this is not quite the occasion. And Timothy has been reading to you, I gather. Yes: one of his little stories. I understand. I see too, that we have intruded. . . . Agnes, my dear."

Pamela abounded with reassurances.

"Dear Master," she said, "as if you were not always welcome! There were just a few friends to dinner, and now we are to have a little music. It was the happiest thought of yours to look in. Yes, Mr. Tim has just read us one of his tales. Such a pleasant voice. Now let me find you a comfortable chair. . . ."

Tim, meanwhile, had edged his way out of the circle and joined Agnes.

"Oh, Tim, this is frightful!" she said. "The unluckiest accident. My dear, I'm so glad to see you. Aren't you enjoying it all tremendously?"

"Of course I am. But I want to enjoy it with you. Can't you come round some afternoon, if I'm not to be asked to come to you?"

She shook her head.

"Difficult," she said. "Alan would hate it. . . ."

"But some afternoon when Pamela is being dictated to," said he.

"I'm doing the dictation again," she said. "And even if I wasn't—I'll send you a line. Things may get better. But this evening is tragic. I don't know what effect it will have on him."

"Just because I've been reading to them?"

"Yes: it's the way Alan takes things. I'm not a bit happy about him. Ah, here he is."

Guests were arriving, and Alan had disengaged himself from Pamela. He came up to where the two were standing, but appeared not to see Tim.

"My dear," he said to her. "We have done a very awkward thing. We have clumsily arrived at a party without invitation. Good Pamela kindly extends it to us now, but it will never do to remain. Had she wanted us, she would have asked us. We must insist on being allowed to go home."

Tim had no intention, if Alan did not see him, of pointing himself out, and would have slipped away. But, even as he turned, Alan, with a visible effort, held out his hand.

"My dear Timothy!" he said. "We all rejoice . . . yes, quite so. . . . I am very busy just now, but we shall see you again some time, I hope. I will invoke, Agnes will invoke the wizard for me. A quiet evening, and if afterwards—my dear, we must slip away. Perhaps we might even omit our salutation to our hostess. Her friends and her other duties occupy her. Most natural. Good night, Timothy. Some time then . . . ."

Tim knew as well as Agnes why her eyes grew suddenly bright and dim together at that: it was compassion and comprehension that gleamed there and was clouded, compassion for Alan, comprehension of what this difficult civility cost him. As she turned to follow Alan she looked at him once more, appealing to his pity.

The room was filling fast, but Alan with a groping swiftness sidled and squeezed through the tide of incomers. Pamela, as hostess, was close by the door, but he passed her on the far side of an entering group. Agnes gave her a head-shake and a smile of departure over Mr. Blewitt's head, who had planted himself near the doorway to salute desirable acquaintances.

" Alan wants to get home," she said, " so we're off."

Mr. Blewitt whirled round, malicious and elate.

" Dear lady, if possibly my appreciation of that wonderful young man . . ."

Agnes permitted herself to stop and raise an eyebrow of wonder.

" Yes," she said. " What do you mean, quite ? "

" A little wholly natural envy of the young generation," said Blewitt. " The shadow that inevitably falls. So sad and so utterly natural."

Agnes moved a step on.

" Are you speaking of my husband ? " she asked. " Surely not ! I remember so well your charming little poem ' Spontaneous lark.' I must read it over again to see just what you said. We liked it so much. Good-night, Mr. Blewitt."

There were too many people of distinction to be greeted to allow Mr. Blewitt time or energy to be angry just then. But he made a note of it.

Alan had already stepped into a discharged taxi when she got out. They drove home in silence, but she felt that some tense situation underlay his share in it. For herself, she could say nothing which would really bring her close to him. She could reach him superficially, could swathe and bandage a hurt, could shelter him from any external disturbance or intrusion, but she could not get between him and himself. . . . On reaching home, he left her to pay the taxi, and was half-way upstairs when she followed him.

" We will sit in the work-room to-night," he threw over his shoulder to her, " if that is agreeable to you. There is time, is there not, perhaps, for a little dictation. . . ."

She took up her usual place.

" Yes, dear, it's only just after ten yet. There is plenty of time before us. Shall I read ? "

" Before we begin," he said. " I have an observation or two to make, which I would ask you to regard, dear, as an expression of my wish. I will just state them, and if you want to discuss them with me, you are of course at liberty to state your views, but I should be grateful to you if you will say your word now and not re-open the subject again. My first observation is this. After our experience of this evening I feel that it would be no use my attempting to dictate to Pamela again—Mrs. Probyn, I think, for the future, should we have occasion to allude to her. She led me to think that my work was the subject— quite unworthily—of her supreme admiration. We find on the other hand that she applies the identical expression of her appreciation to work of which she knew my opinion. At present, she is under promise to come here on Wednesday. I do not wish to inconvenience her in any way, so perhaps, dear, you would write a note to her to-morrow morning, and say that I find I am otherwise engaged then. That will be perfectly true. I shall be engaged, I hope, in dictating to you. . . . Well, dear ? "

" I have nothing to say to that except that I will write the note," said Agnes.

" Thank you. My other observation relates to Timothy. I know, dear, that you admire Timothy's work, and the knowledge of that, it is idle to deny, has much upset me. I hope, with an effort, to circumscribe that knowledge, to shut it up in my mind, to . . . to incapsulate it. With Mrs. Probyn's defection, I am forced to ask you to resume your work with me, and if I allowed myself to dwell on my knowledge, even to let it leak through into my mind, I should be unable to concentrate myself on our task. You, on your side, will not ask Timothy here. If my work is to be worthy of myself, I must put out of my head altogether the thought of him and the amazing inexplicable enthusiasm that has greeted him. Well ? "

" I agree not to ask Tim here," said she. " Do you mind my seeing him elsewhere ? He stayed with us, you must remember, Alan, for many weeks. We both liked him, and . . . and I think he liked us."

Alan's face was adamant.

" I live largely in my imagination," he said. " Unless you promise me that you won't see him, I shall always have the uneasy feeling that you have been doing so, and reading and admiring fresh stories of his. I shall not be able to do my best, when I am dictating to you, unless I feel sure that I have your whole mind. What is done, is done, and we cannot help that. But I deliberately ask your promise to take no steps to see him, and to refuse any request from him that you should do so. Well ? "

" Alan, I think that is unreasonable," said she.

" That is because you do not understand me," he said. " A creative artist like myself demands cer-

tain conditions, tranquillity and a freedom from distracting thoughts, if he is to do his best work. . . ."

He got up with a quick movement and began walking up and down the room, clenching and unclench-
ing his hands.

" Exercise your imagination a moment," he cried,
" and try to see with my eyes, and feel with my
nerves. I have the defects of my qualities, and you
must try to bear with them. I thought I had found
one who was in complete sympathy with me and my
work : she gave me just the stimulus and encouragement I needed. Her eagerness to help me permitted
me also to give you a greater liberty from tasks that
had long become of second-rate value in your eyes. I
make no complaint about that : I am simply stating
the fact. Now I am driven, unwillingly I confess, to
ask you to resume your place. But you must, if you
are to help me, do your best to sympathize and
identify yourself with my aims. You must not hanker
after the trash that wins cheap applause to-day. Our
work, though your part in it is only to take down
what I say, will be impossible if I think your heart is
not with me. I am not, as you know, over-rating my
sensitiveness : never have I done better work than in
this last week when I thought that my coadjutor was
with me in all I did. You must make me feel at ease
about you, and the side which you have chosen. I
cannot afford to have other traitors in my camp."

He was working himself up to an incredible pitch
of nervous excitement.

" I have nothing personal, you must understand,
against my cousin Timothy," he said. " But he is
example and symbol to me of the vile illiterate rubbish which even educated critics now admire and hail
as the work of genius. My life has been devoted to
the production of work which will live when these
gutter-snipe hulloballooings are forgotten. My

powers have never been more ripe and vigorous than they are to-day, and I consecrate them wholly to the war I have ever waged. I will never parley or surrender. If you are not with me in this, you are against me. In that case, I shall have to make some radical change in my life. I do not know what: I should have to consider."

She got up and went to him, alarmed at the violence of his agitation.

" My dear, I have chosen," she said. " You know that perfectly well. Of course I am with you now and always. I have never failed you yet, you know, and you have no right to think it possible that I shall fail you now. But you must not let yourself get in such a state of excitement. Sit down and be quiet."

She coaxed him down into his usual chair, and sat on the arm of it.

" So here we are again, Alan," she said. " You and I are alone, and we will go back to the old days before anyone came in from outside to encourage you and then disappoint you. How many books have you and I seen through first writings and revisions and correction and proof-reading from title-page to finish, ever so happily and tranquilly? And you feel in the full ripeness of your powers still. You couldn't give me better news than that."

He answered to her touch: his voice abated its shrillness, the alarming brightness of his eye seemed to sheath itself.

" Yes, I'm in my full vigour still," he said, " and while it's there I must make the most of it. I cannot expect to remain at this pitch of mental activity many years more. Most men of my age have seen their flames die down, and only the smouldering ash remain. They have wiped their pens, and have their harvest gathered in. They can only look back on the fruitful years, but I am looking forward still, and

more eagerly, I think, than ever. Indeed, many men
much younger than I have already lost the keenness
of their creative or critical faculties. Poor Blewitt,
for instance; I regard what Blewitt said to me to-night
as the maunderings and babbling of senility. Poor
Blewitt! We must be kind to Blewitt. We must
ask him to dinner one of these Sundays."

" I'm not sure that I shall allow that," she said.
" You're under my care again now, Alan."

He patted her knee.

" Yes, my dear," he said. " And I am not sure
that I was right in seeking aid and encouragement
anywhere else. Good, kind Agnes! But we must
make the most of those powers which, up till now,
show no sign of slackening. I shall soon be old, dear,
and then those that look out of the windows shall be
darkened, as that wonderful chapter in Ecclesiastes
has it. My eye will not see with its old keenness.
Yes . . . how does it go on? The sound of the
grinding shall be low: my mills of assimilation will
grow rusty and run slow. And desire shall fail: I
shall not have that intense love of my work any more,
and I shall say ' much study is a weariness of the
flesh.' I have so much still to do. I should regard
myself as criminal if I let slip in idleness the hours
while it is still day. I think, for instance, we will
no longer make a holiday of our Sundays. A man
of my vigour requires no such often-recurring holiday."

He had taken and clasped her hand, but the pressure was not for her. It was the urgency of his own
egoism that tightened it.

" You must forgive me, dear, for ever thinking that
your choice could possibly be other than it has been,"
he said. " I know better now, and I shall look to
you to shelter me from any external distraction and,

not less, to spur me on if you see signs of faltering on my part."

"But I shan't allow you to overdo yourself," she said. "It is very false economy of force to work when you are tired."

"Aha! I see you mean to keep a close hand on me. But now we must waste no more time. If you will go to your desk, dear, and give me the Flaubert paper-knife——"

She glanced at the clock.

"But had you better work to-night?" she asked. "Won't you go to bed, and be very fresh in the morning? You have had an agitating evening. That sort of thing tires you, though you may not know it at the time."

He laughed.

"But it is that very agitation which I am proposing to use now," he said. "Economy, my dear. The matter is hot within me: it will come out blazing now, whereas if I put it off till to-morrow I should have to rake among my emotions and fan them into flame. It is not my new story that I propose to go on with now: that, I agree, demands tranquillity and concentration. But the idea has come to me that I will write an article about modern fiction and its woeful scrappiness. It will be, I think you will find, my *Credo*, my confession of faith. There will be the whole weight of my work and experience to back it. Such a manifesto will come with authority from one who for nearly forty years has set before him and practised the most exalted principles of Art. Besides, to do this will be to purge myself of much perilous stuff. The froth, the turbid water will run off. That will be no small gain in itself. And shall we, aha, shall we send it to good Bristowe to publish in that magazine of his? Bane and antidote together: we will consider that later. Now, dear, if you are ready."

There they were again, he with his shuffling step and his stroked paper-knife, and she waiting for his word.   The episode, the excursion was over, they were entrenched again between the walls of the work-room,   never   again   to   be   violated   by   external presences.   The wheels of life had jolted back on to their stable smooth-running rails.

" The disintegrating influences of the war," he said, " have not been confined to mere material up-heavals; a defenceless Germany, a bankrupt Austria, the ruined chaos of Russia were only the more evident and obvious of its destructions and perhaps will prove the easiest to repair and stabilize again.   Deeper foundations have been shaken : traditions which we hoped were imperishable have been imperilled—the whole future of our art and literature topples and is like to fall in crash of irremediable ruin."

" Full stop and paragraph," said Alan.

" It is on the subject of literature that we feel it our duty to give a protesting word of warning.   The hallowed laws are being overthrown, a void and form-less anarchy, a regime of sheer literary Bolshevism take their place.   In the most admired publications of to-day, hailed not only by the ignorance of a sensa-tion-loving public, but by the accredited critics of the press,   we   find   this   tyrannical   disorder.   Style, technique and construction are all thrown overboard as antiquated and unmeaning formalism, and should the wraith of some master of delicate and fanciful prose, like the late R. L. Stevenson, visit the scenes of his faithful service to literature, we may permit ourselves to picture the dismay with which he would look on the desecration of his beloved shrines."

Alan chuckled to himself.

" Aha," he said.   " I think that will perhaps bring home to poor Blewitt a hint, an inkling of the truth.

That is not bad, dear, for a pure improvisation. Perhaps you would read from the beginning."

But after this he fumbled over his phrases, and a half hour of erasure and repetition followed.

" I think that will do for to-night," he said, " and indeed it is past your bedtime already. I must not overwork my amanuensis, though for myself I feel as fresh as ever. I will do an unusual thing, dear. I will take up to my room some slips of scribbling-paper, and I should not wonder if to-morrow morning the whole article was planned and plotted."

This was her business again now. She had circumscribed her life with his : he bounded and contained her.

" I'm not at all sure that I approve of that," she said. " Good work demands good rest, Alan."

" Yes, my dear. When I have got this little protest off my mind, we will go back to our rule. . . . At least, we will keep to the principle. I will never work when I am tired : will that satisfy you ? I see I am to be kept well in hand."

Agnes left him there, expecting soon to hear his entry into his dressing-room and, after a while, the quiet creaking of the door of communication, which betokened that he was ready for bed. Then for a moment there would be the oblong of light thrown into her dark bedroom, and after that the rustle of his getting into bed, and the click of the quenched light. But she lay long awake, and still there was no sign of his having come upstairs. She waited with a still impatience for that, for she had had a van-load of thought to unpack, and she wanted the sense that she would be undisturbed in her unloading. There was private luggage, there were things that must be fitted into the life that she had chosen. For that she wanted the knowledge that nothing would break in on her.

She held her mind in suspense waiting for the indication that Alan had gone to bed.

There were certain things she could think about while he still lingered, and of these the first was the stimulus which this awful evening had brought him. The fact that the trusted Pamela had had a dinner party in honour of Tim, the fact that they had come in unexpectedly to find Tim reading aloud from his book of stories, had stirred Alan up from his defensive silence to a violent offensive. Hitherto he had ignored, he had waited in his fortress; now, in this projected article, he came out into the open. He came out to fight, and it was a phantom host which was now deploying. People didn't care what Alan was, or what Alan wrote—there was the truth of it—he might strive and cry, and for all the effect of his protest, he was but a breeze whistling among the dry sedges of his books. But what was she to do? If she demurred to his article and his attitude, he would reckon her as the worst of his deserters. Yet all the time she knew that he had become a phantom.

There came the sound of his door opening and shutting. He had come up to bed anyhow. She heard him moving about; he had gone to his washstand, there was the hiss of a tooth-brush. He would go backwards and forwards a few times yet, and then the communicating door would softly open a few inches and a bright strip of light would pencil itself across the floor. Then there would be a rustle and creak as he got into bed, a click from the switch and darkness.

At last it came. She was alone now and would not be disturbed; she could let her body lie quite relaxed, and let her thoughts burrow into the subaqueous dusk of her mind. . . . As she and Alan made their entry into Pamela's music-room, she had forgotten Alan's presence altogether. There had been Tim

straight in front of her, and her heart had leaped to
him. He had looked up at her, and for that moment
they were alone in some glade of Eden. Then with
a swirl of recovered consciousness, as if she had come
back from some immense distance she was aware of
the tenanted room again, and of Alan. But the recovery only emphasized the unreality of what she had
come back to compared to that which she had left, and
all that was softly swarming round her again now in
the darkness. She drew long breaths of it, filling
herself with the sweetness and soft fire of it. . . .
It filled the moment, and she knew it would fill the
moments of the anxious, difficult days which stretched
interminably in front of her. It would feed her
starvation with secret manna, and in the strength of
that meat she would walk strong and undismayed.
She thought with incredulous wonder of the past years
when she had not known the thrill of this hunger of
the heart, when she had not felt the sting of this infinite need. She had been drowsily content to let the
years flow softly by her, wanting them neither to
hurry nor to linger. Now they gleamed with a new
significance : she was inspired to labour for Alan by
just that for which she starved. Love turned to gold
its own renunciations.

A faint familiar noise caught her ear, whisking her
back to the full sense of the actual moment. Turning
she saw that the door between her room and Alan's
was closed again. Instantly her mind was all alert
as to what this meant. There was a tiny chink of light
below it, and presently, intently listening, she heard
the sound of his step, softly padding up and down.
Sometimes it stopped for a moment, and she thought
he had gone to bed again, but the cessation was not
for long. As clearly as if she was in the room with
him, she divined his occupation. He was pacing up
and down, framing phrases and sentences for this

attack on modern fiction, and pausing to put them down on his slips.

She was sitting up in bed now, with her light on, intensely debating with herself. Should she go to him, and try, at the risk of his annoyance at an interruption, to persuade him to get his night's rest? It was utterly unlike him, when he had once gone to bed, to be thus wakeful and active in brain. Usually he slept uninterruptedly whatever his absorption in his work had been. Anxiety for him, urgent and presaging, stirred in her. Yet if she broke in upon him, she might only throw him out, and delay the working out of some train of thought which he was determined to follow to the end before he slept. How could she help him best? . . .

She got out of bed eagerly listening, as once before she had listened for the creak of the board outside Tim's door. She remembered that now, contrasting that secret deep content and yearning with this yearning and this dim, dark anxiety. She knew she was not given to causeless apprehension: why then was this disquiet of hers so deep? Next moment she made up her mind, and throwing a wrapper about her, she knocked at Alan's door. He answered and she went in.

He was seated at his dressing table: her first glance shewed her that he had Tim's book open by him and was copying on his slips some sentence from it. He finished it, looking at the book and writing again before he turned.

" My dear, you ought to be in bed and asleep long ago," he said. " What does this mean? Not ill, I hope?"

" No—but Alan, who else ought to be in bed and asleep?" she asked. " Why are you working now?"

He closed Tim's book, and shuffled some papers over it, with a tongue-click of impatience.

"Ah, I am much relieved to know you are not ill,"
he said. "I was frightened for a moment. . . .
Dear me, what was that phrase? It aptly expressed
my comment on. . . . Well, dear, I think I will
just finish what I was at."

"Oh, do go to bed," she said. "You will be
much fresher in the morning for a good sleep."

He shook his head.

"I can't sleep till I've settled the arrangement of
two or three points. I promise you that you will think
the result worth an abbreviated night."

She still lingered a moment, and he turned with
impatience to her.

"I must ask you to leave me," he said. "I am
proposing to get through with this now. Your interruption, dear, only keeps me up the longer."

The studious days began to pass in monotonous
procession : just so had they filed by from the
year they married till when Pamela had wedged
herself into the work-room. She was gone again
now, but Agnes could see how, in Alan's mind,
her place gaped for her. She was like some friend
of his who had gone wrong, who had disgraced and
alienated herself. Her name never passed Alan's lips
(it was not even necessary to remember to allude to her
as Mrs. Probyn), but to Agnes it was clear how much
he missed her stimulating adoration. She had gone
after false gods with apostasy far more intimately
grievous than Blewitt's. From close quarters she had
dealt a bitter blow at his egoism, and if she had come
with bell and candle to be shriven and reinstated, he
would have withheld his absolution.

The days in procession . . . they and their
quiet industrious faces, pacing slowly by. . . .
That for Agnes was the image that outwardly presented itself. She would have said that they were

unaffected by the passage of time which each
symbolized, so like they were in garb and feature to
their unnumbered predecessors. There was the
morning of preparation, the stroll, the walk, the dictation before dinner, and the dictation after. Only at
night did they differ from the hosts that had gone
before them, for now, as she lay awake, hour after
hour, she could hear his tread going softly up and
down in his room, and she waited for the opening of
the door which shewed that at last he had gone to bed.

The days wore masks which shewed the features of
their forerunners, and she could only guess what lay
below. There was something menacing behind those
cowled quiet faces. . . . Or was it only that now
she looked at them with presaging eyes, imagining
that no tranquillity could be as real as that which
apparently presented? She had made her choice,
and now she gave no voluntary thought for her
own concerns, though sometimes out of the curtain
that she drew in front of them, Tim's face, this
love of his eager eyes would look out mute and
enquiring. Sometimes, especially at night when the
house was still, and the door at last had been opened,
shewing that Alan had gone to bed, it would come
close to her in the darkness, and from the very comfort of its imagined presence, she had not the will to
banish it. But by day she would never look at it :
all her faculties had to employ themselves over Alan,
and her work of ministration.

There was this article about modern fiction. He
had never devoted more meticulous care to any work
of his. Over and over again he dictated and erased
and revised, until every sentence bristled with stings.
And none would feel them : there was the worst and
the best of it, for him the worst of it, for they revealed
him not as the stinger but the unutterably stung, and
for others, the best of it, since those jabbing strokes

were so pathetically innocuous. Agnes alone winced
at them, for again and again he quoted sentences, he
witheringly analyzed plots from modern stories, to
show the decadence of literature, and all these scape-
goats came from that little flock of Tim's. Alan had
read no other contemporary book except that; it was
that alone which he had torn to bits, never quoting
it by name, but holding up these anonymous fragments as instances. . . . At last it was finished,
and as she came to the end of the final reading of the
typed manuscript, he got up and chuckled to himself.

" Well, dear," he said, " I think that will reasonably astonish some of those who think that we older
writers have declined from our ancient vigour. Something of a shock, eh, to good Bristowe when he
receives it to-morrow for his magazine? But after
the shock has passed, good Bristowe will chuckle, I
think, at getting it. It will cause—cannot you see
good Bristowe rubbing his mercantile hands when he
reads it?—it will cause a tremendous sensation. I
shall certainly sign it; I wish the world to know it
comes from a recognised and authoritative source.
Perhaps Bristowe will think better now of his caution
about the collected edition. But whatever the effect
of it, I will be bothered with no interviewers. I throw
if off *en passant,* and now after my gesture, sincere,
as you know, passionately sincere, I go back from
necessary destruction to construction again, to the
building of the palaces of Art on the site we have
cleared. *Cras ingens iterabimus aequor.* We shall
float out again on the favouring tide; we shall resume
our book that will testify for us of our constructive
aims. *Cras ingens* . . . ah, yes, I think I have
just quoted that wonderful line."

" And you won't work to-night when you ought to
be asleep? " said she.

" No, no, my dear. I have every intention of

taking a good rest. Indeed, I feel I need it. Something within, functioning from the inner consciousness, suggests that, though on the surface I palpitate with vigour. Good-night, dear Agnes."

She woke that night long after she had gone to sleep. Half unconsciously, she turned to assure herself that the door was open. But it was shut, and she heard his step from the other side of it, eternally moving up and down his room.

CHAPTER IV

THE November fog advanced and was repulsed by some current of moving air; when that was still, it mobilized its forces again. All the morning there came these alternations of gleams and returning darkness and renewed gleams. Sometimes the electric light must be switched on, and half an hour afterwards a patch of reddish frosty sunshine lay on the carpet of the work-room. . . .

Alan always choked and coughed if there was fog abroad, and after lunch, about the time of his usual start for the walk, a thick orange darkness veiled the trees outside the window. It was now or never, for in an hour's time the short daylight would die, and he finally settled not to go out. But he had plenty of slips to occupy his meditation for the dictation after tea, and he urged Agnes, on this Saturday afternoon, to go out for a brisk turn alone : a brisk turn would do her good. Usually, when he did not want her, he had little concern with her occupations, but of late he had become more solicitous for her. She was now an essential part of the machine of production, and it must be kept in good working order.

"I insist, dear," he said, "I insist not only on your going out, but on your taking our longer walk. You will feel the benefit of it, that I guarantee you, when I make you toil and scribble for me this evening. You must be as fresh as I, for I promise you there is a long journey for your pen to-night. If you are back here by half-past four that will be perfectly convenient. Go out, and have a good, long, brisk walk."

She was in two minds where to go, when she stood,

desperately heavy-hearted, at the bottom of the square. Once more she could choose the streets, could revisit some populous station, as she had done once before when she had left him at the Athenæum for his weekly tea, and see the crowd of busy folk going on the week-end holiday. But now there seemed no medicine there for her assimilation. She did not crave for a crowd in order to heal a loneliness. It was not a crowd that could comfort her; her imagination did not put that picture to her. It was better to take the "longer walk": the Park would be empty and she could perhaps arrive at some sort of bodily fatigue by swift walking. She wanted her body to be tired, to subside into some kind of acquiescent fatigue.

. . .

The sun hung like a red-copper piece, already below the tree-tops, as she crossed the ride below the Serpentine. There had been a frost the night before, and the horse-hooved earth was a sea of stiff billows of frozen mud. The gulls had come back for their winter sojourning, but she had forgotten to take out the bag of broken crusts to feed them. There were a few loungers by the edge of the lake, and, as she got close, she saw that one of them was Tim.

They met without any word of greeting, only that long look. . . .

"Just out for a walk," she said. "Alan is staying at home. It's so very long, Tim. . . ."

"Not since that night at Pamela's," said he.

"Yes."

Then the greeting came.

"My dear, how are you?" she said. "How is all going? What a brain-wave that sends you here, just here and just now!"

His mouth smiling, made him boyish.

"I have these brain-waves on Saturday," he said.

"I had one last Saturday and the Saturday before.

I get the day off on Saturdays, and in the afternoon I just look round here. You were here last Saturday with Cousin Alan."

" And you too ? " she asked.

" Yes, I was here. You fed the gulls and took the shorter walk. Which walk are you taking now ? I am coming with you."

All the silence of these weeks evaporated like a frosty breath in her reply.

" But you understood, Tim ? " she said.

" Of course. If I hadn't, shouldn't I have done something ? It was just because I understood . . . Let's go the longer walk."

It was a pure accident that she had met him thus. She had not sought it, and yet she hesitated.

" I know all that," said Tim impatiently. " It's not your fault. But I'm going to have a good hour's walk with you. I want to know what you're doing, and what you're being."

" I am being nothing," she said. " I'm being dead. . . ."

He had moved a step in front of her.

" Come on, Agnes," he said. " It's too cold for you to stop still. Let's walk. Or will you come to St. James's Place and talk over the fire ? "

" No, my dear."

She fell into step by his side.

" Tell me all about it," he said.

She came out, surrendering.

" Yes, there's nothing I want more than to tell you," she said. " Alan, you know. . . . Oh, it is terrible, my dear. Where am I to begin ? Well, we came back that night, and he . . . I'm frightened about him. He at once began writing an article about modern work. It was all about you. He copied and recopied it, and sent it to that magazine which first published your stories. It was sent back to him. He sent it right and left, and every time that it came back, he was more and more certain that no-one dared publish it. . . . Dared, you know. . . . Now, he is splitting it up; he is putting it into the mouth of characters in his new book. . . . He works half the night, Tim. It is as if something relentless drove him. He has to make a stand against the drivel of to-day. That's what he calls it. There's that awful activity: no brain will stand it. . . ."

He stopped with a half-turn towards her.

"Oh, my dear," he said. "Pour it out: give me my share. . . . I know I can't share: oh yes, I know that. But . . . beastly for you. . . . Go on."

"Tim, his brain isn't standing it," she said. "For all his vigour, there's something self-destructive. . . . I don't know how to say it. Sometimes he tells me that he wants no more preparation, and then he dictates morning and afternoon and evening. And he keeps repeating himself. Word for word there is a paragraph in the evening which he has already dictated before. And if I remind him of it he says he knows he is repeating, in order to emphasize his point. And he won't see any doctor and he says he has never been better in his life, never so well. . . . You poor thing, why am I burdening you with troubles that may come to nothing? Perhaps they are imaginery. But something will happen, so I tell myself, and I shall for ever know that I might have done better for him. . . . My stupidity, my inefficiency, my want of love. . . ."

This time it was she who halted and faced him.

"But is there anything you can do which you have left undone?" he asked.

"Not that I know of. But I ought to know more. I am so feeble . . . it isn't from within that I

approach Alan.   And there is no-one to help me.
My mother . . . well, never mind that.   But as
regards Alan I am so utterly alone.   That's the real
loneliness, my dear, to be close to someone, and yet
not be able to touch him.   He doesn't love me, you
know.   He never did.   And I am all that he has got.
It's tragic for him : you don't know how I pity him.
. . . And he doesn't want me just because I am I.
My dear, what an unutterable relief to be able to say
this !   And now let us get free of it all for this
hour.   Tell me quite all about yourself."

" You know quite all that is worth knowing," said
he.

She flashed her answer to him in the smile and the
meeting glance.

" Then tell me what's not worth knowing," she said.
" I want to be able to picture you and your ways
and your doings.   Your writing, for instance : is the
book still being a huge success?   And what are you
writing now?   Anything, Tim : just babble.   What
did you have for breakfast this morning?   What are
you doing to-night?   But your stories, chiefly."

They worked back into natural talk, as of two
friends who have not seen each other for a period.
Tim was giving up his work in the City in a few
weeks from now, and taking up writing as his profession.   The book of stories had been prodigiously
successful in America : he was busy now on a second
collection.

" And you'll be here?   You'll stop in London? "
she asked.

" That depends.   Shall I ever see you? "

Her lip quivered.

" Oh Tim, you understand, don't you? " she said.

" I suppose I do."

" Well then——"

" If I can't be of any help to you, and if I can't

see you, I shall go to Rome for a month or two soon,"
he said.

"Ah, Tim, what a good plan. You'll enjoy it: I
shall love thinking of you there."

"That's my plan, then," he said and paused.

"Agnes, have you got any right to maim yourself
and me like this?" he said. "He doesn't want you:
you said it yourself. But I——"

For a moment across the fog which had gathered
and thickened about them, there came to Agnes's
eyes some inner vision of the sparkle of late Southern
sunlight, the green serge of sharp cypresses, and of
herself with Tim. The Angelus was flowing on to
the still air from a hundred towers. She shook with
the lure of it. She laid her hand on his.

"O Tim, his helplessness, his loneliness," she said.
"How can love flower out of cruelty?"

They had come to the bridge, and she leaned on
the wet balustrade, steadying herself. The water below
was invisible through the thick air, and for the
Angelus there was the hooting of a motor snailing its
way on the road. . . . Soon she straightened herself up again.

"We must go on," she said. "Straight ahead,
my dear, not faltering nor turning aside. And you
don't know what good it has done me to meet you
and talk to you. . . . Thank you, dear Tim,
for your sympathy and, and your love. I bless God
for you. . . ."

She patted his shoulder, comrade fashion, and let
her hand dwell there a moment.

"Look how the fog has swallowed us up," she said.
"We must grope our way home. When the fog is
thick like this in London, it makes me think of some
great tired brain, and we who creep about in it are
the brain's drowsy thoughts. When we've all crept
home it can sleep. Supposing we got lost, but we

mustn't. . . . Would Alan send out a search party
to follow the route of the longer walk? I should pretend you didn't belong to me, Tim."

She had taken the danger out of perilous things
with that. He could handle her safely now.

" But I do," he said. " What's the use of pre-
tending ? "

It was on the frank note that they parted, and with
the closing of the house-door, she entered again into
the secluded absorbed existence of Alan. To-day he
was charged with matter to deliver; she who so often
had to sit with idle pen in hand for minutes at a time,
could scarcely keep pace with the outpourings. There
were no erasures, no struggling over exact and perfect
expressions to convey his meaning, no reading over in
order to sweep forward again. Paragraph after paragraph was poured out, vague interminable conversa-
tions, long descriptive scenes; for a couple of hours
his voice hardly ceased.

" Aha, a long book this time," he said. " I see it
all clearly before me. We have already exceeded, I
suspect, our usual limits, and I doubt whether we are
really more than half-way through. I anticipate a
triumph this time, Agnes. . . . Somehow, dear,
your presence is proving wonderfully stimulating to
me. Your choice, my dear; you have no idea how
that warmed my heart. I am beginning to feel your
eagerness and sympathy. I wonder to myself how it
was that I ever came to dictate to anyone else. Well,
those days are over, and we sweep forward with all
the splendour of full sail. . . . Ah, that phrase
will serve me : that is just what I wanted. Take down
a few words more. Are you ready ? Write please."

" ' Like some ship moving forward towards the
sunset, under the splendour of full sail, she swept
along the shining——' . . . let me see . . . I
had it all in my mind just now. . . . Curious ! It

was as if a shutter came down and hid it from me.
. . . But we will not worry over it. It will come
back to me. . . . Dear me, these two hours have
gone in a flash.—I think to-night I shall not dress.
I shall just run over my notes while you are upstairs,
so as to be ready when we resume again after dinner."

Then, another day, this voluble tide would cease to
flow altogether, but whether he progressed well or
not, there was the same exaltation of egoism.

" It is only out of patience and unremitting effort,"
he would say, "that any great work emerges. I
could so easily evade this difficulty which blocks our
way. I could make a *détour* round the obstacle,
but there must be no curves or *détours* in our high-
road. It must run inexorably straight from first to
finish. Perhaps, dear, you would play me one of
those divine little morsels of Bach or Mozart. Some
little inevitable tune. Inevitable : yes, all Art is inevitable when once it is done. . . . Ah, inevitable : let me think. That perhaps gives me the key
to what I want. . . . I thought I got it then !
No, it is off again. Patience, my dear : we will not
send a line out to the world, that is not perfectly
fashioned. As long as . . . I have thought sometimes of writing an essay or an article on the deplor-
ably unfinished work that writers send out now-a-days
for fools to admire. Of course, now I remember that
article I wrote a few weeks ago. The new one would
cover much the same ground. Repetition : that is
the only way to get a thing into people's heads. . . .
But all that must wait till we have got through with
our present book."

But below this vigour and this unremitting work
Agnes began to divine a supreme fatigue. It was as
if the lords and rulers of thought slept on their secret
thrones : they gave no mandates. It was not they
who ruled and governed, it was only the habits, those

servants of the will, trained to automatism, who went about their accustomed tasks, hewers of wood and drawers of water, moving like armies of imperturbable ants on their well-worn roads. All these years his employment and his passion had been in writing, and habit turned out these battalions of well-equipped sentences. He built up his paragraphs, he ranged them into chapters . . . but . . . there was nothing there. Recalling her impressions of this swift dictation, Agnes could find nothing to attach her mind to. Fugitive images were recorded, they walked in a mist, lost, getting nowhere. . . .

But there might be some great surprise in store, some flash of sunlight and buffeting of fresh wind which blew the mists away, and you would see the purport of those glimpses. Had Alan, according to his gospel of fiction, been hinting for you and preparing for you, so that at the end, even before the sunlight broke through, you would be gasping with wonder at what you knew was to be revealed? Was this the meaning of these repetitions which she had thought to be forgetfulness on his part? Was something tremendous about to emerge? He had never seemed so certain of himself, so authoritative and sure.

She distrusted every conclusion she came to : she was in a nightmare of indecision. She did not know whether she ought, somehow or other, to force him to see a doctor, who might forbid this abnormal output of energy, this untiring industry. On the other hand his physical health seemed excellent. He was vigorous in the daily walks, he ate well, he moved with unusual briskness. Perhaps the lords and rulers were not asleep at all, but splendidly alert, and the normal habits were whisking about their business, because they knew that great things were a-foot, and they must make smooth running of their jobs.

Then came a snowy day in mid-December, and after the morning's preparation, he said he would take tea that afternoon at the Athenæum. The weather was too inclement for walking, and a taxi was ordered.

"A crowd, my dear!" said Alan, as he stood in the hall waiting for her to put on a cloak. "I wonder if you would tell our driver not to go through the Green Park, but down Piccadilly and that street—let me see, down Saint—ah, yes, St. James's Street, and so along to Pall Mall. You can guess my reason, I have no doubt. I know you have seen that I am preparing for a lost, hurrying sense. . . . Ah, you would pull me up over my want of precision. Quite right. But there is coming a chapter, as I am sure you know, when our poor Eva finds herself among hurrying strangers, to whom she is nothing. We must go down Piccadilly, dear. I want to see—yes, I have my glasses—how the faces of strangers look. Let us go."

"But your coat, Alan," said she. "Put on your thickest coat, please. It is snowing : there is a bitter wind."

"Indeed! I had not perceived any wintriness. Yes, dear, I see when I look out of the window that you are right about the snow. But I shall do very well as I am. If one does not think one is cold, one is not cold."

"Oh, my dear, I insist," said she. "It is a real day of winter. You must wrap up."

"And I insist," said he. "I feel very warm and comfortable. Snow! What is snow? Think of it as swansdown. . . ."

He took a step to the window.

"Ah, the beautiful thing!" he said. "Softly, softly it falls, a core of moisture feathered by the frost. I did not know that snow was so beautiful.

My glasses. . . . No, I see it best without them.
Let us have our taxi open. I will put on my coat,
dear, if it pleases you. I should like to see it fall on
my coat and disappear. . . . Little emotions, little
frozen emotions that thaw and pass away. . . .
What wonderful things suggest themselves. I marvel
at their origin. Do the winds of God blow them into
space? Do they freeze with the contact of our cold
planet, and thaw again when they light on human
habitation and come near to human hearts? I must
remember that. Will you remember it for me, dear?
We shall make it doubly safe like that."

Even while he spoke, she made up her mind.
While he was in the Athenæum she would go straight
to his doctor, and tell him all that made her so apprehensive. He might laugh at her—she prayed God
he would laugh at her—but if he took it gravely, they
could hatch out some plan for him to see Alan. . . .
Probably he would be engaged, but she would send
in her card with " urgent " written on it, and during
the course of the hour or so which Alan spent at the
Athenæum, she could get a minute with him, sandwiched between other appointments. Dr. Brock had
always attended Alan : he was an eager admirer, too,
of his books, and it was an old complaint of Agnes's
that when Dr. Brock came to see him for some small
ailment, they discussed his work instead of his complaint. He lived in Buckingham Palace Road, close
to Victoria station. The fact of her resolution took
a weight off her mind. . . . If Dr. Brock was
disposed to be serious about him, if he wished to see
him, the plan formed itself. . . . He could come
to see her over some minor ache or pain, and thus see
Alan. . . .

Alan consented to his coat, on condition of the taxi
being opened.

"Down Piccadilly, dear," he said as he stepped in. "Will you be so kind as to make that a positive order? Ah, kind Agnes. . . . The snow, my dear! It suggests all sorts of things. How it whitens what it falls on. . . . The dull drab pavements are clad in it. The passengers only make holes in it, and it covers them up again. Soft—irresistible! I do not like its being interfered with. I should like to see it in the country, on fields where no footfall disturbs it. It would be lying now, if there is this severe weather there, on the garden at Playden. A nice lawn; we used to walk there,—ah, yes, poor Pamela and I, not you—when my morning's preparation was done. Pamela: dear me, I said 'Pamela.' I suppose my thoughts took their tune from those days which I spent there with her. They were very fruitful. The preface to 'The Tyro,' for instance. But then she cut herself off from me. No, dear, not painful; anything that restored you to me could not be considered painful."

His hands were bare: he rubbed the back of one with the fingers of the other, like a child conscious of some discomfort, and only instinctively localizing it. She noticed that those beautiful hands were very white, that the fingers were drawing themselves together like the claw of a dead bird.

"Oh, Alan, you haven't come out without your gloves?" she said. . . . How useless it all was!

"No, dear Agnes," said he, "I have got my gloves. If I feel cold I shall put them on. Aha: here is Piccadilly! My glasses! Glasses more important than gloves. . . . Look, dear, at the faces of the passers-by. I want to use your eyes as well as my own. Let us see what strangers look like."

He peered through his glasses, disappointed at the rareness of the hurrying figures.

"I thought there would be more of them," he said.

"And they have put up their umbrellas. That is not fair of them. But how should they know that we drove down Piccadilly in order to see how strange faces looked? But still I have formed some very distinct impression. Here we turn down by that big hotel. Our driver goes by a side-street, but we shan't lose much. We shall turn into Saint—yes, St. James's Street again in a moment. . . . I told you so, my dear. Here we are. We cross over, you see. We drive on the left side of the street. That is the English rule. Compact little streets on each side. . . . There is St. James's Place, is it not? Then we shall swing round into Pall Mall, and in a couple of minutes more we shall be at the Athenæum. Will you amuse yourself, dear, for an hour, or shall we say an hour and a half, and then call for me? No doubt you have a little shopping to do. But let us be on the safe side : if you will come back for me in an hour and a quarter, that will be quite convenient. Then we will drive home again, and have a long splendid evening in the work-room."

There was a block of vehicles at the bottom of the street, and they waited to turn into Pall Mall while a couple of vans lumbered across the road. A taxi with luggage on the top, heading a little to the right, as if to go through St. James's Park, had drawn up exactly parallel to them, and, like them, was waiting for the passage of the vans. A head from inside it, bobbed forward and back again, and Agnes saw who it was. Then the stoppage was relieved, and they slid forwards down Pall Mall.

"An hour and a quarter then, dear," said Alan, as they stopped at the door of the club. "Amuse yourself well."

She had got out first, and saw him disappear into the hall. She had already paid the driver, but now beckoned him back again, and gave Dr. Brock's address. . . .

He could see her, so she ascertained, in half an hour, sparing a few minutes for her. There would be time for everything, and she went straight to the station. Just outside it, sheltered by the glass-roof over the pavement, was a flower-seller, and she bought a little bunch of chapped roses. By the platform the long Continental Express was waiting.

Tim was standing outside the carriage where he had taken his seat. He had finished the registration of his luggage, and was stowing tickets and passports into convenient pockets. She came alongside of him before he saw her.

" Tim ! " she said, and he turned.

" I saw you pass," she said. " I was taking Alan to his club. Only half a minute, my dear, to wish you all good things. . . . Such tired little roses, Tim. Throw them into the sea. Have a good time, and God bless you."

Even as she spoke, she turned, knowing that she could not stand more. But she could not have done with less.

It seemed that Tim could not do with so little. In two steps he was abreast of her again.

" Perfect of you," he said. " And if you want me, you know at any time . . ." Their hands were clasped.

" Oh, don't I know it ? " she said. " But I must go. Be busy and happy, Tim. . . . It was a lovely chance that let me see you pass. . . ."

She mingled in the crowd, and without looking back she went to the doctor's house. On the table was a copy of an old magazine, and ' Cricket ' was the first story in it.

There were discreet noises, the quiet opening and shutting of doors, and soon she was telling her story to the doctor. He asked unexpected questions, questions of which she could not see the bearing, and sat drumming his fingers when she had answered.

" I'll come and have a look at him," he said, after a dozen of these. " And if he won't consent to see me about himself, he must see me about you. Now that's a good idea of yours. Have a feverish feeling, Mrs. Graham, send for me at seven o'clock to-night. Then I can take an observation or two."

She did not know how keen her anxiety was that Alan should see somebody till now, nor how deeply the fangs of it bit into her.

" Ah, that's a great relief," she said. " And can you tell me what you suppose . . . ? "

He laughed.

" My dear lady, if I could tell you that, I shouldn't have to come and see him. Quite possibly I shall only be wasting my time and his too. But we can't take risks and chances with people like Mr. Graham. Colossal brain, you know, and marvellous vitality it appears. I shall expect to be rung up then by you at seven."

He fussed her cheerfully to the door.

" A privilege to see him in his work-room," he said. " And there's another of your husband's name who has made a stir lately. Wonderful stories! I read on in bed last night, till I had finished them. Shocking example for a professional man, who is always telling his patients not to read anything absorbing at night. Some relation of your husband's, so I saw in a paper, and so probably untrue. . . . Eh? . . . Not to mention them to your husband I see, I quite understand : not a word. Yes. At seven o'clock then."

The appointed hour and a quarter had still ten minutes to run when she got back into Pall Mall.

The snow had ceased, but the wind was bitterly chill, and Agnes engaged a taxi and sat in it for shelter till his time was up. She had it drawn up a little beyond the entrance so that she could see him the moment he came out on to the steps of the club. . . . By now Tim would be whirling through the whitened fields and orchards of Kent: he would wake to-morrow among the cypresses of Southern France. . . . What a lovely chance it was that brought their taxis side by side, and enabled her to see him off!

The cold wintry day was drawing in, the lights in the streets only illuminated its dreary inclemency. . . . Patches of snow lay here and there, but most of it was trampled into brown slush. She kept her eyes on the door alert for Alan's exit, and let her thoughts range as they would. Sometimes they sped after Tim, but returned shivering and laden with loneliness. . . . Alan still lingered: he must have found some friend in the club and lost count of time, for the hour and quarter had already long been overstepped.

A motor came up to the porch, and its occupant ran quickly up the steps, leaving the door of it open. She wondered why he hurried so: a man going in for a leisurely hour would not hasten like that. The chauffeur put out a hand and swung his door shut, and backed a little, so as to leave the entrance clear. Agnes found herself noticing all this with extreme vividness, as one notices minute details of the surroundings in some great emotional crisis. And then suddenly she knew that this was so: a tense and terrible agitation at Alan's delay rose upwards into her consciousness from within her. What could be the matter? Then an interpretation of the hurrying visitor flamed into her mind.

She got out and ran up the steps.

"Would you please tell Mr. Graham that I—Mrs.

Graham—have been waiting some time ? " she said to
the hall-porter.

He had the telephone receiver at his ear, but instantly laid it down.

" I've been trying to get hold of you, ma'am," he
said. " Mr. Graham has been taken suddenly ill.
In the library, ma'am : the doctor is with him. This
way, please."

Alan was lying back in a long arm-chair. He
turned puzzled agonizing eyes on her, some sort of
smile convulsed his mouth. There was full recognition there and panic and utter dismay. He was trying to speak. . . .

He had lain now for a fortnight in his own room at
home; there was no sign yet of any return of power.
One side was paralysed and no intelligible word had
passed his lips. He could make little purring con-
tented sounds when they had hit on something that
he wanted, and querulous mutterings when they failed.

Agnes alone seemed to be able to guess his wants
correctly, and by degrees it became clear that nothing
was right unless she did it. If his nurse arranged
something for his comfort, he muttered and grumbled,
but if Agnes put her hand to it, it was well, and that
twitch of a smile crossed his face.

She had been guessing famously this last day or
two, and now as witness of her brilliance, the apparatus of toilet had been moved out of sight and the room
within his area of vision was filled with the furniture of the work-room. The writing table and her
chair were there, and no one might sit in that but she.
If his nurse even rested a tray on the seat of it, the
protesting gruntings and growls began. That chair,
then, was Agnes's and hers alone; she sat in it at
once when she came into the room, and talked to
him from there. Then, one day, she had idly taken

up a pen as she sat there, and that was a great success. Whatever household businesses must be conducted, she now transacted them sitting there with a pen in her hand.

He never took his eyes off her while she was in the room. He looked at her as a dog, dumb and emotional, looks at its beloved mistress. When she left the room he jerked and fidgetted, unquiet always till she came back. Amid many demonstrations of approval she had brought out his sheaves of notes from the drawer of the table, and spread them over its surface, so that it presented the appearance it always used to wear when dictation was going on. Another day, she had put the dictation book in which the interrupted work was written on the table, and had seen an agonized tenseness of expectation come into his eyes. She thought she was on the right track now, and saying " Now, dear, I'm going to read to you," she began. At that, the twitching jerk of a smile played on his face like some telegraphy of dots and dashes. . . . Presently she came to the point where Pamela had taken it up : there was hardly an erasure now, and she went swimmingly on. But that did not suit him at all : his face grew puzzled and protesting. She tried again and once again, before she guessed. Then turning the pages over, she found the place where she had taken up the dictation again. Instantly his face cleared. . . . That gave the clue, and when they came to the broken end of the manuscript she had ready other books, so many of them, in which she had written to his dictation. Hour after hour she sat there and read the old forgotten pages, which he had so sedulously preserved. . . . But if she began reading to him after lunch, he would soon get unquiet and worried again. The solution of that was difficult, until the solving of it made it appear easy.

" I shall leave you now, Alan," she said, when the happy guess occurred to her. " It is bright and sunny this afternoon, and I shall take the longer walk. Would you like me to do that ? Ah, how stupid of me not to have thought of that before."

She would leave him then, and sometimes she would go out, sometimes, if she felt too tired to move at all, she would merely go downstairs, and wait, perhaps in the bow-windowed room by the front door, for a couple of hours, till it might be supposed that she had come in again from her exercise ; then putting on her cloak and hat she would return to him. . . . Those hours which she passed away from him went by in some kind of vivid inertness. She seemed a spectator of her own thoughts, which moved across a lit screen, and she could sympathize or demur, but always as part of the audience. . . . There were some dreadful adventures there, and worst of all was the memory of how, late on the evening of Alan's stroke, he had been brought home, and lay in a drugged sleep, while she had gone across to her mother, hands open and heart open in the desolation of it all. She had sobbed out her story, sitting on the floor by her mother's knee. Before it was done, she felt that that knee was as one of the granite gods of Egypt, and she looked up at her mother's face. There was a granite god again, archaically smiling, and sniffing up, so it seemed, the odour of a human sacrifice.

" Yes, Agnes, you are in deep waters," she said. " Terrible trouble has come upon you. I do not want to make things worse for you, but I cannot spare you the remorse which must be yours."

She stood up menacing as a Greek Fury.

" You suffer, and so does Alan, for your folly," she said. " You let him think himself, all these years, a lord of language. . . . Now he is dumb.

You have been no helpmate to him; you have taken the smooth, easy path of flattering his egoism, until there was nothing left of him but this. . . . It's justice. . . ."

Agnes had never seen anyone so terrible. It was her mother who summed up dead against her. . . .

There was another picture, that of Tim. She had not written to him to tell him of the trouble. He was free of it all, anyhow; whereas, if she wrote to him, he would either carry a heavy heart with him instead of an eye enchanted, or, more probably, would come back here, waiting to see if he could help. But he helped more by being unaware and away.

The awful loneliness: that was the next picture. There was no use in telling Dora, who was, as usual, in Paris. Agnes smiled to herself as she imagined Dora sending, as she certainly would, some box of peaches, or what not, for Alan. Peaches expressed Dora's sympathy with illness . . . the graver the illness, the larger the peaches. . . . Dora did not like Alan : she had always been frictionally disposed towards him. . . . No-one could stand beside Agnes in this desert of destiny, unless he came with a comprehending compassion. Alan had wrecked on the rock of his own egoism, and was derelict, battered to pieces on it.

Then there was Pamela. . . . Pamela had heard, though no public announcement had been made, of Alan's illness. She telephoned half-a-dozen times a day to know how he was, and usually in her inquiries she modulated on to Tim. Tim was abroad, was he not? Pamela had rung him up at his flat, and they said he was in Rome. She meant to go to Rome soon after the New Year, and it would be nice to see him. Was it true that he was at work on a new volume of short stories?

Picture after picture appeared and melted away again, and at the end she was always left with the situation of Alan lying there between the quick and the dead, and of herself the only real link between him and the living. She knew all that doctors could tell her. He might remain in that condition for months and perhaps years. He could receive impressions from the outside world, but he could not transmit them. It was not at all impossible that he should regain the power of speech, and of movement, but he would be a cripple in mind. Never again could he weave and construct, or follow a coherent train of thought. There was no more work for him : at the most, he would be like a child, pleased or displeased, well or ailing. The child had got its innumerable connections with life to be formed : its growth would establish them, but Alan could not follow a child's growth. He might possibly become like a child again, babbling and elementary, but that was all.

There were already indications that he would not struggle back even so far as that into the animate normal world. Though his right side was untouched by his stroke, he would make no effort to use what was left him. It was certain, for instance, that it was in his power to write, to communicate his wishes and his distastes on paper, even though he could not find the spoken words for them. But any suggestion that he should do this worried him. Even if Agnes gave him paper and pencil, and asked him to give her some message, his face grew puzzled and furrowed, and he whimpered and made the querulous noises. Sometimes, so said the faculty, a man stricken like this got on an upward grade again and sometimes he remained stationary, as Alan was doing, without any sign of recovery. In that case he sank lower, often slowly, sometimes quickly. You could not tell . . . some physical function might atrophy.

He gained no ground certainly, and there came a
week of fogs and chilly darknesses. Agnes read and
re-read the old manuscript books: she had found
that it did not matter what she read, so long
as he had dictated it to her. She had found, too,
that he was more content if he held the Flaubert
paper-knife in his hand. He could grasp it, and
rub the nerveless fingers of his left hand with
it. Somehow, in that dim withdrawn cave of consciousness and blurred memory, he felt himself com-
posing and dictating again. . . . But the fog
distressed him; he would make weak passes with his
hand across his face, as if to disperse it, when it had
stolen in through chinks of ventilation: he would
feebly blow at it, and pant with the effort. . . .
And then she perceived that there was something new
in his mind, some incommunicable idea that crept
about his brain.

"Fog;" she said, "you hate it, Alan, don't you?
I wish we could keep it out of your room. My dear,
it makes you cough, doesn't it? What can we do?"

She left her seat at the table, and came close to his
bed, for there was something stirring in him, which
would not be satisfied with the reading. . . .
And then an idea came to her.

"Somewhere where there isn't fog?" she asked.
"Somewhere out of London?"

He purred and gave little pleased squeals.

"I don't know if it can be managed," she said,
"but you must let me know what you want, and then
we'll see. A particular place, is it? Somewhere
where we have spent our holidays? Littlestone?"

That was no good. It certainly was not Littlestone,
and she tried other places where they had been
together. It was like a guessing game, and a heart-
break for every wrong guess.

"Long ago?" she asked. "No? Not long ago?

And you worked there? . . . A book? No?
. . . Ah, Alan, the preface to ' The Tyro.' . . .
Playden, is it? You want to go to Playden again?
And am I to be there this time? . . . I've got it,
haven't I?"

His face twitched with pleasure, and again it grew
clouded and fretful. What did he want exactly?
She began to see.

" You want to go to Playden with me," she spelt
out. " Yes, I understand. . . . Nobody else
. . . is that it? You mean if Pamela will let you
and me go there."

His lips moved and strove and were triumphant.
" Aha," he said.

Agnes felt no touch of embarrassment in proposing
to Pamela that she wanted the loan of the Playden
cottage without her company. It was such a common-
place that Alan must have everything he wanted
. . . for weeks that had been the motive which
dominated and controlled her life. She ran off with
Alan's " Aha " in her ears to " invoke the wizard "
and followed her message herself. " Something
about Alan : a great favour you can do us " was the
preliminary, and she thought she detected a real relief
in Pamela's announcement that she was off to Rome
to-morrow : so glad Agnes had caught her. . . .
Evidently the spectre of dictation had hovered in her
mind. But when once that was laid, Pamela was
delightful : certainly the cottage was at the Master's
service : she would never forget the wonderful days
they had spent there. Already it was consecrated to
him, said Pamela finely.

" If only I could be there, too," she said—her
departure for Rome had made it unnecessary to
explain that she was not wanted—" and see that the
Master had everything comfortable, but you will see

to that, dear Agnes. It is lovely to know that his thoughts turn back to that happy time. How is he?"

"There's no change," said Agnes. "He's not getting his speech back yet. But he said ' Aha ' this morning, just as he used to."

"And the doctors? They are hopeful? They allow him to be moved, anyhow. That is something," said Pamela brightly.

"I don't know about that yet," said Agnes. "I came straight off here to ask you first, whether it would be possible from your part."

Pamela thought, in parenthesis, that she would have a couple of lines in the social columns of the press about it. Everyone had already been informed that she was off to Rome, where Mr. Timothy Graham was busy on his new stories.

"Dear Agnes, you might have taken that for granted," she said. "I shall long to know whether his doctors will allow it. Mind you ring me up and tell me, and then I will telephone at once to my care-taker down there. The preface to ' The Tyro ' ! All that was done there. Beautiful writing."

"I'm ever so grateful," she said. "And you're off to-morrow. My best love to Tim, please."

The consent of the doctors was instantly granted. It would be perfectly easy to move him mattress and all into a motor ambulance and have him carried down. It was clear that the fog was trying to him : the sooner he was moved out of it the better. And next day this was done. There was no doubt that he recognised the place with pleasure : he made little purrings of delight when he was carried into the room which had been his work-room, where he was now to lie, for it looked on to the garden, and caught the morning sun. Here the cold windless weather which caused the fogs in town, was of translucent

winter brightness, frosty at night, but warmed up by
noon so that the long window could be open, and the
air spiced with the smell of wet earth, and mellow with
sun, streamed in. For Agnes, sometimes a whole day
seemed to pass like a moment, or again an hour
seemed to be pulled out into the length of a life-time.
Time had no significance : there was just this arrested
existence. . . .

And then a change began. His vitality was on the
wane, diminishing as the flame of a lamp burns low
and yet lower when the oil is exhausted. He no
longer cared to be read to : all that he appeared to
want was to have her close beside him. Sometimes
his hand would creep towards hers like a wounded
animal crawling into a thicket for shelter, and there it
would lie encircled by her fingers. For hours he
would lie thus, his eyes never quitting her face.

One night when it was time for him to be settled
down, he would not let her go. He paid no attention
to her persuasion in which usually he acquiesced, but
whimpered and moaned. Something about him made
his nurse anxious, and she telephoned for the doctor
to come. . . . Alan's hand was resting in
Agnes's again, for she meant to wait for his arrival.

" No, dear, I'm not going to leave you," she said.
" Quite comfortable ? "

His eyes brightened, and the smile on his mouth
broadened softly and quietly without twitch or jerk.

" Aha," he said.

He made a movement, as if to raise his head, but
sank back again. His hand fell out of hers. . . .

He was to be buried here in the cemetery on the
side of the hill. The notice of his death had duly
appeared, but she expected to be the only mourner.
Dora was abroad, her mother had written to say she
could not come down, and he had no relations nearer

to him than Tim and Tim's father. From the latter she had not heard at all, and Tim was in Rome. . . . She had never before so realized Alan's loneliness and her own, and despite herself she dreaded the hour that was coming. She had thought of telegraphing to Tim, just one word, "Come," and she knew he would have hurried as fast as steam and steel could bring him. But it was doubtful if he could have got here in time, and even so, it would have been selfish of her, just for that hour's comfort, to bring him back across Europe.

She was strolling in the garden : where the lawn lay in shadow, the spikes and crystals of a fairy frost still lingered, but here under the housewall it was warm, and a fly buzzed in the still sunshine. She heard the wheels of a motor crunch the gravel on the other side of the house, and the door-bell ring : probably the undertaker's men had arrived. There would be soft shufflings of heavy footsteps and whispered words from the room there, creakings and muffled noises. She would remain out here, she thought, till they told her that everything was ready.

A passage door opened into the garden at her back as she walked. She heard someone come out and turned.

He was there, dusty from his long journey, and she ran to him. There were no words at first, just the close-held hands.

" I saw it in some paper out there," he said. " I had luck : I just caught the Paris express."

" Oh, Tim. . . ."

www.ingramcontent.com/pod-product-compliance
Lightning Source LLC
Chambersburg PA
CBHW020423030726
47495CB00006B/1635